I0658482

'85 Love Affair

80s Love Affairs, Volume 1

Joshua Fields

Published by Joshua Fields, 2022.

'85 LOVE AFFAIR

First edition. December 9, 2022.

Copyright © 2022 Joshua Fields.

ISBN: 979-8986504018

Written by Joshua Fields.

Table of Contents

"What I have written I have written." ~ Pontius Pilate, The Gospel of John 19:22.

E aster morning ushered in blustery, chilly weather as the sun flitted amongst the clouds. The afternoon warmed to the low forties by the time Elliott Warden drove to his sister's house for a four o'clock Easter dinner. It was four thirty.

Macayla Barnes, Elliott's new girlfriend, prattled endlessly about everything from the insufficiency of her disability checks to the new blue high heels she wore. She also burned through two cigarettes on the trip. Attempting to tune out Macayla, Elliott changed the station from Oldies 104.3 to Z 95.5 and caught the beginning of Paul Davis's "'65 Love Affair".

"The year I started dating Donna," Elliott reminisced. Macayla failed to detect his drifting attention, his thoughts meandering into memories of a relationship long past. He listened to the lyrics and identified each and every parallel between them and his own high school romance but then said to himself, "Long gone, idiot."

Elliott arrived at his destination seconds after the song ended and the disc jockey transitioned into a commercial. He exited his red 1975 Ford LTD – the last car his father ever drove – and stared at the grayish-blue clouds rushing across the Michigan sky.

"Em's gonna kill me," Elliott muttered as he closed the car door. Six-foot-two-inches tall and lean-bodied, the thirty-seven-year-old sported black hair and a constant five o'clock shadow. He wore his characteristic jeans and t-shirt, blue and black respectively, but also donned a battered navy pea coat with the collar turned up and the buttons unfastened. Making his way to the passenger door, Elliott opened it for Macayla.

"Are you sure Em's okay with me coming?" asked Macayla as she climbed out of the car and the wind tussled her voluminous mass of blonde curls. She immediately produced a lighter and stuck a cigarette between her bright red lips. Three years Elliott's senior, Macayla's attractiveness was intact yet frayed subtly around the edges.

"Yeah, just don't call her Em," Elliott said while studying Macayla's curvy figure. She lit the cigarette and inhaled as he added, "And finish that cigarette before we go in the house."

Macayla stopped, tilted her head and pondered Elliott's statement with a billowing cloud of smoke. She wore an acid-washed jean jacket and skirt with a blue, low-cut blouse that curved over each breast and then plunged to reveal her substantial cleavage.

"You didn't tell her, did you?" asked Macayla in mild irritation as she exhaled more smoke. Elliott quickly shifted his gaze from her breasts to her face.

"What?" Elliott asked. He thought her silver, large-hooped earrings and blue eyeshadow excessive but said nothing about them.

"You didn't tell *Emma* you were bringing me today, did you?" queried Macayla. She held the cigarette away from her body.

"Eh, she'll be nice to you," Elliott replied. He lifted his eyebrows and said, "I'm the one who'll catch hell tomorrow when-."

"Oh, shit, the wine," interrupted Macayla. Reaching into the vehicle, she grasped the necks of two bottles and lifted them proudly into the air. She looked positively trashy holding them up with a lit cigarette between her lips.

"Well, like I said, Em usually likes beer," Elliott replied. He focused his thoughts on Macayla's latest sexual performance and thought, "It's worth it."

"Yeah, but she's really gonna love this stuff," Macayla insisted while shifting one bottle to her other hand and holding the pair in her long fingers. She grabbed her cigarette from her mouth and flicked ashes onto the lawn.

"I could bail," Elliott said to himself hopefully. Remembering the empty state of his refrigerator, his spirit dipped and he conceded, "Nah, that's not gonna work. But it'll be worth it."

"Elliott, it's chilly," whined Macayla while childishly hopping up and down.

"Sorry, let's get you inside," Elliott replied while escorting her towards the house. She struggled to walk up the driveway on her high-heeled shoes. Wrapping an arm around her waist to steady her, he said to himself, "It'll be worth it."

• • • •

EMMA HASTINGS WAS BEAUTIFUL. Her comely countenance, her strong yet effervescent personality and her large eyes, which seemed to flicker between green and blue, enraptured all who met her. The dirty-blonde was tall, five-foot-nine to be exact, and possessed an alluring slenderness with curvy hips. Emma wore a dressy teal sweater and jeans, the working mother preferring a casual approach to holidays.

Emma did not, however, feel particularly beautiful or effervescent when she looked out the dining room window. She instead felt a tide of vileness arise within her heart.

"Holy big hair," Emma snarled as her brother opened the car's passenger door and Macayla disembarked from the vehicle. She watched the pair and sneered, "Seriously, Elliott? Macayla Barnes?"

"Ya' think he'd mix it up, maybe throw a redhead in there once in while," replied her husband, David, a brown-haired, broad-chested and bearded bear of man standing six-foot-four-inches tall. Emma turned and punched his shoulder.

"Ow," said David with a chuckle as he fled the room.

"You'd better run," Emma warned him before turning her attention back to Elliott. She wrinkled her nose and watched his approach with disgust, muttering, "And so should he. *Idiot.*"

Straightening her body and breathing deeply several times, Emma calmed herself and prepared to indulge her brother's latest romantic whim. She set down the water pitcher on the dining room table and moved to the front door.

"You can do this," David encouraged her, the words of her rock stifling her sour mood at the last second. Elliott knocked and opened the door.

"You're late," Emma snapped while hugging him and kissing him on the cheek. She centered herself before allowing her eyes to settle on Macayla; with a poorly-feigned tone of welcome, she said, "And you brought a guest."

"Yeah, you remember Macayla, from the club," said Elliott. He stepped behind Macayla and pulled the front door closed.

"Oh, yes, can't forget Macayla," Emma replied. She said to herself, "Easily one of the three biggest sluts who hang out in my club."

"Hi, Emma!" exclaimed Macayla, the towhead failing to detect Emma's deceit. She held up the two bottles in one hand like an experienced party girl and announced proudly, "We brought wine!"

3

"Oh, goodie!" Emma exclaimed. Macayla attempted to hug her but Elliott grabbed her by the coat to prevent it.

"Hey! Elliott!" griped Macayla as she stumbled backward. He caught and steadied her.

"Just gettin' your coat, Cay," Elliott said as he slid it off and hung it on one of the foyer's open coat hooks. He removed and hung his own coat to complete the performance.

"*Cay*," Emma thought bitterly.

"Oh," replied Macayla as she readjusted her outfit, "thank you."

David appeared in the foyer wearing a Detroit Tigers jersey and baggy jeans. He held out his hand to Macayla.

"Hey, I'm Dave, Em's husband," he said. Macayla's eyes sparkled and she took his hand.

"Wow, you got yourself a lotta man here, sister," said Macayla as she hungrily appraised David's physique. He felt the heat of his wife's anger and immediately pulled his hand from Macayla's grasp.

"Hey, let's uncork that wine," urged Elliott as he pushed Macayla past the Hastings and into the kitchen.

"Yeah, I'll take some," David said quickly despite despising wine. He grabbed his wife by the waist and ferried her into the dining room, his strength barely enough to restrain her from pursuing Macayla.

"If she calls me sister again," Emma warned.

"Stop being so pushy," protested Macayla as Elliott swept her further into the kitchen.

"Pushy? Nah, I just wanna try that wine," Elliott replied. He searched for a corkscrew and thought with less certainty, "It'll be worth it."

· · · ·

"SO, ELLIOTT, YOU READY for opening day tomorrow?" asked David's father, Tom, in an effort to break the awkward silence. He knew David's mother, Rose, was uncomfortable with Macayla's presence especially given her experiences with Elliott's past girlfriends. Feeling trapped between Elliott's latest fling, who sat to his left, and his wife, who sat on his right, he told Macayla, "We're huge Tigers fans."

"Cool, so I am," Macayla replied. She loudly gulped some of her cheap white wine.

"You guys are crazy," answered Elliott with a chuckle. He forced down some of Macayla's terrible wine, coughed and then said, "The *high* is gonna be in the thirties tomorrow."

"Davie and I haven't missed one in over thirty years," Tom replied proudly after taking a long pull from his bottle of beer. He bore a striking resemblance to his son despite his thinning hair, graying beard and developing beer belly. Rose was pretty and predictably tall with a long face and lengthy, blonde locks. They both dressed conservatively, Tom in a white shirt and blue tie and Rose in a pastel-pink-and-gray sweater and black slacks.

"You and Dave look so much alike," commented Macayla. Elliott braced for an inappropriate remark but it failed to materialize. He exhaled in relief.

"You should see pictures of Tom in his thirties," responded Rose as the tension slowly evaporated. Emma's eight-year-old daughter, Tessa, skipped into the room as Rose added, "They look like the same person."

"Who do *I* look like?" asked Tessa while taking a seat next to Elliott. He, as usual, sat at the end of the table farthest from the kitchen.

"You have your mother's face and your father's eyes," Rose answered. She smiled at ten-year-old Lanie as she entered the room and said, "Your sister does, too. But that beautiful, dark brown hair comes from your Great Grandma Hastings."

"She's dead, right?" asked ten-year-old Lanie as she parked herself in the chair next to Tessa.

"Damn, Lanie, *blunt*," uttered Elliott with a smirk. Rose opened her mouth to correct him but her granddaughter beat her to the punch.

"Swear jar!" Lanie shouted. Elliott gave her a dubious look and rummaged around in his pocket. Producing a dollar, he laid it on the table.

"Here, that oughtta buy me a few more," grumbled Elliott.

"Naughty boy," Macayla rebuked Elliott in jest.

"All right, let's eat," Emma said as she set a large dish of steaming scalloped potatoes on the table. David entered the dining room behind her with a huge platter of sliced ham. A chorus of delighted compliments followed.

"This all looks and smells so awesome," said Macayla while offering Emma a grateful smile. She offered the same grin to Elliott, touched his arm affectionately and said, "I haven't eaten this good in a long time. I really miss family dinners since my parents have been gone."

Emma, feeling an unexpected empathy for Macayla, seated herself next to David who took his spot at the head of the table. While the family passed around dishes and began its meal, Emma watched Elliott and Macayla flirt like teenagers. He served her from each dish before serving himself and the chivalry reminded Emma of their father. She experienced a rush of nostalgia and a twinge of guilt.

"Tessa, you can't just eat corn," said Emma when she noticed her youngest child heaping corn onto her plate.

"Corn's good for you, Mom," Tessa countered. She shoveled a spoonful into her mouth and said through her food, "Mrs. Lucas says so."

"At least you're listening in school," Emma responded with a begrudging smile. Much to her surprise, the holiday meal proved to be a pleasant experience despite Macayla's presence; in fact, Elliott's girlfriend said nothing objectionable during dinner. Lanie and Tessa chattered away, amusing the adults with their silliness and allowing their elders to fill in the conversational gaps with simple questions and quick comments.

"I almost forgot," Elliott said suddenly. He rose from the table and added, "Excuse me for a second."

Emma tensed as she saw an engagement ring in her mind. She looked to Macayla who seemed as clueless as she was.

"Heads up, girls," Elliott said when he returned. He tossed a plastic egg to each of his nieces. Rose winced at the throwing of objects over the dinner table and Emma rolled her eyes. The girls eagerly snagged them from the air and popped them open. Elliott said, "Happy Easter, munchkins."

"Wow, ten bucks!" blurted Lanie. She held her prize high in the air.

"Awesome! Look, Mommy!" yelled Tessa while waving the bill at her mother.

"All right, girls," Emma corrected her daughters. Pointedly looking at her brother, she said, "We don't throw things at the dinner table, Uncle Elliott."

"Yeah, Uncle Elliott," agreed Macayla with a gentle smack of Elliott's hand.

"But that was awful nice," Emma said, "so what do you say?"

"Thank you!" chirped both girls. They leapt out of their chairs, bounded up to Elliott, one on either side, and hugged him.

"Love you, Uncle Elliott," Lanie said.

"Me, too," Tessa added.

"Yeah, yeah, everybody loves me when I throw cash-filled eggs at them," said Elliott as he playfully disentangled himself from his nieces' embraces. The moment touched all those who saw it, including Emma, until she saw the light dancing in Macayla's eyes. Her emotion faded.

"I'm gonna put mine in my room," declared Tessa as she moved towards the hallway. Lanie, however, stopped next to Macayla and stared at her chest.

"What's that?" asked Lanie, the youth intrigued by the barely-visible edge of a tattoo on Macayla's right breast.

"What's what, sweetie?" Macayla replied. Lanie pointed at the tattoo.

"What's on your boob?" asked Lanie with her usual forthrightness.

"Lanie!" Emma and Rose exclaimed in unison. Tessa walked back to where her sister stood.

"Yeah, what is that?" Tessa inquired.

"Oh, it's okay," said Macayla with a proud grin. She pulled her top sideways so that her vibrant Smurfette tattoo was fully visible and asked Lanie, "Pretty cool, huh? Can't hide it with this rack."

Emma and Rose watched in horror while David and his father speechlessly gawked at Macayla's tattoo. Elliott looked defeated and drained his wine glass.

"*So* cool," replied an awestruck Lanie. She reached out her hand and asked, "Can I touch it?"

"*No*, you *may* not," Emma insisted.

"Mommy, can I have a Smurfette tattoo when I get boobies?" Tessa asked with a thoughtful mien.

"Did it hurt?" queried Lanie, the child fascinated with the tattoo.

"Time for pie and ice cream and coffee!" Emma announced, an early dessert presenting the perfect excuse to evacuate her daughters from the dining room. She addressed the girls, saying, "You can each pick out two pieces of your Easter candy for dessert."

"Can I have ice cream, too?" asked Lanie.

"Yes," Emma replied quickly, her assent surprising David and his parents, "now go."

The girls scampered towards their rooms with cheers and laughs. Emma used the distraction to escape.

"I'll just get these dishes," said David. He scooped up as many dinner plates as he could and rushed into the kitchen.

"More wine for me!" exclaimed Macayla. She grabbed the open bottle in front of her and emptied it into her glass. Pausing as if struck by a thought, she said, "Maybe I'll grab a smoke first."

Rose cringed but Tom's hand on her thigh preempted a verbal response. Macayla stood up and headed for the door.

"I'll go with you," said Elliott as he followed on her heels. He imagined his sister's enragement and said to himself, "Not worth it."

. . . .

"JUST TAKE IT EASY," said David as he entered the kitchen with a high stack of dirty plates. Emma waited until Macayla and Elliott left the house and then unloaded her angst.

"I can't take it anymore, Dave, I just can't," Emma complained as she uncovered a cherry pie on the counter. She flicked on the coffee maker and continued, "Is that what we want our daughters exposed to? Boob tattoos, slutty clothes and cigarettes. It's like he's intentionally throwing all these bar whores in my face just to, like, piss me off."

"So she's a little rough around the edges. She doesn't seem that bad, at least compared to some of the others," replied David while setting the plates in the sink. Emma stopped and stared at her husband.

"Oh, because she didn't ask your mom for a joint like his last winner?" Emma asked. She retrieved a half-gallon of vanilla ice cream from the freezer and said, "That's a Christmas memory I'll never forget."

David shrugged.

"The girls seem ta' like her," countered David feebly.

"That's because all three of them like cartoons and haven't finished grade school yet," Emma said. She efficiently assembled the pie, ice cream, dessert plates and utensils on a tray and suggested, "Maybe Auntie Macayla can take them to get their first titty tattoos."

"Hey, I didn't bring her here," replied David with his hands raised in front of him. Emma exhaled sharply and dropped her shoulders.

"I know. I'm sorry," Emma said. She embraced David and explained, "He's just been wandering aimlessly since Daddy and Mom died. And not just with his relationships. He's like a ghost floating through life that's, that's . . . like waiting to die."

Emma permitted herself some tears and clung to David. He held her until she stopped.

"This is bullshit," Emma declared while drying her eyes. She shook free of her sadness and said angrily, "I'm throwing her out. Right now."

"Nope," said David. He grabbed Emma around the waist and interrupted her march from the kitchen, suggesting, "Let's just get through dessert, huh?"

Elliott appeared in the doorway. His face became grim when he saw Emma seething.

"You ready to tag out, man?" asked Elliott. Emma fought her way out of David's arms and began attending to the dishes.

"Please," David replied. He wasted no time in grabbing the dessert tray and exiting the kitchen. Emma rinsed plates and utensils and placed them in the dishwasher.

"Look, Em," said Elliott, "I know-."

"You're done, Elliott," Emma curtly interrupted him. Refusing to look at her brother, she continued loading the dishwasher and stated, "From now on, you can either show up alone or don't show up. Your trashy girlfriends aren't welcome in my home anymore."

"Hey, what's your problem?" snapped Elliott. Emma slammed the dishwasher shut and accosted her brother with wild eyes.

"What's *your* problem, Elliott?" Emma replied. She opened a cupboard and, one by one, began slamming coffee mugs onto the counter. Firing him a sneer, she said, "Maybe you could bring a stripper to Thanksgiving this year. Or why just one? *Bring two*."

"It's not like she flashed her tits at the table," scoffed Elliott. He attempted to approach Emma but she retreated as he said, "She just wanted to show the girls the tattoo. I'll talk to her about it. She doesn't have kids so she's not real clear on where the lines are."

"She knows where they are when they're made of white powder," Emma said acerbically.

"Hey, that's just a rumor," countered Elliott, "and it's not true."

"I'm not having this conversation anymore," Emma replied as she picked up all six coffee mugs with her fingers. She walked around the kitchen island to avoid him and uttered, "Let's just get through dessert."

"Nah, I wouldn't wanna subject you to any more of Macayla," said Elliott as he turned his back on Emma, "so we'll just leave."

"Elliott, no. Stay for dessert," Emma implored him, her vitriol ebbing as she unsuccessfully tried to block his exit. Elliott left the kitchen with her in tow and ducked into the dining room to bid David and his parents farewell.

"*Elliott,*" Emma beckoned.

"Well, all, we gotta fly," announced Elliott apologetically.

"You're leavin' already?" asked David. Elliott gave his brother-in-law a half-hug, kissed Rose on the cheek and shook Tom's hand.

"Yeah, man, sorry, I totally lost track of time," Elliott lied. He pointed at Tom and said, "You guys enjoy freezing your balls off tomorrow."

Tom chuckled.

"Elliott, *please stay,*" Emma begged, her hands still holding the mugs.

"Thanks for the grub, Sis," Elliott said. He grasped her by the shoulders, kissed her forehead and said, "Say goodbye to the little monsters for me."

Elliott brushed past his sister and hung a left into the foyer. Seconds later, the door closed and he was gone. David and his parents avoided eye contact with Emma who, stunned by her brother's departure, stood paralyzed.

"Damn it!" Emma finally exclaimed.

"Swear jar!" shouted Lanie from her bedroom.

• • • •

EXHAUSTED BY THE ORDEAL of Easter dinner, Emma lay on the couch and nursed a beer. Though she looked at the television, her eyes were hazy and she saw nothing but a blur. The kitchen telephone rang and David, after plucking a cold beer from the refrigerator, answered it.

"Hel-lo," said David. He paused while the caller revealed her identity and then replied, "Oh, hey . . . yeah, I'll get her."

"Unless the club's on fire, tell whoever it is to go away," Emma instructed her husband. She took a sip of her warm beer and grimaced, muttering, "Yuck."

"It's Donna, hon," said David as he stepped into the living room and held up the telephone. Emma spun into a sitting position and placed her beer on the coffee table.

"Oh," she replied with a quizzical mien. She rose to her feet and hurried to the telephone. Taking it from her husband, she held the receiver to her shoulder and kissed him.

"Thanks, babe," Emma said. David took her place on the couch and changed the television channel with the remote. Returning the telephone to her ear, Emma said with concern, "What's wrong?"

"Nothing's wrong," replied Emma's best friend, Donna Kirkinshaw, as she plopped into a loveseat. She wore a yellow bikini top with a towel wrapped around her waist. Emma's best friend was uniquely pretty with prominent eyebrows and an angular jaw. Her eyelashes were dark, her eyes hazel and her curly hair light-brown with blonde highlights.

"Then why're you calling me at ten o'clock on Easter Sunday?" Emma asked. Holding the receiver between her neck and her head, she walked into the living room with a bottle opener and removed the cap from David's beer.

"It's only seven here," countered Donna with a smirk. Throwing her legs over the arm of the loveseat, she bragged, "I'm tired though because I sat by the pool all day."

"Don't you dare tell me the temperature out there," Emma said as she returned to the kitchen with her bottle of warm beer. She poured the remainder of its contents into the sink.

"Hotter than you'd like, trust me," replied Donna before shifting the receiver to her other ear, "and pretty hot for early April, too."

"Soooo, what's up?" Emma inquired impatiently as she stuck the magnetic bottle opener to the refrigerator. She detected a hint of seriousness in Donna's tone and suspected a Michigan visit was imminent.

"I'm coming home next week, Em," answered Donna.

"I knew it! That's awesome!" Emma exclaimed with her usual toothy smile. Taking a seat at the kitchen table, she continued, "Listen, I know your brother's gonna want you to stay there, but why don't you stay with us for a few days?"

"You know the girls hate giving up their rooms," said Donna. She pulled at the drying curls of her hair.

"Well, that's too bad for them," Emma said, "but they won't have to, anyway. Believe it or not, Dave finally finished the room in the basement."

"You're welcome," called out David while holding up his beer bottle. Donna heard his voice and laughed.

"I'll talk to Mark about it," said Donna with hesitation in her voice. Emma knew Elliott was the cause of her reluctance. Donna added, "He and Beth might need me to watch the kids."

"I'm sure he can spare you for a few days," Emma replied. She brushed strands of her hair over her ear and said, "You and I can sleep in the new room and we'll leave the girls up here with Dave. Ya' know, have a couple of girls' nights like old times. How long are you staying?"

"Forever," said Donna bluntly. She squirmed in the loveseat in anticipation of Emma's response.

"You're hilarious," Emma said with half-smile. She picked up a pen and began doodling on the front page of The Detroit News while asking, "But seriously, how long?"

"I mean it, Em, I'm coming home for good," replied Donna. She felt anxious and her palms were sweaty.

"No way," Emma scoffed as she set down the pen.

"Yes way," said Donna with a sigh.

"What about Kenny?" Emma asked. Donna's pause let her know Kenny's fate.

"We broke up," answered Donna.

"*Noooo*," Emma replied. Standing up and beginning to pace the kitchen, she peppered Donna with questions: "What happened? Was it the not wanting kids thing? Wait, what about your house? And your job?"

"I sold the house last month," said Donna. She scanned the hills of stacked boxes in her living room and added, "and Friday was my last day of work."

"You little sneak!" Emma exclaimed.

"I've got some money saved up and I'm gonna stay at Mark's until I find a job and get my own place," explained Donna. She stood up and maneuvered through the maze of boxes, saying, "He's already helped me set up a few interviews for later this month."

"Why didn't you tell me?!" Emma queried in disbelief. Gesticulating as she paced, she admonished Donna, "I'm your best friend for god's sake!"

"I'm sorry, Em," answered Donna remorsefully. She uncorked a half-full bottle of red wine and added, "But don't feel bad. Only Mark knew so he could help me on the Detroit end, and you're just too busy for me to lay all of that on you. I mean, I just told my mom about it, like, two hours ago."

"Okay, missy, you need to tell me what's going on with you, right now," Emma demanded.

"I've decided I need some big changes in my life," began Donna while obtaining a wine glass. Filling it with Merlot, she expounded disappointedly, "I'm thirty-five, unmarried and childless and *I want a family*. My career's good, I guess, but there's more to life than that."

"You still have time for a family," Emma assured her.

"Yeah, but it's running out fast," interjected Donna with a determination foreign to her character. She sipped her wine before continuing, "We're the same age but you have a great husband, and two beautiful girls and a happy home. I don't have any of that, and I just don't think I ever will if I stay out here."

"Well, okay then, honey. *Come home*," Emma said lovingly. She asked, "When do you get here?"

"I love you," said Donna, the support of her best friend meaning the world to her. She re-corked the wine bottle and explained, "I fly into Metro next Sunday morning. Mark's got a whole family dinner planned with his family and Crystal's family – Mom and Dad may or may not show up – but I thought maybe we could meet up on Monday . . . if you're not too busy."

"Of course I'm not too busy," Emma insisted. A plan began forming in Emma's head and she suggested, "Maybe we could invite the boys and make it a foursome for dinner."

David rolled his eyes.

"I know I'm making really big changes," replied Donna, "but I don't know if I'm ready for *that*."

"Ya' know, Elliott's not even dating anyone right now," Emma lied convincingly. David scolded her with a look but she glared at him, waved dismissively and asked, "Can you believe that?"

Donna remained quiet for several telltale seconds. Emma smiled with a happy deviousness.

"Wow. Well, look, I need to call my sister before she goes to bed," replied Donna to change the subject.

"Okay, sweetie," Emma said, "you let us know if you need anything on this end."

"I will," replied a grateful Donna. She grasped her wine glass with both hands and said, "Love you, Em."

"Love you, too, *ya' sneak*," Emma replied. She paused for a second and then squealed, "I'm getting my best friend back!"

"Bye, psycho," said Donna with a laugh. Emma hung up the telephone and meandered into the living room while deep in thought. David looked at her.

"What're you gonna tell Donna when she eventually runs into Macayla?" asked David pointedly.

"That tramp'll probably dump him after tonight," Emma replied as she insinuated herself onto the couch next to David, "and, even if she doesn't, when Elliott sees Donna, he'll throw out that trash."

"You sure about that?" queried David.

"*Positive*," Emma replied with the utmost confidence.

Along Comes a Woman

"That seat's taken, sweetheart," said the white-haired old man. Wearing a 1970s powder blue suit, he patted the barstool next to him and added with a leer, "This one's not, though."

"Oh, I'm sorry," Nora Billingsley replied sheepishly as she slid off the barstool. Looking at the old man with eyes as blue as his suit, the twenty-two-year-old, golden blonde glossed over his licentiousness and asked, "Was someone sitting here?"

"No, that's Elliott's seat. See?" said the old man as he pointed to a burnished nameplate attached to the bar reading: RESERVED above ELLIOTT WARDEN. He sipped his bourbon and suggested, "But you can sit by me."

"Oh, uhhh," Nora said, the young woman unable to muster any other words. The waitress who initially greeted her breezed up to them with an empty tray. The petite, raven-haired forty-year-old was attractive but age weathered her face.

"Ignore him, honey," said the waitress. She placed a hand on her hip, threw daggers at the old man with her big, hazel eyes and admonished him, "She can sit wherever she wants."

"How about on my lap?" the old man suggested. He patted his thigh.

"It's 1985, Don," said the waitress, "buy a new suit."

"You'd better be nice to me, Brandy," warned the old man, "or no tip for you."

"You couldn't get it up to give me the tip," countered Brandy with a satisfied smirk, her remark horrifying Nora. The tension caused her to squirm but, as quickly as it started, it ended. Don and the waitress laughed and, lowering the tray to her side, she kissed him on the cheek. Nora sighed in relief.

"They're all bark and no bite," said Brandy with a smile as she walked backward for several steps. Before spinning around, she told Nora, "I'll go get Emma for you."

"Thanks," replied Nora. A new patron walked through the front doors, one of which was propped open due to the warmth of the late April afternoon. Immediately to the right of the doors was an area for the bouncers and hostesses to operate and a small coat check room. Next to it was the long, straight bar which ran nearly the length of the building though a hallway at its end permitted access to the kitchen and restrooms. A well-organized counter was attached to the wall behind the bar, above which were shelves copiously stocked with liquor and below which were numerous cupboards and beer coolers.

"That's a lot of booze," commented Nora as she scanned the back wall of the bar. She heard the words in her father's voice.

"We drink alotta booze, honey," Don said. He drained his bourbon, shook the glass and then slurped out the remainder of the liquid. Wiping his mouth with a handkerchief, he asked, "Buy you a drink?"

"Oh, no thank you," declined Nora. The old man began telling Nora a story to which she responded with polite nods and smiles. When his meandering tale drifted too far so did her attention and she studied the rest of the club. It contained three areas of tables which bordered three sides of the wooden dance floor. Beyond it there was an elevated stage for the bands that played the club several days a week. Memorabilia from area sports teams - with a heavy emphasis on the Detroit Tigers - adorned the walls but so did signed photographs of the many local bands that played within Johnny Dubs' walls.

"Here comes Emma now," said Don. He rested his folded arms on the bar and gushed, "She's pretty, that one."

"She's gorgeous," replied Nora with admiration. Though she scrunchied her hair into a messy bun and wore a tank top and jeans, Emma shined brightly in the darkness of the club. Her presence made Nora feel self-conscious and she said to herself, "Wonder if she's the reason this place is so popular."

Nora watched Emma deftly work her way down the line of customers at the bar. She boisterously bantered back and forth with them as she made and served their drinks.

"Who's Elliott?" inquired Nora as she waited for Emma. Don gave her a dubious look and turned away. He grasped his glass with both hands.

"I think I'd better let Emma explain that," Don answered.

. . . .

EMMA RAN JOHNNY DUBS, a popular club in the City of Taylor, Michigan. Her father, John Warden, established a bar on the location upon his return from World War II and she had waited tables and bartended there since high school. Emma assumed ownership of the bar after John's death a decade earlier.

"You must be Nora," Emma said after setting another bourbon before Don. She whisked away his old glass and then swiftly washed and dried it. Toweling off her hands, she extended one of them to Nora and said, "I'm Emma. Sorry about the wait. I had to check in a food shipment and my afternoon bartender's off today."

"That's okay," replied Nora. She acutely felt the older woman's magnetism and was surprised by the strength of her handshake.

"So, Nora," Emma said as she studied the young woman's round face and fleshy cheeks. Nora felt as if she read her mind like a book when she asked, "Why do you wanna work here?"

"Well, uh, I've been, like, waitressing in bars for a few years now and, uh, the tips are, like, really good," began Nora with little nervous tremors in her voice. All the men at the bar watched the quasi-interview with great interest.

"You guys gettin' all this?" Emma interrupted as her stern gaze rolled over the length of the bar. Each man quickly turned his attention back to his drink or the television mounted on the wall. Nora blushed. Emma chuckled and shook her head, saying, "Sorry, go ahead."

"Oh, well, yeah, the tips are really good, and this place is, like, *so* busy at night. It makes it fun and the shifts go by fast," continued Nora as the telling of her story bolstered her confidence. Emma drifted down the bar and switched out two empty beer bottles for full ones as Nora expounded, "See, I wanna go back to college. I only finished a semester at U of M Dearborn and then quit. Waitressing is good for working a school schedule around. And I don't mind working weekends."

"College girl, huh?" Emma asked as she approached Nora. She flashed the younger woman a knowing look and said, "We might even be able to schedule work around your school."

"That'd be awesome," Nora gushed.

"You gonna stay for the whole four years or whatever you have left?" Emma queried.

"That'd be *really* awesome," replied Nora with a big, beautiful smile. Feeling good about Emma and her employment at Johnny Dubs, she ventured, "So does this mean I've got the job?"

"Well, I assume you have waitressing references, and that they'll check out, right?" Emma inquired. She possessed her father's talent for evaluating employees and knew she could trust Nora.

"Oh, yeah, totally," agreed Nora with a hopeful expression. She pulled a folded paper out of her front pocket, opened it and handed it to Emma.

"Great," Emma replied as she took the paper. She read through the list of names and numbers and then said, "Then there's just one more thing."

"I told you not to sit in the golden boy's seat," said Don.

"Butt out, Donald," Emma snapped. Don raised his right hand in a sign of surrender.

"This is about Elliott, isn't it?" suggested Nora cautiously.

"Good guess, college girl," Emma replied. She folded her hands, placed her elbows on the bar and explained with a trace of irritation, "Elliott's my beloved older brother and, as part of your duties here, you'll need to watch out for him like he's your brother."

"Um, o-kay," said Nora. Emma's manner of speaking about Elliott made her uneasy.

"He'll wander in here about six o'clock almost every day, hit the bar and order his usual . . . a Grumpy Old Man," Emma continued, her sentence punctuated with an eye roll. Nora tilted her head and offered her a puzzled expression.

"A Grumpy Old Man?" asked Nora, her words catching the ear of a grizzled, older man further down the bar. Wearing a dirty baseball cap, a flannel shirt and jeans, he took a moment to give Nora a once-over.

"Right here, cutie!" shouted the old man with a goofy grin. Nora giggled and waved to him. Emma feigned a scowl.

"Go back to your beer, Mark, ya' old perv!" Emma yelled back. She placed her hands on her hips and said, "She's only . . . how old are you?"

"Twenty-two," answered Nora.

"She's only twenty-two!" Emma scolded him. Mark laughed as she winked at him. She looked back to Nora and thought, "She *is* really cute, and seems like a great kid. But way too young for Elliott."

"I guess I should learn how to make a Grumpy Old Man," said Nora as she disentangled herself from the conversation about her age. Emma stood up and threw a threatening finger at Mark who grinned deviously at her.

"She can make this grumpy, old-," began Mark.

"Don't, Mark," Emma warned him. He laughed again and snuck another glimpse at Nora before returning to his beer. Emma gestured towards Mark and asked, "See what you're gonna have to deal with?"

"Brandy said they're all bark," said Nora with another giggle. Brandy strode past them and held up her hand for a high five. Nora met it with her own and asserted, "I can handle it."

"I don't doubt it," Emma said. Grabbing a glass, she began making a Grumpy Old Man and explained, "So, it's easy. Old fashioned glass . . . fill with ice . . . full shot a' bourbon, and then a splash of lime juice . . . top it off with Vernors and . . . *viola*."

Emma set the glass in front of Nora. She motioned to the drink.

"Go ahead, try it," Emma urged her. Nora hesitantly indulged in a sip.

"It's good," Nora said with a smile. Emma watched her expectantly until she sipped it again and added, "It's a unique taste."

"Yeah, it is, just like Elliott," Emma said. She stretched out her arms, grasped the edge of the bar with both hands and leaned forward, expounding, "While he's working on that first one, get him to order dinner and get it in right away so he's eating with his second drink."

"Is he an alcoholic?" asked Nora gingerly. Her expression became serious and she said softly, "My Dad's one, so I've had lots of experience dealing with it."

"No, thankfully, but if he has more than two without eating, he gets stuck in his own head and tries to drink himself out," Emma answered. Worry became evident on her face though it faded as she continued, "That usually leads to bad things, so he's cut off at three, though he almost always stops at two. Anyway, if you ever think he's had too much, call him a cab and send him home. He won't fight you on it because he knows he'll have to deal with me if he does. But I'll be here most of the time, and the rest of the crew knows Elliott and the routine, so you'll probably be spared that chore."

"I don't mind dealing with it," replied Nora, the new waitress still processing her unexpected duties concerning Elliott. She inquired, "How old is he?"

"You'd think he's, like, a day past twenty-one, right?" Emma asked as her characteristic energy returned. She said with disapprobation, "But he's thirty-seven. He's not an obnoxious drunk or anything. Just a little. . . *dark*. And stupid. Likes to pick up bar whores stupid."

"Gotcha," said Nora as she faked a grin.

"He's really not that difficult to deal with. Like I said, just watch out for him like he's your own brother," Emma said. She gave Nora a penetrating look and asked, "Think you can do that?"

"Yeah," said Nora with affirmative nods and all the confidence she could muster, "I can do that."

"Then welcome to the team, honey," Emma said with a muted grin. She maintained it as she spoke but threatened Nora, "Oh, one last thing. If you sleep with him, you're *absolutely* fired."

. . . .

"THIS IS MY LUCKY DAY," said Don as a second attractive young woman walked into the bar. He took a drink of his bourbon and swiveled his barstool around to face her, saying lasciviously, "Hey there, beautiful."

"Uh, hi," the woman replied with a disturbed half-smile. Her light-brown hair was cut boyishly short and she possessed large, energetic blue eyes. She was also taller than many of the men in the bar and slim-figured save for her broad hips. Dressed in a blue, long-sleeved t-shirt and stonewashed jeans, she asked Don, "Is the manager here?"

"Down there," answered a miffed Don as he pointed at Emma. She stood at one of the club's two cash registers and spoke to Nora who, due to Brandy's suddenly sick child, started her first shift sooner than expected. He sipped his bourbon, raised his hand and added in annoyance, "I know, I know. She's gorgeous."

"Yeah, I guess she is," Toni replied as she appraised Emma who, after instructing Nora on the cash register, disappeared into the hallway at the end of the bar and then quickly reemerged with a tray of food. Dexterously holding it aloft, she hurried down the aisle between the bar and the tables. Toni met her halfway.

"Hi, I'm-," began Toni.

"One sec, hon," Emma said as she dodged Toni and rushed past her.

"Oh-kay," said Toni with a shrug. Sitting down at a table, she rested her chin in her palm and waited patiently. Emma attended to several tasks throughout the dining room and then worked her way back to Toni.

"Sorry, what can I do for you?" Emma asked with a pleasant grin. Toni stood up but then paused, the young woman taken aback by Emma's unique eyes.

"Uh . . . hey, I'm Toni . . . Toni Cullen," said Toni. Emma gave her a blank look which prompted her to add, "I'm with the band, Morning Cloak? Billy Jakes sent me."

"That's right, my Country Night replacement," Emma replied. She shook Toni's hand and gushed, "I'm sooo glad you guys can fill in. I planned this Country Night and then my best country band finked out on me. Billy Jakes said you guys are good, and you especially."

Toni blushed.

"Billy may be a little biased," said Toni modestly as, like Nora, she noticed the strength of Emma's handshake.

"His eyes did twinkle a bit when he was talking about you," Emma replied with a smirk. A sudden realization struck her and she commented, "You're tall."

"Five ten and three quarters," answered Toni, her expression conveying that the question was one she was often asked. Emma continued to study her, the scrutiny making her mildly uncomfortable.

"T-shirt and jeans girl, I see," Emma remarked. Toni chuckled.

"Sometimes," answered Toni. Emma's intrusiveness became less discomfiting and more amusing.

"What do you do for a living?" Emma asked with a serious mien. Toni laughed.

"I'm a nurse over at Heritage," said Toni with a gesture to the northwest as if Emma could see the hospital from where they stood. She asked, "Do you usually give your bands the third degree?"

"Nah, I just have a brother I'm trying to marry off," Emma said matter-of-factly. She seemed to decide against Toni as a potential mate for Elliott and explained, "I was just getting this vibe from you, like the two of you would really hit it off. But, now that I think about it, you're probably too young. And he'd bore you."

"I *am* twenty-seven," replied Toni as she jokingly played along. Emma wrinkled her nose.

"Yeah, still too young," Emma sighed. She shook her head and added, "I think a decade's too much."

"My loss," said Toni playfully. Emma decided she liked Toni nonetheless.

"You want a beer or somethin'?" Emma asked. When Toni offered her an uncertain look, she added temptingly, "On the house."

"Sure," said Toni. She considered her options and asked, "Bud Light in a bottle?"

"Can you excuse me for a minute? There's the girl who's not too young for him," Emma said as she noticed Donna walk into the bar. She pointed to Toni as she approached the front doors and yelled to Nora, "Bud Light for Toni, on the house."

"Comin' up," replied Nora. Emma hurried up to Donna.

"Hey, you!" Emma shouted when she arrived. The two women squealed and hugged in an obnoxious display. Several bar patrons began clapping when she said, "It's so good to see you!"

Nora dropped off the Bud Light for Toni but kept her eyes on her new boss and her friend. Toni followed her line of sight to Donna.

"So that's the chosen one," said Nora. Toni took a pull of her beer.

"Excuse me?" asked Toni.

"She's looking for, like, the perfect girl for her brother," answered Nora. She tilted her head and said slowly, "And I think that's her."

"She must not be that sure about it," said Toni with a simper, "because she was just interviewing me for the job."

"Emma told me if I slept with him I'm 'absolutely' fired," Nora said.

"She thought I was too young for him at twenty-seven," remarked Toni, "so I think it's an age thing."

"Well, Emma said he shows up just about every night, so I'll at least get to meet the mystery man soon," replied Nora. She looked to Toni and said sweetly, "Let me know if you need anything else."

"Thanks," said Toni. Nora scurried towards the bar to attend to her patrons as Toni watched Emma and Donna's reunion and drank her beer. She queried quietly, "Every night, huh?"

Toni fingered the label on her beer bottle. The smallest twinge of guilt turned her thoughts back to her own boyfriend, Bobby, and she soon forgot about the plight of Emma's brother.

• • • •

HER INTEREST PIQUED by Donna's arrival, Nora kept an eye on her as she went about her duties. She believed Emma's longtime friend to be an acquired taste in the looks department.

"Definitely not as pretty as Emma," thought Nora.

"It's been way too long," Emma gushed. She examined Donna's toned arms and shoulders, her tanned skin and cute green sundress, marveling, "Arizona's been good to you. You look fantastic."

Donna blushed. Something about her response told Emma Arizona was not as good to her as it appeared.

"Hey, sweetie, my name's Don!" yelled Don from his barstool, the old man clearly intoxicated. He held up his glass and shouted, "How 'bout you let me put the Don in Donna?!"

The entire bar, including Donna, erupted in laughter. Nora placed her hand over her mouth to stifle a surprised chuckle.

"I will throw you out of my club," Emma replied with a pointed finger. She managed to restrain her own laughter for a few seconds before muttering, "These guys, I tell ya."

"You sound just like your Dad," said Donna as the patrons returned to their drinks and conversations. She looked around the bar and walked into the past, saying wistfully, "I still miss him."

Emma's countenance darkened and her eyes watered. She took a moment to compose herself.

"Me, too," Emma finally uttered. Shaking off her sadness, she motioned to a large picture of John Warden behind the bar and declared proudly, "But Daddy's always here."

"Sorry, Em," said Donna as she saw the picture. She breathed deeply and then exhaled, saying, "Coming here brings back so much."

"Remembering him is always a *good* thing," Emma said. She noticed Toni waiting and added as she pointed at her with both hands, "I've gotta handle something real quick and then I'll be back with beer. Sit wherever."

"Oh, we can catch up later," replied Donna. She watched Nora hustling a food order out to a table and said, "Looks like you're a little shorthanded."

"Nah, me and the new girl got it," Emma countered without the least bit of concern. She walked backwards a few steps and asked, "Whatcha drinking?"

"Will I be in trouble if I say Merlot?" replied Donna.

"Normally, yes. But today I'll let it slide," Emma said with mock irritation. She turned around as she arrived at Toni's table and explained, "Hey, my best friend who I haven't seen in forever just got in from outta town. Mind if we cut this short?"

"Oh, sure, no, problem," replied Toni.

"Nine or ten 'til one or so with the usual breaks," Emma advised. Toni attempted to finish her beer as Emma continued, "Same terms as Billy, pay and everything. And if you keep this place full through your whole set, I'll throw in an extra $20 each for you and your guys. Fair?"

"Oh, definitely," confirmed Toni. She rose to her feet and said, "We're not tryin' to make it big or anything. We just love to play."

"Sounds good," Emma said as the pair shook hands. Toni caught a glimpse of Donna.

"Good luck with your brother," said Toni. She felt awkward as the words passed her lips and wondered why she said them.

"Thank you," Emma replied. She glanced at Donna and said, "but I think everything's gonna be alright now. See ya' in two weeks."

"See ya' in two weeks," Toni repeated before turning and exiting the bar. Both Emma and Donna watched her leave and felt a strange sensation in their hearts. They looked to one another but each woman quickly averted her eyes. Nora noticed.

"That was weird," she thought.

• • • •

MANY OF THE CLUB'S patrons, seemingly realizing that Emma wished to speak with her old friend, finished their drinks, threw down their cash and exited the club. Few of them remained and Nora interacted with them as if she worked at Johnny Dubs for years.

"She's so meek but she just mixes right in," Emma said as she watched Nora serve her customers. She and Donna sat at a two-person table next to the south wall, the vantage point providing them a view of the entire club.

"Yeah," said a distant Donna. Her eyes were on Nora but her mind was on Elliott.

"So are you gonna ask me about Elliott or what?" Emma inquired impatiently.

"I don't know, Em," replied Donna before lifting the wine glass to her lips and taking a drink. Clearly conflicted, she said, "It's been *fifteen years*, and we've both changed and . . . I just don't know."

"What's left to know?" Emma challenged her. She drank a Miller Light and argued, "You're single, and still in love with him, and he hasn't dated anyone for more than three months since you guys broke up."

Donna winced and her expression became sour. She took several gulps of her Merlot.

"That doesn't mean anything," countered Donna. Her face flushed as the old memories and emotions – both good and bad – flooded her mind and her heart.

"The hell it doesn't," Emma said with intense eyes. She reached over the table, grasped Donna's forearm and insisted, "He's been a revolving door of relationships because none of them were with you. He knows he screwed up."

"Did he say that?" asked Donna skeptically.

"Not in so many words," Emma replied as she released Donna's arm, "but I know my brother better than anyone and he knows he shoulda' stayed with you."

"How are you so sure he's still interested, after all this time?" asked Donna. She wanted so badly to believe Emma but old wounds made her wary.

"Daddy always loved you like his own daughter," Emma answered. She took a sip of her beer and continued, "To him, you were already family. He was always telling Elliott to make it official."

"'Son, get off your ass and marry that girl,'" repeated Donna with a warm smile. It faded and she returned her attention to Emma, saying gravely, "But that doesn't mean Elliott's still interested. And you know your Mom didn't agree with your Dad. I mean, she was always great to me, too, but she didn't believe I was the one for Elliott."

"She was wrong," Emma asserted in a bitter tone. Drawing herself up, she stated resolutely, "I'm gonna lean on him this time."

"So you're gonna twist his arm and make him be with me?" asked Donna sharply. She drank her wine, looked away and added, "Geez, Em, why don't you just get a shotgun?"

"Daddy should've," Emma snapped.

"Just let things happen as they happen" begged Donna, " . . . *if* they happen."

"Look at me," Emma demanded while grasping Donna's arm again. Donna reluctantly obeyed as her friend added, "I'm going to help him make the right decision. The decision he messed up in 1970."

"Does he know I'm back?" queried Donna. Emma released her arm and returned to her beer.

"No, and *we* are going to use that to our advantage," Emma assured her.

"I don't want to trick him into it, either, Em," objected Donna.

"We're not going to trick him," Emma said. She took a long slow drink of beer, narrowed her eyes as the gears of her mind spun and declared, "But Elliott's wasted fifteen years. I'm not letting him waste any more."

Donna's lip quivered and she gently bit it. She shifted in her chair.

"Maybe it's too late," suggested Donna. Emma jerked her head towards her friend.

"*It's not*," Emma scolded her. Donna turned towards Emma and rested her folded arms on the table.

"It's not just me you want for him, it's the whole family thing," said Donna shrewdly. The distress was evident on her face as she argued, "If Elliott and I conceived a baby tonight it'd still be a high-risk pregnancy. What if I can't carry a baby to term? My mom lost two pregnancies."

"She was sixteen and nineteen, not thirty-five," Emma countered despite the kernel of doubt created by Donna's reasoning. She insisted, "And you want a family just as much as I want one for you and Elliott. Everything will be fine."

"Maybe he needs someone younger," offered Donna as she turned her attention to Nora.

"Stop it," Emma demanded. She took Donna's hands in her own and squeezed them reassuringly, saying, "You and Elliott will get married, have kids and build a life together. You'll be happy, he'll be happy. He just needs a little work and a little motivation. That's all. I promise."

"Okay, Em," said Donna with a convincing smile, "but just give me a little time, first."

"You got it," Emma replied, "but not *too* long."

The dinner rush started early and ran late and, even with the night waitresses and bartender hustling at full speed, Emma asked Nora to work until it ended. When it did, she left the club in the capable hands of her seasoned staff and led Nora into the hallway at the far end of the bar.

"You did great today," Emma lauded her.

"Thanks," replied Nora while blushing. The hallway granted access to the kitchen and, beyond that, the men's and women's restrooms. Across from the bar there was another door which led to an external yet enclosed stairway. It was up this flight of steps that Nora followed her new boss.

"No one but me, my husband and Sean have keys to my office," Emma advised. She inserted the key into the deadbolt, turned it and then paused, adding, "And no one else is *ever* allowed in here without me, except maybe Elliott."

"Got it," replied Nora. Pushing open the door, Emma revealed her large office. Opposite the door sat a cluttered desk and chair with two guest chairs in front of it while to the right against the near wall was a worn leather couch. A full bathroom and a walk-in closet dominated the far-right wall.

"Now we honor tradition," Emma announced while closing the door. Motioning to one of the chairs in front of the desk, she circumvented it and said, "Have a seat."

"You're not going to hit me, are you?" asked Nora half-jokingly. She slowly seated herself as Emma used another key to open a cabinet behind her desk. Emma left the keys dangling from the lock.

"I'm not gonna hit you," Emma said with a sly grin, "but this might."

Keeping her eyes on Emma, Nora watched her anxiously as she placed an unmarked bottle of clear liquor on the desk with one hand and two shot glasses with the other. Emma opened the bottle and filled them both.

"Every new employee since Daddy opened this place has had a shot of this with him, or me, at the end of their first shift," Emma explained with pride. Happily traveling into the past, she continued, "I had my first shot at sixteen when I started waitressing here. Mom would have killed him if she knew about it. But it was our little secret."

Emma handed one shot glass to Nora and picked up the other. Feeling a sense of occasion, Nora rose to her feet.

"Daddy used to toast 'all the boys who never made it back'," Emma said, "but I always toast him."

Emma and Nora raised their glasses together. Emma's eyes glistened with emotion.

"To John Warden," Emma said loudly with a compelling strength in her voice.

"To John Warden," repeated Nora. Each woman drank her shot. Emma easily handled the liquor but Nora did not, croaking, "Oh . . . god."

Nora struggled to recover from the spirit's harsh sensation. She fell into her chair as Emma eased into her seat.

"Well, you've seen how this place works now," Emma said. She stifled a smile as Nora sputtered and coughed and expounded, "The old guys, the retirees, the bar flies who've been coming in for years and years, they hang out here from opening until around dinner. Some stay and eat, some don't, and you'll never know who's staying and who's going because they don't even know. Dinner's usually busy but manageable, and then there's always a lull before the younger crowd starts showing up around nine, nine-thirty. It's packed in here most nights, especially Thursday through Sunday when the bands come in."

"Awesome," said Nora with a raspy voice, the twentysomething still feeling the effects of the liquor.

"You'll be bumping around on shifts depending on your school schedule, at least to start, but you'll do just fine no matter which one you're on. You're pretty, and nice, and you put up with their bullshit, so the geezers – *which I say affectionately* – will all fall in love with you, and so will all the young idiots who come in at night," Emma said. She wavered on whether to assess Nora's fitness as a girlfriend but the younger woman beat her to the punch.

"Hey, about that sleeping with your brother thing," said Nora sheepishly.

"What about it?" Emma asked. She feigned ignorance.

"I'm not like that, I swear," said Nora with all the earnestness she could muster.

"Oh, sweetie, I know you're not. I don't hire bar whores, I just serve 'em. Ya' just gotta keep 'em on the right side of the bar or you lose money," Emma replied as she stood up. Replacing the cap on the bottle, she whisked it and the shot glasses away and said bluntly, "And when it comes to Elliott, I love my big bro, but he's damaged goods and needs a particular type of girl . . . no, a particular type of *woman*."

"Like Donna," said Nora. She felt strange saying Donna's name and experienced an unpleasant sensation not unlike the taste of the liquor. Nora attempted to hide it.

"*Exactly* like Donna," Emma said while evaluating Nora's reaction. She returned everything to its place, locked the cabinet and added suggestively, "Now, if you were ten years older, well, I might just reconsider. Of course, you do seem pretty mature for your age . . . ."

Turning back to Nora, Emma let her scintillating eyes wash over her. They intimidated Nora greatly and she desperately wanted to flee. A knock at the door prompted her to sigh in relief.

"Thank god," thought Nora, "someone to rescue me."

· · · ·

"YOU IN HERE, EM?" ASKED Elliott after he opened the door to his sister's office and cracked it a few inches. Nora looked to the door and then back to her boss with an expectant expression.

"Shit," thought a wide-eyed Emma. She hesitated. While she intended to introduce Nora to Elliott, she did not want to do so in the intimate setting of her office. She instead wanted the cacophony of the club to interrupt any chemistry between them.

"Earth to Emma," beckoned Elliott. Nora watched her and wondered if she would respond. When she did not, Nora turned her head to view the door.

"Yeah," Emma finally replied in defeat, "come in."

"What the hell, Em?" complained Elliott in response to her tone. He opened the door wide and asked, "You sleepin' one off in here?"

"I don't ever do that," Emma objected with a glance at her new employee. Neither Nora nor Elliott heard Emma's response, however, as their attentions fell upon each other. The instant attraction was palpable.

"Oh, sorry. Didn't realize you had someone in here," said Elliott. He drew himself up to his full height and gazed on Nora with penetrating eyes. She thought him ruggedly handsome while he thought her irresistibly adorable.

"Nora, uh, this is, uh, my brother," Emma stammered.

"*Elliott*," interrupted Nora in a breathy voice. She noticed the mole on his right cheek, the imperfection endearing him to her even more. Nora said, "I thought so."

"Hey, Nora," said an intrigued Elliott as he strode up to her and extended his hand. He wore his usual old jeans and a black t-shirt.

"Hi," gushed Nora. She allowed him to guide her to her feet. They outwardly remained calm and exchanged pleasant smiles but their trembling hands and shimmering eyes betrayed their true feelings. The pair quickly released their handshake, each one fearing the intense focus of the other's sexual magnetism.

"Well, this sucks," Emma said to herself as she regained her senses. She leapt to her feet, walked around her desk and wrapped an arm around Nora's shoulders, saying, "Nora just hired in today."

"Yeah, I can smell the Taylortucky 'shine," replied Elliott sardonically. He looked to Nora and added, "Tastes like shit soaked in gasoline, doesn't it?"

Nora tilted her head from side to side in tacit agreement and giggled. Emma gave her a subtle shove forward and then ushered her towards the door.

"It's an honor, Elliott, and one that she definitely earned today," Emma declared, her brother's dig clearly prickling her. Moving Nora into the stairwell, she told her, "But now you're finally free for the night so we'll see ya' tomorrow."

"Uh, okay, bye," replied Nora. She managed a feeble wave at Elliott.

"Bye, hon," Emma said quickly. Elliott returned the wave before Emma closed the office door and then leaned against it. Nora lingered on the steps and listened carefully.

"Geez, Em, why didn't ya' just throw her down the stairs?" asked Elliott. He sat in the same chair as Nora and put a foot against Emma's desk.

"What?" Emma countered as if she failed to grasp his meaning. Nora's light, sweet scent lingered in the air and Elliott indulged in it.

"Don't you think you're getting a little aggressive in screening my love interests?" asked Elliott with a glance over his shoulder. He folded his hands on his stomach and queried, "What gives?"

"He doesn't know Donna's here yet," thought Nora. She felt guilty for eavesdropping but could not pull herself away from the door.

"I told you, I'm tired of you bringing trashy sluts into my home, and you should be ashamed about what they've exposed your nieces to," Emma responded. She returned to her desk and sat down, ordering him, "And get your foot off my desk. You're always leaving shoeprints all over it."

"Look, I'm sorry about Easter," said Elliott earnestly. He dropped his foot to the floor, scooched up in his chair and placed his folded arms on Emma's desk. He reasoned, "What can I say, Em? She's fun to be around. I mean, we're just hangin' out. Well, *were* just hangin' out."

"What happened?" asked Emma despite knowing the answer to her question. She was thrilled Elliott's relationship with Macayla had ended but also felt bad for him.

"I told her she needs to tone it down around the munchkins," expounded Elliott, "and she told me what part of the human anatomy I am and that I needed to go have sex with myself."

"Way to avoid the swear jar," Emma said with smirk. Her expression became serious and she said, "Didn't you learn anything from the *Mandy* incident? You wasted three months of your life on that girl and I lost one of my top earners because you couldn't keep it in your pants."

Nora, intrigued by the references to Elliott's sexual mischief, placed her ear against the door. The speakers in the club roared to life and made hearing difficult.

"Damn," Nora whispered in frustration.

"Nora's not like Mandy or Macayla," argued Elliott.

"You're picking the wrong girls, Elliott, because you get infatuated with them and overlook obvious problems," Emma asserted forcefully. Gaining momentum, she pointed at the door and ranted, "That girl is only twenty-two. *Twenty. Two.* You were, like, in high school when she was born. When she started kindergarten, you were a junior in college. You're just old enough to be her father, idiot. *Seriously.*"

Nora cringed as the age difference sunk into her brain. Elliott shrugged.

"Drama queen," replied Elliott.

"Cradle robber," Emma shot back. She glared at him and demanded, "*If you meet her in this club, don't date her.*"

"So, we doin' the Memorial Day thing?" asked Elliott as the tension between the siblings vanished. Puzzled by the change in tack, Nora wrinkled her nose.

"Yes, and we're cooking out that Sunday, not on Memorial Day," Emma stated. She attended to a few quick tasks on her desk as she explained, "I'd like to just hang out with my girls on Monday and do whatever they wanna do. Remember, you're bringing chips and dip and some of that weird beer Dave likes. And just get the cheap dip, nothing fancy, or your nieces won't eat it."

"You closing that Sunday, too?" asked Elliott in surprise.

"No, but Sean's getting her first shot at running a 'big' night," Emma answered. She signed two checks and then returned her attention to Elliott.

"Supermom taking two days off in a row?" asked Elliott facetiously. He chuckled and added, "You dyin'?"

"I just want a nice family weekend," Emma said, her tone conveying her desire for one. She leaned back in her chair and added, "Dave's parents are coming, too. You, Dave and Tom can watch the Tigers game."

"I think they're in Seattle so first pitch isn't until, like, ten o'clock that night," advised Elliott. He asked with a straight face, "Can I bring Nora?"

Nora felt a heated rush of anxiety and grabbed her mouth. Emma fumed.

"I will kill you," Emma warned. Elliott laughed and pretended not to notice the unusual fire in her eyes.

"I'm just yanking your chain, Sis," said Elliott. Nora, her feelings tweaked by Elliott's words, composed herself and quietly descended the steps.

"He's too old for you, stupid," Nora chastised herself. She heard no more of the conversation.

"You know why I do it, right?" Emma asked, her anger dissipating.

"Yeah, I know," Elliott replied. He stood up and thrust his hands in his pockets, saying, "I just wish you wouldn't worry about it so much. I'm alright, I promise."

"You eat yet?" Emma inquired.

"Nope," answered Elliott.

"Elliott, it's almost eight o'clock at night," Emma scolded him. Sighing and shifting the paperwork on her desk, she lamented, "God, you're like having a third kid."

"Relax, I had a late lunch. I'll go downstairs and get something," replied Elliott with his hands raised in a sign of surrender.

"I'll fix you something," Emma insisted. She rounded her desk and followed Elliott to the door.

"You have cooks who do that, remember?" asked Elliott. Emma hugged him and he wrapped an arm around her shoulders.

"I like to cook for you," Emma countered, "and I'm gonna do it until I . . . until *you* find someone to do it for you."

"Ain't ever gonna happen," replied Elliott merely to irritate his sister. The expected explosion did not occur and she instead opened the office door.

"We'll see about that," Emma said, her manner of speaking making Elliott suspicious. She playfully pushed him through the doorway and ordered, "Now move it, mister. Time to eat."

• • • •

ELLIOTT MADE HIS USUAL inconspicuous entrance at his usual time and sat on his usual bar stool. His first visit to Johnny Dubs since meeting Nora, however, felt decidedly unusual.

"And there she is," he thought as he immediately located Nora and tracked her as she darted amongst the tables and deftly delivered orders. It seemed to Elliott that, in the week since he met her, she darted in the same way through his thoughts.

"I gotta get that girl outta my head," Elliott tried to convince himself. He endeavored to look around the bar, desperately searching for another comely face on which to rest his affections, but his eyes always returned to Nora. Appreciating her youthful energy, he thought, "*Em's right*. She's just too young."

His rapt attention to her every movement prevented Elliott from detecting Brandy as she strode up behind him. She shifted her tray to her left hand and rested her right arm on his shoulder.

"I remember when you used to hawk me like that," said Brandy with a smirk.

"That was ten years ago, Brandy," Elliott responded while dropping his gaze to the bar.

"Em thinks she's too young for ya', ya' know," said Brandy while demonstratively chewing her gum.

"Yeah, yeah, I know," Elliott complained. He conveyed his annoyance to Brandy through the mirror behind the bar.

"I didn't say *I* think that, hon," said Brandy pointedly. She placed her lips near his ear and said softly with warm breath, "I think that sweetie pie'd be good for you."

Brandy patted Elliott twice on the shoulder before spinning away from him and back to her duties. He risked one more glimpse at Nora and their eyes met.

"Uh oh," Elliott replied as Nora struck him with an exuberant smile and an excited wave. She hurried behind the bar, addressed the bartender and then quickly fixed Elliott a Grumpy Old Man. He muttered, "I really hope she sucks at making those."

"Hey, stranger," said a beaming Nora. She set the drink before him and asked, "Em told me you come here almost every day but you haven't been here in like, a week. Are you avoiding me?"

Nora instantly regretted her remark. She blushed and her cheeks warmed.

"Not at all. Just a busy week," Elliott lied, the true reason for his absence being his strong yet disquieting attraction to her. Nora watched him intently while he sampled her work, savored it with a thoughtful expression and said, "Tad strong on the bourbon but pretty good for a first attempt."

"Aww. I was hoping it'd be perfect the first time," said Nora disappointedly.

"We'll have other first times," Elliott remarked. His inadvertent innuendo embarrassed them both but Nora pretended to miss his meaning.

"So, whatcha eatin' tonight?" inquired Nora. She managed a pleasant yet neutral expression and dropped her trembling hands behind the bar.

"Don't let him fool you, Nora, the bar's not in your section," interrupted Emma with a nod towards the dining area.

"Hey, I'm trying to order here," Elliott scolded his sister.

"Sorry, Em," said Nora sheepishly.

"It's okay, sweetie, you're new," Emma said in a sugary tone. Walking backwards, she pointed at Elliott and added with a glower, "But you're not."

"Seriously, Em?" asked Elliott with a gesture of irritation. Emma remained silent but chastised him with her eyes before turning around. A rattled Nora attempted to flee but Elliott snagged her sleeve and asked "Where ya' goin'?"

Despite enjoying the interaction, Nora squirmed out of his grasp and playfully smacked his hand. Elliott attempted to regain his grip but she dodged the attempt.

"You're gonna get me in trouble!" said Nora in a hushed tone. She waved at Elliott and said, "I'll see ya' later, okay?"

"Yeah, okay," Elliott conceded. Nora pretended to complete a few tasks as she proceeded down the bar and disappeared into the busy dining area. Elliott failed to see Emma double back to him.

"Don't make me fire that girl," Emma threatened him. She slid onto the barstool next to Elliott.

"Stay outta my love life," countered Elliott as he faced forward. Setting his elbows on the bar, he gulped his drink and then warned, "It's none of your damn business."

"The hell it's not," Emma said while poking Elliott's shoulder, "and this is not the place for you to meet someone. *You know that.*"

"And where is the right place? Church?" asked Elliott. He added bitterly, "Thanks for the advice, *Mom.*"

"*Don't* call me that," Emma snapped. Pausing to let her angst dissipate, she changed her strategy and said, "Look, I'll make you a deal."

"A deal?" asked Elliott suspiciously with a sidelong glance. He took another drink.

"Yeah, a deal," Emma said. Elliott heard the whirring mechanics of her mind as she expounded, "If you haven't found someone in six months . . . hell, by the end of the summer . . . someone you really like, I'll back off. You can date Nora's brains out and I won't fire her."

"Are we talking the end of meteorological summer, which would be September twenty-second, or the more commonly accepted Labor Day weekend?" inquired Elliott with a straight face. He stared at the liquor bottles behind the bar and sipped his drink.

"Labor Day, *idiot*," Emma said, Elliott's cheek irking her. He shook his head.

"You're not gonna let me date her," said Elliott. He placed his thumb and his forefinger on his lips and pondered Emma's offer.

"I swear I will," Emma insisted. Elliott rotated his barstool and squared his shoulders to his sister. Earnestness sparkled in her eyes.

"So, if we make this deal – and I'm not saying I am – I can date her with your blessing?" queried Elliott skeptically.

"You can date her," Emma said with disapprobation and a sour expression. Hopping off the bar stool, she continued, "But no bullshit. If you find someone you like, you date her and forget about Nora. That's the deal."

"You realize I could just wait you out, right?" inquired Elliott.

"You could," Emma said. She declared with particular relish, "But a pretty young girl like that? She'll be dating someone her own age by June and you'll just be alone."

"Oh, I get it now," replied Elliott. He finished most of his cocktail before saying, "You're just trying to keep me away from her until she can find someone else."

"If she's so hung up on you, smart guy, she won't find someone else," Emma replied with a cold half-smile. Her grin faded and she added with the utmost seriousness, "She'll wait for *you*."

Elliott considered his sister's deal carefully while knowing she would manipulate he and Nora at every turn. Driven by her smugness and his growing desire for the young waitress, however, he made his decision.

"All right, Em," said Elliott while intensely gazing at Emma. He took a long, hard look at Nora and she offered him the most adorable of embarrassed smiles before turning away. His heart stricken, he said, "*Deal.*"

· · · ·

TAKING EVERY OPPORTUNITY to engage with Nora, Elliott arrived earlier and stayed later at Johnny Dubs as the week progressed. Emma kept close tabs on their interactions, however, and Nora quickly began shying away from Elliott if his sister was within sight. Fortunately, the Friday night crowd arrived early and provided Nora a plausible excuse to avoid him.

"I gotta run a few errands and then I'm gonna pop in and see the girls for a few minutes before they go to bed," Emma advised Elliott as she threw an arm around his shoulders. Playing her part to perfection, she said, "Why don't you come with me? You haven't seen them in, like, two weeks."

"I've been busy," replied Elliott in annoyance.

"Yeah, stalking a twenty-two-year-old who you promised you'd stay away from," Emma countered bitterly. Nora noticed the siblings' terse exchange and repeatedly snuck glimpses of their interaction.

"No, I promised I wouldn't date her," said Elliott. Emma embraced his head and kissed him on top of it.

"Cross the line and she's gone," Emma warned. She released him and exited the club. Nora made her way to Elliott, the twentysomething delivering drinks along the way.

"You're gonna get me fired, Elliott," complained Nora. She remained calm but castigated Elliott with her eyes.

"Only if you sleep with me," Elliott countered with a shit-eating grin.

"*Elliott*!" squeaked Nora. Her protestation garnered the attention of several nearby patrons.

"One date," Elliott implored her, "just one date. We can get away with one without her finding out."

"I can't," insisted Nora.

"Yes, you can," Elliott countered emphatically. She wished to embrace him and stay in his arms but the specter of Emma held her at bay. She glanced at the front doors.

"*I can't*," declared Nora angrily. Visibly conflicted, her gaze lingered on Elliott before she tore herself away from him. Nora marched down the bar and hung a right into the hallway at its end. She met Brandy who held two bags of trash.

"I'll take 'em," said Nora as she swiped both bags from Brandy.

"Hey!" objected Brandy but, before she could protest further, Nora turned, opened the door by backing into it and disappeared. Brandy shrugged and said, "Okay, whatever."

Nora stepped into the parking lot and stopped in the yellowish glow of its exterior lights. Holding a trash bag in each hand, she shivered in the chilly air and began crying. The door clicked closed behind her.

"I can get another waitressing job," said Nora with a sudden surge of courage. It left her as quickly as it appeared and, feeling foolish, she walked towards the dumpster with slumped shoulders and her head hung low. Her tears fell to the pavement but she made no effort to squelch them. Nora chastised herself, "Oh, just stop it. He's not that special."

Nora dropped the bags on the concrete and opened the dumpster's side door. A black-and-white cat leapt from the opening, bounded off Nora's shoulder and fled into the night. She froze as she processed the assault, shivered violently and then screamed.

"Nora!" Elliott yelled. Dashing around the corner of the building, he saw the cat stop at the tree line. Elliott growled with a wave, "Get outta here."

The cat vanished into the trees. Nora shook like their leaves.

"Oh my god," said Nora. She trembled and looked to him, whimpering, "*Elliott*."

Nora charged Elliott and crashed into his arms. He embraced her, the two of them fitting together as if God designed their bodies for that very purpose.

"You're alright," Elliott assured her. She laid her head on his shoulder as he added, "It was just that damn stray."

"It scared the hell outta me," said Nora with two quick swipes at her watery eyes. She shamelessly indulged in the protection of Elliott's arms and griped, "Stupid cat."

"Em needs to trap that damn thing," Elliott said. Nora squirmed against his grasp and offered him a worried look.

"Don't hurt it!" exclaimed Nora, her feeling for the mischievous feline instantaneously turning from contempt to concern. The pair looked at one another and, after a pause, began laughing. Elliott tightened his grip on her.

"You're somethin' else," he said. The moment struck them both like a snake and, in a scene out of a romantic movie, they engaged in a passionate kiss.

A pair of drunken bikers stumbled out of the club. One of them noticed Elliott and Nora and grabbed his friend by the forearm. Both men stopped to gawk at them.

"Couldn't make it to the backseat, huh?" he shouted. The bikers roared with laughter. Their incursion tweaked Nora's conscience and she came to her senses.

"*I can't*," pleaded Nora anxiously. She pushed Elliott away and scurried towards the club. Elliott inhaled to speak but stopped himself. Nora pulled the back door open just enough to slide through it. It closed on its own and muffled the music coming from inside.

"Damn it," Elliott sighed. Nora's escape amused the bikers.

"Chase that tail, fool!" said one of them. They again erupted into laughter.

"Yeah, thanks for the advice," Elliott shouted with disdain. He muttered under his breath, "*Assholes.*"

The bikers mounted their motorcycles and, with a roar of engines, soon departed. Elliott placed his hands on his hips and lingered in the parking lot. A final exhale sent him on his way.

"Oh, just stop it," Elliott said sourly. Walking slowly towards the club, he continued, "She's not that special."

· · · ·

EMMA'S BODY TENSED and then flooded with rage when Elliott and Nora kissed. She did not park her car in her reserved spot and her position on the north side of the club allowed her to witness their impromptu tryst.

"*Idiot*," Emma snarled while hitting the steering wheel. Normally, she would rush to the defense of Elliott but, when the bikers interrupted their kiss, she did nothing but watch. She said, "It's about time those two losers made themselves useful."

Emma read Nora's lips as she said "*I can't*". She sat up in anticipation of Elliott's response.

"Good girl," Emma said when Nora shoved Elliott away and dashed inside the building. Her lips settled into a muted smile and she uttered, "*Smart* girl."

"Yeah, thanks for the advice," Elliott shouted in response to the biker's taunt.

"Now beat it, morons," Emma said. The bikers obliged, fired up their motorcycles and rolled out of the parking lot. Emma's heart melted when a dejected Elliott sighed and slowly returned to the club.

"Hang on, big brother," Emma said. Loathing the loneliness that emanated from Elliott, she stated resolutely, "Little sis' is gonna fix this."

• • • •

"HEY, BABE," A PLEASANTLY surprised Emma said when David met her at the front door. He engulfed his wife in his strong arms and ardently kissed her. The sudden affection swept her off her feet and when David paused their kiss, she uttered, "*Wow*."

"You've been gone way too much lately," David said with longing in his eyes. He finished their kiss and then released her.

"I know," Emma answered with remorse. She set her keys on a small table near the door and asked, "What're you doing up?"

"Just wanted to see your pretty face," answered David.

"Even at three in the morning, when I look like this," Emma said with outstretched arms. Disheveled and smelling of cigarette smoke, she wore the exhaustion of a busy day on her face. She patted his cheek and added, "Guess you do love me."

"Guess so," said David with a quick tilt of his head.

"How did the girls do today?" Emma inquired. She headed to the kitchen with David in tow.

"Mom said they did fine and had a good day at school. They pooped out early so I went to bed when they did," replied David as he followed Emma into the kitchen. She set her purse on the kitchen table before obtaining a glass from a cupboard and filling it from the faucet. David continued, "I got a good five hours in so I figured I'd just get up and wait for you."

Emma drained her glass. She refilled it again and drank half of its contents.

"Well, I'm glad you did," Emma said with a warm grin. She set down the glass, wrapped her arms around David's neck and kissed him. Nodding towards the living room, she suggested, "Let's go sit for a while."

"Aw, hon, I know you're tired," replied David.

"I need to wind down anyway or I won't sleep," Emma said, "and I want you to hold me."

The married couple proceeded to the couch and Emma nestled herself in David's arms. They shared the details of their days and spoke of their daughters before falling into a comfortable silence twenty minutes later. Emma was the first to break it.

"Are there any good, single guys at the shop, maybe mid to late twenties?" Emma inquired. Her eyes glazed and she continued, "You know, stand-up guys who you'd let date the girls if they were old enough."

"Why, you on the market?" countered David with a wry smile.

"Absolutely not. I have my good man," Emma answered as she cuddled into David. She fiddled with her wedding ring and said, "But that new waitress I hired, Nora, she's a real sweetheart. Cute, nice, fun . . . but unattached."

"Em, you just met the girl," scolded David with a look of disbelief.

"Hey, I just like to see people happy and loved, like I am," Emma declared with an air of righteousness. She added innocently, "That's all."

"So she caught Elliott's eye, huh?" asked David. Emma's countenance soured.

"Yes. *Idiot*," Emma griped. She folded her arms like an angry child and pouted, "She's fifteen years younger than him, Dave. And they have *nothing* in common. But that's the one he heads right for."

"She must be interested in him at least a little bit if you're trying to knock her outta the race this early," commented David, his shrewd assessment irritating Emma. He suggested carefully, "Maybe you should see where it goes. That May December shit works sometimes."

David regretted the words as soon as they passed his lips. Emma sat up and looked at David crossly.

"I thought you agreed with me that Elliott and Donna should be together," Emma said. Her eyes rippled with blue-green energy as she waited for his response.

"I do, I do," backtracked David. He threw his right arm over the back of the couch and explained, "But if you let it play out, Elliott won't feel railroaded. You know how he hates that."

"He needs to be railroaded," Emma insisted. She gently but repeatedly poked David in the chest as she ranted, "Everything was perfect the first time and he still screwed it up. But now it is again. He's not playin' around with some bimbo, Donna's finally back here to stay, *and* still loves him *and* can still have a baby on the right side of forty. I'm not letting him screw it up again."

Knowing Emma would not be gainsaid on the matter, David refrained from further comment. She stewed for over a minute but then calmed down and cuddled into him again.

"So, are there any young guys down at the shop worthy of that sweet, pretty girl?" Emma inquired in businesslike fashion.

"Well, I guess the new guy, Bart. He seems like a good kid. Hard worker. Good attitude," answered David. Emma made an unpleasant face.

"Bart?" Emma asked. She protested, "His name is Bart? I don't like that."

"I don't think he'll change his name to date Nora, babe," said David blithely, "pretty or not."

"I guess it doesn't matter," Emma conceded reluctantly. Pondering the matter as she spoke, she said, "Maybe you can get him in for an after-work beer this week and we'll introduce 'em. Then you can encourage him to ask her out."

"You're relentless," said David with a chuckle. He hugged her tightly.

"It's one of the reasons you love me," Emma said while laying her head on his shoulder.

"One of the many, lady," said David, his answer igniting Emma's libido. She slithered out of his grasp and rose to her feet.

"C'mon, handsome," Emma beckoned as she clasped his hands. Pulling him off the couch, she said with desire, "Let's go burn off the last of the energy I have left."

D avid lumbered through the doors of Johnny Dubs, one of which was characteristically propped open due to the day's eighty-degree temperature. He wore a gray-and-blue uniform smeared with dirt and grime.

"I'll catch ya' later. Dave's here," Emma told a customer when she noticed David. She stood at the far end of the bar but, before greeting her husband, she yelled into the kitchen, "Hey, Nora, come here for a minute!"

"Okay, one sec," shouted Nora. Emma hurried towards David and met him halfway down the bar.

"Why are you dressed like that?" Emma asked with disappointment in her voice.

"Great to see you, too, sweetheart," replied David.

"He's not coming here straight from work, is he?" said Emma as her interrogation continued.

"Well, yeah," answered a puzzled David.

"C'mon, Dave," Emma said as she demonstratively threw her hands in the air. Wrinkling her nose, she chastised David, "You're dirty and *you stink* and he's gonna be dirty and stink, too. You couldn't have had him clean up first?"

"I'm not gonna ask a guy from work to clean up to have a beer with me. He'll think I'm gay," David replied in frustration. Emma's countenance softened.

"I'm sorry," Emma gushed. She kissed him on the lips and said, "But you really do smell."

"Because I've been working in a garage all day in the heat," said David, his frustration teetering on anger. Emma noticed a young man walk through Johnny Dubs' doors and embraced David.

"Hey, honey," Emma greeted her husband in a sugary tone. Beaming with adoration, she kissed him and then asked, "Does my hardworkin' man need a beer or three?"

"Layin' it on a little thick, don't ya' think?" whispered David. Emma ignored the question, disentangled herself from David and moved past him. He rolled his eyes.

"And who's this handsome young man?" Emma asked as she approached him with an extended hand. Her magnetism and aggressive welcome cowed him.

"Bart, ma'am," replied Bart. He stood as tall as David but was leaner with blonde hair and a square jaw. He also wore the same dirty uniform as David but, in Emma's opinion, smelled much better.

"Thank god for that," Emma thought. Bart took Emma's proffered hand and shook it firmly yet respectfully. She patted his shoulder and said jokingly, "I am *not* old enough to be called ma'am."

David stifled a chuckle and shook his head at his wife's performance. Bart squirmed.

"Oh, I'm sorry," blurted an embarrassed Bart, "I don't think you're old."

"You're fine. Just call me Em," Emma said with grin. She took Bart by the arm and waved from one end of the club to the other, asking, "So, whaddaya' think of my place?"

"Wow, you own all this?" asked Bart with wide eyes. Emma noticed his muscular arms.

"That I do," Emma answered as she turned and placed her hand on David's back. Guiding he and Bart back towards the front doors, she sat Bart in Elliott's reserved seat and inquired, "Watcha' drinking, Bart?"

"Miller Light?" replied Bart as if asking permission. David's amusement faded into befuddlement over Emma's surrender of Elliott's barstool.

"Same for me," added David.

"Two Miller Lights, comin' up," Emma said. Nora suddenly appeared at the far end of the bar while drying her hands on a white bar towel. Emma motioned to her and asked, "Hey, Nora, will you get the boys Miller Lights?"

"Sure, Em," said Nora while throwing the towel over her shoulder. David raised his eyebrows when he saw her. Bart was instantly smitten.

"No wonder Elliott fell for her," thought David. Nora walked down the other side of the bar and grabbed two Miller Lights from the cooler. Bart's eyes remained glued to her.

"Perfect," Emma said to herself when she noticed Bart's rapt attention. Nora deftly opened the beer bottles and set them in front of her newest customers.

"Nora, this is my husband, Dave," Emma explained proudly.

"It's so awesome to finally meet you," said Nora with an infectious smile. She excitedly shook David's hand.

"Em's been tellin' me how everyone loves you here," David replied. Nora blushed. Emma pounced.

"And this is Bart," Emma said. She placed her arm on his shoulders and continued, "They work together at Dave's Dad's shop."

"Hi, Bart," said Nora in her usual bubbly manner of greeting patrons.

"Uh, hey," offered Bart feebly.

"Oh, shit, I almost forgot, David, I need you to fix the door in my office real quick," Emma said. She removed her arm from Bart's shoulders.

"I just fixed it last week," responded David. He picked up his beer and took a swig."

"Not the office door, babe, the bathroom door," Emma informed him. She tugged on his arm and said, "C'mon, grab your beer and I'll show you."

"Sure, hon," relented David. Leaving his beer behind, he rose to his feet and muttered, "*Obvious.*"

David winced subtly when Emma covertly pinched him. She pulled him towards her office.

"Nora, will you keep Bart company for a few minutes while Dave fixes the door?" Emma inquired with as much innocence as she could feign. Ushering David away, she added quickly, "Thanks."

"Be right back, man," David assured Bart. He and Emma soon vanished into the stairwell. Bart said nothing and an awkward period of silence followed. Nora finally broke it.

"So, you're a mechanic?" Nora queried.

"Yeah," answered Bart with a nod. Unable to speak, he took refuge in his beer several times before saying, "Like Mrs. Hastings said, I work with Dave."

"Cool," Nora said. Suddenly realizing that Bart sat on Elliott's barstool, she moved David's beer to the next spot on the bar and asked, "Hey, can you move over one?"

"Why?" inquired Bart.

"That seat's reserved," Nora answered with a flutter in her heart, "for Em's brother, Elliott."

"Uh, okay," said Bart with a shrug. He switched seats and received a grateful smile from Nora.

"Thanks," said Nora. She motioned down the bar and explained, "Hey, I've gotta get everybody another round. I'll be back in a minute."

"Sure, okay," replied Bart. Nora moved away from him and refreshed drinks as slowly as possible.

Emma and David returned from her office several minutes later. Her mien soured when she saw Bart sitting by himself on a new barstool and Nora flitting amongst the tables and delivering dinners.

"It's worse than I thought," Emma said.

"Swing and a miss, hon," said David as he brushed past his wife and walked to Bart's rescue.

"This isn't over," Emma declared.

• • • •

THE EVENING TEMPERATURE remained in the low eighties as the wind lessened and the clouds thickened. Lanie and Tessa tirelessly played in their inground pool, the girls expending the pent-up energy from a week of school.

"Oh, so sorry!" Elliott shouted as the foam ball he threw to a leaping Lanie bounced off her head and she splashed into the pool. Tessa laughed and ran to retrieve the ball.

"My turn!" declared Tessa. She picked up the ball and lobbed it to Elliott. It flung water at him as it spun in his direction.

"Hey! Watch it!" Elliott protested after the spray hit him. Tessa gave him little time to recover as she jumped into the air. Elliott chucked the ball at Tessa and she snagged it before crashing into the water.

"You suck at throwing," griped Lanie after swimming to the shallow end of the pool and standing up.

"She caught it," countered Elliott while pointing at a surfacing Tessa. He sat in a chair on Emma's backyard patio and kept the company of a Grumpy Old Man. A Domino's pizza box, three plates containing pizza crusts and two cans of Coke littered the patio table.

"Whatever," replied Lanie. She climbed out of the pool, wrapped herself in a nearby towel and plopped into a chair at the table. Eager to avenge the slight, she smirked and taunted him, "Mommy said you like one of the waitresses at her club."

"Oh, she did, huh?" Elliott said. He took a drink, the reminder concerning Nora and her rejections an unpleasant one. Tessa, always seeking to be like her big sister, quickly exited the pool and, cocooning herself in a large beach towel, joined them.

"Yeah," interjected Tessa in a serious tone, "*and* she says you're bobbin' the cradle."

Elliott chuckled and shook his head. Lanie grabbed her Coke and drained it with loud gulps.

"That's *robbin'* the cradle. *Robbin',*" Elliott corrected Tessa. He took another drink and set down his glass, adding, "And your mommy's wrong. That's *not* what I'm doing."

"What does it mean?" asked Tessa.

"It means dating someone younger than you," Lanie answered proudly, "*a lot* younger."

"Well, how old is she?" inquired Tessa, the eight-year-old intrigued by the concept. Elliott, feeling cornered, paused and pondered his response.

"Uh, I don't know," Elliott lied with a dismissive gesture.

"Mommy said she's twenty-two," said Lanie snottily. Tessa gave Elliott a puzzled expression.

"How old are you?" asked Tessa.

"He's thirty-seven," answered Lanie. She grinned in satisfaction. Tessa grew quiet and worked out the math in her head.

"I think that means you *are* robbin' the cradle, Uncle Elliott," said Tessa gently to spare his feelings.

"We're not dating," Elliott responded in frustration, "and I don't even know why we're talking about this."

"Is she pretty?" queried Tessa. Elliott saw the perfect picture of Nora in his mind's eye and his mien softened into a muted grin.

"Yeah, kid, she's very pretty," Elliott replied fondly.

"Heads up!" announced Lanie before burping loudly. The girls cackled with delight.

"Nice," Elliott said while shooting Lanie an incredulous look. Wanting to move the conversation away from his love life, he asked, "More swimming or ice cream and TV?"

"Swimming!" bellowed both girls in unison. They threw off their towels, ran to the pool and jumped into it.

"Little maniacs," Elliott muttered with a chortle.

• • • •

THE POST-DINNER LULL settled over Johnny Dubs, its only three customers being regular barflies without anywhere else to go. Though Emma and her staff busied themselves in preparation for the evening crowd, there was soon little for them to do but wait. Nora sat in Elliott's seat and read a Psychology textbook assigned for one of her summer classes. Her attachment to Elliott's barstool prickled Emma.

"Need a beer to make that stuff interesting?" Emma asked as she plopped onto the next barstool. She held a beer bottle in one hand and offered a second one to Nora with the other.

"I kinda like this stuff," replied Nora. She accepted the beer despite having no desire to drink it. The glass was ice cold so she quickly set it on the bar, saying, "Maybe I'll be a shrink someday."

"I hated school, but Daddy still made me go if I wanted to work for him," Emma said before drinking her beer. She lingered briefly in a memory and then, glancing at Nora, asked, "Soooo . . . what'd you think of Bart?"

Nora became visibly nervous and took a sip of her beer. The taste was unappealing and she again set it on the bar.

"He was nice," answered Nora with a shrug. She paused, considered her first encounter with Bart and then added, "Kinda quiet, though. He didn't say much."

"He's a good lookin' guy though, right?" Emma said with a pointed look and a half-smile. Nora blushed.

"Well . . . yeah," admitted Nora with a guilty grin. It faded when she thought, "But so is Elliott."

"He's really likes you," Emma advised. She drank her beer but kept her gaze on Nora.

"Really?" asked Nora with a befuddled expression. She closed her textbook and added, "I don't know how he could. We hardly talked at all."

"Trust me, he does," Emma insisted. She leaned towards Nora and stated, "Dave said he wants to ask you out . . . but he's worried you'll say no. Ya' kinda blew him off that day."

"No I didn't," squeaked Nora, the young woman taking offense at Emma's assertion. She fiddled with the corner of her textbook and said, "But he was so quiet, and it was a little awkward, so I, like, bailed."

"How about this?" asked Emma as she pretended to contemplate a solution. She offered Nora a thoughtful expression and suggested, "We'll make it a double date with me and Dave. If you guys don't hit it off, we'll be there to keep it from getting weird. And we'll treat, so you'll get a free dinner outta the deal."

"I never said I'd go out with him," countered Nora with a shake of her head.

"Oh, c'mon, it'll be fun," Emma said dismissively. Nora hesitated. She knew what Emma was doing but felt powerless to stop it. The images of Elliott in her head became more intense yet so did her doubt. She punted.

"Where's Elliott tonight?" asked Nora.

"He's watchin' the girls so Dave can play poker," Emma answered. She set her beer on the bar and said in irritation, "But we were talking about Bart, the hot guy who's *not* old enough to be your father *and* wants to date you."

Nora's mien dimmed. Emma watched her closely and waited for her response.

"If I said yes, Elliott can't know," stated Nora resolutely.

"Why does *that* matter?" Emma inquired. The scene of Elliott kissing Nora replayed in her mind and her irritation became anger.

"I mean it, Em," answered Nora with a conviction that disarmed Emma's ire. She explained with angst, "Look, I know he's too old for me, and we don't have much in common, and we can't . . . can't *be*. But, whether you like it or not, I . . . I care about him. I really do."

"Elliott'll be fine," Emma said feebly. Nora's concern for her brother made her doubt her plans to keep them apart.

"I'm actually afraid to date him," said Nora as she bowed her head. She trembled and then exhaled.

"Look, I've been too hard on you about him," Emma conceded. Nora returned her attention to her boss.

"It's not that," replied Nora. She battled tears and continued, "I'm afraid *not* to date him, too. He makes my feelings get all, like, tangled up, and I don't know what to do about it. Or him."

The two women broke eye contact, both of them quietly sipping their beers and immersing themselves in thoughts of Elliott. Emma stirred first and returned her attention to Nora.

"What if I promised you Elliott's gonna be okay?" Emma inquired. Nora's eyes flashed to her.

"I don't want him to just be okay," said Nora curtly before changing to a softer tone, "I want him to be happy . . . even if it's not with me."

Emma's face became grim. She did not expect such a heartfelt outpouring from Nora, especially one tempered with wisdom beyond her years.

"Then date the cute guy your own age," Emma said, "and let me take care of Elliott. He'll be happy if you do, it may just take a bit."

"Promise?" asked a tearful Nora.

"Promise," Emma assured her. Sensing victory, she raised her bottle for a toast and said warmly, "To Elliott being happy."

Nora felt uneasy but, trusting her superior, she clinked bottles with Emma. Her first attempt to speak failed.

"To Elliott being happy," repeated Nora finally with an aching heart and Elliott still on her mind.

• • • •

SITTING AT HER DESK, Emma poured herself a shot of vodka and slammed it. Self-doubt and guilt crept over her as she contemplated her manipulation of so many hearts. The telephone on her desk rang.

"Who could that be at this hour?" Emma asked aloud. Few people knew the number for her direct line and she assumed it was either David or Elliott. She picked up the receiver and said, "Hello?"

"Hi, Em," said Donna. She reclined on the living room couch at her brother's house and snuggled in a blanket. The shifting bluish light from the television illuminated her.

"Hey, you. What're you still doing up?" Emma inquired. She poured another shot but did not pick it up.

"Couldn't sleep," answered Donna. She squirmed uncomfortably.

"Thinkin' about Elliott, huh?" Emma said. Forgetting about the vodka, she leaned back in her chair and put her feet up on her desk.

"*No*," insisted Donna. She pulled in her legs and, holding the telephone between her head and her shoulder, hugged her knees and confessed, "Well, yeah."

"You're ready to see him, aren't you?" Emma replied with a grin.

"Part of me . . . *yeah*," said Donna. Conflicted and anxious, she asked, "Em, are you sure he's gonna want to see *me*?"

"Yes, and I already know when it's gonna happen," Emma declared.

"Really?" replied Donna. The confidence in Emma's voice allowed her to relax and she laid down again.

"You're coming to my little Memorial Day shindig on the 26th, right?" Emma queried though her tone conveyed it was expected.

"Well, duh, of course," said Donna. She trembled with the anticipation of seeing Elliott.

"That's the day, girlfriend," Emma said. Taking her feet off her desk, she sat up and advised, "And you need to wear something that'll get his attention. One of those west coast bikinis you love. If it's warm enough."

"You're terrible," replied Donna with an embarrassed giggle. Her anticipation morphed into arousal.

"And you're a little hottie," Emma said. She poured the vodka back into the bottle and demanded, "So use that smokin' bod to seduce my brother."

"Emma Renee!" exclaimed Donna in the same manner that Emma's mother once scolded her. She immediately recoiled when she realized the volume of her voice, admonishing her friend quietly, "Don't make me do that. Everyone's sleeping here."

"I mean it in a good way," Emma replied in a snarky voice. She screwed the cap on the vodka bottle and explained, "The 'take me now and then marry me and live happily ever after' way."

"You are too much," replied Donna with a slow shake of her head.

"Stop by the club tomorrow," Emma insisted.

"Okay, after my interview," replied Donna.

"That works," Emma said. She switched the phone to her other ear and said reassuringly, "Now relax and get some sleep, sweetie."

"Good night," said Donna with an appreciative smile. Each woman returned her receiver to its base.

"Now I just gotta keep Elliott from finding out about Nora and Bart," Emma said aloud. She stopped, tilted her head and then sat up straight. Emma uttered, *Wait.*

She considered the possibility of intentionally allowing Elliott to learn of Nora's date and the effect of that knowledge on his feelings for Donna. A slow grin came to her lips.

"Maybe a little jolt to the heart is exactly what he needs," Emma reasoned. Her eyes became hazy and she plotted for several minutes. A knock at the door interrupted her scheming.

"It's me, Em," announced Brandy.

"C'mon in," Emma responded. She felt elated and it showed on her comely face. Brandy opened the door and approached Emma's desk.

"Uh, oh," said Brandy with a half-grin, "I know that look."

"I need you to spring me for a few hours tomorrow," Emma told Brandy.

"Really? On a Saturday? With one day's notice?" scoffed Brandy.

"Give me four hours, and I'll pay ya' for eight," Emma replied.

"Can't Sean handle it?" asked Brandy with noticeable dissatisfaction though the lure of double time piqued her interest.

"I think so," Emma said, "but I want a trial run before Labor Day weekend and I need you to keep an eye on her. Plus, I'll be in town if anything happens."

"All right, Boss Lady, but you owe me," said Brandy. Emma nodded in assent as Brandy took a seat and inquired, "What's the occasion?"

A light bulb illuminated in Emma's head. The perfect opportunity presented itself in the form of Brandy's loose lips and she seized it.

"Dave and I are taking Nora and one of Dave's workers to dinner at Mexican Gardens," Emma answered nonchalantly. She picked up a paper on her desk and pretended to read it.

"Elliott know about it?" inquired Brandy with a dubious expression.

"No," Emma quickly responded. She warned Brandy with a pointed finger, "And I want it to stay that way. Got it?"

"Got it," said Brandy.

. . . .

BRANDY UNABASHEDLY arrived at Elliott's apartment and knocked loudly on the front door. Unwilling to wait for him to open it, she took a seat at his patio table, pulled out a cigarette and lit it. The morning was warm and muggy though the sun's rays had yet to creep over the top of the apartment buildings.

Elliott lived most of his adult life at Continental Plaza Apartments on Beech Daly Road. The two-story buildings were constructed of mottled bricks in various shades of reds and browns with black-shingled mansard roofs. Manicured hedges bordered small patios and shade umbrellas hovered over many of them.

"I always knew you'd be back," Elliott said when he opened the door. He was disheveled, wore shorts and a wrinkled t-shirt and had clearly been sleeping when she arrived.

"You wish," scoffed Brandy. Holding up her cigarette, she said, "I like coffee with my cigarettes. And an ashtray, sleeping beauty."

"Nothing in it, right?" Elliott asked. He rubbed his eyes and then the radix of his nose.

"Uh, yeah," said Brandy as if Elliott should have known the answer.

"I'll be right back to take your order," Elliott muttered. He disappeared inside the apartment and returned three minutes later with two coffee mugs and an ashtray. He held it out to Brandy who twisted out her cigarette in it.

"Want one?" asked Brandy while retrieving another cigarette. Elliott set the ashtray and a coffee in front of her.

"You know I don't smoke," Elliott grumbled. He zombie-walked to the other chair and slumped into it. Sipping his coffee, he leaned back and inquired, "So, to what do I owe the privilege?"

"You really want a shot with Nora?" queried Brandy bluntly. She exhaled a plume of smoke and then sampled her coffee.

"Damn, you couldn't let me get one mug in first?" Elliott griped. He doused his grogginess with caffeine.

"Do ya' or don't ya'?" demanded Brandy. Elliott averted his gaze and exhaled. His mien then darkened but he chuckled nonetheless.

"All right, fine, we can do this," Elliott replied. He set his coffee down on the table, looked Brandy squarely in the face and declared steadfastly, "Yeah, I do."

"Even though it's gonna start a war with Em?" inquired Brandy shrewdly. She paused for more nicotine and caffeine before adding, "And probably get that little sweetie fired."

"I'm still gonna poke the bear," Elliott answered with a devil-may-care attitude. Brandy took a drag of her cigarette and chortled.

"That's more like hitting the bear with a two-by-four," said Brandy. Her casual attitude and intrusion into his love life prickled Elliott.

"Is there a reason why you care or does my pain amuse you?" Elliott asked. He crossed his legs and massaged the heel of his bare foot.

"Oh, it amuses me," joked Brandy. She then became uncharacteristically serious and explained, "You know I love you. I love all you crazy Wardens. Your old man was the best. And I think, maybe, just maybe, that chick might be good for you. Maybe she just might make you smile like you used to. Ya' know, make you happy again."

Elliott, uncomfortable with the rare emotional depth displayed by Brandy, looked away. His consciousness drifted. Brandy allowed him the journey.

"Tell all that to Em," Elliott replied after bringing himself back to the moment with a swig of coffee.

"*You* tell that to Em," countered Brandy. She indulged in a rush of nicotine and said, "And if you want that girl, go get her before your sister gives her to someone else."

"Whaddaya mean?" Elliott asked in puzzlement.

"Mexican Gardens, tonight at six," advised Brandy. She held Elliott in an intense gaze and repeated, "*Go get her.*"

• • • •

ELLIOTT CASUALLY WALKED into Mexican Gardens wearing his usual getup and, as a counter to Emma, his father's old army jacket. Her wrath be damned, he wanted a relationship with Nora and decided to put the young waitress's feelings to the test.

"I'm not giving her up that easy," Elliott thought defiantly. He stepped into the hive of activity that was the waiting area and adjoining bar.

"Hi," the hostess greeted Elliott with a warm smile. She checked her seating chart and asked, "How many tonight?"

"My people are already here," Elliott replied with a nod into the first dining room.

"Oh, go on in," said the hostess with a gesture before turning her attention to the next party. Elliott walked forward, dodged other patrons and scanned the crowd for Nora. He stopped in his tracks when he found her.

"Shit," Elliott muttered. Nora sat next to Bart, the pair laughing and conversing with another couple. Elliott noticed the accentuated blush on Nora's cheeks, the brighter lipstick on her lips, and the cute denim outfit she wore. A weight fell on his heart and he said, "Guess she couldn't wait."

The world seemed to slow down, the waitstaff, busboys and restaurant patrons moving around Elliott like he was not there. He extricated himself from his funk when he saw Emma and David sitting across the table from Nora and Bart. His anger rose like a wave but then passed just as quickly and he chuckled.

"I'm gonna crash anyway," Elliott said while approaching the table, "so I might as well kamikaze the new guy on the way down."

"Oh, boy," uttered David when he saw Elliott.

"What?" Emma asked him. She turned her head and acquired her brother in her field of vision. Pretending to be confused, she said, "Oh, hey, Elliott."

"Hey, *Em*," Elliott answered pointedly as he castigated Emma with his gaze. She feigned a guilty expression. Nora's eyes widened and she froze.

"Hook, line and sinker," Emma said to herself. The rush of satisfaction she experienced when Elliott sauntered up to the table vanished. The realization that he wore John Warden's jacket slapped her in the face and she thought, "Oh, god. Daddy's jacket."

"How we doin', kids?" Elliott asked.

"Hi, Elliott," said a shocked Nora. She fidgeted and added uneasily, "What're you doing here?"

"Beats the hell outta me," replied Elliott. He grabbed a tortilla chip from the basket sitting in the middle of the table and said, "But it looks like you're on a double date with my conniving little sister."

"Conniving?" protested Emma, the hurt in her voice having more to do with her father's memory than her brother's slight. Elliott looked to David.

"Accessory before or after the fact?" asked Elliott. He popped the chip in his mouth. David retreated to his beer while Emma tussled with memories of her father.

"Well, ya' see, I, um, well, Emma thought, uh, it was like . . . ," stammered Nora. Dishonesty, however, was not her strong suit and she was unable to muster a cover story. Elliott grabbed another chip as Nora sighed and confessed, "Yeah, it's a double date."

Bart, who bristled during the initial exchanges, stood up and confronted Elliott. Elliott, in turn, shifted the chip to his left hand and held out the other.

"Elliott," Elliott said. He nodded to Emma and added, "Emma's brother."

"Bart," replied the suspicious young man as he shook Elliott's hand. The moment was tense as both men stared each other down and battled for the firmest handshake. Nora trembled.

"Nice to meet ya', kid," Elliott said. He surrendered and allowed the younger man to end the handshake on his terms. Elliott relented, "Well, I'll let you guys get back to your *double date*."

Elliott popped the tortilla chip in his mouth and snagged another. He lifted it in the air as if making a toast.

"*Enjoy your meals*," Elliott said in a snarky tone while crunching obnoxiously. He spun around and walked away. Nora watched him depart and, visibly distressed, slid out of the booth.

"Excuse me for a minute," said Nora with her eyes on Elliott. She pursued him to the waiting area.

"Where's she goin'?" asked an irritated Bart.

"Relax, I'll handle this," Emma assured him while motioning for him to sit down.

"Take it easy, man. It's all good," David urged Bart. He reluctantly sat down but, unconvinced, he watched Elliott and Nora closely.

"Elliott," Nora beckoned. He stopped and turned around but the sour expression on his face cowed her.

"So who's the guy?" Elliott inquired. Nora averted her gaze, the twenty-two-year-old unable to bear his wounded mien.

"He's from Dave's shop," answered Nora sheepishly. She felt ashamed and, sensing her angst, Emma hurried to her rescue. Nora blushed and admitted, "Emma fixed us up."

"No shit," Elliott said. Holding out the tortilla chip and threatening her with it, he said, "Guess that kiss didn't mean a damn thing."

"Elliott, don't," pleaded Nora. Her face went from red to white and she began to inwardly panic. Emma quickly interceded.

"Nora, can I talk to Elliott for a sec?" Emma asked. Nora moved to touch his arm but he subtly stepped back.

"Yeah, you should get back to your new guy," Elliott said with a scowl.

"He's not my new guy!" Nora objected. Several nearby patrons became aware of the burgeoning lovers' quarrel.

"Okay, you two, just bring it down a notch," interjected Emma. Glancing at Nora, she realized she was on the verge of tears and thought, "Keep it together, sweetheart, keep it together."

"Well, you'd better tell him that, because he looks like he wants to kill me right now," Elliott said while ignoring his sister. He waved at Bart who began to rise. A word from David returned him to his seat.

"Nora, you'd better get back," Emma insisted. She nudged Nora but, though swaying with the contact, she refused to leave.

"It's just a first date," pouted Nora.

"You lead him on with a kiss, too?" Elliott rejoined. His callous words shocked her.

"You're a jerk," snapped Nora. Angered by Elliott's cheek and her own guilt, she snatched the tortilla chip from Elliott's hand and stormed back to the table.

"Hey, I was gonna eat that!" Elliott called after her. He placed his hands on his hips and tracked her departure.

"Elliott, just let her go," urged Emma. Elliott glared at her.

"Yeah, you'd love that," Elliott grumbled. He turned on a dime and exited the restaurant. Emma said nothing until he left her sight.

"It'll all work out, Elliott, I promise," Emma sighed. She stared at the door and added, "*Almost there.*"

I Won't Hold You Back

Emma, with great effort and the comedic assistance of David, managed to carry the evening past Elliott's impromptu appearance while keeping the mood light and the conversation moving. Her thoughts remained on her brother, however, and she wondered if she pulled the trigger on her plan too early.

"Lookin' forward to summer on the boat, that's for sure," declared Bart when the topic turned to the warming weather. His statement piqued Nora's interest.

"You've got a boat?" Nora asked in a sudden burst of energy.

"My old man's got a *nice* boat," answered Bart proudly, "but he doesn't use it as much anymore so I take it out all the time."

"My Dad sold his boat last year," Nora said before indulging in her margarita. She sighed and reminisced sadly, "I was *soooo* bummed out. I *loved* going out on that boat, ever since I was little. I miss the water, swimming on hot days, out on Lake Erie. Summer's just not the same without it."

"I can take you out on the lake," offered Bart, his excitement restrained but palpable. Emma sat up.

"You can?" Nora asked with an uncertain smile. Bart drained his beer.

"And there it is," Emma thought, her apprehension subsiding as dinner progressed. Nora and Bart settled into spirited conversation and their youthful energies seemed to align. Emma and David shared a quick glance, remembered the days of their own courtship and clasped hands under the table.

"My parents have a party *on* Memorial Day but what about Saturday or Sunday that weekend?" asked Bart. Nora pouted and slumped in her chair.

"I'm working both days," Nora replied with an apologetic expression. Emma whisked her out of her disappointment.

"I think I can spare you for one day," Emma quickly interjected. She sipped her margarita before continuing, "How about that Sunday? If the weather's nice."

"My folks might want to be out with us that day, though," said Bart. He eagerly awaited Nora's reaction.

"That's fine with me," Nora said. She was not ready to be completely alone with Bart and the presence of his parents was reassuring.

"Then it's a date," Emma said with wide, enthusiastic eyes and a grin.

"My wife's crazy," thought David. He squeezed her hand and added, "Beautiful, but crazy."

The waiter arrived to deliver the bill. Emma took it from his hand before Bart could reach for it.

"Uh-oh, reality," Emma said. She sighed as the waiter cleared plates from the table, "Guess I'd better get back to the club."

"Are you sure I can't get that?" asked Bart while his eyes darted between Emma and the bill.

"Of course. I said it was our treat," Emma admonished him gently with a wave and a half-grin.

"Oops, I got a little ways to go on this margarita," Nora said as she noticed her glass was three-quarters full.

"Why don't you two just move to the bar?" Emma suggested with a nod over her shoulder. She beamed and said, "You need to finish planning your boat day."

Nora and Bart looked at each other expectantly, each waiting for the other's response. They simultaneously and sheepishly grinned.

"Okay, but I can't have another one of these," Nora said. She sipped her drink again and said, "I have to drive home."

"So it's settled," Emma stated to seal the deal. Nora and Emma rose to their feet and shared their first hug.

"See ya' tomorrow, Em," Nora said.

"Good night, kids, have fun," Emma replied. Dave and Bart stood up together and shook hands over the table.

"See ya' man," said David. He waved at Nora and added, "Bye, Nora."

"Bye, Dave," Nora said. She scooped up her drink and, with Bart in tow, headed towards the bar area. David returned to his seat.

"Those two have great chemistry. You can *feel* it," Emma commented with great satisfaction. She retrieved her wallet from her purse and said, "And all it took was a boat and some childhood summer memories. *Perfect.*"

"Don't you think you're going a little too far with all this?" inquired David. Emma turned towards her husband.

"No," Emma stated bluntly. She pulled a stack of bills from her wallet, counted them out and tossed them down on the table, saying, "Not one bit."

Melting David with her powerful eyes, she grabbed his cheek and planted a loving kiss on his lips. He returned it.

"I hope you're right," replied David. They stood up to leave.

"Give the girls goodnight kisses for me," Emma said. She stuffed her wallet back in her purse.

"I'd get right home tonight and get some sleep if you can," advised David. He wrapped an arm around her waist and warned, "They've got a whole plan for your Mother's Day breakfast tomorrow and they're *really* excited about it."

"So am I," Emma said with wonderful thoughts of Mother's Day morning in her head.

• • • •

THE BAR CROWD THINNED as Nora and Bart bonded over their love of boating and childhood memories of perfect days on Michigan's lakes. Elliott, however, remained an uncomfortable prickle in her consciousness and she winced when Bart mentioned him.

"So what's the deal with Emma's brother?" asked Bart, the young man frustrated by Nora's deft avoidance of his hints about Elliott.

"You're gonna make me talk about him, aren't you?" Nora replied discontentedly. She lifted her glass of water and slowly drank from it. Bart leaned closer to her.

"Look, I like you, and I wanna spend time with you, and maybe more," admitted Bart, the nervousness evident on his face. Nora held the water glass at her lips as if hiding behind it. Bart gently moved it aside and said, "But I wanna know if I got a shot or if this guy's already got you."

Nora set down the glass. She offered him a look of pity.

"He doesn't *got* me," Nora countered. Her mind raced as she pondered how to handle the situation but, as always, she settled on honesty. Nora steeled her resolve and explained, "We've been, like, flirting a little bit. And we kissed. *Once.* But Emma doesn't want us going out so nothing's happened other than that."

"Is somethin' gonna happen?" replied Bart pointedly.

"Don't like the competition?" Nora teased him with a smirk. Bart's face soured and she instantly regretted the question.

"What is he, like fifty?" queried Bart sharply. Nora's expression became incredulous and she tilted her head.

"Thirty-seven," Nora corrected him.

"Still *way* too old for you," argued Bart. Her incredulity evaporated.

"I know," Nora said grudgingly. The pair broke eye contact and remained silent for thirty seconds. During the pause, Nora made a decision that would affect them all.

"Okay, this is the story," Nora announced firmly. She stood up and placed her hands on Bart's broad shoulders, declaring, "I'm not committing to anyone right now. Not Elliott. Not you. Not anyone. I just can't with school, and work . . . just everything. So if you wanna go out, have some fun this summer, and see where we're at in the fall, I'd *really* like that. But if you want a full-time, exclusive girlfriend, it's just not me. I mean, I'll understand. There won't be any hard feelings."

Nora returned to her seat. Bart stared at her with adoring eyes.

"But it's just not me," Nora repeated. Bart smiled.

"So, you comin' out on the boat with me or not?" Bart asked, the matter being settled in his mind. Nora hesitated and struggled to contain a grin but, after considering the invitation, shook her head in the affirmative.

"Yeah," Nora said. The prickle that she felt eased and she stated, "I am."

• • • •

ELLIOTT NEATLY AND respectfully folded his father's army jacket and placed it in the back seat of his car with great care. His spine tingled in a rush of sorrow and his eyes watered.

"God I miss you, Dad," he said. Climbing out of one well of depression and casting himself into another, he thought of Nora and said, "Wish I could get your advice on that one. And maybe you could get Em to back off. You were the only one who was good at that. I don't know, Dad. Maybe's she's right."

Responding to the growing coolness in the air, Elliott pulled a zippered sweatshirt from his trunk and slipped into it. He parked in a farmer's field on Wick Road northwest of Detroit Metropolitan Airport. The spot offered a great view of incoming and outgoing flights, the bustle of the airport and the twinkling of its multitudinous lights. He retreated to it often when he needed time to think.

"I gotta figure out what I'm gonna do about her," Elliott said to himself. He turned the volume knob on the radio before climbing onto the hood of the car. Resting his back on the windshield, he clasped his hands behind his head and thought, "A girl hasn't gotten into my head like this since, well . . . ."

Elliott searched his memory but found there was no comparison to be made. The thought bothered him.

"Since never," Elliott said aloud. The piano opening of "I Won't Hold You Back" by Toto emanated from the radio and interrupted his ponderings, the notes picking his heart strings like a guitar player. Elliott pictured Nora and Bart together in the restaurant, first hearing her laugh in his head and then her stinging words.

"You're a jerk."

"Why did I have to meet her?" Elliott asked. He stirred and folded his hands on his stomach, saying, "All the Mackaylas combined've never made me feel like *this*."

Toto's ballad was meant for established lovers at the end of a long romance but, in spots, its words aligned with Elliott's fledging relationship with Nora. The lead singer at one point sang that he was alone. Elliott identified with that sentiment as, despite being near the commotion of the airport, the immediate vicinity seemed quiet and he felt awash in solitude. He wished Nora was with him, her youthful energy making the spot not isolated but peaceful, not desolate but beautiful.

"It'd probably just bore the hell outta her," Elliott scolded himself.

The song ended.

"That's all I'm doing, just holding her back," Elliott said aloud. His slid down the hood and sat on the bumper, reasoning, "I should just let her be a kid. Date a guy her own age, have fun. Not pull her into all my old man bullshit."

His decision made, Elliott ceded the rest of Saturday to the night. He climbed into his car, turned off the radio and drove out of the field. Turning right onto Wick Road, his car disappeared into the bustle of the suburbs.

. . . .

A SLEEPY, DISHEVELED Elliott opened the door to his apartment. Squinting in the Sunday morning light, he wore a wrinkled white t-shirt, rumpled gray sweatpants and no socks.

"Truce?" inquired Nora uncertainly as she held up a brown paper bag and two coffees in a cardboard tray. Elliott, noticing her bleary, puffy eyes and her hastily tied ponytail, surmised she had a rough night.

"Yeah, sure," Elliott finally replied. He stepped aside and motioned for her to enter his apartment. The instant she crossed the threshold both their hearts dropped, each of them apprehensive as to what might happen next. Elliott closed the door and inquired, "So, what's up?"

"First things first," answered Nora. She walked to his round dining room table and set down the bag and the coffees. Turning back to him, she asked, "Got plates?"

Elliott nodded and, after a dramatic stretch and a yawn, proceeded into his small kitchen. He procured two plates from a cupboard and brought them to Nora.

"Cream and sugar?" asked Nora with an expectant grin. Elliott handed her the plates and returned to the kitchen.

"Anything else?" Elliott replied. He collected a sugar bowl, a spoon and a half-gallon of milk and set them on the table.

"Can we sit?" asked Nora. Elliott nodded his head and seated himself as she swiftly served them each a coffee and a donut and arranged everything to her liking. Nora handed Elliott a napkin and added, "I just got chocolate glazed. I didn't know what you like."

"That'll work," Elliott said. He pulled back the tab of the coffee lid and sent some caffeine into his veins. Unwilling to start the conversation, he took a large bite of his donut and then looked to Nora. She, with her eyes glued to him, drank from her coffee and then collected herself.

"I wanna talk about last night," declared Nora. Elliott sighed and slumped in his chair.

"Look, I shouldn't've barged in there like that," Elliott admitted. He gripped his foam coffee cup with both hands and added, "It's none of my business who you're dating. I'm sorry."

"I'm not dating him, we just went on *one date*," countered Nora. Elliott took another swig of his coffee and averted his gaze as she emphasized, "*A double date*. I wasn't even alone with him when he walked me to my car. The restaurant was really busy, there were people everywhere and-."

"Still, none of my business," Elliott interrupted stubbornly, the details of Nora's date grating on him. He refused to look at her and focused on pulling apart his donut and popping the pieces into his mouth.

"Why did you do it?" asked Nora with curious eyes. Elliott squirmed in his seat and his countenance became grim. His silence prompted Nora to goad him, "Seriously. Why?"

"Can't you just punch me in the balls instead?" complained Elliott. He took several gulps of coffee.

"Please," begged Nora. Elliott stewed for twenty seconds.

"All right," Elliott said while setting his cup on the table with a thump. Glaring at Nora, he ranted, "You wanna know why? *Fine*. I'll tell ya' why. I did it because, like an idiot, I'm really falling for you. Like I thought you were falling for me, but I was obviously wrong so it doesn't matter anyway."

Nora's entire body tingled as her emotion for Elliott surged. She carefully considered her response.

"You're not wrong," admitted Nora. She reached out and touched his hand, saying, "I really care about you, too. *A lot*."

"Then why the hell did you go out with *him*?!" Elliott shouted while pulling away from her grasp. His abrupt reaction startled Nora and, biting her lip to keep it from quivering, she battled tears. Standing up, Elliott said, "Don't answer that."

"You know why. Because of Emma," mewled Nora. Elliott turned his back on her as she said, "She's been so crazy about this whole thing."

Elliott's anger instantly evaporated. He turned back to her.

"I can fight her off, I've done it before," Elliott replied as if Emma were a minor concern. The gears of his mind spinning, he said, "I just wanna know you're with me before I start that war."

The full weight of Elliott's feelings for Nora fell upon her. He waited impatiently for her response. She faltered.

"I don't know, Elliott," said Nora. She lowered her voice and said, "I really need my job, and I *don't* want to fight her. And then there's the age thing. Doesn't that bother you, at least a little bit?"

A nasty smirk came to Elliott's lips and he shook his head slowly. He chuckled.

"Ah, I see, you don't date old guys, huh?" Elliott said sardonically. He picked up the bag of donuts and tossed it to her, saying as she mishandled them and they fell to the floor, "Well, ya found yourself a young one, so go take him donuts."

"Don't be a jerk," snapped Nora with a wavering voice. She picked up the bag to conceal her falling tears.

"Oh, that's right, I'm a jerk," Elliott said. Gesturing emphatically, he loudly declared, "That's *three* reasons not to go out with me, so just don't go out with me. See, simple answer. Why are you even here?"

Elliott took a few seconds to calm himself. His face twitched with a sadness of his own.

"Why did you even kiss me?" Elliott queried. Nora lost her composure and began openly weeping. She searched her mind for an answer but, even if she could have found one, she could not muster the words.

"*Elliott*," whimpered Nora.

"Did you kiss him?" asked Elliott quietly and gravely. He exhaled in frustration when she did not answer and said, "Ya' did."

Nora dried her tears with a napkin. Standing up and walking to Elliott, she steeled her will.

"I wanna date you both," announced Nora firmly. Elliott's shoulders drooped as she pled her case, saying, "I don't have time for a hot and heavy relationship right now. I have work, and school – but I like you both. Why can't we just, like, take it slow and have fun? Just see what happens. See how we feel. And if we really feel the way we think we do, and the whole age thing isn't a big deal, we'll still feel that way in a few months."

"I know how I feel now," Elliott said.

"So it's now or never?" asked Nora though she suspected she knew the answer to her question.

"*Yeah*," Elliott said, "and I don't think that's asking too much."

"I can't get into anything serious right now, Elliott," Nora insisted.

"Then don't," Elliott said dismissively. They lingered, each one waiting for the other to make a concession. When neither of them did, Nora sighed.

"Well, I gotta go," said Nora.

"Yeah, sure," Elliott said. He picked up his coffee, held it aloft and said, "Thanks for breakfast."

"Any time," said Nora with a weak smile. Elliott, as if by silent agreement, walked Nora to the door and opened it for her. She stopped on the porch and turned around.

"I did kiss him," confessed Nora. Elliott's anger flared but, before he could express it, she added, "But not like I kissed you."

Turning on a dime, Nora hurried down Elliott's walk and hung a right past the hedge. He listened to her car door open and close and then heard her engine start.

"Well, what now?" Elliott said. Feeling horrid and more alone than ever, he closed the front door.

• • • •

NORA MARCHED INTO JOHNNY Dubs and directly to Emma. The older woman felt the emotional heat of her advance and squared her shoulders to her. Several patrons sitting at the bar noticed the tension and turned their heads.

"Just chill out," Emma instructed her in a knowing tone. Sensing the attention of her patrons, she intercepted Nora and guided her to a table in a far corner of the dining area.

"You promised he'd be okay, Em," said Nora through angry tears and running mascara. The pair sat down as Nora slapped her hand on the table and continued, "But he's *not* okay."

Her spirited response was seen by everyone in the bar, patron and worker alike. Emma cowed the gawkers with a sweeping, stinging look before returning her attention to Nora.

"You went to his apartment, didn't you?" Emma admonished Nora. She pretended to be disappointed in her young mentee despite being ecstatic that her fledgling relationship crumbled. Nora bowed her head like a guilty child.

"Yeah," admitted Nora sadly. Emma pulled two napkins from a metal dispenser on the table and handed them to her.

"And you had a fight," Emma said like she witnessed their donnybrook, "and Elliott acted like a jerk."

"Uh-huh," confirmed Nora. She took the napkins and blotted her eyes with them.

"Look, Elliott'll be fine," Emma assured Nora. She motioned to the bartender and mouthed "water" while pointing at her. Emma placed a comforting hand on Nora's arm and added, "*You'll* be fine."

Allowing Nora to compose herself, Emma looked on her with pity. She hated to see her struggle.

"Two weeks, sweetie," Emma thought, "and then you'll both be moving on. Just hang in there."

"I told Elliott I wanted to date them both," said Nora as she crumpled the napkins and set them aside. Emma's eyes widened in astonished disbelief.

"You actually said that to him?" Emma asked. Fate was handing her another unexpected boon.

"I just don't want anything serious right now," whined Nora. She shrugged and explained, "I like them both, so I thought I'd just hang out with them both this summer. You know, see how things went."

She paused.

"Give us all some time to figure things out," said Nora hoarsely.

"Elliott's not big on competition," Emma advised with a dubious expression on her face. The conversation then took an unexpected turn.

"This sounds bad but Bart, he's, like, a sure thing," Nora said pensively. Emma merely watched her employee for thirty seconds before speaking.

"Did you tell Elliott *that*?" Emma inquired. Nora's brutal honesty was foreign to her way of thinking.

"No," answered Nora defensively, "I'm not that stupid."

"You're not stupid at all," Emma corrected Nora. She folded her arms on the table and explained, "You're actually being very smart about this whole thing. Look, Bart stayed even after Elliott pulled his bullshit, and kept watching you with those little twinkles."

Blown by the drafts of Emma's encouragement, the dark cloud lifted from Nora's mood. The bartender arrived and set a glass of ice water in front of her.

"Thanks, Luke," Nora said sadly. Emma waited for him to pass out of earshot.

"Bart's definitely a sure thing," reasoned Emma with burgeoning hopefulness, "and he's your age, and he loves the water just like you do and, ding ding, he's even got a boat. There's a lotta potential there, girl. *Long term* potential. I'm talking, like, taking your kids out on the boat just like your parents took you out. That's good stuff."

Nora's eyes glazed and she pondered Emma's words. The thought of a future with Bart was alluring but, as always, Elliott clawed his way back into her contemplations.

"What about Elliott?" queried Nora. Refocusing on Emma, she said, "I don't want him to hate me."

"Trust me, he'll get over it," Emma replied. She sat up and said, "You'll get the cold shoulder for while – just be ready for that – but he'll eventually come around."

Emma stood up and motioned for Nora to join her. She smirked.

"Besides, he's just as pissed at me, so I'll get most of it anyway," continued Emma.

"I'd like to still be his friend," said Nora. Emma bristled at the desire in her tone but choked down words of chastisement.

"It'll all be fine. Come on," Emma replied as she waved Nora upward. When the twentysomething hesitated, she laid a hand on her shoulder, saying, "Let's go up to my office and you can get cleaned up for your shift."

"Okay," agreed Nora. She gulped from her water, rose to her feet and allowed Emma to lead her away.

• • • •

"HELLO?" ELLIOTT MUTTERED into the phone. Freshly woken from a vibrant but forgotten dream, he laid in bed with his eyes closed.

"Are you still in bed?" asked Emma pejoratively. She sat on her living room couch with her slippered feet propped on the coffee table and a mug in her off hand.

"It's Sunday, Em," griped Elliott as he shook the tangled cord to create more slack in the line. He opened his eyes, squinted and then shielded them, griping, "What the hell do you want?"

"Haven't seen ya' all week," said Emma in an injured tone.

"Overtime," Elliott replied curtly. Emma knew he rarely worked overtime but ignored his lie.

"Wanna grab a late breakfast before I head to the club?" suggested Emma. She sipped her coffee and then held the warm mug to her chest.

"With Dave and the kids?" Elliott queried suspiciously. Their presence or absence would reveal his sister's intentions.

"No, just you and me," answered Emma. Elliott threw his covers aside, sat up straight and set his feet on the floor.

"I don't wanna talk about her," Elliott grumbled. He discovered he was unable to call Nora by name. Elliott's mood worsened as he stood and stretched and he sneered, "Or your devious role in the whole thing."

"Just give me ten minutes," begged Emma. Elliott said nothing and exhaled in frustration. Emma continued, "Ten minutes, Elliott, and then that's it. I promise."

"I'll give you as long it takes for me to eat breakfast," Elliott said as he walked to the window. He opened the blinds and stated flatly, "Senate in a half hour. You're buying."

Elliott hung up the phone. Emma exhaled dramatically and looked to David who entered the living room with a bowl of cereal.

"This is gonna suck," said Emma as she blew a draft of air straight up. It lifted a strand of her hair.

"You made your bed," David said before shoveling a spoonful of Fruit Loops into his mouth.

"Shut up and eat your cereal," replied Emma.

• • • •

EMMA AND ELLIOTT SAT at a booth in Senate Coney Island on Ecorse Road. They spent many breakfasts there throughout their lives and it conjured fond memories of their parents. Those memories were clouded by Elliott's mood and Emma's apprehension.

"All right," Emma said, "let me have it."

"Hey, you're the one who wanted to talk," Elliott said with raised hands.

"All right, then," said a surprised Emma. The chastisement she expected was not forthcoming. She drank her coffee, collected her thoughts and confessed, "I meddled, like I always do and . . . and I shouldn't have. I'm sorry."

"Excuse me?" Elliott replied. Though stunned by his sister's rare contrite attitude, he took considerable pleasure in watching her squirm. It was the fake apology, however, and not remorse that tortured her.

"I said I'm sorry, okay," said Emma. Elliott watched her skeptically and sipped his coffee as she explained, "But, seriously, Elliott, Nora is just too young for you. It wasn't right, and it wouldn't last. It would just waste precious time. You need to settle down, get married, have kids. And that all starts with finding the *right* woman."

"Yeah, and my oldest kid'd be graduating high school as I collect my first Social Security check," scoffed Elliott with a smirk. He threw his right arm on the back of the booth's bench.

"Not true," Emma countered. Her eyes began to sparkle as she said, "If you met someone this year, and dated for a year or so, and then got married, enjoyed each other for another year or so and then had a kid, you'd be thirty nine . . . and you wouldn't even be sixty when John graduates."

Elliott laughed heartily. His mirth garnered several puzzled looks from nearby tables.

"You've put a considerable amount of thought into that," Elliott said. He chuckled and asked, "And John?"

"Somebody has to," Emma admonished her brother. She said in a loving yet serious tone, "And you have to name him John. First born son of a first born son. Just like Daddy."

"You're insane," said Elliott, though the idea of his son carrying on the family namesake intrigued him. Emma had no chance to respond to the slight as the waitress arrived with their meals.

"Western Omelet for the lady," said the waitress as she set a plate in front of Emma. She then gave Elliott his meal and said, "And corned beef hash and biscuits for you. Be back in a sec with coffee."

"Thanks," Elliott said. He appraised Emma's meal and commented, "Just like Dad."

"Always," said Emma. They shared a reminiscent smile before she launched her first salvo, querying gently, "What about Donna?"

"Where'd *that* come from?" Elliott asked with a furrowed brow.

"I just talked to her the other day, and I thought about you two back then," answered Emma wistfully. She gave Elliott a poignant look and gushed, "She really loved you, Elliott. You were her world."

"But I didn't love her," Elliott argued and, after pulling apart a biscuit, he said, "and you just wanted her to be your best friend *and* your sister-in-law."

"So you didn't care about her at all?" queried Emma searchingly. She sliced into her omelet while Elliott slathered butter on a biscuit half and asked, "Not one little bit?"

"Okay, I guess I loved her, for a while," Elliott conceded. He bit into the biscuit and, after swallowing, added, "But that was almost two decades ago, Em."

"You ever thought about, like, reconnecting with her?" asked Emma as innocently as she could. They ate in silence for over a minute while Elliott contemplated his old flame.

"My feelings for her faded, Em, and they'd never get back to where we were at when it was *really* good," Elliott finally replied.

"You don't know that," countered Emma. She sipped her coffee and stated slowly, "I can tell you from experience, you can build caring into love, with effort and time."

Emma averted her gaze and became still and stone-faced. Elliott watched her closely and wondered at her fey mood.

"Wait. Are you telling me you didn't love Dave in the beginning?" Elliott inquired. Her revelation was stunning.

"*I love him now,*" insisted Emma. She grasped her coffee mug with both hands and said ardently, "He's a wonderful husband, a loving father and a good man . . . and we've built a strong family together. *I want that for you.* Don't you ever wonder what could've been?"

"What could've been?" asked Elliott with a confused expression.

"If you'd married Donna back then," Emma said. Elliott bowed his head. He did, in fact, wonder about how different his life would have been had he wed Donna but loathed the thought of admitting it to his sister.

"Yeah, I've thought about it," he said. His spirit died and he stared at the table, admitting, "I bought a ring."

"You never told me that!" Emma exclaimed, her eyes scintillating blue and green. Her outburst drew the attention of the patrons at the surrounding tables. Grabbing Elliott's arm, Emma demanded, "When?"

"That summer I graduated from college," replied Elliott. Emma released his arm and watched his face with rapt attention as he said, "But when it came time to propose, I just couldn't do it. Over and over again, I'd plan it but then not go through with it."

"You idiot!" Emma chastised him. Unconcerned with the annoyed looks of nearby restaurant goers, she declared, "She would've said yes!"

"I know that, Em," grumbled Elliott. He sat back and folded his arms, saying, "And I've considered where I'd be right now if we took the plunge."

"You'd have a big, happy family of your own," Emma said.

"Sorry, I thought I had one," countered Elliott.

"You know what I mean," Emma rejoined. She continued to process Elliott's near-engagement and exclaimed, "Damn it, Elliott!"

"I couldn't give her the ring because it wasn't for her," said Elliott curtly. Emma narrowed her eyes.

"So did you sell it?" Emma asked intently.

"No," answered Elliott reluctantly, "I still have it."

"Donna's still single, after all these years, and still in love with you – trust me on that – *and* you still have the ring you should've given her back then," said a flabbergasted Emma. She took a deep, calming breath and asked, "How many more signs do you need, Elliott?"

Elliott considered his sister's arguments carefully. Donna was a sure thing and he knew it.

"She's a sure thing," Emma said slowly and thickly as she remembered her conversation with Nora about Bart. Elliott's eyes darted to her face when she used the words "sure thing".

"It doesn't matter," Elliott declared as he disentangled himself from Emma's webs. He downed the rest of his coffee and said, "She's two thousand miles away, so it doesn't matter."

"I guess you're right," said Emma in a fake concession. She was content to merely plant the seed in his mind. She waited for the waitress to refill their coffees and continued, "How's work going? You haven't said anything about it."

"What's to say?" Elliott said while resting his cheek on his fist. He droned, "I'm a cable TV installer. I install cable TV all day, every day."

"I thought you were up for supervisor," said Emma.

"Yeah, supposedly," Elliott uttered. Given his disinterest in the topic, Emma decided to solidify the next plank of her plan.

"You're still coming on Memorial Day weekend, right?" asked Emma as if there were only one answer to the question.

"That depends," Elliott replied.

"On what?" asked a perturbed Emma.

"On whether there's going to be someone there you've been wanting me to meet," Elliott said. Though he was joking, his proximity to the mark unnerved Emma. She deflected.

"I'm just gonna let you find your *own* girl," said Emma snottily. Elliott offered her a half-smile.

"I'll be there," Elliott conceded.

"Good," said Emma. She pointed at him and added, "And remember-."

"Yeah, yeah, I know," Elliott interrupted her in a mocking tone, "bring chips and dip and that weird beer Dave's likes. And I'll get the cheap dip so your little monsters will eat it."

Brother and sister grinned at one another with fondness and then shared a laugh. Everything was good between them once again.

Who's Holding Donna Now?

The Sunday temperature rose into the eighties as the sun shined and the southwest wind blew. Elliott basked in the warmth after disembarking from his car and grinned when he heard his nieces' shouts and splashes in the pool. The smell of the hamburgers and hot dogs that David grilled soon wafted over him. A sudden sadness fell upon Elliott, however, and he shivered despite the heat.

"Too bad Mom and Dad couldn't be here for this," Elliott thought as he gazed up at the beautifully blue sky. A shrill scream from Lanie brought him back to the present and he said with gratitude, "At least I get to be."

Elliott grabbed the six pack of David's "weird beer" and two plastic bags containing potato chips and sour cream dip from the front passenger seat. He then closed the car door with his foot.

"You're late, big brother," Emma playfully scolded him when he strolled into the foyer of her house. She rushed from the kitchen to the dining room carrying a large, plastic bowl of macaroni salad with both hands.

"Hello to you, too, little sister," said Elliott.

"I'm glad you're here," Emma said earnestly as she returned from the dining room. She embraced him and kissed him on the cheek, asking, "Wanna drink?"

"Nah, thanks, I'm good for the moment," replied Elliott. Emma did not continue into the kitchen as he expected but instead stood in front of him to block his advance. He lifted the beer and the bags and queried with a smirk, "Mind if I join the party?"

"Remember when we talked about Donna the other day?" Emma inquired. Though she restrained her excitement, Elliott could sense it percolating beneath her emotional surface.

"Wouldn't it be smarter to get a few in me before bringing that up?" asked Elliott with a befuddled expression. Emma showed no intention of relenting so he reasoned, "It's been fifteen years, Em. You *really* need to give up on that one."

"She never stopped loving you," Emma countered.

"Okay, look, I let that one slide the other day but c'mon," said Elliott. He offered Emma a dubious look and rebuked her, "That's bullshit and you know it."

"She's been hung up on you since the day you broke her heart," Emma advised him. She shook her head and said, "I just never told you."

"Why are we even having this conversation?" asked an irritated Elliott. He nodded over his shoulder and said dismissively, "She's in Arizona and I'm here."

"No, she's not," Emma said while beaming. Her eyes shimmered. Elliott's face went pale.

"What did you do, Ray?" asked Elliott with the *Ghostbusters* line.

"She's back, Elliott," Emma replied enthusiastically.

"In Detroit?" asked Elliott with a raised eyebrow.

"In the back yard," Emma said.

"You're evil," said Elliott. Emma smacked his shoulder but her zest did not fade one iota.

"Is it evil to want my brother to be happy?" Emma inquired in a mock wounded tone.

"It is when you're involved," answered Elliott. Unable to be angry in the blinding light of Emma's zeal, he chuckled and said, "I should know better than to tangle with you. I think I'll have that drink."

Elliott moved past Emma and carefully edged his head around the corner of the living room. Donna, clad in a turquoise beach coverup, played and laughed with his nieces while David grilled and his parents sat at the patio table.

"You gotta admit, she looks fantastic," Emma said. Donna disappeared from view so Elliott quickly moved to the far side of the kitchen. Emma added, "Arizona's been good to her."

"Yeah, but that was never the problem," replied Elliott while setting the six-pack and the bags on the kitchen table. Emma began preparing a Grumpy Old Man.

"She's nervous about seeing you again," Emma warned Elliott. His heart thumped in his chest and, to his surprise, his palms grew sweaty.

"I know the feeling," replied Elliott. Emma finished fixing his drink and handed it to him. She then gave him a nudge towards the sliding patio door.

"Go say hello, and remember you hold my best friend's heart in your hands," Emma instructed him. She nudged him again and said, "I'll be out in a minute."

"What, you don't have a script written out for us?" asked Elliott with a harsh over-the-shoulder glance. He did not appreciate being ambushed. Emma, unconcerned with his annoyance, waved him away.

"*Go*," Emma ordered firmly. She jammed one of David's beers in Elliott's back pocket and said softly, "And don't screw it up this time."

Elliott started at the cold sensation in his pocket but it provided him an excuse to delay his entrance. Urged forth by Emma's expectations, however, he soon walked to the door.

"At least there's no pressure," muttered Elliott as he stopped at the door-wall screen and took three large gulps from his drink. His thoughts turned to Nora and he said to himself, "I think I'm about to drive a Donna-sized nail in that coffin."

• • • •

NORA SUNBATHED ON THE front of Bart's parents' speedboat, the twentysomething soaking up the glorious rays of the late spring sun. Because it was her first time meeting his family, she chose a modest one-piece swimsuit in black.

"Guess the bikini woulda' been okay," Nora told herself when she saw Bart's mother, Helen, wearing a sexy, floral-print two-piece. The older woman lay several feet away from her as she, too, indulged in the sun's heat and light. Bart and his father, Dennis, chatted with some mutual friends, their boats tied together and anchored in a small bay. She glanced at Helen and added, "They're in pretty good shape for their age."

Dennis and Helen were both attractive, tall and lean people and, in that sense, Bart was clearly their offspring. However, they seemed more intelligent and social than their son: Dennis was a high-level salesman at a large auto parts supplier and Helen was an accountant. She wondered how the pair could produce a down-to-earth mechanic.

"Oh my god," Nora thought as a lightning bolt of anxiety struck her. She abruptly sat up and said to herself, "*Today's* the day Em was gonna spring

Donna on Elliott. That's why she took the day off and *that's* why she pushed me to go out on the boat with Bart today."

Nora had successfully stashed Elliott in a far corner of her mind until that point. He now flooded her thoughts, however, and they were pressurized by her inability to reach him and powerlessness to stop Emma's plan. Nora felt lightheaded and the world spun.

"Just calm down," Nora thought. Focusing on her breathing, she composed herself. She rose to her feet and watched Bart who, at one point in his conversation, looked to her with an adoring smile. She forced a half-smile in return and studied his handsome face. Using his image to chase away the phantom of Elliott, she thought, "He's a nice guy, attractive, strong, *your age* . . . and he really likes you."

Nora's efforts failed. She replayed her passionate kiss with Elliott in her mind. The memory still tethered her heart to him.

"I'll just kiss Bart like that . . . tonight," Nora promised herself though the mere prospect caused her to shiver. Moving towards him, she stopped at the cooler to get Bart and his father fresh beers. She focused intently on Bart's physique and thought, "On this boat, with him, is, like, exactly where you're supposed to be."

Bart and Dennis ended their conversation as Nora walked up to them. They cast off the other boat's lines and bid their friends farewell.

"Here ya' go, Dennis," Nora said.

"Look at this," replied Dennis while tossing his empty can into the trash with a clatter. He happily accepted his beer and wrapped an arm around Nora's shoulder, announced proudly, "Now, this is daughter-in-law material! Always bringing Dad another beer."

Bart winced.

"*Dad*," Bart scolded Dennis. He knew of Nora's alcoholic father and warned Dennis about making his characteristic, alcohol-based jokes. She squirmed under his arm.

"Oh, shit. I'm sorry, honey," apologized Dennis as he released her. Hearing the exchange, Helen stood up as he uttered, "Me and my big mouth."

"Honestly, Dennis," Helen chastised him while shaking her head with disapprobation.

"Oh, so you told him," Nora asked, the revelation embarrassing her.

"I'm sorry. I just didn't want him doing what he just did," said Bart. He offered his father a frustrated glare and added, "But he did it anyway."

"I'm really sorry," said Dennis.

"It's okay, really. I bring beers to people all the time. It's my job, remember," Nora said as she deftly maneuvered out of her discomfort. Bart wrapped a supportive arm around her waist. Her first instinct was to avoid it but, swiftly suppressing the urge, she allowed him to pull her closer. Buttressed by Bart's caring attitude, Nora smirked and said, "Besides, my dad's a whiskey drinker."

Nora let the smirk spread into a wide grin to put Bart and his parents at ease. Her strategy worked.

"So, whaddaya wanna do now?" asked Bart.

"Take me swimming," Nora said as she playfully pushed Bart away.

"That's a great idea, Nora," Helen replied. She plopped down in the seat opposite the captain's chair and informed Dennis, "We want to go swimming."

"I know the perfect spot for that," said Dennis. He sat in the captain's chair and started the boat.

"Yeah," Nora thought as she and Bart sat down next to each other with the bare skin of their legs touching. Wallowing in the physical contact and letting any thoughts of Elliott flit away on the wind, she declared, "We're both exactly where we oughta be."

• • • •

DELAYING HIS REUNION with Donna as long as possible, Elliott hung an immediate left after stepping onto the patio. He offered a hand to Tom but felt her presence behind him and heard her playing in the pool with the girls. Sneaking repeated peeks at Elliott, Donna trembled with anticipation.

"Donna!" Tessa yelled while splashing her. Donna forced her attention back to the eight-year-old.

"Hey, Tom, how are ya'?" asked Elliott. David's father sat at the patio table, smoked a cigar and held a half-full, condensation-coated glass. Tom shook his hand.

"Doin' great, Elliott," Tom replied. He pulled Elliott towards him, leaned forward and said in a low tone, "And you will be, too, if you play your cards right."

"Started early today, did we, Tom?" queried Elliott. Tom released his hand and laughed heartily. Elliott maneuvered towards David's mother and kissed her on the cheek, asking, "And how are you, beautiful?"

Rose grabbed his arm and moved her lips to his ear. Elliott cringed.

"That girl's a delight, young man," Rose whispered. She gave him a pointed look and added, "Don't let that ring gather any dust."

"My god, she recruited all of 'em," thought Elliott. He drained his drink, felt the rush of the alcohol and set his glass on the table.

"Did ya' get me my Cheese Whiz, boy?" David asked in reference to *The Blues Brothers* line. Elliott produced the beer bottle from his back pocket and tossed it to him. David quickly opened it with a bottle opener and took a long pull.

"Uncle Elliott!" bellowed Elliott's nieces as they climbed out of the pool. He turned to face them but was still unable to lift his gaze to Donna.

"Little monsters!" yelled Elliott in response.

"Heads up!" Lanie shouted as she hurled the wet ball at Elliott. He snagged it from the air but the resultant spray hit the adults.

"Lanie!" Rose scolded her. David and Tom chuckled.

"Time to eat," Emma announced as she appeared on the patio. She scooped up towels and handed them to the girls, instructing them, "Dry off and go wash your hands. And stop throwing wet balls at your grandparents."

The girls vanished into the house, the sisters picking at each other the entire way. David and Elliott snickered. Emma shook her head.

"You're both twelve," Emma admonished them. Her irritation proved to be short-lived as she looked to David and asked, "Are they done, babe?"

"Yep, comin' off now," replied David. He took another pull of his beer, opened the grill and used a spatula to pile hamburgers and hot dogs onto a large white plate.

"Hi, Elliott," Donna said cautiously as she ascended the pool steps. Her words, despite the gentleness of her tone, ripped through the air and struck every nerve in Elliott's body. Emma caught her breath while David and his parents watched with great interest.

"I didn't expect it to be like this," thought Elliott. Donna wowed him with a strapless bikini of neon green and black. The soft, girlish body of her youth was gone, replaced by the lean, toned figure of a woman, and prompted Elliott to comment, "Em was right. Arizona's been good to you."

The comment brought smiles to the adults' faces and Emma watched their reunion with shimmering eyes. Donna melted.

"Elliott," Emma called. Garnering his attention, she nodded to a neatly folded towel on a nearby lounge chair and asked, "Would you grab Donna's towel for her?"

Emma's conspirators quickly moved into the house as he complied with her wishes. She kept her gaze on Elliott and Donna until David herded her inside.

"Let's go, crazy lady," David playfully directed her, his beer in one hand and the plate of cooked meat in the other.

"All right, all right," relented Emma with several rearward glances. Though the cacophony of the Hastings clan still emanated from the house, Elliott and Donna were soon alone and, free of prying eyes, he re-examined her.

"Wow, you two're really playing hardball," said Elliott.

"You don't like my suit?" Donna asked impishly. A stiff breeze blew through the backyard and caused her to shiver.

"I'm definitely not saying that," answered Elliott as he reflexively wrapped the towel around her. He smirked and added, "I hate to cover it up."

The former lovers looked to one another, suppressed the urge to kiss and then fell into an awkward silence as Donna dried herself. Despite his anxiety over their first meeting in fifteen years, Elliott spoke after a long exhale.

"I'm gonna be honest, Donna," admitted Elliott, "I don't know what to do with all this."

"I know, it's kinda surreal," Donna agreed. She finished drying off, grabbed her coverup from a chair and slithered into it, saying adoringly, "But it's really good to see you again, Elliott."

"Yeah," concurred Elliott. Donna's desire for him was obvious and, though not to the same degree, he also felt a yearning for her.

"Why don't we just do what Emma expects us to do?" Donna suggested. Elliott's eyes grew wide and he stared at her in disbelief.

"Excuse me?" asked Elliott.

"I meant go in and eat dinner," Donna said with the smile of a nervous schoolgirl. Elliott shook his head, relaxed his body and grinned.

"Right," replied Elliott. Another pause followed.

"A hug wouldn't be asking too much, would it?" Donna inquired gingerly.

"Not at all," Elliott answered. He embraced her and they both indulged in the physical contact for longer than expected. Donna pecked him on the cheek before Elliott wrapped an arm around her shoulders and said with mock incredulity, "Ya' know, you didn't tell me how good I look."

"You look old and tired," Donna joked. Elliott was surprised that his once meek sweetheart risked the slightest misinterpretation of her intentions. They both laughed and Elliott ushered her forward.

"Nice," he said with feigned annoyance, the word echoing in his head. He remembered them walking together in high school, in exactly the same manner, and thought, "Yeah. That about covers it. *Nice.*"

. . . .

BART'S PARENTS DEPARTED shortly after their arrival at the marina – Nora believed it to be by design – and she assisted him in closing the boat for the night. When nearly all was done, she changed out of her swimsuit and into more comfortable clothing in the boat's small cabin.

"You gotta do it, Nora," she told herself as she tied her hair in a ponytail. She began to exit the cabin but stopped on the middle of the steps. Noticing that the marina still buzzed with activity as the Michiganders enjoyed the warm, late spring evening, Nora thought, "But you can't do it out here."

"Ready?" asked Bart. He tossed a duffle bag onto the dock and offered her his hand, saying, "Just gotta lock the cabin and put the cover on and we can head out."

"Hey, can you come down here for a minute?" Nora requested. Her anxiety was palpable and Bart detected it in her tone.

"You alright?" said a concerned Bart. Nora descended the steps and he followed her. She lured him to the middle of the cabin and, when she did not turn around, he placed a hand on her shoulder and beckoned, "Nora?"

Nora trembled before spinning around with an upward lunge and planting a sultry kiss on Bart's lips. Infusing it with as much passion as she could muster, she attempted to recreate the moment she shared with Elliott and fell into Bart's strong embrace.

"Whoa," uttered a stunned Bart. Nora shook like a leaf in a stiff wind as a realization struck her: the kiss, while pleasant and even arousing, paled in comparison to the one she and Elliott shared.

"Oh, no," Nora thought. She quickly kissed Bart again.

"Uh, I thought we were, like, taking it slow," said a confused Bart when she released him and stepped back.

"I'm sorry. We are," Nora mewled. Scrambling to cover the reason for her sudden aggressiveness, she forced a half-smile and said, "Sometimes girls get carried away, too . . . especially with guys that look like you."

Nora blushed and sat down on a cushioned bench. Bart laughed off the compliment.

"I'm not ready to let you go yet," admitted Bart, the young man glossing over Nora's advance.

"I'm not ready to let you go, either," Nora replied. She genuinely wished to be with him in the present but, to her dismay, could not see him in her future.

"Wanna get some food?" queried Bart.

"Yeah," Nora answered. Shaking free of her doubt, she decided to focus on the here and now.

"Then get off your butt and let's go get some food," teased Bart. His lighthearted nature set her at ease and she giggled. Offering him her hand, Nora allowed him to pull her to her feet. She pecked Bart on the lips.

"Another kiss?" asked Bart.

"You earned that one," Nora said. She then scurried out of the cabin, saying, "C'mon, I'm hungry."

• • • •

DINNER PROVED AN ENJOYABLE experience for Elliott as he was able to converse with Donna in a comfortable, familiar atmosphere without either of them being the sole focus of the conversation. Lanie and Tessa provided comic relief and frequent interruptions as the party moved back to the pool area and, once David's parents departed and the girls tired of swimming, the four remaining adults retired to the hot tub for cocktails.

"It is *so* awesome to have you back," Emma gushed. She cuddled into David, who wrapped an arm around her shoulders, and held a beer in her hand. Pulling her feet onto the hot tub's bench, Emma asked excitedly, "Isn't it awesome, Elliott?"

Elliott rolled his eyes and David squirmed. He and Donna sat at a safe distance from one another, close yet not too close.

"Leave him alone, Em," scolded Donna. Her tone was lighthearted but her face was uncharacteristically stern. She sipped a glass of wine and fought the urge to jump into Elliott's lap.

"She's right, though, Donna," Elliott interjected, "it *is* good to see you again."

Emma's eyes lit up and she squeezed David's thigh. Donna looked to Elliott with delighted surprise but, before she could respond, the telephone rang.

"I wonder who that is," Emma said. She handed David her beer and exited the hot tub. Grabbing a towel on her way to the door, she dried herself and then disappeared inside the house.

"We all know who it is," replied David with a dubious expression. Emma soon returned.

"That was Sean," Emma said. She explained in exasperation as David stood up, "There was a fight in the parking lot and the cops are there."

"Oh, no," replied Donna.

"Nothing big, just some regulars acting like assholes," Emma grumbled.

"I'll get my keys," sighed David. He retrieved his own towel and dried himself while walking to the house.

"I'll have Dave drive me up there if you guys could stay here with the girls until we get back," Emma explained. Elliott shook his head in disbelief as she continued, "They're passed out in front of the TV and, with how hard they played today, they're dead to the world."

"Yeah, of course," said Donna while nodding in the affirmative. Emma refused to look at Elliott for more than a second or two. She quickly turned and hurried into the house.

"Thanks, you two," Emma said over her shoulder.

"I don't know how she does it," commented Donna with respect and admiration for her best friend. She finished her wine and set the glass on the cement, saying, "Running a successful business and raising a happy family. She and Dave've built such a great life."

Elliott and Donna heard David start the car, pull out of the driveway and accelerate down the street. She pressed her lips together and then bit them before sliding closer to Elliott. Donna let her thigh touch his thigh but he instinctively moved his leg.

"Emma strikes again," Elliott said. He took a drink and then set his glass aside.

"Is it really that bad to be alone with me?" asked Donna in an injured tone.

"Donna, we're here because my sister wants us to be here," argued Elliott. Donna, in a move uncharacteristic for one of her meekness, threw a leg over Elliott, sat on his lap and went nose-to-nose with him. He sensed her anxiousness, felt her trembling and knew she was forcing the action.

"*I* want to be here," Donna declared. She captured him in her ardent gaze and, cognizant of his erection, said with a seductive yet unconvincing smirk, "And it feels like you do, too."

"Lanie and Tess could wake up at any time," warned Elliott as old yearnings stirred within him. Fighting the urge to take Donna at that very moment, he said, "All it takes is someone wanting a glass of water and we're busted."

Donna grasped Elliott's cheeks and engaged him in a long, sultry kiss which he eagerly returned. Maintaining her grip on his face, she pulled away and let her loving eyes paralyze him. Donna's façade of confident sexuality suddenly vanished.

"We're not having sex, Elliott," Donna advised him, his former girlfriend clearly conflicted. She climbed out of his lap and slumped down next to him.

"Wait, we're not?" asked a befuddled Elliott.

"No, I shouldn't even be doing this," Donna answered.

"Doing what?" queried Elliott.

"Tying to seduce you," Donna said. Elliott's resentment of Emma's meddling, fueled by his frustrated sexual desires, boiled beneath his emotional surface but he said nothing. Donna panicked and, standing up, she demanded, "What do you feel, right now?"

"Come on, Donna," Elliott replied.

"Don't think, just tell me," insisted Donna. Studying her face, Elliott knew she would not relent.

"I think you're being too intense about us," Elliott said gravely. Donna deflated.

"What's wrong with intense?" mewled Donna. Reluctant to admit her love for Elliott, she said awkwardly, "I, I . . . I still have . . . *really strong* feelings for you. Even after all this time."

"Nothing's wrong with it," Elliott answered, "until you mix it with desperation and my sister's scheming."

Donna's face spasmed with a sob and she jumped away from Elliott. She sloshed towards the hot tub steps but Elliott caught her arm.

"Donna," Elliott pleaded, "wait."

Donna whirled around and started to cry. The former lovers stood face-to-face in the center of the hot tub.

"You devastated me," whimpered Donna through tears. She attempted another retreat but Elliott grasped both her hands. She exhaled with a shiver and said, "I loved you . . . so, so much. And when you ended it, I was crushed."

"I know, Dee," Elliott said. He massaged her hands and added, "Emma told me."

Elliott's hearkening back to her high school nickname, one that he used for their entire relationship, impacted them both. Donna's mood improved.

"No one's called me that in while," said Donna, "not even Em."

"Why did you come on so strong if you felt this vulnerable?" Elliott inquired.

"I don't know," replied Donna while averting her gaze. Elliott recalled Emma's admission that her love for David was not immediate but developed over time. He also thought of Nora and, driven to action by the pain of losing her, he asked a dangerous question to which he knew the answer.

"Are you still in love with me?" Elliott asked bluntly. Donna steeled her will, summoned her courage and held back her remaining tears.

"I never stopped loving you, Elliott," answered Donna softly.

"I loved you once, too, I'm sure of it," Elliott began. Before Donna could lament her unrequited love for him, he continued, "And I never stopped caring about you, really caring about you, and I still thought about you."

The image of the engagement ring he bought for her arose in his mind. He stifled the thought.

"Swear it?" asked Donna.

"Yeah," Elliott answered, "I do."

"What're we gonna do, Elliott?" pleaded Donna. Collapsing into his arms and then wallowing in his embrace, she again wept but said firmly, "I don't want you back just to lose you. I can't do that again. I won't make it."

Elliott's mind flooded with old memories and old feelings inundated his heart. He surrendered.

"Let's just take it one date at a time, and build on what we already feel for each other," Elliott said. They pledged their commitment with an embrace and another kiss. The kiss was not one of ardent love but one of deep affection and, in that moment, Nora passed to the back of Elliott's mind.

• • • •

BUILDING ON THE SUCCESS of The Club's first County Night, Emma scheduled them throughout the summer. Elliott hated country music but, when the first band began playing, he ignored it and kept his eyes on Nora. Emma noticed his hawking of her waitress, marched up to him and smacked the back of his head.

"Hey!" protested Elliott as he spun his barstool around and faced his attacker. Emma leaned into him and spoke in his ear.

"I swear to god I'll kick you out if you don't stop," Emma snarled. Disregarding the patrons swirling around her, she threatened, "And I'll kill you if you hurt Donna again."

Elliott held up his hands in a sign of parley. His odd reaction halted Emma's assault and he in turn spoke in her ear.

"It's not what ya' think, Em," Elliott said. She stepped back, bumped into a patron and glared at him.

"Upstairs," Emma yelled, her words barely carrying above the band. Maneuvering though the bustling crowd and the smoky air, the siblings made their way to the outer stairwell.

"Uh-oh," Nora said to herself as she noticed the tension between Elliott and his sister. Emma unlocked the door and held it open for him.

"Let's go," she said with a nod to the stairs. Elliott complied and, after Emma locked the door, the pair ascended the steps.

"That can't be good," said Nora while placing drinks on a tray at the bar. Curiosity chewed on her mind but her duties soon carried her away and she saw no more of the siblings' interaction.

"No witnesses up here, huh?" said Elliott with a chuckle when they reached the top of the stairwell. Emma remained icily mute, her coldness prompting Elliott to joke, "You still don't have Dad's old revolver in your desk drawer, do you?"

The noise level faded when Emma unlocked the door and she and Elliott entered her office. He started when Emma slammed it. Placing his hands on his hips, Elliott turned to face the wrath of his sister.

"Take it easy, Em. You win," said Elliott preemptively. His declaration halted the acerbic words on Emma's tongue.

"What?" Emma asked, her anger morphing into confusion.

"You heard me," said Elliott slowly and firmly. He thrust his hands in his pockets, shrugged and repeated, "You win.

"I do?" Emma asked suspiciously.

"That was the deal. If I found someone, I forget all about Nora, at least as a girlfriend," replied Elliott resignedly. He paused and drifted mentally for twenty seconds before refocusing on Emma and saying, "I'm just here to make peace with her."

"Does Donna know that?" Emma inquired sharply. Her ire returned.

"Why would I tell her about Nora and I, Em?" asked Elliott incredulously. He pulled his hands from his pockets and said with a demonstrative gesture, "She'd just be hurt there was someone else, and she wouldn't be happy that you lied to her about it."

"Yeah, I guess so," Emma conceded.

"Like I said, Emma, you win, so that's it. And besides, I'm picking Donna up in a half hour and we're gonna catch a movie," Elliott said. Emma grinned. Her designs were coming to fruition and it made her happy.

"Whatcha guys gonna see?" Emma inquired.

"Well, I thought about *Rambo II*, but I decided to spare her so we're gonna see the new Bond flick, *View to a Kill*," Elliott answered.

"Good choice," Emma said before placing her hands on his shoulders and planting a kiss on his cheek. Gazing on him with her unique, sparkling eyes, she announced, "Remember today, Elliott. June 1, 1985. Your second first date with Donna and *the day your life turned around*."

• • • •

NORA CLOSED THE STAIRWELL door. She caught her breath when she noticed that Elliott awaited her on the third step.

"What's going on, Elliott?" asked an anxious Nora.

"I wanna talk," Elliott replied. He was nervous as well and deeply exhaled to center himself.

"I didn't think you wanted to see me anymore," said Nora with a pained expression, "and I sure didn't think Emma'd let me near you."

"We both changed our minds," Elliott answered with a weak smile. He patted the space next to him and said, "Pop a squat."

"Uh . . . okay," agreed Nora. She realized that Emma painted them both into corners, she with Bart and Elliott with Donna, but wondered how Elliott would respond.

"Can we just skip all the hard stuff and go back to being friends again?" Elliott blurted. The question stunned Nora but she quickly recovered. She sighed in relief and relaxed her body.

"*Yeah*," replied Nora. She asked with a caring smile, "Good friends?"

"Yeah, I think we can do that," Elliott replied with several nods. The band hit a crescendo and the crowd roared, the cacophony rescuing he and Nora from the moment.

"I'm getting outta here. I can't take all this hillbilly crooning," Elliott said as he stood up. Nora laughed and joined him.

"What, you're leaving me here alone with all of 'em?" asked Nora puckishly.

"Hey, you're getting *paid* to endure this country hell," Elliott replied with a smirk.

"Welcome to Taylor-tucky," said Nora. They embraced tightly to seal their truce. She pecked him on the cheek.

"All right, Nora, catch ya' later," Elliott said as he released her. The pair stared at each other for a moment but Elliott soon broke eye contact, opened the stairwell door and proceeded into the crowd. Nora leaned against the doorframe and watched Elliott depart.

"Bye, Elliott," whispered Nora with a sad smile. Taking a final glance at the stage, Elliott saw Emma take the microphone.

"Next up we have Morning Cloak," Emma announced. The crowd cheered as Toni and her bandmates took the stage.

"Well, ain't she purdy," Elliott thought in a southern drawl. He soaked in the beauty of her smile and her engaging presence. Nora traced his line of sight to Toni and then back to him. She shivered.

"Get going, Elliott," Nora rebuked him in her mind. His unusual expression made her uneasy. A drunken patron bumped into Elliott.

"Sorry, man," said the patron. Elliott, however, did not hear his words. Instead, he sensed Nora's attention and turned to her. She had a look of disapproval on her face and, suddenly uncomfortable, Elliott threw her a quick wave and fled into the night.

A cool breeze washed over Elliott and Donna as they laid on the hood of his car with their backs to the windshield. A six-pack container holding four bottles of beer sat on its roof.

"I missed the cool Michigan air," commented Donna as the pair watched flights arriving at and departing from Metro Airport. She drank her beer and wrinkled her nose. Her tastes had changed since their college years and beer was now too bitter for her palette.

"Yeah, just wait six months," Elliott remarked.

"I said cool, not cold," replied Donna with a half-smile and an elbow to Elliott's ribs. She covertly poured out her remaining beer and added, "I know why the snowbirds flock to Florida and Arizona now."

Donna returned the bottle to its container but did not procure another one. She and Elliott fell into what was, for him, a comfortable silence and she cuddled into his body. Donna, however, stirred several times and he knew something was on her mind.

"I've kept something from you," admitted Donna after several minutes, "and I don't feel good about it."

"We've both been with other people," Elliott said, his thoughts immediately going to Nora. He felt morally slimy with Donna attached to his side but Nora attached to his mind.

"Of course we've both been with other people," replied Donna though the words tasted bitter on her lips.

"Really?" Elliott inquired with mock jealously.

"Stop it, Elliott. I'm serious," said Donna. She struggled to find the courage to confess and said, "It's something else."

"You're serious," Elliott said when he saw the distress Donna's secret caused her. The images of Nora in his mind faded and he focused on his girlfriend. She exhaled, scooted away from Elliott and sat up with her legs crossed.

"I was at your parents' funerals," said Donna as she folded her hands in her lap. She bit her lip and anxiously awaited his response.

"I thought you had pneumonia for Dad's and the plane broke down for Mom's," Elliott replied with a furrowed brow.

"I lied," said Donna. Elliott finished his beer as she added guiltily, "Twice."

"Let me guess," Elliott said while shaking his head disapprovingly and exchanging an empty bottle for a full one, "it was Em's idea."

Donna studied Elliott, gauged his mood and mulled over her response. She lowered her eyes before speaking.

"No," replied Donna, "it was mine."

"It was you, Dee?" Elliott queried. He pulled a bottle opener from his jacket and said, "I mean, it'd been a few years at that point."

"I was really busted up, Elliott," said Donna, her shame evident. Elliott popped the cap off his beer with a hiss but kept his gaze on her as she expounded, "I panicked over seeing you again. And I didn't wanna add anything to what you and Em were already going through. I went to your dad's funeral and then came back a few weeks later after everything had settled down and spent two weeks here with Em. I came back for your mom's, too."

"Wow, I had no clue," Elliott said. He stared at the lights of the airport and allowed them to blur, saying, "You came up after Lanie was born, too, right?"

"I spent a lot of money on airfare that year," Donna said with a weak smile.

"I guess I was too out of it to notice," Elliott said as he searched his mind for any hints as to Donna's presence. He skirted around the painful memories of his parents' funerals.

"I'm so sorry, Elliott," apologized Donna. She moved closer to him again and grabbed his arm, saying, "I was still hurting over us but I made a bad decision."

"No, you didn't," Elliott replied supportively. He took her hands in his own and said, "Who knows how we each would've dealt with it? Besides, you took care of Em."

"I should've taken care of *you*," insisted Donna. She reversed his grip and instead held his hands, saying, "Em had Dave to help pull her through all of that. You had no one, no one close who hadn't suffered the loss, anyway. I really regret that and I'm just . . . I'm just really sorry."

"Don't be," Elliott corrected her gently. He looked down and began running his fingers along hers, stating, "Em lost both her parents in less than six months, too, and had a baby in the middle of it. Thank god for you and Dave."

"Especially Dave," said Donna. She snuggled under his arm and added, "He'd do anything for her."

Remorse welled in Elliott's heart as he remembered the horrible year that was 1975. It caused him to miss Donna's continued distress and that she prepared to speak once more.

"If anyone should be apologizing, it should be me, to her," Elliott said before she could say a word. He took a long, slow pull of his beer and explained, "I mean, how can I blame her for being so crazy about family when ours was torn apart like that? But she's so strong, too, strong like the old man was. And she stitched us back together, remade the family and raised two little girls while resurrecting Johnny Dubs. It's a helluva lot more than I did, which wasn't much."

Elliott's raw emotion and vulnerability shattered Donna's defenses and, seeking nothing but to heal his hurt, she hugged Elliott tightly to console him. Unable to muster soothing words, she took a different tack.

"I'm ready, Elliott," said Donna. She pulled him into a passionate kiss.

"Yeah, I guess we can go," Elliott said, his venture into the past dulling his perception. He chugged his beer, twisted around and returned it to the container.

"No, Elliott," Donna said emphatically. She took his chin with her forefinger and her thumb and held it fast as she gazed into his eyes and repeated, "*I'm ready.*"

Donna kissed Elliott again and she soon melted into him. He quickly realized her desire and felt the rush of sexual arousal throughout his own body. Her forthrightness surprised him, however, as she never initiated sex during their first relationship.

"You sure?" Elliott asked though he himself was more than ready. Donna pressed her hand into his erection as he asked, "Here?"

Donna squeezed him and then grabbed his hand. She slid off the hood while maintaining her grip and pulled Elliott to his feet in front of the car.

"Why not?" asked Donna playfully. Wrapping her arms around his waist, she reminded him, "It's where we had our first time."

"In the back seat of a car," Elliott added with a smirk. Donna's countenance became intense.

"And it's where we should have our second first time," Donna urged Elliott. Leading him to the driver side door, she then waited as he opened it for her. The reunited lovers slipped inside Elliott's car, into the backseat and into one another's arms.

· · · ·

"I NEED YOUR ADVICE," said Donna. She dipped a brush into a can of black paint, she and Emma doing some touch-up work on the club's exterior.

"I'm so glad I started doing this myself," Emma said as she carefully moved her brush up and down. She paused, surveyed her work and then continued painting, saying, "That last contractor really messed this up."

"*Anyway*," replied Donna, "I need some advice about *your brother*."

The mention of Elliott instantly garnered Emma's attention. She stopped painting and looked to Donna.

"What'd he do?" Emma asked, Elliott's sibling mildly annoyed with him.

"Nothing, Em. Stop it," Donna admonished her. She finished the section on which she worked while saying, "I'm thinking about, like, talking to him about something, and I just wanted to get your opinion."

Emma's mild anger morphed into worry. She set down her brush on the top of the can.

"Is he okay?" Emma queried. Donna squinted as the sun blazed behind her friend and converted her into an intimidating silhouette.

"Yes, Emma, he's fine," answered an irked Donna. She hesitated for a moment, however, and wondered if her statement was accurate. Emma watched Donna closely as she explained, "Well, I think so. I mean, you know him. He's never been a real active or outwardly happy guy."

"But that's why you're so great for him," Emma countered reassuringly. Deciding that all was well with Elliott, she resumed her painting and continued, "It never bothered you."

"But he's . . . I don't know . . . regressed a little, maybe," suggested Donna carefully.

"How's that?" Emma inquired while deftly moving her brush in steady, smooth strokes.

"Never mind," answered Donna. She, too, resumed painting and shook her head, saying, "It's probably just me. I shouldn't've said anything."

"Oh, just say it," Emma replied as she dipped her brush in the can of paint and again lifted it.

"I think he's really depressed," Donna said quickly. Emma flashed a harsh yet panicked expression at her. Paint dripped from her brush onto the pavement.

"Don't say that," Emma snapped, the sharpness of her tone surprising Donna. Moderating her response and her expression, Emma stated, "He is *not* depressed. He's just gone through a lot and hasn't had the support I have."

Emma went cold and reapplied paint to her brush. Donna deemed the time unripe to discuss Elliott's mental wellbeing.

"You're probably right," declared Donna. The pair painted in silence for several minutes until she said, "I think I'm gonna push him to be a little more social and, ya' know, try some new things. It'll be good for him."

Emma slathered paint on the building and processed her best friend's new attitude. The change discomfited her but she concealed it.

"Sounds good," Emma said with a positive air and a forced grin. She set down her brush and wiped her hands on an old rag, adding, "He's thirty-seven, not sixty-seven."

"Except for how he dresses," said Donna with smirk. She rolled her eyes and expounded, "He's still wearing t-shirts and jeans like he's in high school. Like it's his uniform or something. I wanna mix up his wardrobe a bit."

"Yes, *thank you*," Emma agreed heartily. Surprised at Donna's burgeoning backbone, she asked, "So what's bringing all this on?"

"The first time around, all I did was bleed for him," began Donna. She continued thoughtfully, "I wanted to be near him every second of every day, and I don't think that was healthy. There needs to be more give and take between us."

Emma became stone-faced and silent and her normally brilliant eyes dimmed. Donna's worship of Elliott was much of the glue that she hoped would bond them until he again fell in love with her.

"I still love him, so much," said Donna as if reading Emma's mind, "but I've grown up, Em, and I want more . . . *equality* in our relationship."

"Wow, okay," Emma replied. She searched for but could not find any other words and focused instead on her painting.

"I never once initiated sex when we were together the first time," Donna said. She set her brush on the can and wiped her hands on the rag.

"You usually don't have to with young guys," Emma said in irritation, "because they're humping your leg every five seconds. Dave's finally started to move outta that phase, thank god."

"Well, I did the other night," said Donna with pride, "and it was nice."

"The same rule applies as before, girlfriend," Emma said while pointing her paintbrush at Donna. Though smiling, she narrowed her eyes and warned, "We can talk about your sex life with him but *no* details."

"It's not just about sex," insisted Donna. She stepped further away from Emma, retrieved her brush and began painting a new section, saying, "I wanna pull him outta that shell, get him outta his routines. Not all the time. But once in a while? Yeah. There's this party on the 4th . . . ."

Emma lost track of Donna's words and pretended to be engrossed in detailed painting. Her mind raced. Donna's newfound desire for a more balanced relationship with Elliott and his social betterment was an unwelcome development and one for which she was not prepared.

"So whaddaya think?" asked Donna.

"Just be careful with him," Emma said ominously. Donna nodded in agreement as both women returned their full attention to the task at hand and let the chirping birds continue the conversation.

. . . .

ELLIOTT AND DONNA WADED hand-in-hand through the crowds at Southland Mall on a Saturday afternoon, the mall teeming with all manner of patrons. He followed her into a few stores, letting his mind drift as she perused the merchandise and nodding in response to her comments. An hour later, they arrived at the entrance of the JC Penney department store.

"I thought you wanted to eat at Hudson's," Elliott said in puzzlement.

"Whaddaya say we do some shopping for you today?" suggested Donna with a slight crack in her tone. The old compulsion to please Elliott was strong and it warred with her decision to improve on their past relationship.

"Shopping for me?" Elliott asked. Looking at the JC Penney sign above the wood-paneled entrance, he said, "I don't need anything."

Donna pulled Elliott from the flow of humanity entering and exiting the store, the couple shielded by a low wall surrounding massive planters. She took his other hand and held them both tenderly as they faced each other.

"My brother's boss is having a big Fourth of July party," said Donna. She squared her shoulders to Elliott and straightened up, adding, "I'd like to go to it."

"Okay," Elliott replied. He remained cagey and hoped the invitation would not materialize.

"I'd like *us* to go to it," declared Donna firmly in response to Elliott's non-committal attitude. He felt her hands shaking as she said, "And I'd like you to, ya' know, dress up a little."

"For a Fourth party?" Elliott queried. Reading Donna's conflicted expression, he took her by the arm and guided her to a nearby bench in a secluded spot. Elliott asked with a smirk, "New clothes, new people. What're you and Em up to now?"

"Em's got nothing to do with this," stated Donna emphatically. The pair sat down on the bench.

"Well, what exactly is *this*?" Elliott asked. Donna paused to collect her thoughts, exhaled deeply and then returned her attention to him.

"Elliott, I was like a little puppy before," Donna said. Elliott chuckled but Donna grabbed his hands again and continued in earnest, "*I mean it*. I did whatever you did, followed you everywhere, and wanted everything that you wanted. I was happy just to be with you and missed you every second we weren't together. But I've changed in the last fifteen years and, well, I think we can do better than that. We're not kids anymore."

"We just got back together," replied Elliott. Donna never questioned their relationship in the past and it both concerned and annoyed him. He extricated his hands from her grasp and queried, "How can you be unhappy already?"

"*I'm not,*" Donna said dramatically. She reestablished her hold on his hands and implored him, "But I really, like, think we could be more than we used ta' be. A lot more."

"I liked what we were," said Elliott. He paused as a group of noisy teenagers passed and then explained, "There was no pressure. Nothing we had to do. We just were. We actually liked each other."

"Liked?" interjected Donna. She released his hands.

"*Loved,*" Elliott conceded though the interruption irked him. Standing up, he thrust his hands in his pockets and shrugged, saying, "I don't know, Donna. It was cool. We could just be happy hanging out and doing nothing. You didn't care what I wore, and you didn't give a damn about any parties. My friends' girlfriends were all trying to run their lives. You just let me be who I was."

A pall fell upon Elliott. He stared at the tiled floor.

"This is just . . . weird," Elliott said. He stated in a low, almost sad tone, "Man, Arizona's really changed you."

"Yeah, it did. It made me stronger, and smarter, and more independent," rejoined Donna with a surge of confidence.

"Hey, I never kept you from being those things," Elliott insisted. Donna sensed his angst and it made her nervous.

"Not intentionally, no," said Donna. Elliott inhaled sharply to rebuke her but she quickly added, "Elliott, look, I used to worship you, and that wasn't good. But I eventually found a good guy out there and, though you're still the man I'll always love, I had something with him, something good. But what I didn't have was a family, and he didn't really want one. We used to talk about it. A family. Remember?"

"Yeah, but we were young and dumb," Elliott answered bitterly. The years of hounding from his father and Emma had blunted the desire for a family and he stated, "We had no idea of what that meant."

Donna's face turned white. Her confidence abandoned her.

"Did you change your mind?" squeaked Donna. Elliott swiftly rejoined her on the bench.

"Hey, take it easy, Dee," Elliott said as he took her chin in his hand. Looking deeply into her eyes, he said, "I didn't say that. I just look at it differently now, that's all."

Donna mulled Elliott's words. Offering him a muted grin, she stood up, pulled Elliott to his feet and planted a kiss on his lips.

"C'mon, let's get lunch," said Donna. The tension between them eased and she exuded a sudden joy.

"So we're done talking?" Elliott asked in relief. It was short-lived.

"Oh, no," answered Donna while beaming. She reversed course and headed towards Hudson's while pulling Elliott behind her.

"Awesome," Elliott sighed.

. . . .

NORA HURLED THE BOWLING ball down the lane with a jerky, unbalanced motion. It hurtled upward and outward, traveled a short distance and then hit the wood with a loud crack. Wobbling down the lane, the ball staggered and fell into the gutter like a drunken old man. Nora's shoulders fell in disappointment and she slowly rotated around with her arms at her sides.

"I suck at this," Nora said dejectedly. Bart, an avid league bowler, convinced her to try the sport and the couple joined a group of his friends at Taylor Lanes. Her first foray into bowling proved a spectacular failure.

"Let me help you," pleaded Bart. The angst on Nora's face struck his heart and he desperately desired to rescue her. His friends and their significant others stifled grins and laughs.

"O-kay," Nora pouted. She secretly wanted his help but felt foolish needing to be taught like a child. A grade schooler on the lane next to Nora bowled a strike and cheered, his success almost bringing her to tears.

"All right," said Bart. He picked up the ball when it came spinning out of the return and carried it to Nora.

"I feel stupid," Nora complained. She loathed her dual status as the outsider and the novice and added, "I *look* stupid."

"No, you don't. You've just never done this before," countered Bart. His strong, steady demeanor lessening Nora's embarrassment, he assured her, "You can do this. And I'll walk ya' through it."

"C'mon, Nora, you can do it," shouted one of the girlfriends. The short, stout brunette clapped several times in encouragement.

"We're gonna go with the four-step approach, because that's the easiest for beginners to pick up," said Bart as he melded his body with Nora. She instantly appreciated the feel of his athletic figure, his scent and the gentle strength with which he guided her.

"Okay," Nora replied. She glanced up at him with a schoolgirl's smile and then turned her head forward. Bart transferred the ball to Nora's hands.

"Now, stand with your left foot just ahead of your right, with your left knee bent a little, right hand under the ball, left hand on its side, arm straight out," instructed Bart as he gently nudged Nora's legs into position with his own. His physical direction surprised her at first but she soon enjoyed it. He pressed down on her right shoulder and said, "Lower that shoulder a bit, and eyes forward. Feel alright?"

"Yeah," Nora answered. She concentrated on the pins and stated, "I'm ready."

"Good. We'll practice it once and then do it for real," said Bart.

"Whaddaya talking about, Bart?" shouted Bart's friend Seth. His girlfriend, a tall leggy blonde with feathered hair, smacked his shoulder.

"Shut up, Seth," yelled Bart with scowl. Returning his attention to Nora, he said, "Forget him. He's an idiot."

"Then we have something in common," Nora replied while concentrating on the end of the lane, "'cuz I feel like one."

"First step with the right foot, ball moves up," said Bart as they began their dance. Nora moved in perfect synchronization with him as he guided her and added, "Then, second step with the left, ball moves down."

Bowling balls striking pins echoed throughout the alley. The immediate vicinity grew quiet, however, as Bart's friends and even those on adjoining lanes spectated.

"Third step, ball moves all the way back," instructed Bart firmly as Nora slowly maneuvered towards the lane, "and fourth step, ball moves down, release it when it passes your ankle, and then the follow through as the right foot slides behind the left. Got it?"

"I don't know," Nora replied with a wrinkled nose. Giving Bart an uncertain glance, she lowered the ball.

"I'm gonna do it with you," said Bart reassuringly, "except a little faster and you'll release the ball at the end."

"Okay," Nora replied. She and Bart returned to the starting position. She pursed her lips and took a long, slow exhale.

"Here we go," said Bart. The pair moved through the proper motions with Bart repeating the instructions, ". . . release the ball and follow through."

Nora released the ball. She swept her right leg behind her, the dramatic motion causing her to lose her balance. Bart, however, deftly held her upright and concealed her faux pau.

"Oh, oh, oh!" Nora exclaimed as the ball hit the lane, rolled forward and remained on target. It struck the pins and knocked down all of them but the ten pin. Nora jumped up and down in excitement and hugged Bart. His friends and the surrounding bowlers rowdily cheered, clapped and laughed. Several held up their beers in a loud salute.

"Ready for another game?" asked Bart.

"I'm ready for chili cheese fries," Nora answered. Bart laughed.

"All right. You earned 'em," said Bart as he and Nora proceeded through his group of friends who threw high fives and overzealously slapped their backs. He advised them, "We're out this game."

Mock incredulity ensued but Bart and Nora ignored it while dodging patrons on the crowded thoroughfare. Ducking into the bar, they sat at a two-person table.

"You heard anything from Elliott?" asked Bart, a question that took Nora by surprise. She looked to him and prepared an admonishment. The worry festering in Bart's eyes stopped her.

"Bart, I'm having a great time with *you*," Nora asserted, "so let's not talk about *him*."

"Why?" queried Bart, the hurt and suspicion evident in his voice.

"I told you, he and I are friends," Nora explained, "*just friends*, and I talk to him at the bar a couple times a week. He doesn't come in as much anymore because, and pay attention to this, he's dating Em's best friend. Remember, the one he dated in high school and college? The one Em wants him to marry?"

Discussing Elliott and his love life tugged at Nora's heart strings but she hid it. She slid out of her chair, sat on Bart's lap and kissed his cheek.

"Those two will be married by the end of 1986, you watch," Nora predicted while looking directly into Bart's eyes. The words, however, tasted sour on her tongue so she muttered, "If Em doesn't weld 'em together before that."

"Whatever," grumbled Bart. A sly smile came to his face and he said, "I wanna know if we'll be married by then."

"*Bart*," Nora chastised him with a dramatic tilt of her head. She looked around to see if anyone heard her and then stated firmly, "I told you I don't want anything hot and heavy right now."

"Doesn't mean I can't think about it once and a while," uttered Bart. Meticulously studying his countenance, Nora considered a future where they lived as husband and wife. She decided it was a pleasant future, that she cared deeply for Bart and that walking down that path, albeit slowly and cautiously, was not such a bad thing.

"Well, you're closer to marrying me right now than anyone else," Nora offered with a coy grin. Her concession was enough for Bart and the tension between them vanished.

"Seriously?" Bart asked as a grin slowly spread across his handsome face.

"Seriously," Nora answered in a sweet voice. They clasped hands and Nora, suddenly anxious over her revelation, asked, "So can I have my chili cheese fries now?"

"Anything you want, babe," replied Bart earnestly. They both stood up and he hurried away to search for a waitress.

"He's a good man and he'll do anything for you," Nora thought as she watched Bart approach the bar. She bit her lip and asked herself, "How can you do better than that?"

• • • •

"DID YOU HEAR ABOUT that airplane that was hijacked yesterday?" Donna inquired after she and Elliott were seated. He fidgeted, the more formal atmosphere of Hudson's restaurant making him uncomfortable.

"Nope," replied Elliott. He cared little for current events unless they touched on his own life.

"TWA 847. It's horrible. They have like a hundred and fifty hostages," Donna said before launching into a summary of the news accounts. Perusing the menu as she spoke, she failed to notice Elliott meticulously studying her face. He met her gaze and nodded each time she looked at him but then returned to his examination when her eyes fell.

"Wonder why she cut her hair," thought Elliott. Donna's hair once cascaded past the middle of her back but now it barely hung past her shoulders and had lightened several shades. He noticed the small mole on the right side of her jaw: it was one of the unique features that first attracted him to her.

"Are we ready?" asked the young waiter before Elliott could comment on Donna's beauty mark. The couple placed their orders and the waiter departed.

"So whaddaya wanna talk about?" Elliott inquired. His apprehension was palpable.

"This doesn't have to be painful," replied Donna.

"You wanna talk about the past, don't ya?" Elliott said. He started tearing up his straw wrapper into little pieces and stated, "There's a lotta pain back there."

Keeping his eyes on the pile of shredded paper, Elliott's mood darkened. Donna offered him a sympathetic expression but soldiered forward.

"And a lotta great times, too," argued Donna. Elliott grinned as he walked down the pathways of his mind.

"Yeah, there were," Elliott admitted, his concession garnering a satisfied grin from Donna. Some of his best memories were of them spending summer holidays with his parents and Emma. Donna's smiled faded.

"Why did you break up with me?" asked Donna bluntly.

"Hey, I *know* we talked about that," Elliott replied. He still bore the emotional scar of breaking Donna's heart and carried the horrible memories of her desperately begging him to stay. He said thickly, "I remember it."

"Once, Elliott. We talked about it once," countered Donna. She took a drink of water before expounding, "But I spent so much time fighting you on the breakup that we never *really* talked about why."

Donna remained outwardly composed. Elliott, however, believed he could feel the rapid beating of her heart.

"We did, Donna," Elliott said dismissively. The dread of unearthing old wounds hung on him.

"We didn't," rejoined Donna. She bit the inside of her mouth to prevent her tears, absorbed the pain and then continued, "You just kept saying it didn't feel right. But that's all you said."

Elliott's eyes glazed and he drifted away with an exhale. Donna concernedly yet patiently allowed him to collect his thoughts.

"Everyone was so mad at me over it, and Dad was already pissed at me over the whole Johnny Dubs thing," Elliott said. His intense gaze fell on Donna and he added, "Hell, Emma didn't speak to me for a month."

Elliott recalled the isolation he felt during that trying time. He then remembered his rock.

"Except Mom," Elliott said with a faint smile. He reached across the table, grabbed Donna's straw wrapper and began shredding it, saying, "She and Dad didn't fight much, and she deferred to him on almost everything, but not during all that. She took on Dad and Emma, if you can believe it. If she caught them hassling me about it, she'd go all mamma bear on 'em. God, I miss her."

"I didn't know," Donna replied. She remembered every shred of evidence that Lillian Warden believed she was wrong for Elliott. She kept the memories to herself.

"I think it really started when Dad started his bullshit about marrying you," Elliott volunteered.

"He pressured you way too much," Donna said.

"He's where Em gets all her crazy from, that's for damn sure," remarked Elliott, "and she fell right in line with him. It just spread from there. Everyone kept pushing me, everyone assumed we just had to get married. Again, except Mom. But I just didn't feel ready."

"Did you feel it from me, too?" Donna asked gingerly. Elliott hesitated.

"Yeah," admitted Elliott reluctantly. Donna deflated, her sadness causing Elliott to swoop in to rescue her. He said earnestly, "But you didn't know you were doing it. You were just a sweet girl dreaming about your wedding day."

"I'm sorry, Elliott," Donna replied while on the verge of tears.

"Hey, you were nothing but good to me," scolded Elliott gently, "and you have nothing to be sorry about. It was just me. I'm just . . . *weird*."

Elliott took a long drink of water to avoid speaking. Donna shook free of the melancholy of the moment.

"Elliott, I want to marry you, always have, and I think – I know – you and I are supposed to be together," declared Donna with a serious mien. It soon softened, however, and she added lovingly, "And I'd like to be married before I'm forty. But you don't have to feel any pressure. If . . . ."

Donna subtly winced.

". . . and hopefully *when* you decided you want to marry me, then we'll get married," continued Donna. She said, "Until then, let's just be us. I mean, don't get me wrong. We can both make changes for the better. But that doesn't mean it can't be like it was, that we can't have those great times again."

"Wow, you have really changed," Elliott replied.

"I like to say I've *matured*," said Donna.

"You sure your best friend will accept the delayed nuptials?" Elliott asked with a smirk.

"If your Mom can handle your Dad and Em, I can handle just her," Donna assured him. Feeling protective of Elliott, she rubbed her leg against him under the table and said supportively, "You just do whatever you have to do and take all the time you need. *I mean it.*"

The couple exchanged adoring looks before the waiter appeared bearing their lunches. Digging into their meals and engaging in pleasant small talk, Elliott and Donna returned from the past and spoke no more of it that day.

The outside temperature dipped into the sixties as the clock rolled past 9:00 pm but the bustling Johnny Dubs crowd made the inside temperature sultry. Despite being Independence Day Eve, the club was full and its vibe was electric; Emma's booking of Morning Cloak for a special show served its purpose.

"This is so crazy," yelled Nora to Elliott as she scurried past his barstool to grab her next order. He smiled at her and tried to keep his feelings in check.

"Damn, could she be any sexier?" Elliott thought. She wore overall shorts and a red-and-white-checkered tank top with a matching bow in her mussed hair. It prickled him to observe every patron drool over and flirt with her but, watching them as they forked over wads of cash, he conceded, "Guess I can't blame them. And she's cleaning up on tips."

Elliott wanted to watch Nora but wrested his thoughts away from her. Facing the bar, Elliott lowered his eyes and sampled his second Grumpy Old Man.

"You've got your own sexy girl, *woman*," Elliott admonished himself. Images of Donna's fit body arose in his mind and he added, "So fantasize about her."

A well-built, fortysomething man sitting halfway down the bar hopped off his barstool and blocked Nora's path as she returned with a food-laden tray. The sudden movement caught Elliott's attention.

"Your parents shoulda' named you Angel, not Nora," said the man. His movements betraying his intoxication, he stated, "You're gorgeous."

"Thank you, Gregg," replied Nora with a polite smile. When he failed to step aside, she asked meekly, "Can I get past you? I gotta get this food out."

"I will if ya' go out with me," Gregg said. She managed to deflect his frequent advances in the past but he had never been so aggressive with her.

"I told you, Gregg, I have a boyfriend," replied Nora.

"I'm not movin' 'til you say you'll go out with me," announced Gregg with a conceited grin. Nora exhaled in frustration and turned around to take an alternate route. Gregg abruptly and unexpectedly delivered a hard slap to her left butt cheek and laughed. A friend joined him in his mirth.

"Ow!" squeaked Nora, Gregg's assault causing her to drop her tray. The clatter drew everyone's attention and the crowd grew quiet. Elliott, meanwhile, leapt from his bar stool and maneuvered through several patrons. Nora grabbed her buttock and, with a pained, embarrassed expression, mewled, "That hurt!"

Several of Nora's regulars moved towards Gregg but none with the speed with which Elliott fell upon him. He spun Gregg around with his left hand and hurled his right fist into his jaw, the violent contact sending him sprawling. Gregg crashed into a table full of food and drinks and overturned it. The commotion caused the crowd to let out a collective gasp and stare at Elliott as time seemed to stop.

"Oh, hell yeah," Brandy said unabashedly. Gregg sat up but his head reeled and his vision blurred. Realizing what happened, the crowd erupted into applause and raucous cheers. Nora gaped at Elliott.

"What *in the hell* is going on?" Emma demanded while examining the scene, her question again silencing the audience. A mortified Nora fled into the bathroom.

"I got her, Em," Brandy assured Emma. She slithered through the crowd after Nora.

"Elliott, go up to my office," Emma directed him. Coming out of his rage, he obeyed her and slowly proceeded upstairs. Emma glowered at Gregg with her intense eyes and growled, "*And you.*"

"Go to hell," Gregg said as he stood up and brushed food and other debris from his shirt. The regulars who moved to Nora's defense closed in on Gregg, all of them upset by the disrespect shown to Emma. She, however, strode up to him and kicked him in the testicles. He fell to his knees in agony but managed to groan, "I'll call the cops, bitch."

Another round of cheers ensued. Emma lifted Gregg's chin with a finger.

"Let me tell you somethin', pal, before you get yourself in even more trouble," Emma sneered. She brushed a stuck French fry from his shoulder and explained, "There're at least ten guys in this place right now who will beat the living shit outta you if you don't get the hell outta my club right now."

"That's right," the bouncer, Jeff, confirmed in a deep voice while looming behind Gregg.

"So, pay your tab, leave a great, big tip for Nora," Emma stated, "and get out."

Gregg fumed. Emma scowled.

"And don't you *ever* show your face in here again," Emma warned. The man hesitated but, thinking better of further conflict, stood up. He dug out his wallet, pulled out a fifty dollar bill and, after tossing it to the floor, stormed out of the club to a thicket of boos and hisses. Jeff followed on his tail.

· · · ·

BRANDY OPENED THE STALL door farthest from the restroom entrance and found Nora sitting on the toilet and crying. Her body was tense and she hugged herself in between swipes at her tears with a matted stack of napkins.

"He's always been a jerk but I didn't think he'd . . . ya' know," whined Nora. She displayed a chaotic mix of anger and sadness as she declared, "I'm never wearing anything sexy in here again"

"You'd take a *big* hit on your tips if you do," Brandy remarked with a smirk. She leaned on the doorframe and folded her arms, saying, "Little skin for the win, know what I mean?"

"You're not helping," snapped Nora. Traffic continued to flow in and out of the restroom as they spoke.

"Oh, come on, honey, he slapped your ass. So what?" Brandy said dismissively. She squatted in front of Nora and said, "I've been manhandled in this joint so many times. And if they cross the line, you smack 'em as hard as you can. That usually does it. And if they don't? That's when you sick Em on 'em."

Brandy chuckled. Nora grimaced.

"This sucks," Nora griped as she let Brandy's advice pass over her and float away. Still distressed by the incident, she continued, "It just, it just happened so fast, and it hurt, and, it was, like, so embarrassing. How do I go back out there?"

"No one cares about all that. They're all drunk," Brandy said. She stood up and readjusted Nora's bow, saying suggestively, "And sweetie, there're a lotta good guys here who'll always come to your rescue."

"Oh, god, Elliott," sighed Nora. She began processing his actions. It blunted her sadness and lessened her tears.

"That's right, Elliott," Brandy said. When Nora failed to respond, she asserted, "If you haven't noticed, that boy loves you."

"No, he doesn't," countered Nora. Her tears ceased and she blotted her eyes, saying in annoyance, "Besides, I'm with Bart, he's with Donna. We've been through this."

"Elliott, who doesn't get into scraps, *ever*, *with anybody*, just walloped some dude to defend your honor, princess," explained Brandy with a serious mien. She guided Nora to her feet, saying, "In this hillbilly burgh, that's love."

"We gotta get back on the floor," insisted Nora. The discomfort of discussing Elliott was greater than the prospect of returning to the scene of the crime.

"I was the one who told him about your double date," Brandy stated while refusing to move. Shock came to Nora's face.

"Why would you do that?" asked Nora incredulously.

"To get you two together," Brandy stated flatly. She gesticulated dramatically and said, "But he screwed that up. He shoulda punched Bart in the face and walked outta there with you that night."

"That would've been terrible!" objected Nora. The events of the night and the two competing men in her life discombobulated her and she wanted nothing more of it. She stated firmly, "And I'm not talking about this anymore."

"Hey, are you two finished?" asked an irritated blonde who waited for the stall. Decked out in her country finest, she wore tight jean shorts, a flannel tied up to expose her midriff and sequined cowboy boots.

"Get lost," Brandy replied with a scowl. Lingering in the stall doorway, she pointed towards the front of the club and warned, "You're a great girl, Nora, but don't take too long. Ya' never know when the next great girl's gonna walk through those doors."

"*I gotta get back,*" said Nora emphatically, Brandy's advice sticking in her heart like a splinter. Nora pecked her on the cheek and said, "Thanks for checking on me."

"I'm not the one you should be thanking," Brandy replied with unforgiving eyes. Nora, intimidated by Brandy's assertive campaigning for Elliott, scurried from the bathroom. The blonde folded her arms and stamped her foot. Shaking her head, Brandy stepped aside and nodded to the stall, uttering, "Well, go on."

• • • •

THE ENERGY IN THE ROOM spiked as it neared 10:00 pm, the crowd reacting to Toni and her band as they took the stage and readied to play. Brandy, standing at the bar in a rare moment of rest, indulged in a quick cigarette and surveyed the crowd.

"That's one place Emma's got the old man," Brandy thought. She exhaled a plume of smoke and remarked, "She's one hell of a rainmaker."

Brandy's gaze passed over the sea of patrons and landed on the front doors. She smiled devilishly.

"Oh, this is too good," Brandy said aloud as her eyes fell on Donna. Elliott's girlfriend spoke with Jeff who pointed at the door to the exterior stairwell. Brandy extinguished her cigarette in a nearby ashtray and moved to intercept Donna as she waded through the crowd. Donna noticed her first.

"Hey, it's Brandy, right?" asked Donna when she arrived in front of Brandy. The older woman sensed her anxiousness.

"In the sexy flesh," Brandy replied. The women spoke in raised tones amidst the cacophony of the club.

"The bouncer said Elliott was in a fight," stated Donna, her worry palpable. Brandy looked at Nora interacting with customers and then back to her.

"It wasn't much of a fight," Brandy replied, the waitress toying with Donna.

"Is he okay?!" exclaimed Donna, her worry becoming fear. Brandy patted her shoulder but she, in her angst, missed the condescension.

"Oh, yeah, he's fine," Brandy said. She expounded with a satisfied grin, "Some asshole slapped Nora on the butt so Elliott came to her rescue and socked him in the face. Sent him ass over tea kettle. It was awesome."

"Elliott did that?" inquired Donna in utter disbelief.

"Crazy, isn't it?" Brandy replied. She motioned to Nora as she peddled drinks and added, "But the guy was messing with his little princess."

"What?" asked Donna with a befuddled expression. Her head on a swivel, she looked from Nora to Brandy and back again.

"You don't know about those two?" Brandy queried as she perfectly feigned ignorance.

"Oh my god," squeaked a panicking Donna. Brandy shook her head in disagreement.

"It's not like that," Brandy assured Donna. She returned her attention to Nora and explained, "But before you showed up, those two were flirtin' something fierce. Lucky for you, though, Em was *not* havin' it. She slid Bart in there under Elliott's nose and he was just the wrench she needed for that machine."

"She broke them up?" asked a mortified Donna. Brandy again shook her head in the negative.

"Oh, no, don't worry. They were never together," Brandy began while gently pushing away a patron who came too close to her. She commented with a smirk, "Em made sure 'a that."

Donna trembled and Brandy watched the first traces of angry tears appear in her eyes. The waitress struggled to maintain a neutral expression as she wallowed in her success.

"Excuse me," Donna growled. Swiftly departing, she maneuvered through the hustle and bustle of the club and disappeared into the stairwell.

"Sorry, lady," Brandy said with a twinge of remorse as the stairwell door closed, "but you're just not the one for him."

• • • •

EMMA SLUMPED INTO HER desk chair. She looked at Elliott who sat on the middle cushion of the couch with a hand resting to either side.

"What happened, Elliott?" Emma inquired. She studied her brother's pensive face and said, "You've never punched anybody in your adult life. That's not like you at all."

"He had it coming, trust me," grumbled Elliott. Unwilling to discuss his defense of Nora, he stared into the floor and added, "Don't worry about it."

"If the cops show up, I'll hafta tell them something," Emma explained. Elliott's intense eyes snapped upward.

"He slapped Nora on the ass, all right," growled Elliott. Throwing a hand towards her, he passionately asserted, "He hurt her, Em."

"You know that's a rite of passage in this place," Emma countered, albeit in a conciliatory manner. Elliott lowered his hand as she explained, "And it'll probably happen again, Elliott. But she'll learn how to handle it. All my girls do."

"Bullshit!" barked Elliott, his determined response surprising Emma. She had no time to respond, however, as Donna burst into her office, the force of her entrance causing the door to bang against the wall. Emma jumped.

"What the hell, Donna!?" Emma griped. Elliott sat up but said nothing as Donna marched to Emma's desk.

"Was there something between Elliott and Nora when you fixed us up?" inquired Donna sharply. The question petrified Emma save for the widening and scintillating of her eyes. An expression of shock on her face, Donna gasped, "Oh my God, there was."

"No, there wasn't," Emma insisted. Paralyzed by the precariousness of the moment, Elliott did nothing but breathe.

"Swear it on the memory of your dad," demanded Donna. Discombobulated by her best friend's assault on her emotional jugular, her armor cracked and she confessed.

"Okay, they were flirting a little bit," Emma said, her answer causing Elliott's feelings for Nora to burgeon. Recovering from Donna's unusually aggressive approach, Emma counter-attacked, "*But it didn't mean anything, Donna. He was lonely, and alone, and she was young and naïve. He's old enough to be her dad for Christ's sake. But I took care of it and they're both better off now."

"What do you mean 'took care of it'?" asked Donna. Emma's countenance darkened when she realized her mistake and her friend stated, "Oh my God, Em, you kept them apart so he'd get back together with me."

"That's not true," Emma asserted. Donna waved her off.

"Shut up, Em," snapped Donna. The words, which she previously had only spoken to Emma in jest, rendered her friend speechless.

"Donna," Elliott said softly. Donna turned to him and he urged her, "Nora and I are just friends and since we've been together I *only* see her here. That's it. She's got a boyfriend, too."

"Well, of course, Elliott. Emma 'took care of it'," Donna said while shifting the heat of her emotion to him. Feeling betrayed by everyone involved, she asked him, "Do you still have feelings for her?"

Elliott looked upon her with pity. He stood up and hazarded a few steps forward.

"Just calm down, Dee," Elliott said. Donna exhaled with a dramatic shudder and wept.

"You're only with me because you couldn't be with her," declared Donna sadly.

"*He's with you*, Donna," Emma interjected forcefully, "and that's *all* that matters."

"How can you say that?!" mewled Donna.

"Hey, Em, you ready for the band to go on?" inquired Nora as she swept into Emma's office. She froze when all eyes fell on her and she uttered, "Oops. Sorry."

"Actually, it's good that you're here," Donna said in a feigned sugary tone. The sight of Elliott and Nora standing next to one another pierced her heart.

"Don't," Emma warned Donna.

"Emma, *for once*, shut up," said Donna. The pain etched on her face cowed Emma and she clenched her jaw. Donna approached Nora who stepped behind Elliott.

"Is it true you almost went out with Elliott?" asked Donna.

"Nothing's happened between us since you've been with him," Nora said. Peeking out from behind Elliott's shoulder, she continued, "I swear it. And I'm dating one of Dave's friends. He's the *only* guy I'm seeing right now."

"I know," Donna replied. She looked to Elliott wistfully and said, "Elliott wouldn't do that to me."

"That's right," Elliott asserted while shaking his head in agreement. Donna returned her focus to Nora.

"But I asked if you two almost went out," Donna said. She stuck her hands in the back pockets of her jeans and asked, "Maybe the better question is: if I wasn't with him and you weren't with . . . what's his name?"

"Bart," answered Nora reluctantly.

"If you weren't with Bart," Donna continued, "would you two be together right now?"

Nora turned bright red and averted her gaze. Emma felt nauseous.

"There's my answer," Donna said with a wounded grin. She took slow, steady steps towards Elliott and stopped when her nose was just inches from his face. She shed a tear and queried, "Have you kissed her?"

"Seriously, Dee," deflected Elliott. The memory of kissing Nora plagued his conscience, however, and it was seared into his brain.

"The truth, Elliott," Donna requested. She looked to Nora, who cowered behind Elliott and kept her gaze on the floor, asking, "Have you kissed her?"

"Yes, damn it!" shouted Elliott. Emma winced. Launching herself into Elliott, Donna engaged him in an ardent liplock and then retreated.

"Now. Whose do you want more?" queried Donna with a razor-sharp tongue.

"C'mon, Donna, this isn't a soap opera," scoffed Elliott.

"Donna, listen to me," Nora interjected. She stepped out from behind Elliott and said, "Even if Elliott and I had gone out, I was going to date Bart, too. I didn't – *and I don't* - want anything serious."

Nora paused. She decided against revealing Elliott's desire for an exclusive relationship but instead released a rash thought into the air.

"And now, especially now, I realize there's no future for him and I," said Nora, her words filleting Elliott's heart. His defense mechanisms, honed through years of practice, engaged and his face turned stony and pale. He swallowed his emotions as she expounded, "Do I care about him? Yeah. I do. But don't let what happened between he and I – what *little* happened between he and I – ruin what you two have."

"I know this isn't easy for you, so thank you for being honest," Donna said with gratitude. She turned her attention to Elliott and appraised his countenance.

"Sure," replied Nora feebly. Donna placed a tender hand on Elliott's cheek.

"I love you, Elliott Warden, but we're over," Donna said as she, too, withdrew all her emotions deep within her. Emma sharply inhaled as she added, "For good this time."

"Donna, no," Emma pleaded desperately.

"I love you, too," Donna said forlornly, "but I think I need a little time without Wardens."

Donna walked to the door. She paused.

"I'll call you, Em," Donna said without looking at her best friend. She then turned the corner and descended the stairwell. Elliott's gaze shifted from the vacant doorway to Nora. She met it coldly.

"I gotta get back to work," said Nora with a hard swallow. Seeking to flee the consequences of her rejection of Elliott, she, too, vanished into the stairwell.

"I gotta remember to lock that door," Emma said blithely.

"Yeah, you do," replied Elliott.

Emma sighed and accepted the defeat. Retrieving the moonshine bottle and two glasses from its locked cabinet, she poured herself a shot. Emma slammed it back and felt the burn spread from her mouth, down her throat and into her chest. She refilled her glass and the second one as Elliott closed and locked the office door.

"You want one?" Emma asked.

"I want two," replied Elliott. He approached his sister who watched him with apprehension until he picked up the glass and held it aloft. He forced a weak grin and said, "Here's to runnin' outta options."

. . . .

ELLIOTT, INTOXICATED by just two shots of Emma's moonshine, stumbled to his barstool and claimed it. Intent on sobering up and then limping home to lick his emotional wounds, he ordered a black coffee and turned his back to the stage.

"Now if I can just avoid Nora until I leave," Elliott said to himself. She shared his sentiment, gave him a wide berth and kept her eyes elsewhere. His apathy burgeoned and he remarked, "Well, that's easy. She won't even look at me."

The crowd suddenly roared to life. Glancing over his shoulder, Elliott saw the band take the stage. He shook his head.

"Great," Elliott sighed, "country music."

"Well, hello there, Johnny Dubs. You ready for some Morning Cloak!" shouted Emma into the microphone while Toni slipped into her guitar strap. The crowd cheered its raucous approval. Addressing the entire audience, Emma said with an edgy flare, "And sorry we're late. I had to take out the trash first."

Emma's patrons shouted their approval while simultaneously heckling Nora's absent assailant. Elliott chuckled and accepted his coffee from the bartender.

"That sister a' mine's something else," he told Luke as they shared knowing smiles.

"But now, without further ado, Morning Cloak!" announced Emma. Another wave of applause and shouts washed over the club.

"You guys are great, thank you so much," Toni gushed while beaming with her hand on her heart. She motioned to Emma and said, "And how about that Emma? I didn't think a girl that gorgeous could be that tough!"

Thunderous clapping, stomping and cheering ensued. Emma feigned embarrassment and mouthed "thank you".

"Ya' know, we usually start with something upbeat," Toni explained, "but tonight the guys and I are gonna play something a little different. Can I tell you a quick story about it?"

Driven by the sincerity of the request and Toni's radiance on stage, the crowd cheered in the affirmative. Elliott, as if moved by an unseen force, rotated his barstool around.

"Damn, she really shines on up there," Elliott thought. He watched Toni pull a stool to the center of the stage as he said to himself, "They love her."

Elliott set down his coffee on the bar. Leaving the pain of his evening and two failed relationships behind, he joined the audience in basking in the aura of Toni's warmth.

"Well, not many people know this, but I grew up in Montana, in a mining town called Butte," Toni explained with a half-smile. The rowdy crowd shouted and clapped. When the noise subsided, Toni said, "I lived there 'til I was ten, when me and my Mom moved here. I got a lotta memories there. Some wonderful . . . ."

Toni eyes became watery and her grin disappeared. Elliott, as did every soul in Johnny Dubs, felt the depth of her emotion and her acute sadness. She composed herself.

"Some not so wonderful," Toni continued, her heartfelt monologue keeping every single person's gaze riveted to her. The Club fell eerily silent as she allowed a few heavy seconds to pass and then continued, "But I guess a little piece of my heart will always be in Montana, in that old mining town, even though I haven't been back to Butte in a long time. But trust me, there's so much more to Montana than Butte. The mountains, guys, the bluest sky, the cleanest air."

"She's got every person in this place . . . hook, line and sinker," thought an amazed Elliott while appreciating the rapt attention on each and every face.

"So, when this next song came out, I knew I had to sing it," Toni said. The dimness of her mood evaporated, her beaming smile returned and she explained, "So I took a little vacation from work and practiced it for three days straight. And I think I got it down. So, would you guys give it a listen for me and let me know if I do?"

The crowd erupted and resoundingly answered in the affirmative. Toni laughed with sparkling eyes that paralyzed Elliott.

"Now it's a duet, one about love, so my special guy's gonna help me sing it," Toni said to another round of cheers from the crowd. She waved forward a man who jogged up on stage as she said, "C'mon, Bobby."

Toni's positive energy struck Elliott's heart dumb but her introduction of her lover sliced it open. Bobby, who carried another stool to center stage, possessed black hair that was thick and wavy and enigmatic gray eyes. He wore the dress of an urban cowboy *sans* the hat: blue jeans, a broad leather belt with a large, blue buckle and a western shirt with the top three buttons unfastened.

"I can't get him to join the band, but I conned him into singing this one with me, so . . . here it is," said Toni. She kissed Bobby and the pair took their seats. Elliott, though he did not know why, felt sick. The audience erupted again but then quickly became quiet.

"You're lucky I'm doing this," countered Bobby.

"I'm just lucky," Toni replied with adoration for Bobby. Elliott coveted that look and he contemplated an impromptu departure to escape the desire. He glanced at his chest.

"You're just gettin' pummeled tonight," Elliott thought. The band commenced its cover of "Meet Me In Montana" by Dan Seals and Marie Osmond. Seconds later, Bobby launched into his portion of the song.

"Country sucks," Elliott said. Thoroughly unimpressed with a man singing a country love song, he plucked his keys from the bar and stood up. Toni's voice suddenly joined the first chorus and its melodiousness rooted him to the floor.

"She's good," Elliott gushed aloud. Toni began the second verse and the power of her voice rendered Elliott mute. Weak in the knees, he fell back onto the barstool and gaped at her. The atmosphere of the moment, the lingering buzz of the alcohol and Toni's brilliance overwhelmed him.

"She's good," said Nora to the bartender. The song's message of reunion tweaked Nora's heart and she glanced at Elliott. Jealousy prickled her as she watched his intense focus on Toni. It throttled her when Elliott hurried to the door, threw a last, desperate gaze at Toni and fled from her voice.

"You shouldn't like the way he was looking at her," Brandy said ominously as she appeared next to Nora. Nora scowled at her.

"Haven't you done enough tonight?" snapped Nora, her ire with Brandy on full display.

"I gave you an opening, princess," Brandy countered with a wink and a devilish smirk, "*so don't waste it.*"

You Can't Get What You Want
(Till You Know What You Want)

Elliott's head throbbed and his sheets were wet with perspiration. Light filtered into his room through the blinds and, though not direct sunlight, it stung his bleary eyes. The stale scent of alcohol drifted in the air.

"Today's gonna be rough," Elliott muttered, his speech revealing the dryness of his mouth. He sat up, the motion causing the room to spin. Elliott paused to regain his equilibrium and sighed, "Really rough."

Elliott gingerly slid out of bed and set his bare feet on the dark beige carpet. Wearing only his underwear, he walked the path of crumpled clothes strewn from his bedroom door to the bed. Elliott ducked into the bathroom and flipped on the light.

"Ugh, damn it," Elliott groaned in response to the brightness. He turned on the faucet and drank greedily from the tap until he could no longer endure the pounding of his headache. Opening the medicine cabinet, he obtained a bottle of Tylenol and opened its cap. The shrill ring of his telephone abruptly ripped through the air and Elliott moaned with a wince, "Uh, god."

He quickly shook two capsules from the bottle, popped them in his mouth and then took another drink from the still-running faucet. The telephone continued its ear-splitting summons.

"Hang on," Elliott grumbled in response. Fumbling with the lid, he managed to affix it to the bottle and return it to the medicine cabinet. Elliott subsequently moved to the telephone on his nightstand and picked it up after the eighth ring. He uttered pathetically, "Hello."

"Eight rings," answered Emma pejoratively. Clad in a turquoise bathrobe, she sat at her kitchen table with a half-full mug of coffee. Emma raised it to her lips and said before drinking, "You were starting to worry me, Big Bro."

"You're always worried," Elliott said in mild irritation. The events of the previous night slowly seeped into his mind and, along with a healthy dose of curiosity, prompted him to ask, "You talk to Donna?"

"No," said Emma with a dramatic exhale. She stretched her legs out before her, wrung the stiffness from them and stated, "I want to call her, *so bad*, but I think it'd make things worse. I'm gonna give her a few days."

"Good idea," Elliott commented. He plopped onto the bed and added, "She was in a bad way last night. I've never seen her like that before."

"Me either," said a concerned Emma. The pain in Elliott's head gave away to his angst over Donna and Nora. Neither he nor his sibling spoke for twenty seconds.

"Elliott, I'm strongly considering firing Brandy," Emma said in a serious tone.

"What?" Elliott inquired sharply, the force of his response tweaking his aching temples. He massaged one of them and asked, "Why?"

"She told Donna about you and Nora," Emma explained, "and it wasn't an accident. I think she was trying to break you two up."

Elliott recalled his conversation with Brandy and her encouragement of his pursuit of Nora. It pleased him that at least one person thought it a good idea.

"Is that really any different than you trying to keep Nora and I apart?" Elliott challenged Emma. Brandy was the longest tenured employee at Johnny Dubs and he doubted Emma would terminate her employment.

"*Yes*, it is," snapped Emma.

"You know what, Em?" Elliott asked. He tilted his head to the side until his neck popped and said, "My head is killing me, I'm dehydrated, and exhausted, and right now, neither one of 'em wants me. I'm off 'til Monday and I don't have to leave my apartment until then. I think I'll just hole up and forget it all."

"I don't like it but I guess I can't blame ya," conceded Emma. She twirled her finger in the telephone cord and inquired, "But what about Brandy?'

"Well, maybe you should ask yourself what Dad would've done," Elliott suggested shrewdly.

"He'd scold her, feel bad about it and then give her a raise," replied Emma. She unwound the cord and said, "He always had a soft spot for her, though I don't know if it was in his heart or his head."

"Well, there ya' go," Elliott said. He thought of Nora and, worried about her, queried, "Was Nora okay?"

"I thought you wanted to forget about all that," responded Emma with a sour face.

"Emma," Elliott growled. Startled by his harsh tone and use of her full name, she relented.

"All right, *Elliott*," answered Emma begrudgingly. She stood up and pushed in her chair, continuing, "She was a little shook up, but I think she'll be okay. I gave her tomorrow off, so she'll have a nice little break from the club."

Elliott felt a slight panic in his heart. Emma sensed it.

"I think she and Bart are going out on the boat today," offered Emma. Elliott's heart plummeted into his stomach but he concealed his emotion and deflected.

"So, what's the Hastings family up to?" Elliott inquired to prevent Emma from volunteering any more information. Knowing that her swing landed, she grinned impishly.

"The Detroit Zoo," replied Emma with mock excitement.

"On the Fourth of July?" Elliott asked with a dubious tone. He shook his head and remarked, "You're nuts. That place'll be a madhouse."

"That's what my little darlings want to do, so that's what we're gonna do," said Emma. She asked, "Wanna come with?"

"I don't think I could handle that much natural sunlight in my condition," Elliott uttered. Tasting the remnants of the moonshine in his mouth, he griped, "And I don't know how you drink that gasoline the old man called moonshine. Makes my stomach queasy just thinkin' about it. Yuck."

Emma snickered. She could always hold her liquor better than her brother.

"You only had two shots of it," teased Emma.

"That was enough," Elliott countered.

"Elliott, don't give up on Donna," pleaded Emma in a sudden change of tack.

"I wasn't the one who gave up," Elliott argued.

"Just don't," urged Emma. She leaned against the kitchen wall and said, "I'll talk to you tomorrow. Love you."

"Love you, too, maniac," Elliott replied, "and have a good time."

"Enjoy your hangover," said Emma playfully. The siblings each hung up their telephones after which Elliott sprawled out on the bed. Drifting back into sleep, he complained aloud, "Things were never this complicated with Macayla."

. . . .

INDEPENDENCE DAY PROVED warm yet cloudy, the sun only occasionally peeking from behind the fluffy white ceiling. Bart and Nora took his parents' boat out early and were meeting them at Portside Inn in Wyandotte for a late lunch. After heading south on the Detroit River, they turned north and puttered along the Michigan shoreline.

"Even without the sun, it's so nice out here," Nora gushed. She cuddled into Bart as he drove the boat. A stiff yet refreshing breeze rolled over them.

"Yeah, it's warming up pretty good," replied Bart who wore a stylish pair of swim trucks, a blue polo shirt and deck shoes. He rubbed Nora's shoulder and asked, "Sure you don't wanna get a swim in?"

"Not before lunch, if that's okay," Nora answered. She wore acid-washed jean shorts and a white tank top under a fishnet coverup. Her curly, bushy hair was tied in a side ponytail, the wind tussling it as the boat cruised forward.

"My buddy Kevin was at Johnny Dubs last night," offered Bart carefully. He glanced down at Nora.

"Great," replied Nora with a defeated exhale. She bowed her head and braced herself for the expected tiff with Bart.

"Are you okay?" asked Bart, the concern evident on his face.

"Yeah, I'm fine," Nora answered. She extricated herself from his arm and slumped into the passenger seat. Turning it toward Bart, she explained, "It just scared me, because it like, happened so fast, and it hurt a little. It was embarrassing."

"Who did it?" asked Bart as his protective instincts flared. He squeezed the steering wheel of the boat until his knuckles turned white.

"Relax, Bart, it's over," Nora implored him as she folded her arms. Her countenance became sad and she said, "I'm okay. I just wanna forget all about last night. I *need* to forget about it and-."

"I guess Elliott took care of it, huh?" interjected Bart bitterly.

"There was a line of guys waiting to kick that guy's butt," Nora explained. More touched by Elliott's chivalry than she allowed Bart to know, she said, "If Elliott hadn't've done it, somebody else would've. He got there first, that's all. Now can we *please* just drop it."

Nora suddenly smirked.

"Em kicked the guy in the balls," Nora said with a chuckle, "and banned him from Johnny Dubs forever. So, there's nothing to worry about."

"Yeah, I heard," said Bart with a smile of his own. It faded and he continued, "But you know there are more guys like that in there, and when they're drunk, well."

"I'm not getting another job," Nora insisted. She watched some ducks paddle by the boat and said, "I make good money and Em works my shifts around my school schedule. Besides, it's like having another family and I'd miss it. Except for Brandy, maybe."

"I don't like all those drunks gawking at you, and you getting hit on like that," said Bart though the propositions were the least of his concerns. Nora read his face and sifted his words.

"Bart, I told Elliott there was no future for us," Nora revealed bluntly, her heart aching as she spoke. Bart lifted his chin.

"Really?" inquired Bart suspiciously.

"Really," Nora replied. She looked away, pondered the moment she told Elliott and then turned back to Bart, saying, "No matter what, he and I are just not gonna happen. I mean it."

"What does he think about that?" queried Bart jealously.

"I don't know," Nora replied with a shake of her head, "and it doesn't matter. But that doesn't mean anything changes for us. I still want us to take it slow. Ya' know, enjoy our summer together."

"That's cool," said Bart with a shrug. Nora stood up and insinuated herself underneath his left arm. Bart eagerly welcomed the physical contact.

"Good," Nora said. Focusing on Bart's muscled torso and his manly scent, she hugged him and tore her thoughts away from Elliott.

• • • •

ELLIOTT'S KEPT HIS existence low-key for over a week as he recovered from the July 3rd debacle. He ventured into public only to work and then returned home to wallow in self-pity and emotional pain. Emma called a few times to check on his wellbeing but, if she spoke to Donna, she was not revealing it and Elliott did not ask.

"I don't think I'll have to worry about seeing her for a while," Elliott repeatedly told himself. He said it for the last time as he arrived home for another weekend in hiding.

"Hi, Elliott," Donna said. Her sudden appearance in Elliott's apartment scared him and, at the last second, he grabbed the door frame to avoid tumbling onto his porch. His mail hit the floor and scattered.

"Jesus, Donna!" exclaimed Elliott. He righted his ship, stepped inside and closed the door, asking, "How did you get in here?"

Donna sat in the middle of his couch, which was positioned on the far living room wall, with her hands clasped in her lap and her legs folded beneath her. She seemed completely composed and even her eyes were dull.

"Emma lent me her key," Donna answered. The entertainment center, which was angled into the corner to the right of the front door, housed a television that was on but muted.

"Good thing she's stopped interfering in my love life," replied Elliott as he knelt and collected his mail. Glancing at Donna, he said, "She failed to mention you two'd buried the hatchet."

"We didn't," Donna corrected Elliott. He stood up as she continued, "I told her I wanted to talk to you and I didn't want her involved. She only fought me on it for about ten minutes."

"But she still gave you the key to my apartment," replied Elliott with a dubious smirk. He walked into his dining area, which formed an "L" with the living room, and slapped down the stack of envelopes on the table.

"Oh. Well . . . yeah," Donna said sheepishly. Elliott returned to the living room and watched the soundless nightly newscast on Channel 4.

"Want somethin' to drink?" queried Elliott. When Donna shook her head in the negative, he dramatically dropped into his recliner with a sigh. Spreading his legs out before him, Elliott hung his arms off the rests like an exhausted king on his throne. Donna marked the dark circles clinging to

Elliott's eyes and his pale countenance. He yawned before asking, "So, what's up?"

"Know that I'm not apologizing," Donna began carefully. Elliott nodded his head slowly while she explained, "but confronting you and Emma at the club and then just walking off was the wrong way to handle things."

"You were hurt," reasoned Elliott with a shrug and a simultaneous gesture of each hand. Donna averted her eyes as he added, "I get it."

"I acted like a high school kid," Donna countered with obvious disappointment in herself. She looked to Elliott and said, "I should've talked to you first, not Emma. And cornering Nora? That wasn't cool. She didn't do anything wrong."

"Ya' know, Brandy telling you wasn't an accident," advised Elliott to shift the conversation away from Nora.

"Yeah, I figured that out after the fact," Donna said. She gazed at Elliott wistfully and said, "Do you know why she did it?"

Elliott tilted his head from side-to-side while raising his hands to convey his uncertainty. He hesitated but Donna waited eagerly for his response.

"You really wanna know all that?" inquired Elliott. He hoped Donna would relent.

"Yeah, Elliott, I do," Donna answered while scooting to the end of the couch closest to Elliott. She rested her elbow on its arm and pulled her legs onto the cushion, saying, "I wanna know why someone who's known you for as long as Nora's been alive thinks you two should be together."

"Brandy's just crazy," scoffed Elliott. He explained with a peeved expression, "She enjoys stirring things up and then watching everything go to shit. It's her way. Ask Em. She'll tell ya."

"When it comes to you, she likes Nora and hates me," Donna replied. She grabbed a throw pillow and hugged it, inquiring, "Why?"

Elliott withdrew into himself and stared at the carpet. Donna again waited for his response, her persistence pushing him closer to truths he wished to avoid.

"Damn it!" barked Elliott as he jumped out of his chair, his abrupt ascent startling Donna. He placed his hands on his hips and began pacing back and forth in the small living room.

"Elliott, *tell me*," Donna pleaded. She stood up but kept her distance, imploring him, "Say it. Get it out."

"It's not important, Dee," replied Elliott as he stopped in front of her. He struggled to contain his emotions.

"*It is*," Donna insisted. She touched his arm and expounded, "No one let you just talk about us last time, about how you felt, and you bottled it all up and then exploded and I lost you. And from what Emma's said, you ran and hid, and you haven't come out since. You can tell me."

"It's always too complicated for me, okay!" blurted Elliott while pulling his arm away from her. Donna remained composed and watched him closely. Gesticulating emphatically, Elliott launched into the monologue she desired and explained, "We already talked about the old days. You and I were good and then everybody got a hard-on for us gettin' married and I hated that. I hated that pressure. I hated that we couldn't just, just . . . *be us*. So I bailed. But all that did was piss everyone off, and I spent a year taking everyone's bullshit over you."

Elliott paused. Walking to the window, he bent down the dusty blinds and peeked outside. Donna returned to the couch and allowed his angst-fueled fire to burn.

"And after that, I don't know," continued Elliott as his eyes glazed. He said, "Maybe I didn't want the pressure, or went with the wrong girls, or I just didn't care . . . I don't know. Maybe all of it. And through it all, Em just got crazier and crazier, especially after Mom and Dad died. Hell, I think in the last few years, I just started picking up good lays who I knew would drive her nuts. And it worked for me. I took what I needed from 'em, gave 'em back as little as I could . . . and stopped caring."

Fascinated by the tsunami of Elliott's emotion, Donna sat quietly and spectated as if he performed a heart-wrenching play. Elliott chuckled.

"That was a decade, a revolving door of bar whores and constant battles with Em," Elliott said. His said blithely, "Which brings us to my living room in July 1985."

Elliott's outburst fizzled out. He dropped himself back into the recliner and felt even more exhausted.

"Something changed when you met Nora, didn't it?" Donna suggested carefully. Elliott's angry eyes flashed to her.

"Let's not go there," said Elliott. Donna leaned forward but he insisted, "No, check that. We're *not* going there."

"I want to. I want you to talk about it," Donna implored him.

"Did you become a shrink or somethin' while you were out there?" asked Elliott incredulously. He left the safety of his chair, knelt before Donna and placed his hands on her thighs, saying, "Dee, right or wrong, somethin' was brewing between Nora and I before I had any clue you were coming back, and then Emma ambushed me with you, and pulled every trick in the book to get us back to together."

"More than you know," Donna confessed forlornly.

"She decided for us," replied Elliott as he released her thighs, "but I wasn't ready. Were you?"

"I love you, Elliott," Donna pleaded before accepting his premise. She pulled her legs into an embrace and conceded, "No, I wasn't."

"So now what?" asked Elliott.

"I'd still like to give us a chance," Donna stated with a conviction that rattled Elliott. The ghost of Nora began swirling around him.

"I thought we were over," replied Elliott.

"I was really hurt, and I overreacted," Donna admitted. She studied him as if to read his mind and added, "But I think we can still do this."

"How's that?" asked Elliott. He felt Donna painted him into a corner.

"By taking off the pressure," Donna answered. She reacquired the throw pillow and, though starting with uncertainty, slowly gained confidence as she stated, "If you want to date Nora, then date Nora. I met this really cool guy at the 4th party you were supposed to go to with me. He asked me out – he doesn't even know about you – but I've politely held him off . . . so far."

Elliott acutely felt the emotional ties Donna latched to him years ago. She was cutting some, and he sensed each one snap, but others remained affixed to him as tightly as ever. He remembered a similar conversation he had with Nora. He laughed.

"That was Nora's solution, too," began Elliott with misplaced mirth. He said with dismissive amusement, "*See other people.*"

Donna froze. Her face went pale and she immediately regretted her strategy.

"*Elliott*," Donna whined.

"Well go get 'em," replied Elliott with a gesture towards the door. Donna's disapproving look prompted Elliott to say, "Hey, I made the same decision for Nora, and look where she's at now. Happy as can be, with the other guy. Kinda feels like a theme, doesn't it?"

"That's not what I meant," Donna argued. Elliott's bizarrely calm demeanor stunned her. Standing up, he walked to her, lifted her to her feet and hugged her.

"You'll thank me for this, trust me," said Elliott. Before Donna could return to her senses and participate in his embrace, he moved her to the door. She resisted, albeit feebly, and found herself staring into the warm July afternoon.

"Elliott!" Donna protested. Her resistance became stout but, no match for his strength, she was ushered to the porch. Elliott turned her around, kissed her on the forehead and fixed his gaze upon her.

"I'd hide Mr. Right from Em until she accepts reality," Elliott stated. He added with a fey smile, "A decade or two oughta' do it."

Elliott closed the door. Shocked by his uncharacteristic behavior, Donna stared into it and trembled. She burst into tears and hurried away.

• • • •

WHEN HE FINALLY VISITED Johnny Dubs, Elliott chose a night he knew Nora to be off work. He missed his sister but, more than anything, he desired to see the picture of his father behind the bar. The sight of John Warden entranced him and he approached his barstool, standing quietly behind it and gazing on the photograph. Elliott felt an emptiness in his chest.

"Hey, do you want somethin', man?" asked the stool's occupant after several galled glances at Elliott. He was a wiry man with a bristly black beard, a long moustache and little patience.

"Yeah, get the hell outta my seat," Elliott droned, the emptiness suddenly filled with ill will. The man rotated the stool to face Elliott.

"I don't see your name on it," said the man. The ill will became rage.

"Try again, asshole," Elliott sneered while pointing to the nameplate on the bar. He barely restrained the urge to strike the man and hostility burned in his eyes.

"How do I know that's who you are?" asked the man with no inclination to surrender his seat.

"Because I put it there for him," advised Emma. Nodding over her shoulder, she said calmly, "A seat's about to open up down there. Why don't you grab it?"

"What if I don't wanna?" queried the man. Elliott tensed to attack but Emma's hand on his arm stopped him cold.

"Okay, but I was gonna comp your drinks for your trouble," said Emma with a shrug. Elliott's anger fizzled and he wondered at the measured response of his sister.

"Why didn't you say so?" replied the man as his anger, too, evaporated. He hopped off the stool, grabbed his drink and said to Elliott, "All yours, man."

Elliott watched the man depart and then looked to his sister. Emma's expression was withering.

"Don't start fights in my club, Elliott," scolded Emma. He slid onto the stool and rotated it towards the bar. Emma immediately turned it back and queried, "Did you hear me?"

"He was in my seat," Elliott grumbled. He felt vile.

"Look, Nora switched shifts with Laurel so she's here tonight," Emma warned Elliott. Motioning towards the door, she said, "If you wait in your car, I'll make you dinner and run it out to you."

"I was here long before she was," Elliott said. He pointed to where Nora interacted with a large table full of customers and added, "Make *her* leave."

Emma stepped forward and went nose-to-nose with Elliott. The siblings fumed at each other.

"Look, I know things are shitty for you right now," began Emma, "but don't take it out on me and don't start anything in here ... *with anybody.*"

Looking over Emma's shoulder, he noticed a banner hanging on the north wall. It announced dates that Morning Cloak was scheduled to play at Johnny Dubs. Her brother's drifting attention raising her ire, Emma waved her hand in front of his eyes.

133

"Hello? Elliott?" called Emma condescendingly. Elliott lingered briefly in a trance as neurons fired and heart strings tightened and were plucked by some unseen force. Growing impatient with his mental distance, Emma beckoned, "*Elliott.*"

"Morning Cloak's playing here a lot this summer," Elliott remarked while keeping his gaze on the banner. Emma's frustration with him weakened and she offered him a dubious expression.

"They're playing a lot here this *year*. I signed 'em to a contract," stated Emma, "because they're a moneymaking machine. People love 'em, especially Toni. That chickee's something else."

The mention of Toni's name caused an epiphany in Elliott and a sly smile came to his face. He turned his attention to his sister and warmly grasped her shoulders.

"Sorry for being such a jerk, Sis," Elliott apologized. Befuddled by her brother's sudden transformation, Emma gaped at him in response.

"Are you on something?" Emma inquired.

"Nope," Elliott replied. He sat down on his barstool and called to the bartender, "Grumpy Old Man, Luke."

"You got it, Elliott," replied Luke with an emphatic, double thumbs up. Emma, uncharacteristically discombobulated and uncertain of how to handle her brother's weird mood, instead switched gears.

"I need you to watch the girls for a weekend, Uncle Elliott," said Emma, the request greater than the usual overnight babysitting he did for his nieces. She weighed his facial expressions as she expounded, "We're going to Traverse City with Dave's parents for a long weekend."

"Sure," said Elliott without giving it a second thought. Luke set his drink in front of him and he said, "Thanks, man. You know, I should take them to Cedar Point."

"On a weekend?" asked Emma. Elliott's willing entry into a crowded amusement park was proof, at least to her, that something was amiss and she queried, "Who *are* you?"

"The best damn uncle in the world, that's who," Elliott quipped as he raised his drink in a mock toast. Emma's astonishment gave way to a smile of disbelief as she sensed a surge of hope within her brother.

"I still think you're on something," Emma said. Walking backwards and away from him, she pointed and ordered, "Behave yourself."

"You got it, Sis," Elliott replied.

· · · ·

HIS HUNGER SATIATED and his buzz at a comfortable level, Elliott watched Toni as she and Morning Cloak prepared for their first set. She wore a black, collared shirt with its long sleeves rolled up and an extra button undone. Most everything else she wore was black, too, from her belt to her jeans to her cowboy boots; her lipstick, however, was a muted red and her oversized belt buckle, imprinted with the State of Montana, was silver.

"That's a helluva getup," Elliott thought as he appreciated the length of her body and the curviness of her hips. He smiled a half-smile and added, "Bet she's singin' Johnny Cash tonight."

Elliott chuckled.

"The old man loved him some Johnny Cash," he said to himself.

"Hey, Elliott," said Nora sheepishly. She knew she had to break the tension between them but wanted the protection of a public place to blunt his reaction.

"Hey, Nora, how's it goin'?" Elliott replied as his smile widened. It tweaked his heart to see her but, to his surprise and encouragement, it was not as trying as he expected.

"You're in a good mood," commented Nora, her apprehension melting away due to the positive nature of Elliott's response. She nodded to his drink and queried with the slightest hint of disapprobation, "How many of those have you had?"

"Three in two hours, Emma Junior, but my next one's a coffee," Elliott answered good-naturedly. Nora tilted her head: she expected the number to be higher and Elliott to be surlier.

"Really?" asked Nora in puzzlement. She placed a hand on her hip and said, "That's . . . ."

Nora searched her mind for the right word. An amused Elliott waited patiently for her to complete her thought.

"*. . . reasonable*," said Nora finally. Noticing the odd air about him, she asked, "Are you okay?"

"Yeah, I am," Elliott said confidently with a glance at Toni as she sound checked her microphone. He returned his attention to Nora, his eyes scintillating, and queried shrewdly, "Are you?"

"Uh, yeah," replied Nora. Elliott's strange mood disconcerted her.

"Glad to hear it," Elliott said. Nora believed Elliott to be sincere but sensed that his words carried greater import.

"Are you *sure* you're okay?" asked Nora, Elliott's miraculous recovery from their previous encounter prickling her. His grin faded and he became serious.

"Remember when I asked if we could just skip all the hard stuff and go back to being friends again?" Elliott inquired stoically. The question made Nora anxious.

"Uh, yeah," replied Nora. She felt Elliott detaching from her but managed to force an uncertain smile and stated, "Good friends."

"Let's actually do that this time," Elliott replied with several nods. Nora found his behavior deeply concerning but, before she could speak, Elliott saw Toni slip into her guitar strap. Pointing at the stage, he said, "Hey, music's gonna start."

Nora turned her head to the stage. Toni walked to the microphone but dispensed with her usual introduction.

"Hi, I'm Toni Cullen," Toni announced in the same deep tone that Johnny Cash would announce his name. The club erupted in applause and shouts while the band launched into Folsom Prison Blues with Toni playing guitar and imitating Johnny Cash's movements. She began the first verse to another wave of cheers.

Nora watched Toni's electric performance for a few seconds. She then glanced at Elliott, recognized the look of infatuation and traced his line of sight to Toni.

"Oh, boy," said Nora to herself. After the first chorus, Toni stepped away from the microphone and played her guitar with vivacious energy. Nora again glanced at Elliott.

"She actually makes this stuff tolerable," Elliott joked loudly to make himself heard over the music. Nora shivered. It seemed Toni's voice held some magic power that enthralled Elliott. Unable to suppress the sudden urge, she poked Elliott between the ribs.

"Hey!" Elliott objected with a vexed glance at Nora. She plucked his glass from his hand.

"I'll get your coffee," Nora said as she scurried away. Elliott watched her depart with a baffled mien.

"What's her deal?" he asked himself.

· · · ·

NORA NEVER DELIVERED Elliott's coffee and spent the night observing him from a distance as she waited tables. Seemingly hypnotized by Toni, he forgot all about the coffee and did nothing but watch her performance. When Morning Cloak's last set ended, Elliott quietly slipped out the front doors with a pleasant smile on his face.

"How many times do I have to tell you this?" Nora asked herself. She experienced a hot flash of anxiety but swiftly squelched it and muttered, "He's not that special."

Nora meandered through the rest of her shift in a dreamlike state, the waitress merely going through the motions with her customers. When the last patrons exited and the doors were locked, Nora made her way to Emma as she closed out one of the registers.

"Morning Cloak should be named *Gold Cloak*," remarked Emma. She held up a stack of bills as Nora approached the bar and said to no one in particular, "It's gonna be an awesome summer."

"Hey, Em," Nora beckoned as she set her bottle-laden tray on the bar and slid onto a stool.

"Yeah," answered Emma. She stuffed the cash into her deposit bag. The other employees dispersed from the bar area as they attended to their end-of-night duties.

"Did you notice anything . . . *weird* about Elliott tonight?" Nora inquired. Emma zipped the bag with a scowl.

"Not just tonight," grumbled Emma.

"Whaddaya mean?" Nora said, the twentysomething thinking it was she who ran afoul of her boss.

"I think he's on coke," stated Emma in a hushed tone. She unfastened her hair clip and shook out her dirty-blonde locks.

"He's not on coke," Nora countered in a high-pitched voice. Emma shot her an irritated look and Nora, realizing the volume of her denial, sheepishly said, "Sorry."

"Think about it, Nora," said Emma, her annoyance shifting from Nora back to Elliott. Her exotic eyes sparkling, she explained with a serious countenance, "He punched a guy last week and, even though that jackass deserved it, Elliott doesn't do that stuff. And tonight, he almost started another fight over his barstool. Then, just like that, he went from wantin' to kill the guy to calm and happy. And, after *that*, he just sat there and drooled-."

Emma stopped herself. Nora's jealousy peaked and she squirmed uncomfortably.

"You can say it," Nora assured Emma. The older woman hesitated.

"I don't have to if you saw it, too," replied Emma after the pause.

"He was probably just drunk," Nora reasoned.

"He wasn't when he got here, and none of the crew would dare serve him more than three," asserted Emma. Nora gave her a doubtful look and, in response, she admitted, "Well, other than me. But I didn't, so he's gotta be on something."

"Em, he's not on drugs," Nora insisted. She refused to believe Elliott would succumb to substance abuse.

"Look, you don't know all of this, but Elliott changed a little when he broke it off with Donna," explained Emma as if she ate something unpleasant, "and not for the better. Became a little more introverted. Then he changed *a lot* when Daddy and then Mom died. I think now this stuff with you and Donna finally pushed him over the edge and he's going to extremes to cope. *Idiot*."

The two women fell silent and did not look at one another. Emma stared into the bar. Nora finally stirred.

"What do we do about it?" Nora asked concernedly.

"*We* do nothing," answered Emma. She walked around the bar and sat on the stool next to Nora. Setting her foot on the low rail running the length of the bar, Emma said, "I know you care about him, but anything coming from you'll just set him off."

Emma contemplated the wisdom of the words on her tongue and examined Nora's face meticulously for a sign. Receiving nothing, she went with her gut instinct.

"He loves you," conceded a sour-faced Emma.

"*Em*," Nora admonished her. Clearly conflicted, she was unable to find anything else to say.

"I didn't say I think you two should be together," continued Emma acridly, the cutting remark wounding Nora's heart, "or that I think you love him."

Nora's lip quivered and she held back the wateriness of forming tears. Her reaction shamed Emma into a softer approach.

"Besides, you have Bart, and from everything I hear," said Emma, "that's going pretty well."

"Yeah, it is," Nora concurred with slow, forward nods and her gaze on the floor.

"Good," said Emma. She raised Nora's chin and firmly yet kindly instructed her, "So you worry about Bart and let me worry about Elliott. Okay?"

"Go easy on him," Nora pleaded as she again shook her head in the affirmative.

"I'm not an evil bitch, despite what you might believe," objected Emma with a gentle grin. Nora smiled as well when she added, "I'll be nice, I promise . . . until it's time to kick his ass."

. . . .

ELLIOTT, WHO HAD NOW committed Morning Cloak's schedule to memory, promptly arrived forty-five minutes before its set on the following Wednesday. He took counsel with a Grumpy Old Man before dinner, eagerly consumed a cheeseburger and fries and then sipped a second drink while waiting for the show to start. When Toni took the stage, he lost himself in her infectious energy and longingly watched her.

"Eh, probably *too* much energy for me," Elliott thought, though he secretly wished he was wrong. He sighed and told himself, "I guess admiration from a distance will hafta' do."

Emma introduced the band, making sure to send a few veiled optical daggers at Elliott, and then relinquished the spotlight to Toni. She greeted the audience and stomped her right cowboy boot three times before the band commenced Jerry Reed's "Eastbound and Down". The frenetic pace of the song and Toni's enthusiasm sent the crowd into a hand-clapping, foot-stomping fervor. When the song ended, it erupted into cheers and Elliott, too, joined the applause.

"How is she not famous?" Elliott wondered. He felt a sudden chill ripple down his spine and he shivered. Turning his head to the right, Elliott saw through the pulsating mass of patrons and noticed Emma standing in the stairwell doorway that led to her office. She motioned for him to approach with a single, wiggling finger. He returned her scowl.

"Enter the buzzkill," Elliott muttered. Sliding off his barstool, he dodged customers and waitresses to reach his sister. He knew the reason for her ire given his overt gawking at Toni but nonetheless asked with feigned mirth, "What's wrong, Emma?"

"Upstairs!" Emma demanded as she attempted to pull Elliott into the stairwell.

"What the hell?!" asked Elliott while resisting her attempt.

"Whaddaya you think you're doin'?" inquired Emma sharply. Elliott moved into the stairwell after which she slammed the door to close out the cacophony of the club.

"I was watching the band, like everyone else in there," answered Elliott with a nod to the club's main room.

"You weren't watching the band," Emma said accusatorily.

"Okay, technically I was watching the chick singing, uh, what's her name, uh, Toni," said Elliott nonchalantly. Emma groaned at his attempt to play dumb so, deflecting as best he could, he added, "So what? She's got an incredible voice."

"Do you really think I'm that stupid, Elliott?" Emma asked emphatically. Her demeanor became strange and she said, "I see guys looking at girls like that in here all the time. A guy'll hide out in the crowd, in plain sight, watching some girl he sees here a lot. He thinks he loves her, but really, he's never met her, or hardly knows her, and it's just desperate infatuation. He says 'I love you' with his eyes, and prays to God she'll notice him, and when she does, it'll interest her just enough to spark something. And trust me, you're not the only one looking at Toni like that."

Elliott stared at his sister in disbelief and marveled at how she laid bare his designs. He recovered quickly and burst into raucous laughter.

"'Says I love you with his eyes'?" replied an amused Elliott. He folded his arms, laughed again and inquired, "Where in the world did you come up with that soap opera bullshit, Sis?"

"You're using, aren't you?" inquired Emma cuttingly. She hoped the abrupt topic change would disconcert him and lead to a confession.

"Using?" a befuddled Elliott asked. Emma shoved him and he nearly tripped on the first step.

"Coke, Elliott," snarled Emma, "you're using coke!"

Elliott laughed yet again while Emma fumed. Infused with endorphins from his infatuation with Toni, he composed himself.

"Okay, I know you're supposed to be the protective sister and I'm supposed to be the loser brother with the bad picker, but c'mon, Em," replied Elliott. He placed reassuring hands on her upper arms and said, "You're gettin' really whacked out over this. I am *not* on coke, or any other drug. I promise you that, on our memories of Mom and Dad."

Emma, though not entirely convinced, accepted her brother's claim of sobriety for the moment. She decided to probe further, however, on the matter of Toni.

"Okay, I believe you, but only about the coke, and not about Toni," Emma said. She pointed at her face and insisted, "Look me in the eyes and tell me you're not infatuated with her."

"Why does that matter?" Elliott countered with a raised voice. Her on-the-mark assessment and persistence prickled him.

"You can't say it, can you?" queried Emma.

"What can I say? She's pretty," admitted Elliott as he looked and gestured towards the unseen stage. Indulging in Toni's voice as it penetrated the door, he said, "She's got, ya' know, a unique look."

"I said, look me in the eyes and tell me you're not infatuated with her," Emma repeated slowly. Elliott glowered at his sister but she read the guilt in his expression with ease.

"What, I can't look at an attractive woman?" inquired Elliott in a last-ditch attempt to throw Emma off his trail.

"You know I don't want you to be with someone who you look at like that," Emma said earnestly yet bluntly. Her countenance saddened and she explained, "I want you to be with someone who looks at you like that. The same way Dave looks at me. The way Donna looks at you."

"Hey, that was not my fault," Elliott objected with a pointed finger.

"I know," replied Emma. Elliott began to speak, paused to consider the wisdom of his revelation and then opened his mouth.

"But I'm glad it happened," Elliott confessed. Emma smacked his cheek.

"Take it back," ordered Emma through a clenched jaw.

"No, because you need to hear this, and accept it," Elliott advised her. He rubbed his stinging cheek and bit his lip before continuing, "How she reacted made me realize she's not the one for me and that she was right, Em. We're over."

"*You're both wrong.* She's just hurt, and jealous of a younger woman, and she overreacted," Emma stated in a vigorous defense of Donna. She centered herself, stepped to within inches of Elliott and asserted, "I'll bring her around and you two *will* get back together. She needs a little time, that's all. And you need her."

"For once, Emma, you need to be more like Mom than Dad," Elliott stated with a seriousness and a conviction that rendered her speechless. He patted her on the cheek, a gesture from which she recoiled, and said, "She didn't try to pick girlfriends for me, and neither should you. *Butt out.*"

Elliott exited the stairwell. Emma did not regain her senses until the locking mechanism clicked.

"What am I gonna do with him?" asked an exasperated Emma. Wishing for quiet time to think, she ascended the stairs and vanished into her office.

E lliott's infatuation with Toni surged so strongly that it soothed his cares and his spat with Emma faded to a dull, shadowy remembrance. He watched the rest of Morning Cloak's show and pondered the peaks and valleys of his 1985 love life.

"You're in the lowest valley," Elliott thought as he contemplated the shifting nature of his relationships with Nora and Donna. He raised his eyes to Toni and wondered, "Could she be the highest peak?"

Elliott stopped himself. He massaged his forehead with the bases of his palms.

"Damn, Elliott, now you sound like Emma with that romance novel garbage," Elliott rebuked himself. He sensed a presence next to him.

"You keep staring at her like that and you'll burn a hole in her face," quipped Brandy. Elliott thought she appeared more attractive than usual, her hair as black as he had ever seen it and her lipstick a vibrant red.

"I need some advice," Elliott said. He took a sip of cold coffee, grimaced and then set it aside.

"'Bout what, lover boy?" asked Brandy with her usual tactlessness.

"How to get to know a woman with a boyfriend," Elliott answered. He watched Toni and her bandmates take a table at the far side of the bar and continued, "You know, just casually build a relationship but not, like, a romantic one. Just a friendship."

"How the hell would I know about that?" replied Brandy with a dubious expression. She tucked her empty tray under her left arm, placed her other hand on her hip and shifted her weight to her right leg.

"I don't know," Elliott said. He waved in surrender and muttered, "Forget it."

"Spit it out, Warden," said an irked Brandy.

"I want to get to know someone *without* interfering with their relationship," Elliott explained.

"Oh, my god, boys are so dumb," Brandy remarked. She set her tray on the bar and said, "Your best bet with Nora is just keep doin' what you're doin'. Come up here when she's working and talk to her when ya' can. She and that grease monkey she hangs out with won't last. Just give it time . . . but don't get caught in the rebound."

"That's the idea," Elliott agreed, "but I'm not talking about Nora."

"Damn fool, I knew you were gonna say that," responded Brandy. She sat on the barstool next to him.

"So you know, huh?" Elliott asked.

"Everybody who knows you knows, Elliott," insisted an incredulous Brandy. She scolded him with her brown eyes and said, "You've been sittin' here starin' at and droolin' over her like some creepy stalker."

"Can you help me or not?" Elliott snapped.

"Pump the brakes, cowboy," said Brandy. She glanced at Toni and then turned her attention back to Elliott, warning, "That filly's outta your league. *Way* outta your league."

"And Nora's not?" Elliott queried sharply.

"Nora may be a lot younger than you, but she's the deferential type," began Brandy. She rested her elbow on the bar and gestured with her other hand, saying, "You can kinda mold her to what you are. She's not an idiot, but she's a simple girl who'll fit the way you like things to be."

Elliott gazed at Brandy but did not see her. She heard the spinning of his mental gears.

"That one, on the other hand," continued Brandy with a subtle nod to Toni's table, "is a strong, independent woman with a lotta energy."

"How do you know that?" Elliott inquired skeptically despite knowing Brandy's assertion was accurate. She slid an ashtray towards her and produced a cigarette from her pocket.

"How do you not?" countered Brandy. Lighting the cigarette, she took a moment to indulge in it before blowing out smoke and expounding, "Just watch her up there. She runs the show and leads everyone in here by the nose without even trying. She just doesn't abuse it because she's got a big heart, which is one thing she and Nora have in common. And I've talked to her a little bit. She knows where she's going and how to get there . . . plus she's loyal to Bobby, and I mean *loyal*. She's a good Catholic girl, too, and you're not exactly a religious guy."

"So what you're sayin' is a loser like me's got no shot," Elliott uttered.

"No, I'm sayin' be smart and go get the sweetheart, you moron," replied Brandy. She smoked her cigarette and complained, "God, Elliott, you're drawn to the wrong move, like, every time. No wonder Emma's always so whacked out about it."

Brandy casually surveyed the remaining patrons in the bar and quietly enjoyed her nicotine rush. Elliott pondered her words until the light bulb in his head illuminated.

"You know, Em was pretty pissed about that stunt you pulled with Donna," Elliott said.

"Yeah," replied Brandy. She exhaled a plume of smoke and said, "She's hasn't said a word to me since that night."

"She wanted to fire you," Elliott revealed.

"She did, huh?" snarled Brandy with a scowl.

"And guess who defused that bomb," Elliott added pointedly. Brandy offered him a begrudgingly smirk.

"Your old man was never this sneaky," Brandy griped. She ashed her cigarette and said in exasperation, "*All right.*"

Elliott grinned while Brandy narrowed her eyes and drifted into contemplation. She then shook her head in the affirmative.

"I got an idea," announced Brandy.

"I knew you would," Elliott said.

"Don't get cocky," Brandy warned, "'cuz, in the end, you'll screw it up anyway."

· · · ·

LUKE SET FOUR ICE COLD Bud Light bottles on the bar and Brandy, with impressive manual dexterity, clutched two necks in each hand. She turned to Elliott.

"All right, *Elliott*, let's do this," Brandy said. Her use of his first name, and not a derisive nickname, surprised him.

"After you," Elliott replied with a gesture. He managed to project a confident façade but inwardly he doubted Brandy's plan. They proceeded to the table where Toni and her bandmates decompressed after their performance. The foursome talked and laughed against a backdrop of loud conversations and the sound system playing the local country radio station.

"Follow my lead, don't say anything stupid," Brandy instructed him, "and don't stare at her the whole time like some freak."

"No promises," replied Elliott. He watched Toni laugh with the bar lights dancing in the blue of her eyes and felt woozy.

"Moron," Brandy muttered under her breath.

"Hey, Brandy," Toni greeted her as they arrived at the table, the sound of her voice paralyzing Elliott. She glanced at the beers, grinned and asked politely, "What's this?"

"Another round on the house," Brandy answered as she passed out the beers and Toni's band mates eagerly accepted them. Elliott had registered their existence before that moment; however, their exact appearances had been muddled by Toni's bigger-than-life stage presence. Brandy added with a nod over her shoulder, "Compliments of this loser."

Elliott shook his head in disbelief. The three men chortled.

"Thanks, mouth," sniped Elliott. Brandy's slight distracted him from his anxiousness just long enough and he extended a hand to Toni, saying, "I'm Elliott."

Toni showed a flash of recognition and her smile faded. She hesitated, her reaction in turn giving Elliott pause, but she recovered with an exhale and took his hand.

"Sorry about that," Toni apologized, "I just . . . I-."

"She just figured out you're the guy who kicked that dude's ass before our last show," said the man sitting to Toni's left. Elliott recognized him to be the other guitar player. He wore a shaggy, reddish-brown beard with shaggier blonde hair, was tall and lanky and had a broad face and large nose.

"Oh, yeah, sorry about that," said Elliott as he shook his hand. He kept his eyes off Toni but felt the gravity of her attention, saying, "Guess I kinda owed you a round anyway."

"I'm Eddie," the man said. He pointed his bottle at the man sitting across the table from Toni and added, "And that's my brother, Oscar, who's a big fan of your work."

"Wish I coulda' got there first," grumbled Oscar as he and Elliott shook hands. The band's bass player, Oscar did indeed resemble his brother but was heavier in build and sported a long, bristly moustache. Both men dressed alike in blue jeans, plaid shirts and big buckles attached to thick leather belts. Oscar tipped his cowboy hat to Elliott and continued with burgeoning protectiveness, "But you did all right. We can't have anybody pickin' on our lil' darlin' now, can we? At least that asshole got what he had comin'. A good shitkickin'."

Elliott watched Toni in his peripheral vision. She winced at each profane word that fell from Oscar's lips.

"Oscar's a little sweet on Nora," the third man advised as Oscar punched his huge, meaty fist into his other hand. The band's drummer was tall and dark, though not in the traditional way. He seemed somewhat vampiric in appearance to Elliott, possessing messy, wavy black hair, the deepest of brown eyes, pale skin and a withdrawn demeanor. He did not shake Elliott's hand but waved and said, "Ryan."

"So do you work here?" Toni inquired. She read the discomfort on Elliott's face and sought to change the topic.

"Well, you know Emma, obviously," answered Elliott to head nods and "yeahs". He pulled up a chair, turned it backwards and sat down. Folding his arms on its top rail, he revealed, "She's my little sister."

"Ain't nothin' little 'bout that woman," commented Eddie with a mischievous grin. He sampled his beer and then added, "She's one helluva a beauty and a ballbuster."

"Geez, Eddie," Toni rebuked him. Brandy, who remained uncharacteristically quiet during the encounter, chuckled. Elliott noted Toni's dislike of profanity.

"I gotta go push booze," Brandy announced unceremoniously. She subtly kicked Elliott's foot and departed, calling out, "Later."

"Thanks, Brandy," replied Elliott.

"Yeah, yeah," said Brandy. Elliott again surveyed Toni's bandmates, one after the other, and guessed that their ages hovered around thirty. He decided to speak before apprehension froze his tongue but Toni beat him to the punch.

"Thanks for the beers," Toni said while holding up the bottle in her hand. She drank from it while watching Elliott expectantly.

"Yeah, whaddaya want?" asked Ryan pointedly.

"*Ryan*," Toni scolded him.

"Actually, he's right," responded Elliott. Forcing himself to distribute his attention equally amongst the band members, he admitted, "I do have a little bit of an ulterior motive."

Toni and her bandmates shared quick glances, their expressions conveying a familiar suspicion. Elliott furrowed his brow.

"What's wrong?" Elliott asked.

"This is usually where the pass at Toni happens," said Oscar bluntly. Toni maintained a reserved expression but her companions' countenances conveyed annoyance.

"What? No, no, nothing like that," assured Elliott while waving his hands to underscore his point.

"C'mon, man," scolded Eddie. Beginning to panic, Elliott wished Brandy would rescue him but she was nowhere to be found. He turned to Toni.

"Look, I usually hate country music but you," Elliott said before driving himself to look at Toni's bandmates and adding, "*you guys*, I mean, all of you, are somethin' else. That cover of *Folsom Prison*? It was awesome. And Em, she already loves country like my old man did so she really digs your music."

"Man, she loves how we fill this place," Oscar interjected with a smirk.

"Yeah, that, too," conceded Elliott. The three men's interest wavered so Elliott cut to the chase, venturing, "But, like I said, she loves your music – seriously – so I was wondering if you guys would maybe play Emma's birthday party in September."

Toni and her bandmates again exchanged glances. Elliott attempted to read them.

"Paid, of course," added Elliott, "and it's a surprise, so don't tell her."

"If we're free, I don't see why not," Toni said with a shrug. Her gaze darted to the bar. Elliott turned and saw Emma as Toni warned, "Oh, there she is."

"With her usual timing," said Elliott. He rose to his feet and swept up his chair, saying, "I'll let you guys know, soon."

"You know where to find us," said Eddie as he used his beer bottle to point at the banner over his head. Elliott and Toni shared a lingering look and half-smiles before he returned the chair to its original table.

"Right," replied Elliott who casually walked away.

"You'd better nip that in the bud quick," advised Eddie to the nods of Oscar and Ryan.

"Stop it. He wasn't hitting on me," Toni countered with warming cheeks and a final look at Elliott who turned and walked parallel to the bar. Brandy joined him carrying a tray full of last-call cocktails.

"They bite?" Brandy asked.

"Yes, ma-am," answered Elliott in a shot at Brandy's age. Feeling unsettled, he queried, "Think she knows?"

"I think she knows you're an idiot," Brandy answered snidely. She broke away from Elliott and headed to a nearby table, saying, "But everyone knows that."

"*Thanks*," sighed Elliott.

. . . .

"YOU DON'T NEED TO ESCORT me to my car whenever I work," Nora told Bart despite enjoying the chivalry. She did not, however, want him to adjust his schedule for her and it pained her to see the exhaustion in his eyes. She caressed his arm from his shoulder to his elbow and added, "It's almost three in the morning."

"I'm just fine," replied Bart stubbornly as he embraced Nora. He released her but maintained his grip on her arms, asking, "You ready?"

"Almost," Nora answered guiltily. She extricated herself from his grasp and said, "I'll get done as soon as I can."

"That's fine," said Bart with a shrug. He planted himself on a barstool.

"Ten minutes," Nora said apologetically.

"No rush, babe," stated Bart. Wrapped up in one another, the couple failed to see Brandy sitting on the stage. She smoked a cigarette, its red circle of light vibrant in the darkness of the dormant stage area. An ashtray sat to one side of her and a half-empty Vodka and Cranberry on the other. She glowered at Bart.

"You really need to puppy-dog after her so much?" shouted Brandy across the club. Nora and Bart quickly turned their attention to her, Nora being the first to realize Brandy was intoxicated.

"Stay here," Nora instructed Bart with a hand on his shoulder that prevented him from rising. She cut across the dance floor and approached Brandy who harshly surveyed him with disapproving eyes.

"He's just overprotective, that's all," said Nora in an attempt to derail Brandy's foul mood. The older waitress glared at her as she suggested, "It's kinda sweet if ya' think about it."

"Yeah, whatever," Brandy replied, her bitterness tweaking Nora's pride. She ashed her cigarette and took two gulps of her cocktail.

"What're you so mad about?" asked Nora. Brandy pointed at Bart with her cigarette between her fingers.

"He shouldn't be here," Brandy uttered. Hearing Brandy's unfriendly tone, Bart rose to his feet and took two steps toward her. Nora spun around.

"Sit down, little boy," Brandy ordered him. Discombobulated by Brandy's sharp rebuke, Bart stopped in his tracks. Luke, the bartender, nodded towards the kitchen and, at his nonverbal urging, a waitress and a kitchen runner nonchalantly departed.

"Bart, please just wait in the car," begged Nora. Bart hesitated, his gaze darting between a desperate Nora and an angry Brandy. He finally relented but, instead of complying, he pulled out a chair from a nearby table. Moving it into the aisleway, Bart placed it so that he could sit and watch the brewing altercation. Frustrated by his hardheadedness, Nora turned to Brandy and inquired, "What's your problem?"

Luke exited the bar area and slipped into the stairwell leading to Emma's office. Brandy finished her drink.

"*He's* here," Brandy answered as she again pointed at Bart with her cigarette between her fingers. She dropped her arm and complained, "That's my problem. Ya' can't just keep him clear of this place. Ya' know, for Elliott's sake."

"That's stupid, Brandy," argued Nora. Though she did not believe it, she lashed out, "Bart's got just as much right to be here as Elliott does."

Brandy's face went stone cold while Nora's heart sunk into her chest. She looked down, ashed her dying cigarette and then stood up. Brandy's gaze fell on the picture of John Warden and, with old wounds stoking her inner fire, she went nose-to-nose with Nora.

"Don't *ever* say that again," Brandy growled, her vitriol causing Nora to retreat several steps. Emma emerged from the stairwell at that moment and noticed the tension between Brandy and Nora. Donna appeared two seconds later but remained in the doorway and peered cautiously into the club.

"Wait here," Emma said. Donna followed Emma's line of sight to Nora and Brandy.

"Uh, oh," muttered Donna. Luke appeared behind her.

"*Uh, oh* doesn't cover it," he said. Brandy again closed the distance between she and Nora.

"Get him outta here," Brandy demanded with as much intimidation as she could muster. Nora trembled but held her ground.

"He's not hurting anyone by just being here. And besides, Elliott's never here at three am," insisted Nora. Brandy slapped her cheek and the smack echoed throughout the club.

"Brandy! Stop it!" Emma yelled as she hurried to intervene in the altercation between her employees. Bart attempted to rise but Emma threw an index finger in his direction and commanded him, "Nope, sit down."

The young man quickly complied. Emma arrived at the scene, pulled Nora backward and insinuated herself between the two women.

"What the hell are you doing?" Emma demanded fiercely.

"Taking care of our boy," answered Brandy coldly. She glowered at Nora and asked, "Isn't that what we're *all* supposed ta' be doing?"

Nora glanced at a fuming Bart. Feeling protective of him, she decided to take the fight to Brandy.

"Luke said she introduced Elliott to Toni the other night," revealed Nora. The other waitresses and the kitchen staff, unable to contain themselves, filtered into the hallway to watch the spectacle on the dance floor.

"Oh, he did, huh?" Emma replied as she glanced over her shoulder. Luke paused but then nodded his head in the affirmative. Donna inhaled sharply to speak but Emma interrupted her, inquiring, "Is that true?"

"Yeah," replied Brandy unabashedly, "it's true."

"She's been sticking her nose in his relationships a lot lately," griped Nora. Brandy flashed her a vile, heart-stopping scowl.

"Maybe you should worry more about where your own nose is, little girl," Brandy sneered threateningly. She attempted to circumvent Emma but her superior blocked her path. Bristling but unwilling to physically challenge Emma, she snapped, "Like six inches up Emma's ass."

"Toni's over his head and you know it," Emma informed Brandy, her volume lowered to prevent Donna from hearing her words. She added thickly, "You shouldn't be encouraging that."

"Why do either of you care?" Brandy asked. She looked to Nora and said, "You got your young stud over there."

Brandy turned her ire to Emma. The two women engaged in an optical battle from which neither one shied.

"You need to realize that Elliott should be with who *he* wants to be with," Brandy admonished her. She glanced at Donna and called out, "And you're supposed to want him, and then *you* go off with that other people bullshit. What's he supposed ta' do with that?"

Brandy's reasoning cowed everyone in the room. Everyone, that is, save Emma. Irked by the accusations, she made her final decision.

"All the meddling is one thing, Brandy, but overdrinking and hitting another employee?" Emma uttered with disdain. Shaking her head in disappointment, she stated resolutely, "You're fired. Get out."

Emma turned around and motioned to Luke. He was already on his way to the telephone.

"Luke, call Matt to come get her," Emma directed him. A sinister snicker from Brandy chilled everyone who heard it.

"It's nice to see him with a little hope for once instead of hurting and bleeding all over everything," Brandy said dramatically. She let her gaze fall on Donna, and then Nora, and last of all on Emma, sneering, "But he'll never stop bleeding if you bitches keep cutting him."

Flabbergasted by Brandy's hurtful wisdom, Emma and Nora simply gaped at her as she walked to the bar and obtained her purse. However, her words caused Donna considerable distress and she fled to Emma's office to hide her tears. Brandy slapped Luke, who held the telephone receiver in his hand, on the right butt cheek.

"Tell Matt I'm having a smoke outside for me, would ya', hon?" Brandy requested. Seconds later, she threw open Johnny Dub's doors with both hands and never returned.

• • • •

BRANDY LIVED IN ONE of the neighborhoods along the Monroe Boulevard corridor and, like many of its houses, hers was a cookie-cutter, red-brick ranch. Using his lunch to visit the former Johnny Dubs waitress, Elliott pulled up to the curb in his MacLean Hunter service van. He found Brandy sitting in a lawn chair on her front porch and smoking a cigarette.

"Well, if it ain't the belle of the ball?" Brandy said loudly as Elliott exited his vehicle and walked towards her.

"What the hell did you do last night?" asked Elliott accusatorily. He stopped before ascending the porch step.

"Eh, got fired," Brandy said blithely. She lowered her arm and nicked her cigarette in an ash tray sitting on the porch.

"And hit Nora," countered Elliott in exasperation. Brandy set her elbow on the chair's armrest and held her cigarette aloft.

"I just smacked her on the cheek, and I pulled it," Brandy said. She aimed two threatening fingers with the cigarette between them at Elliott and warned, "And if you give me any shit about it I'll punch you in the face and I *won't* pull it."

Elliott rolled his eyes and exhaled sharply. Dousing the fire on his tongue with discretion, he folded his arms.

"C'mon, Brandy, that was extreme," reasoned Elliott, "even for you."

"Alcohol may have been involved," Brandy replied with a sour face.

"Yeah, I bet. But I heard you may have been defending my honor," replied Elliott with a half-smile, "so I can't be too mad."

"You're welcome," Brandy said. She blew a plume of smoke into the air.

"Just don't hit her anymore," pleaded Elliott with an emphatic gesture.

"No promises," Brandy said. A scathing expression from Elliott prompted her to cool her ire and add snottily, "Besides, I doubt I'll even see your little princess anymore."

"True," said Elliott.

"Wanna chair?" Brandy asked.

"Nah," muttered Elliott. He took a seat on the porch step and laid his forearms on his knees with his hands clasped in front of him, saying, "I don't think Em'll take you back, so I'm not even goin' down that road."

"I'm not beggin' for my job, anyway, so don't worry about it," Brandy stated. Elliott did not respond to her comment.

"I do know a few places who need help," suggested Elliott. He stretched his legs out before him and rested his elbows on the edge of the porch, continuing, "And Neil'd always hire ya', especially to piss Emma off. Those two've always hated each other."

"Thanks, but I'm not working for that jerk at his crappy little bar," Brandy informed Elliott. She shook her head and indulged in her cigarette before explaining, "The old man made foreman, so I'm gonna take some time off anyway. Plus my oldest ones are turnin' into real assholes in their teenage years so I need to put the hammer down more often. This'll give me plenty of time to make their lives miserable."

Elliott and Brandy shared a chortle before growing silent and watching the neighborhood's daily activities. She eventually leaned back in her chair and turned uncharacteristically serious.

"Whaddaya gonna do about all your women?" Brandy inquired bluntly.

"Not a damn thing," replied Elliott while shaking his head in the negative, "because none of 'em are mine."

"Not even the country queen," Brandy queried. Elliott folded his arms again, stared into the green lawn and sighed.

"*Especially* not the country queen," said Elliott with a frown, "because I've heard she's a stone's throw away from being engaged."

The pair did not talk for over a minute. A car passed and honked its horn. Brandy waved. Elliott stirred.

"So I guess you're not on team Nora anymore," said Elliott.

"She's decided to make her mistake," Brandy said, her feeling on Nora evident in her tone, "so, no, I'm not."

"And the team you're on now is . . . ." said Elliott.

"Yours, idiot," Brandy replied. Elliott turned to face her.

"Huh?" he said. Brandy fixed a penetrating gaze on Elliott and held her cigarette away from her face. It left behind a trail of smoke that the breeze soon dispersed.

"Enough pussyfootin' around, Elliott," Brandy growled. She counseled him with a sharp tongue, "Do what *you* want to do. Decide which one you want and *go get her*."

"Are you serious?" asked Elliott, his uncertainty etched on his troubled countenance.

"Most likely, given your history, it'll blow up in your face," Brandy said without jest. Her words deflated Elliott but, before he could respond, she asserted, "But leavin' *all three* of 'em on the table when you've still got a shot in the dark . . . I don't know, Elliott. Seems pretty damn stupid ta' me."

Brandy returned to her cigarette and her quiet observation of the neighborhood. Meanwhile, Elliott's vision clouded and he contemplated Brandy's advice. Minutes later, he rose to his feet and stepped onto the porch.

"Thanks," Elliott told Brandy before planting a firm kiss on her cheek. She squeezed his arm affectionately.

"I wanna know how it's going," Brandy said as she released his arm.

"I know," Elliott replied. He, without further engagement of Brandy, slowly walked to his van, boarded it and drove off into the suburban sprawl.

"Good luck, you handsome bastard," Brandy said.

· · · ·

EMMA SET A GRUMPY OLD Man in front of Elliott. Folding her arms, she rested them on the bar and looked lovingly on her wayward brother. He mimicked her posture and returned the look.

"You eatin' tonight?" asked Emma. It comforted her that, despite the siblings' sometimes turbulent relationship, Elliott always returned to the special place she reserved for him.

"Yeah, not sure what yet, though," Elliott answered. He and Emma continued to gaze upon one another. She faltered first.

"Look, Elliott, I-," began Emma.

"Em, everything's fine," Elliott interrupted her with a slow shake of his head. She returned her shimmering eyes to him.

155

"Really?" queried Emma, her countenance conveying her surprise.

"Really," Elliott answered. He grasped his glass and said pointedly, "*You're insane . . . .*"

"Yeah," muttered Emma feebly with a weak grin.

". . . but, in the end, ya' do it because ya' love me," Elliott continued in a measured tone, "and you just want me to be happy."

"*I do,*" insisted Emma in earnest while grasping Elliott's forearm.

"I know," Elliott said. Emma released his arm and stepped back.

"What about Brandy?" asked Emma carefully. She expected a tongue-lashing from Elliott over her termination.

"This is your place, and you gotta do what you gotta do," Elliott said. Emma waited for him to elaborate but he remained mute. Her eyes flashed to her right and she saw Toni approaching them.

"What the hell is this?" thought Emma with a suspicious gaze. She straightened her body and muttered, "Incoming."

Glancing over his shoulder, Elliott did a double take as Toni's long, tall form sauntered towards him. Mesmerized by her presence, Elliott gawked at her. She slid onto the bar stool next to him.

"Hi, Em. Hi, Elliott," said Toni with her usual ardor. Elliott watched her uneasily.

"Oh, hey, Toni," Elliott replied. He channeled every ounce of his energy into faking composure.

"Hello there," said Emma with a forced smile. Barely masking her accusatory response, she asked, "What're you doing here?"

Toni hesitated. She acutely felt Emma's irritation.

"I was wonderin' if I could talk to Elliott for a minute," answered Toni. Elliott's heart dropped into his stomach and he quickly took two slugs of his drink.

"Oh, shit," Elliott thought.

"About what?" Emma inquired sharply without the slightest trace of discretion. Toni grew tense but Emma's treatment of her sparked abrupt indignation in Elliott. He rose to Toni's defense.

"One of the guys at work's gettin' married and I asked Toni and the boys if they'd play the reception," Elliott lied convincingly. Toni's body relaxed.

"Who's getting married?" queried Emma.

"Chuck Anderson," Elliott replied on the heels of Emma's question. Elliott's acting defused his sister's anger and he declared, "I know what I want. Some of those awesome tacos you make. You haven't made those for me in a while."

"Okay, sure," said a puzzled Emma. Toni watched Elliott with an impressed yet muted smile.

"And some for Toni, too," Elliott added. Toni nodded in agreement.

"All right," replied Emma. She looked to Elliott and then to Toni before saying, "Emma's famous tacos, coming right up."

"You're good," said Toni while watching Emma depart.

"Bud light for Toni, Luke," Emma instructed him as she breezed by the bartender. Luke stuffed the remainder of his French fries into his mouth and then wiped his hands on his jeans. Elliott turned to Toni and his anxiety returned.

"So, uh, what's up?" Elliott asked with a sense of dread. Toni paused before speaking. The moment hung heavy in the air.

"This is kinda weird but . . . well, I'll just say it straight up," Toni said, Elliott barely squelching the urge to run out of bar. She exhaled and stated, "There's a rumor runnin' 'round here that you have a thing for me."

"There is, huh?" replied Elliott. He grasped his glass with both hands and stared into it. She struggled to find the right words.

"Sorry," Toni apologized. She let her eyes fall to the bar and said, "I do this enough you'd think I'd get better at it."

"Do what?" said Elliott.

"Tell guys who're infatuated with me that I'm not interested," Toni said, her heart hurting. Her words stunned Elliott as she expounded, "It's nothing personal. You're probably a great guy."

"You might wanna ask around about that," Elliott countered with a dubious expression. Toni did not respond to his remark.

"This is gonna sound *so* conceited, but I swear it's not," Toni said. She paused to let Luke open her beer and set it in front of her before explaining, "I get hit on *a lot*. Which I don't understand, because I'm just an average girl living in an average neighborhood with an average life."

"I doubt that," Elliott scoffed. He took another drink.

"Yes, I am. I really am," Toni said with a hint of distress in her tone. She rotated her bar stool so that she faced Elliott and continued, "But like I said, I get hit on a lot. I think a big part of it is playing in bars. A lotta guys are lonely, most guys are drunk. And being the lead singer, they all focus on me, and a lotta times they get a little starry-eyed, especially if they see me perform a few times."

"So you want me to take my starry eyes elsewhere," replied Elliott, a devil-may-care attitude and a loathing for romantic love arising in his heart.

"Look, I have a serious boyfriend who, hopefully," Toni said while holding up crossed fingers, "will be a fiancée soon, and who I'll spend the rest of my life with."

"Can I be honest with you?" asked Elliott, every word Toni spoke feeling like another stab in the kidney.

"Uh, yeah, sure," Toni answered. She was taken aback by his question.

"You're absolutely right. I'm infatuated with you," Elliott confessed. The statement caused him a rush of relief and, spurred by the emotional unburdening, he continued with growing ease, "*Stupid infatuated.* And I was gonna make a play for you, but try to do it the right way. Ya' know, take a shot in the dark. Be your friend, secretly hope you and that soon-to-be fiancé of yours break up, wait for the right moment, and then sneak in there when you weren't expecting it."

Elliott laughed. An astonished Toni gaped at him.

"Ya' okay there, country girl?" queried Elliott.

"Yeah, I just," Toni began, her head muddled by Elliott's admission, "I just never've had anyone come clean like that."

It was Toni's turn to laugh. Elliott joined her and marveled at the light that shined from within her. Emma hawked the couple from the other end of the bar with a withering mien.

"Brandy was right," said Elliott, "you're way outta my league."

"Stop it," Toni replied with a playful slap of Elliott's shoulder.

"It makes you uncomfortable, doesn't it?" queried Elliott. The pair forgot they were in public as he added, "All the girl worship."

Toni looked away and then to her lap. She nervously fiddled with her fingers.

"I've always hated it," Toni said. She returned her attention to Elliott and explained, "You know how it goes. The tall, dorky girl suddenly *develops* really late and . . . well, you know how guys are."

"Yeah, I do," Elliott replied. He finished his cocktail.

Toni took a moment to appraise Elliott. She grinned softly.

"Another place, another time, I'd've said yes to a first date," said Toni.

"You'd still be outta my league, though," said Elliott, "and, as Brandy would say: 'You'll just screw it up, Warden.'"

"Oh, come on," said a flattered Toni. She wished to comfort Elliott and, the curiosity dripping from her tongue, she asked, "What about Nora?"

"You know about Nora?" Elliott queried in disbelief.

"How could I not?" Toni said. She made a fist and comically threw a mock punch, saying, "You knocked that guy out who slapped her on the, well, on the butt."

"She finally smartened up," said Elliott. The color drained from his face and he said, "She's datin' some guy her own age now."

"Emma still think she's too young for you?" Toni inquired.

"How do you know so much?" asked Elliott.

"The first day I ever walked in here, Emma was scheming to get you and your old girlfriend back together," said Toni. She chuckled and admitted, "She told me I was too young that day, too."

"I'll say it again. My sister is *insane*," stated Elliott with a dramatic exhale. He turned to Toni, his mood serious, and stated, "Look, infatuated or not, I'm not gonna bother you. You're taken, I'm not that much of jerk and I probably need some time to get my head straight, anyway. And if you don't want to play Emma's party, if it'd be weird, it's no problem. You can just forget about it."

"Oh, no, we can still do it," Toni insisted. Her conscience told her to stop there but, egged on by her heart, she added, "And you don't have to stay away from me or anything."

"Get it worked out?" inquired Emma. Elliott thanked God for the interruption.

"Yeah," Elliott said, "Morning Cloak's gonna do it."

"We've never played a wedding before," Toni replied. She smiled a satisfied smile at Elliott, her misgivings about his intentions resolved, and added, "It'll be fun."

E lliott stumbled onto his porch with a mug of coffee in one hand and his radio in the other. Wearing only a pair of blue shorts, he stopped to let the storm door close behind him. His forward momentum, however, caused coffee to slosh out of the mug and over his fingers.

"Son of a . . . ," Elliott griped. Setting down the radio, he switched the mug to his other hand and shook off the coffee. Elliott let his eyes adjust to the light and felt the muggy air, commenting breathily, "Warm already."

Moving to the patio table, Elliott set his mug on it. He slumped into one of its chairs with a yawn.

"Damn it," Elliott complained when he realized the radio remained on the porch. He took a drink of coffee, retrieved the radio and set it next to the mug. Pulling another chair close to him, Elliott sat down and threw up his feet, saying, "If only I could get breakfast delivered."

Fiddling with the radio, Elliott managed to turn it on and tune it to the first station he found. Casey Kasem soon announced the thirty-seventh most popular song in the country, WHAM!'s *Freedom.*

"Wow, how painfully appropriate," Elliott muttered as he considered the kaleidoscope of love interests that were no more. Adjusting the volume knob, he reasoned aloud, "Well, want it or not, I guess I got it. Might as well enjoy it."

The next hour passed quickly as the sun rose higher, the temperature climbed and the clouds gradually increased. Elliott became mired in an unpleasant review of a decade and a half of romantic mistakes and misfortunes. His elderly, chain-smoking neighbor emerged from her apartment and, with coughs and grumbles, wrested Elliott from his contemplations.

"Mornin', Ms. Franklin," Elliott called despite her being partially concealed by the hedge. She stopped watering her flowers and attempted to return his greeting several times but was thwarted by phlegm and repeated coughing. She wore curlers in her thin hair and a gaudy, floral print housecoat.

"Mornin', young man," rumbled Maude Franklin in her raspy yet strong voice. Elliott turned down his radio as she asked, "You reel in that little cutie yet?"

"I told you, Mrs. Franklin," Elliott answered in clear frustration, "she's datin' some other guy."

"What about the other one?" demanded Maude with increasing volume. She resumed watering her flowers and said, "That one you used ta' go with in high school."

"All of em', Mrs. Franklin," Elliott said in irritation as he raised his voice, "they're all datin' other guys."

"Why the hell is that?" inquired Maude bluntly.

"What? Like I'm gonna go up to them all and ask 'Hey, what the hell's wrong with me?'" Elliott rebuked her. He paused as an epiphany washed over him and then posited, "But maybe I could ask them what's not."

"Huh?" asked Maude. A thought formed in Elliott's mind – a sudden, desperate thought – and he stood up. Leaving the old woman behind and his mug and the radio on the table, he rushed into his apartment. Maude shrugged when Elliott did not answer and continued watering her flowers, muttering, "Kids."

. . . .

THE RECEPTIONIST AT Heritage Hospital's main desk confirmed Toni was working that day and directed Elliott, who claimed to be her friend, to her floor. He patiently camped in a waiting area until, twenty minutes later, Toni emerged from a hallway.

"Toni!" Elliott beckoned eagerly as he rose from his chair. Hearing her name, she turned around but then started when she saw Elliott. She wore medium-blue scrubs but otherwise looked the same as she did on stage. Elliott appraised Toni and thought, "Damn, doesn't really matter what she's wearing, does it?"

Toni slowly approached Elliott but her initial attempt to speak failed. She tilted her head in an odd manner and pondered Elliott's strange appearance.

"Elliott?" said Toni as she forced his name from her lips. Discomfited by his visit, she asked, "What're you . . . what're you doing here?"

"I need to ask you something," Elliott said, his intense focus on his question rendering him oblivious to his social *faux pau*.

"On a Sunday morning?" queried Toni. She looked around her and added, "While I'm at work?"

"It'll just take a few minutes," Elliott answered. Descending back to the fringe of reality, he said hurriedly, "I know you're working. But I can wait until you're on a break or lunch or whatever. Yeah, hey, I'll buy you lunch. Whatever you want."

Elliott returned to his seat and settled into it as if he planned on a long stay. Toni thought him to be manic and her nursing instincts engaged. She studied him closely.

"It's slow today," said a hesitant Toni. She folded her arms tightly and meandered closer to Elliott. Though concerned by his unexpected visit, Toni was nonetheless intrigued by it so she stated, "I got a few minutes."

"Did you know I live like, not even a mile that way?" Elliott advised her with a finger pointing to the west. He moved his arms to the armrests of the chair and added, "Continental Apartments, right over on Beech Daly."

"Are you feeling okay?" asked Toni.

"Oh, yeah, sorry," Elliott said. He made an effort to calm himself and stated, "Just hopped up on way too much coffee, that's all."

The pair stared at each other for twenty seconds. Toni squirmed.

"So. . . what's this burning question you have?" asked Toni.

"Remember when you said, ya' know, 'another place, another time', you'd date me?" Elliott inquired with a deathly serious mien. He gripped the arms of the chair and leaned forward. Toni retreated a step.

"I just said I'd give you a first date," replied Toni warily. Elliott glanced downward, processed her words and then returned his attention to her comely face.

"Yeah, first date, that's right," Elliott repeated in agreement. Realizing the extent of his intensity, he leaned back, asking, "Did you mean it?"

"*Elliott*," scolded Toni in disappointment. Her nervousness stripped away, she took a seat next to Elliott and lectured him, "I told you I'm in a serious, committed relationship. I thought you understood that. You have *zero* chance with me."

"Oh, no, it's not like that," Elliott protested with quick waves of his hand. He continued contritely, "I'm not trying to get in your . . . I mean, I'm not trying to woo you. I swear it."

A confused Toni watched Elliott carefully. He rose to his feet.

"I guess what I'm really asking is," Elliott said as he paced in front of her and gestured vigorously, " . . . is *why* would you give me a first date?"

Toni exhaled. Elliott sensed the chastisement on her tongue and swiftly defused it.

"Hypothetically," Elliott insisted with a raised palm. He continued earnestly, "Again, I'm not hitting on you."

"Are you really serious?" inquired Toni. She relaxed, settled into her chair and crossed her legs, querying, "This isn't some ploy to get closer to me?"

"I just wanna know, that's it," Elliott assured her.

"You swear it?" asked Toni with a raised eyebrow.

"I gotta know," Elliott pleaded. Toni accepted the sincerity of his plea.

"If I tell you," Toni began with grave eyes, "we talk about it this *one* time, and you never show up here unannounced again. That just can't happen."

"Deal," Elliott replied in relief. He eagerly held up his hand as if taking an oath and uttered, "Promise."

"Well," Toni began as the gears of her mind began spinning. Her discomfort returned as she considered her opinion of Elliott. He took a different chair, his selection leaving an empty one between them, as she expounded, "Well, I saw you here and there at Johnny Dubs – I didn't even know who you were until you told me – and, I suppose . . . . I guess I thought you were pretty cute. But I didn't think anything more of it."

"Okay," Elliott said. The last sentence tweaked his ego but he hid it.

"I mean, I see a lot of cute guys in bars," admitted Toni. She pondered for a few more seconds and then declared with adoration, "And, even saying that, I only have eyes for Bobby. He's the handsomest man in my world."

"Fair enough," Elliott said. Her feelings for Bobby prickled him but he asked, "So that's why?"

"No, not all of it. I'm not that shallow," Toni said with mock offense. Doubting that Toni possessed any shallowness in her nature, Elliott listened to her as she continued, "The more I saw you, you kinda have this, this . . . dark, kinda brooding vibe."

"And you like that?" Elliott asked, his interested piqued. Toni turned red. Fleeing the moment, she stood up and walked to a window.

"No," she insisted as she folded her arms. Gazing into the early August sky, she relented, "Okay, yes, maybe a little. But that's not usual for me. I can't believe I'm talking to you about this."

"Hey, this really helps," Elliott encouraged her. Riveted to her attractive frame, which was partially silhouetted by the light streaming through the window, he said, "I'll buy you lunch for it."

Toni turned back to Elliott with a dubious expression. He sat up straight and waved his arm like a white flag.

"Just buy," Elliott clarified with a smirk. Amused, he sighed and stated, "I won't subject you to lunch with me."

Toni moved as if to laugh but no sound came from her lips. She surveyed Elliott briefly.

"There's one more thing," said Toni. A little of the redness returned to her cheeks.

"Yeah?" Elliott replied.

"I'm not usually one for the macho stuff," Toni explained, "but the way you defended Nora, how it was just like an instinct for you to protect her . . . that was pretty cool."

Elliott averted his gaze. A similar visit to Nora loomed over him.

"I'm not usually one to *do* stuff like that," Elliott admitted. He looked at Toni, felt his infatuation with her becoming something deeper and offered her a sad smile. He said appreciatively, "You kept your end of the bargain so now I'll keep mine."

Elliott stood up.

"Thanks," Elliott said. Toni walked to him and patted him on the cheek.

"Whatever it means for you," Toni replied, "*good luck, Elliott.*"

Elliott nodded and departed. Toni titled her head and watched him go before resuming her nursing duties; however, drifting into deep thought, she long contemplated the enigma that was Elliott Warden.

• • • •

ENTRENCHED IN AN ENVIRONMENTAL science textbook, Nora sat at a worn oak table in an out-of-the way spot at the University of Michigan – Dearborn's library. A glitch in the Johnny Dubs' waitressing assignments freed her day and she intended to catch up on her studies. The library, as she expected, was empty on an August Sunday.

"Geez, could she get any more adorable?" Elliott thought when he found her. He leaned against a bookshelf and studied Nora. She wore a white headband that held back her hair and only a light application of makeup. Nora's wardrobe doused his admiration in cold water, however; she dressed in high-waisted jeans and an untucked, man's plaid shirt.

"Already wearin' his clothes," Elliott said to himself. The realization made him nauseous. Propelling himself forward, Elliott walked towards Nora with a nervous exhale and muttered, "Here goes."

Though Elliott approached Nora from the front she was so engrossed in her reading that she did not notice him. Her single-minded focus amused Elliott and allowed him to stand next to her.

"Whatcha studying there?" Elliott asked while lifting the book's cover. Nora squeaked and jumped.

"Elliott! You scared me," answered Nora. Embarrassed by the commotion, she scanned the vicinity but found no one to be offended.

"Environmental science," Elliott said while ignoring her admonition. He eased the cover downward and stated, "I thought you were a psych major."

"Science elective," answered Nora, her mortification fading.

"Got a minute?" Elliott asked.

"Yeah. I'm about due for a break," answered Nora. Elliott took the chair opposite her, spun it backwards and sat down as she inquired, "How'd you know I was here?"

"Luke told me you were off today," Elliott replied, "and I figured this is where I'd find you."

"He took over for Brandy in the nosy department," said Nora with an eyeroll. Elliott rested his arms on the top rail of the chair.

"I'm sure he's still feeding her all the gossip, too," Elliott remarked. Nora yawned and stretched as Elliott inquired, "How's school going?"

"Good, but I've got a long way to go," answered Nora. She stuck a piece of paper in the textbook and closed it. Glancing at Elliott warily, she asked, "You're gonna ask me a hard question, aren't you?"

Elliott paused.

"Yep," Elliott confessed. Nora became distressed.

"I thought you said we were gonna skip the hard stuff," complained Nora. She moaned and pouted and her shoulders slumped.

"It's the last and only question I'm gonna ask you about us," Elliott assured her, "whatever *us* was."

Nora squirmed while pondering Elliott's request. A thought struck her.

"If I answer your question, then I get to ask you one," bargained Nora. Reading Elliott's mind, she added quickly, "And you have to answer it."

"Deal," Elliott confirmed. The electricity between them heightened, each of them realizing they were alone with little chance of interruption. Elliott maneuvered away from the temptation and inquired, "Why'd you kiss me at the club that night?"

"Not this again," whined Nora. She dropped her head into her hands and pleaded, "I don't wanna fight."

"We're not gonna fight. I just wanna know why, that's all," Elliot replied with a grave mien. He reached out and tugged on the sleeve of her shirt and said, "You're with him now and I just gotta accept it. No more fights."

Nora pulled free of Elliott's grasp and sat up to avoid his touch. Feeling guilty, she refused to look at the shirt but instead massaged its left cuff between her thumb and forefinger. She hated to see Elliott hurting and decided to help move him along.

"Look, Elliott, you're a good lookin' guy, and I think I got a little infatuated because of the way Emma warned me to stay away from you," explained Nora. She stood up and, moving behind her chair to place distance between them, grabbed the top of it and continued, "I think we both fell into that trap. Ya' know, she told us to stay away from each other so all we wanted was, like, to get closer."

"I see," Elliott said while absorbing her words like wasp stings. He pointed to the area behind Nora and suggested, "You can talk to me from behind that bookshelf if it'll make you feel better."

"Stop it," scolded Nora. Tightly gripping the chair, she continued, "That night in the parking lot . . . that stupid cat scared me and you kinda came to my rescue. It was like, all emotional and romantic, I guess, and I just got carried away. *We* got carried away."

"All right, then," Elliott said while struggling to accept her emotional retreat from him.

"I care about you a lot and-," insisted Nora.

"You don't have to do that," Elliott interrupted her. He rubbed his eyes, saying, "We're good."

The moment lingered. Neither of them spoke.

"Okay, then it's your turn," said Nora to break the silence. She queried, "Why'd you punch Gregg?"

Elliott languidly rose to his feet. He spun his chair back around.

"Just know I'd do it again," Elliott replied with a seriousness that tugged at Nora's heart.

"That's not an answer," complained Nora. Elliott briefly held her in his gaze before his countenance softened.

"Would Bart've done the same thing?" Elliott asked. Nora's eyes fell and she pondered the question. She then raised them to Elliott.

"Yeah, I think he would've," said Nora with swell of appreciation for Bart.

"That's all I needed to hear," Elliott said. He approached Nora and leaned into her. Expecting a kiss on the lips, she recoiled but he instead pecked her on the top of her head. A wave of adrenaline washed over Nora and she felt her cheeks flush. Before she could squelch it and respond, however, Elliott walked away, rounded the bookshelf behind her and was gone.

• • • •

"IN A LITTLE LATE FOR a Sunday, Big Bro," said Emma. She greeted her brother with a hug and a quick kiss on the cheek.

"Busy day," Elliott said as he returned Emma's embrace. She stepped back and appraised him.

"You look good," commented Emma with goofy half-smile, "ya' know, like . . . happy."

Elliott laughed.

"Not diggin' it?" Elliott asked.

"Not used to it," replied Emma. She looked on him with sisterly love and said, "It's a nice change."

"Let's just say I've worked some things out," Elliott replied. Though she wished to question him further, Emma's curiosity evaporated as a more immediate concern entered her mind.

"Uh, speaking of working things out, do you think maybe you could . . . *leave*?" suggested Emma with uncharacteristic sheepishness. Elliott stared at her with amused disbelief.

"Are you finally kicking me outta your club?" Elliott replied. Disinclined to grant her request, he sat on his barstool and said, "I haven't even hit anyone today."

Emma squirmed. Elliott stared at her and awaited an answer with his feet on the floor and his hands clasped between his thighs.

"Fine, I'll tell you, but then you gotta go," relented an irked Emma. She attempted to lift him upward as she confessed, "Donna called a little while ago. She's on her way here with her new guy and you being around is *not* a good idea."

"So she went for it, huh?" Elliott queried rhetorically while resisting Emma's effort to displace him. He felt a twinge of sadness but it passed. Grinning softly, Elliott commented in earnest, "Good for her."

"Good for her?" responded Emma, his easy surrender greatly annoying her.

"Donna's changed, Em, and so have I," Elliott said. He folded his arms and explained, "She's not the naïve girl that followed on my heels when we were young and dumb. She's . . . *smart* . . . and mature. And she needs more than what I am. That's for damn sure."

"But you two-," began Emma in a mild panic.

"There is no 'us two,'" Elliott interrupted her. He called out to the bartender, saying, "Hey, Sean."

Emma's dutiful second-in-command, Sean Richards, stood six-feet tall with her thin, blonde hair tied in a perpetual ponytail. Her face was round and her nose small and pointed, the twenty-seven-year-old a calm and unassuming counterweight to Emma at Johnny Dubs.

169

"Usual, comin' up," replied Sean after receiving an affirmative nod from Emma.

"Let me guess, you're gonna go back to chasin' Nora," sneered Emma.

"Nope," Elliott replied. He rotated his stool so that he faced the bar and set his forearms on it. Emma insinuated herself between her brother and the next barstool.

"Oh, god, not Toni?" asked Emma snottily. Her brother threw her a brief glare.

"I'm not gonna chase *anyone*," stated Elliott, "*and* I don't want anybody chasin' me, *and* you're gonna stay the hell outta my love life, *and* that's all I'm gonna say about it."

Emma prepared to unleash her fury on Elliott but Donna's arm-in-arm entrance with a tall, lean man defused the explosion. His hair was short and styled and he wore a brown leather motorcycle jacket. The mustached man appeared to be several years older than Donna.

"Damn it," exhaled Emma as her vitriol fizzled. Sean approached quickly, set a Grumpy Old Man in front of Elliott and then immediately retreated. Donna's companion removed his leather gloves and stuffed them into his jacket pocket before pointing to Elliott.

"That's him, isn't it?" asked the man shrewdly.

"What?" Donna replied. Realizing her companion's intentions, she asked in horror, "Ben, where're you going?"

"You must be Elliott," said Benjamin Williams in a genuinely cordial manner. He extended a hand to Elliott.

"Uh, yeah," Elliott replied. His gaze fell on Donna, who stared back in utter shock, and then he realized who stood before him. Elliott shook Ben's hand and said, "Oh. And you're *him*."

Donna threw Emma a panicked look. Emma offered her a nonverbal apology in return.

"Look, I'm not trying to cause any trouble," Elliott said while holding up his hands. Feeling no ill will towards Ben or jealousy towards Donna, he added, "Honestly, I had no idea you two'd be here."

"Oh, no, man. It's not like that at all," insisted Ben. He placed an elbow on the bar and leaned into it, expounding, "I don't believe in all that possessive macho stuff. You and Donna were together, and I acknowledge it, man, I really do. It's better for all of us to be open and honest and just, like, be understanding. Let everybody process."

A slow grin came to Elliott's lips while Donna and Emma watched the two men interact with jaws agape. Elliott chuckled but, when Ben failed to react negatively, his smile vanished.

"Holy shit," Elliott said, "you're serious."

"Oh, yeah, man, totally," replied Ben. He motioned for Donna to join him. She hesitated but, after his continued urging gestures, she complied with his wish. Ben wrapped an arm around Donna's shoulders and stated, "Look, I've been seein' this wonderful woman for over a month now, and I really dig her. A lot. But if you two have unresolved issues, man, I won't get in the way of that. Free will, man, that's the name of the game. *I don't wanna force her into anything.* That's how you keep it easy and healthy and loving."

Emma placed her hand over her mouth to stifle a laugh. Elliott turned his attention to Donna; amazingly, he felt a true liking for Ben.

"I like this guy," Elliott remarked with a smirk. Donna again paused but, encouraged by Ben's wisdom, she smiled and nodded her head.

"Yeah, I do, too," Donna said, the admission tasting bittersweet on her tongue.

"Sorry, you must be Emma," said Ben as he moved around Elliott. Before Emma could stop him, Ben gave her a huge hug. It was Elliott's turn to stifle a laugh as Ben released Emma and said, "It's great to meet you, man."

"Likewise, *man*," Emma responded. Ben studied her eyes meticulously, his scrutiny causing her to slide between the barstool and the bar to escape his reach.

"Your eyes are remarkable, like, mesmerizing," commented Ben. He queried energetically, "Hey, why don't we all have a drink together?"

"I'm sure Em's busy," Donna said. She did not mention Elliott and could not even bring herself to glance at him. Elliott grabbed his drink, rotated his barstool around so that he faced Ben and threw an elbow onto the bar.

"Nah, she's got a few minutes, right, Em?" Elliott said with a shit-eating grin. Emma forced a grin of her own as he added, "Let's all have that drink."

"Sure, why not?" answered Emma. Inwardly cringing, she asked with feigned enthusiasm, "Wine for Donna . . . and for you?"

"Gin and tonic," replied Ben.

"You got it," said Emma.

"You guys grab a seat," Elliott said with gesture towards the dining areas. Soaking up the surrealness of the moment, he added, "We'll be right over."

"Righteous. C'mon, hon," said Ben. He respectfully guided Donna into the south dining area.

"What *the hell* are you doing?" muttered Emma without looking at her sibling. She watched the couple select a table and Ben pull out Donna's chair. He waved to them.

"Tyin' up the last loose end, Sis," replied Elliott as he waved back, "just tyin' up the last loose end."

· · · ·

EMMA AND ELLIOTT SPENT an unexpectedly enjoyable hour with Donna and Ben. She was cagey, and asked many questions, but Ben seemed unoffended by and open to her queries. Elliott and Donna spoke little, the former lovers stealing quick glimpses and attempting to read each other's thoughts and emotions.

"Well, I gotta get goin'," Elliott announced. He stood up, as did Ben, and the two men shook hands.

"Great to meet you, man," gushed Ben.

"You, too, Ben," Elliott replied. He gazed upon Donna, nodded to Ben and said pointedly, "Keep this one."

"I plan to," said Donna, a sudden look of veiled vexation on her face.

"I'll walk you out," Emma said as she interrupted their verbal fencing. Once out of Ben's view, she shoved Elliott forward and he stumbled ahead.

"He's an o-kay guy," said Ben in an understatement of his opinion of Elliott.

"He actually seemed happy today," Donna commented thoughtfully.

"Yeah, he's feelin' good right now, on the surface," replied Ben. He grasped his chin and said with a thoughtful expression, "You're right, though. He's depressed. Deep down. Puttin' up a good front but a lotta inner turmoil."

"Do you ever stop being a psychologist?" Donna asked. Ben's diagnosis chilled Donna and she felt conflicted. She loved Elliott, but he was the past, and she saw Ben as the promising future.

"Not really," replied Ben with a chuckle.

Emma and Elliott, meanwhile, exited Johnny Dubs and stepped into the evening air. The siblings passed a motorcycle with two helmets on the way to Elliott's car.

"Can you believe he got her on a motorcycle?" Elliott inquired.

"I'm having trouble believing everything about him," replied Emma bitterly.

"Admit it," Elliott urged her. He pulled his keys from the pocket of his jeans and said, "It might be early but it looks like she found herself a pretty good guy."

"I'm not admitting anything," countered Emma. The traffic light at the Mortenview-Goddard intersection clicked green and, watching the waiting vehicles accelerate away, she grumbled, "I don't like this, Elliott."

"Don't like what?" Elliott asked. He opened his unlocked car door and quickly attempted to slither inside. Emma grabbed his arm to stop him.

"This 'new you' you're throwing out there," replied Emma. She paused to allow a group of patrons to pass and, with the vicinity becoming quiet, she released her grip and said, "Declaring everything's okay. Closing every door. Giving up on Donna so easily."

"All three of 'em have great guys," Elliott reasoned, "guys who're good for 'em. *They* closed the doors."

"*But who do you have?*" inquired Emma emphatically. Elliott's countenance became pensive and wistful, his expression chilling Emma to her core. He recovered, however, and a look of content arose on his face.

"No one," Elliott answered stoically. He took a deep breath and then released it, stating, "But maybe it's time I was all right with that. Maybe it's time I got back to a simple, unattached life."

Elliott reached out and squeezed his sister's arm. Quelling the waterworks but unsure if she could contain them much longer, she yanked her arm from his grasp.

"Love you," blurted Emma as she fled into the club. Elliott's eyes followed her to the door before he lifted them to the setting sun.

"Love you, too, maniac," Elliott said with a sigh. He dropped into the car, closed its door and set his sights for home.

Illuminated by numerous strings of multicolored party lights, Toni led Bobby into a large, crowded backyard on the west side of Taylor. The couple searched for Joan Swartz, Toni's nursing coworker who hosted the boisterous house party. The weather proved typical for a Southeastern Michigan night in the middle of August; temperatures were in the low seventies and the humidity was high.

"Oh, here we go," said Toni as she pulled two cans of Bud Light from a metal wash tub crammed full of ice and various other beers. It had been a long, trying week at the hospital and, as she held out a can to Bobby, she gushed with a grin, "Time to blow off some steam."

"We coulda done that at my place," Bobby responded with a suggestive expression. Toni touched the ice cold can to Bobby's face which caused him to jerk away from it and exclaim, "Hey!"

"Just helping you cool down," said Toni. Bobby took the beer and cracked it open.

"Hey, Ton-nae!" Joan greeted Toni excitedly as she embraced her, the exuberant hug knocking Toni back a step. Joan pulled away from her friend and examined her, saying, "God, you are so gorgeous."

"Hi, Joanie," replied Toni as she blushed. She wore an acid-washed jean skirt cut just above the knee, a white collared shirt and a wide, powder blue belt. Its color matched that of her eyeshadow.

"Here's to Saturday night," Joan announced with a raised bottle of beer. A round of cheers rippled throughout the backyard. Solidly built with short, black hair, Joan wore jeans and a tank top. Turning her attention to Bobby, she released Toni and pointedly asked, "Well hello there, Bobby. You propose yet?"

"*Jooooan*," whined Toni with a wince.

"Back off, ya' lush," said Bobby in feigned jest. Though Joan's sudden embrace masked the trace of hostility in his tone, Toni detected it. A squeal arose from the crowd and a sobbing woman rushed past them and into the house. Some partygoers noticed while others continued their reveling.

"Aw, geez," said Joan in disappointment.

"What's wrong with Natalie?" Toni asked.

"Her fiancée called things off last week," said Joan with a look of pity. A disinterested Bobby took several gulps of his beer.

"*Nooo*!" Toni protested. She looked to the house and then back to Joan, adding, "I didn't know that."

"Yeah," said Joan. Sticking her left hand in her back pocket, she emptied her beer and then explained, "She was tryin' to put on a brave face by coming tonight but I guess she's just not ready. She's really takin' it rough."

"Of course she is," Toni said with deep sympathy for Natalie. She handed Bobby her beer and said, "I'd better go check on her."

Bobby did not accept the can and rolled his eyes. Joan blocked Toni's advance towards the house.

"No, you two enjoy the party," insisted Joan. She pushed Toni's beer back towards her and said, "I'll go console our girl. Hopefully I can get her back out here."

Toni watched Joan disappear into the house with worry on her face. She opened her beer and took a sip.

"That's so sad," Toni said as her gaze lingered on the patio door.

"Hey, a ring's no guarantee," remarked Bobby blithely. Toni's eyes flashed to him.

"What's that mean?" a surprised Toni asked.

"You know it what means. Even if she gets engaged, there's just as good a' chance they get divorced as they won't," commented Bobby. He took a drink and expounded, "They only have a fifty-fifty shot of making it work, Toni. Hell, we only have a fifty-fifty shot."

"*Bobby*," Toni scolded him. Astonished by Bobby's attack on marriage, her cheeks flushed and she felt panicky; in fact, only their presence in public prevented a stronger reaction. She caressed his cheek and inquired concernedly, "Where's this coming from?"

"Sorry, just forget I said anything," relented Bobby. Toni looked around her and, locating a quiet, darkened corner of the yard, pulled Bobby towards it. He reluctantly followed her, saying, "Toni, seriously. It's not a big deal."

Toni stopped next to the privacy fence when they reached the corner. She turned to face him.

"Do you really feel that way?" Toni inquired in a hushed tone.

"'Course not," Bobby answered. Taking offense at Toni's insinuation, he added, "Don't get carried away with it."

"Promise?" Toni asked on the heels of his assertion. Bobby conjured a lie but then faltered under the intensity of Toni's gaze and remained mute. She begged him, "Bobby, say something."

"Look, Toni, I love you, I really do," said Bobby earnestly. He tried to wrap an arm around her but she dodged it. He launched into an impassioned monologue full of gesticulations, first declaring, "*I'm a child of divorce.* I've seen how bad it can get, and I've taken the flak from two parents who hate each other. You've met most of my friends. *They're divorced.* Their cases lasted for years. They battled over kids and money, and some of 'em are still fightin'. Hell, even my grandparents, at a time when hardly anyone got divorced, *got divorced.*"

"I'm a child of divorce, too. *We've got that in common.* And we're not just any other couple," Toni encouraged Bobby. She wrapped her arms around his neck and implored him, "I love you, so much, and I'm completely and totally faithful to you."

"You're an incredible, wonderful woman," Bobby lauded her, "and you and I . . . *us* . . . well that's incredible and wonderful, too."

Bobby grabbed Toni's forearms, squeezed them affectionately and then lowered them from his shoulders. She watched him as the gears of his mind turned and waited for him to speak. He exhaled.

"I don't wanna lose that," said Bobby. Toni returned her arms to his shoulders and gazed deeply into his eyes.

"I don't either," Toni assured him with a soft grin. Her countenance lit up and she reasoned, "Getting married just cements that *incredible, wonderful* bond between us. Makes it deeper. More meaningful."

"That hasn't been my experience," countered Bobby ominously. He looked away and squirmed as if insects scuttled over his skin. Toni's demeanor darkened.

"Are you saying you don't want to marry me?" Toni inquired, the gravity of her question chilling the air. She trembled and swallowed hard.

"I'm saying I want you, more than anything," asserted Bobby. Taking her by the waist with his strong hands, he continued, "Joan was right. You're gorgeous . . . and smart and caring and so many other things. Who *wouldn't* want you?"

"That's not what I asked," Toni replied, her expression one of worry. Bobby searched for the right words but, finding none, he said nothing. His momentary paralysis allowed Toni to slither out of his grasp.

"I'm gonna take a walk," Toni blurted. She swiftly scurried away from Bobby and maneuvered through the partygoers. Passing a table, she set down her beer and then broke into a jog.

"Damn it," grumbled Bobby. Shaking free of his inertia, he followed Toni but soon lost her as the festivities closed around him.

• • • •

TONI LET HER BLUE PUMPS hang from her hand while walking barefoot down the sidewalk. She sought only to put distance between herself and Bobby and contemplate his unforeseen revelations. Headlights arose behind Toni and she recognized the hum of his beloved 1985 Fiero's engine.

"Great," Toni muttered. She added in a defeated voice, "Will this week ever end?"

Bobby rolled up to Toni. She increased her pace to escape him but he easily matched it.

"Toni, get in the car," pleaded Bobby. He leaned towards the open passenger side window and said, "Let's just forget all about the marriage thing for now and go back to the party."

Toni cringed at Bobby's phrasing. She stopped and hugged herself before walking down a driveway. Meeting the red Fiero at its end, Toni composed herself and spoke calmly.

"Everything's okay, Bobby, and we'll be fine," Toni assured him though the flames of doubt burned with her. She straightened her body and explained, "But this is something we need to work out, and I need time to sort out how I feel about it. Why don't you go on home, get a good night's sleep and I'll call you tomorrow? I can get someone to give me a ride."

"You're blowing this way out of proportion," stated Bobby with frustration in his voice. Its presence tweaked Toni's emotions and her composed façade cracked.

"*Go home*, Bobby," Toni demanded while on the verge of tears. She resumed walking and Bobby resumed following her. He swerved to avoid several vehicles parked in the street that escaped his notice.

"Get in the car, Toni," commanded Bobby as his patience frayed. When Toni failed to obey, he asked in annoyance, "How're you gonna get home if I don't take you?"

"I don't know," Toni replied sharply, "but I figure I got a fifty-fifty shot."

"I mean it, Toni, get in the car," shouted Bobby. She ignored his demands, reversed course and walked away from him. Seeing red, he gunned the engine, squealed his tires and roared away. Toni stopped, closed her eyes and clenched her teeth but her anger soon vanished and her tears fell.

"What just happened?" sighed Toni. She began crying as her surroundings blurred and she wandered aimlessly through the neighborhood. Toni stopped at a three-way intersection. Exhaustion crept over her eyelids and her legs felt heavier with every step she took.

"Wait, where am I?" Toni asked aloud. She knew she needed to turn left and take Sharon Street back to Joan's house. Looking forward, however, she felt an unexplainable urge to continue on Kinyon Street. It proceeded straight for a short distance before turning left and disappearing behind several houses. She surveyed her surroundings while the sounds of the party drifted into her ears, saying, "I should just go back."

A sudden realization struck Toni. She bit her lip, paused and shifted her focus between the unknown ahead and the known behind. Deciding on the unknown, she hurried forward into the night.

• • • •

ELLIOTT DOZED ON HIS living room couch with the Tonight Show on the television. He drifted into sleep after watching a rerun of his new favorite show, the police drama *Hunter*, and felt no inclination to climb the stairs and sleep in his bed. The end table lamp, guarded by four empty beer bottles, provided a small halo of light.

A knock at Elliott's front door roused him from his slumber. He sat straight up, the sudden ascent and the beer making him lightheaded.

"What the hell?" Elliott griped. Visitors were a rarity even when he was engaged with one of his flings. Setting his feet on the floor and still not fully awake, Elliott unsteadily walked to the door and peeked through the peep hole. He jumped away from it when he saw Toni's comely face staring back at him. Slapping his cheek, he absorbed the sting and then uttered, "Not a dream."

Elliott slowly unlocked the door and turned the knob. Pulling the door open gradually, he took a deep breath and prepared to face her.

"Hi, Elliott," said Toni with a nervous grin.

"So much for the country girl look," Elliott said while scanning her from head to toe. His appreciation of her body abruptly ended when he noticed she had been crying. He opened the door wider and asked her, "You all right?"

Toni bit the inside of her mouth and then slowly released her jaw. Jerking her body as if to flee, she subsequently paused and then squeezed her eyes closed. Toni forced herself to speak.

"Can I come in?" asked Toni. Elliott experienced an immediate adrenaline rush and his spine crackled with electric sensation.

"Yeah, sure, come on in," Elliott answered as calmly as he could. Toni opened her eyes and he motioned for her to enter. She hesitated again.

"If I come in, you *have to* promise me something," insisted Toni. Her disquiet was palpable.

"Uh, okay," Elliott agreed with an eager nod.

"If I walk through this door, you can't hit on me or try to kiss me or anything like that," said Toni. A confused look from Elliott prompted her to add, "I'm *not* here to rush into your arms or start anything romantic. I just really need to talk to someone and, I don't know why, but I think it needs to be you."

Elliott pondered Toni's request and neatly placed the puzzle piece into his new life plan. His apprehension evaporated and he set his hand on the back of the recliner to the left of the door.

"You sit here," Elliott said. He walked to the couch and dropped onto it.

"And I'll stay right here," Elliott continued. He shrugged with a half-smile and said, "Just two friends talking at a respectable distance."

"Sounds good," said Toni guiltily. She cautiously entered Elliott's apartment and closed the door without looking at him. Moving around the recliner, Toni hugged it tightly to avoid coming too near him and sat down. She pressed her legs together and held her shoes in her lap.

"How'd you find this place?" Elliott queried. He stretched and yawned before rubbing the sleep from his eyes.

"You told me where you live, remember?" Toni replied. She fiddled with her shoes and added, "And your car kinda stands out."

"Oh, yeah," Elliott said. Toni noticed the empty bottles on the end table. Elliott registered the look and asked, "Want a beer?"

"No, thanks," declined Toni. The pair remained quiet for thirty seconds before she suggested sheepishly, "Maybe a glass of water."

"Comin' up," Elliott replied. Tasting the dryness of his mouth, he said, "I think I'll make it two."

Elliott eagerly fled the awkwardness of the moment. Toni shifted uneasily in the recliner but, as she did, she surrendered to its comfort. The exhaustion of her week settled into her bones and her heavy eyelids flickered. While Elliott intentionally dawdled in preparing two glasses of ice water, Toni relaxed her body and closed her eyes. She breathed heavily by the time Elliott returned.

"Ya' still with me there, Toni?" Elliott asked. Toni responded with an abrupt snore. Looking at the two glasses of ice water, Elliott said casually, "Good talk."

• • • •

TONI STARTED OUT OF deep sleep. Her gaze darted around the darkened, unfamiliar bedroom.

"Oh, please, no," gushed Toni as she noticed the oncoming grayness of dawn through the blinds. Rising into a sitting position, she realized she wore her outfit from the night before. She exhaled in relief, glanced upward and prayed, "Thank you."

Toni crept out of the bed and walked as quietly as she could to the bathroom. The squeaking floor betrayed her movements and she stopped outside the bathroom door.

"He's making breakfast," sighed Toni as the scent of bacon wafted into her nostrils. She heard it sizzling through the bedroom door as her stomach grumbled and she chastised herself, "You're so stupid."

Toni used the bathroom but felt awkward relieving herself in Elliott's apartment. While washing her hands afterwards, she studied herself in the mirror and noticed the sad state of her makeup.

"That should be enough to scare him off," said Toni as she worked in vain to fix her face. She spent several minutes tidying herself up, confidently straightened her body and looked in the mirror. Her courage bled away and she finally uttered, "Maybe I can sneak out before he sees me."

Letting her right hand slide along the railing as she descended the stairs, Toni took each step slowly to delay seeing Elliott. Reaching the landing, she halted her approach though Elliott's breakfast preparations prevented him from noticing her. She looked to the door longingly; however, she thought better of escape and meandered into the living room.

"Damn it," Elliott griped when the bacon grease popped and some tiny splatters hit his hand. He saw Toni watching him.

"Well, good morning, sleeping beauty," Elliott said flippantly. He regretted his choice of words and both he and Toni averted their gazes. Elliott swiftly filled a mug of coffee for her and said, "Breakfast's almost ready."

"I am *so* sorry," apologized Toni profusely.

"Cream and/or sugar?" Elliott queried while keeping his focus on the mug.

"Black's fine," answered an unsettled Toni. Elliott handed her the mug and their hands touched. She accepted it but pulled away too quickly and some of the coffee spilled on the floor. She griped, "Oh, shit. I'm sorry."

"You're fine, you're fine," Elliott assured her while coming to her rescue with paper towels. He took the mug from her, set it on the counter and then guided her to the dining room table. He pulled the chair out for her and coaxed her into it, saying, "I got it."

"You should've woken me up and I would've went home," said Toni apologetically. Elliott dried her cup with the paper towel and then set it in front of her.

"You were *out*, and it looked like you needed the sleep," Elliott explained as he wiped the coffee from the floor. He efficiently tossed the paper towel into the garbage, returned to the bacon and flipped it, explaining, "So I just put you in my bed and I slept on the couch."

"Oh, geez, I'm sorry," said a mortified Toni. Elliott grabbed the coffee pot, walked to her and refilled her mug as she continued, "You should've put *me* on the couch."

Toni shook her head and rolled her eyes. Placing her elbows on the table, she leaned forward and hid her face in her hands.

"Or just left me in the chair," added Toni feebly. Returning to the kitchen, Elliott lifted a pancake from the pan and flipped it over.

"I sleep on the couch a lot so no worries," Elliott advised while repositioning the strips of bacon. He prepared Toni's plate and inquired, "How did ya' sleep, by the way? You didn't look comfortable in that belt but I thought taking it off woulda' crossed the creepy line."

"It would've been okay," said Toni. Shivering at the implications of her comment, she watched Elliott slap the finished pancake on top of another one and said, "I have a feeling you would've been a gentleman about it."

Elliott used the spatula to transfer the bacon from the pan to a plate covered in paper towels. He carried it into the small dining room and set it on the table.

"Hey, I carried you upstairs, threw a blanket over you and didn't see you again until now," Elliott said though he was unable to look at Toni. She accepted his chivalrous explanation and a realization struck her: she trusted Elliott.

"I actually slept pretty well," said Toni. Elliott returned to the kitchen, grabbed the plate of pancakes and collected everything Toni would need: silverware, syrup, butter and several sheets of paper towel.

"Yeah, you were dead to the world," Elliott said as he arrived at the table. He quickly assembled everything on it and, tossing down the paper towel, added, "Sorry, ya' gotta use bachelor napkins."

"This is great, thank you so much," gushed Toni as she stole a piece of bacon. Elliott returned to the kitchen to work on his own breakfast.

"Don't wait for me," Elliott urged Toni, "go ahead and dig in."

Toni normally would have insisted on waiting for her host but, as her stomach voiced its displeasure, she complied with Elliott's wishes. She looked at the clock which read 6:33 am.

"You're up pretty early," commented Toni between bites of her pancakes.

"I'm taking Emma's girls to Cedar Point today," Elliott said. He muttered with discontent, "On a Sunday. In August."

"Sounds like fun," responded Toni, the mention of Cedar Point improving her mood. Her countenance gleamed as she reminisced and expounded, "I have some incredible memories of that place. My friends and I hit it a lot in high school and even into college. Those were some really awesome times."

"You should come with us," Elliott suggested while continuing to cook his pancakes.

"Oh, no," replied Toni though the invitation intrigued her. She washed down some bacon with coffee before saying, "I wouldn't want to impose on your special day with your nieces."

"Even numbers are better for the rides, and two sets of eyes never hurt with those two maniacs. They're like squirrels on coke," Elliott countered. Toni chuckled and nearly choked on her breakfast. Cognizant that he played with fire, Elliott nonetheless urged, "Come with us."

"I don't think that'd be appropriate," said Toni. She uneasily added, "Bobby and I, well-."

"It ain't gonna be like a date, sweetheart," Elliott interrupted crassly. His bluntness silenced Toni. Softening his tone, he said, "Not with Lanie and Tess' draggin' us all over the place."

Toni resumed her breakfast while pondering the invitation. Elliott flipped a pancake.

"It'll be good for you to get out, have some fun. Ya' know, forget about everything else for a while," Elliott reasoned. Tossing the pancake onto his plate, he encouraged her, "*Come with us.*"

Elliott waited with bated breath for her response. Toni started to decline again but, with a sudden reversal of intention, stopped herself.

"Ya' know what?" asked Toni. Elliott felt his spine tingle again when she answered her own question: "Sure. I'd love to go."

"Good," Elliott remarked while struggling to downplay his elation. His face became grim and, pouring pancake mix into the skillet, he advised her, "Now, finish up your breakfast. There are two little monsters who are irritating the hell outta their mother, and we need to go rescue them."

"Rescue *them*?" asked Toni in puzzlement.

"If they push her too much when she's on a few hours' sleep, she'll kill 'em," Elliott said facetiously.

Toni giggled. Elliott felt the shimmering of her eyes and the warmth of her smile like a punch in the heart.

• • • •

TONI JUMPED WHEN THE heavy door of Elliott's LTD clicked shut and suddenly felt trapped. His alleged platonic intentions notwithstanding, her presence in the vehicle of another man prickled her conscience. She knew Bobby would be furiously jealous if he learned of her Cedar Point trip.

"You don't need his permission," said Toni to herself. She shifted in her seat and watched Elliott approach, thinking, "And you're not doing anything wrong."

"All right, let's get this show on the road," Elliott announced as he dropped into his seat and closed the driver-side door. He glanced at Toni with a faint smile which she returned, explaining, "We'll hit your house real quick so you can get cleaned up, go get the munchkins and then we'll be on our way to the Point."

The pair remained in uncomfortable silence as Elliott meandered around Continental Circle. He turned right onto Beech Daly and sped north. Toni pinched herself and used the resulting pain to force the words from her mouth.

"Elliott, I owe you an apology," confessed Toni. She turned her head towards him but, unable to withstand his gaze, she looked away.

"For what?" Elliott replied with a quizzical expression. He stopped the car at the Wick Road stop sign and waited for her answer. A car to his left honked for him to proceed but he dismissed the gesture with a wave.

"It wasn't fair for me to do this to you," answered Toni as she watched the vehicle pass them. Uncertain of her intentions, Elliott retuned his attention to the road and accelerated as she expounded, "I knew you had feelings for me, I knew you wouldn't turn me away, and I knew this would give you false hope. But I still did it. And, and . . . I think maybe I should skip Cedar Point. Oh, turn right there. On Wohlfeil."

Elliott flipped on his blinker and turned right. He stole several glimpses of Toni and adoringly admired her faithfulness. She rolled down the passenger window and inhaled the warm morning air.

"As far as I'm concerned, you and Bobby are together and that's the end of it," Elliott said as his field of vision swiveled between Toni and the road. Resting his forearm on the steering wheel and gesturing with the other, he stated firmly, "I'm just a friend taking you for some much-needed R&R and that's all I am. *A friend.*"

"Promise?" asked Toni with a glance and a tilt of her head. Elliott slowed as he neared Gulley Street. Toni directed him, "Left here and then a quick right on Chernick."

"Actually, no," Elliott replied with a serious mien, his unexpected response causing Toni to catch her breath. Elliott made the turns in quick succession before continuing, "When Lanie and Tessa are involved, there is no rest or relaxation."

Toni exhaled in relief. She wrinkled her nose, smiled and playfully smacked Elliott's shoulder.

"You're a mean uncle," ribbed Toni, Elliott's jest and the familiarity of her own neighborhood lessening her apprehension. His disquiet increased, however, as his role in Toni's life came into focus. Steeling his will, he forced himself to comfort her.

"You and Bobby'll work it out," insisted Elliott. His assertion tasted bitter on his tongue.

"Not if he won't marry me," argued Toni as the LTD slowly rolled down the street. She pointed at a driveway and said, "Right there. It's the driveway before the big tree."

"He'll come around," Elliott said matter-of-factly while pulling into Toni's driveway. He shifted the LTD into "Park" and reasoned, "Being without you'll drive him crazy and he'll be back."

Toni watched Elliott in wonder. The engine idled.

"I know I would," Elliott thought despite wanting to utter the words aloud.

"Maybe," replied Toni forlornly. She bowed her head and folded her hands in her lap.

"And you watch," Elliott continued to bolster her spirits, "he'll have a ring when he does. It just might take him a little while. You know us guys is dumb."

Toni studied Elliott with a dubious grin gradually forming on her face. She narrowed her eyes.

"You're either accepting this really well," stated a suspicious Toni, "or you're going with your original plan and I'm falling right into the trap."

Elliott laughed and ran his tongue along the bottoms of his upper teeth. He realized that, beyond any romantic feelings for Toni, he truly enjoyed her company.

"But you'll never know which one until it's too late," Elliott said. He paused to let Toni's mirth fade and, after briefly enjoying the confusion on her face, laughed again, saying, "Kidding. I'm kidding. Geez, Toni."

Thoroughly amused by his trick, Elliott continued to laugh. Toni's irritation melted into a begrudging smile.

"What's Em gonna think when I show up with you?" inquired Toni astutely as she attempted to put Elliott on his heels. The attempt failed.

"That sister of mine doesn't like most of what I do," Elliott said while rolling down his window, "so this isn't any different. But don't worry. She won't take it out on *you*. So, are you in or are you in?"

"I'm in," relented Toni with affirmative nods.

"Excellent," Elliott said. He studied Toni's small, quaint house, a one-story brick ranch, and queried, "So this is home, huh?"

"Yeah, it's my little breadbox," answered Toni with a disappointed mien. She continued absent-mindedly before trailing off, "But I can't wait for Bobby and I to, well, I don't know now, I guess . . . ."

"You can't wait for you and Bobby to get a house together, one you can really call home," Elliott urged Toni firmly. His heart lurched and bled but, for her sake, he endured it.

"Yeah," concurred Toni. She added meekly, "Thanks."

"Go get ready and let's get rollin'," Elliott instructed her.

"Yes, sir," responded Toni. Climbing out of the car, she hurried up the driveway, opened the gate and entered the house via the side door.

"What have I gotten myself into?" Elliott asked aloud.

· · · ·

"HERE WE ARE," ELLIOTT announced as the LTD arrived in front of Emma's house. Lanie and Tessa sat on the front porch and charged the car when it stopped. They both grasped the edge of the car door at the open passenger window and took great interest in Toni.

"Who're you?" asked Lanie with a sour expression. Toni stifled a chuckle.

"I'm your uncle's friend, Toni," Toni said while extending her hand from the window. A suspicious Lanie took it reluctantly as Toni asked, "And, let me guess. You're Lanie, right?"

"Toni's a boy's name," objected Lanie. Tessa nudged Lanie out of the way and the sisters tussled with each other.

"It can be a girl's name, too," Tessa interjected. She held out a hand to Toni and asked, "Do you know who I am?"

"I sure do," replied Toni sweetly. She shook Tessa's hand and said, "You're Tessa."

"You're really pretty," Tessa said matter-of-factly. Toni melted at the innocent compliment.

"Mommy's prettier," Lanie said in annoyance.

"You're right, Lanie, she is," agreed Toni. A puzzled Tessa tilted her head.

"You know our Mommy?" Tessa asked.

"I do," replied Toni.

"Damn, you guys, were you snortin' sugar this morning?" Elliott asked, his tolerance of the girls' antics wearing thin.

"*Elliott*," scolded Toni. She deemed the profanity and the drug reference inappropriate and let him know with a look of disapprobation. It cowed him.

"Let us in!" demanded Lanie as she opened the car door.

"Lanie Michelle Hastings," Emma admonished her daughter from the porch, her voice halting both girls. She dried her hands on a dish towel and threw if over her shoulder. Making her way to the car with the backpacks that the girls left on the porch, she continued, "We talked about that snotty tone. *Be polite, please.*"

Lanie pouted briefly but composed herself. She then offered Toni a polite smile.

"Can I please get in the car, Toni?" inquired Lanie with a sugary voice.

"Toni?" Emma said with surprise. She arrived at the vehicle just as Toni exited it and the girls scrambled inside.

"Hey, Em," said Toni in as pleasant a tone as she could muster.

"Hello," Emma said while stifling her discontent. She subtly bristled and stated, "I didn't realize you and Elliott were friends."

Elliott disembarked from the LTD and slammed the door to interrupt Emma's assault. He quickly circumvented the car and came to Toni's rescue.

"We are," said Elliott firmly, "and I invited her to come today."

"Great," Emma lied convincingly. She handed the backpacks to Toni and said, "Well, they're all yours. Enjoy."

"Let's go, Uncle Elliott!" shouted Tessa.

"Elliott, a moment," Emma said in a polite tone. An embarrassed Toni bowed her head and quickly glanced at Elliott.

"We're kinda in a hurry," grumbled Elliott in response.

"Just for a sec," Emma pleaded. She brushed past Toni, leaned into the car and kissed each daughter on the forehead, saying, "You two behave for Uncle Elliott, you hear me? Love you both."

"It's fine," Elliott mouthed to Toni with a raised palm. She offered him a dubious look.

"Good luck," Emma said to Toni. She and Elliott proceeded to the porch while Toni handed the girls their backpacks and climbed into the car.

"What's *she* doing with you?" Emma demanded in a hushed tone when they arrived at the porch.

"We're just friends, Em," replied an irked Elliott.

"Bullshit," Emma snapped. She watched Toni checking seatbelts before focusing on Elliott and chastising him, "She's got a serious boyfriend, Elliott, and, from what she's told me, the ring could come any time now. I can see you doing something this stupid but I didn't think she was the type."

"*She's not*," snarled Elliott in defense of Toni. His biting response blunted Emma's anger and he rebuffed her, "She's had a rough week and she needs some fun. It's all above board."

"I am *not* letting you use your nieces to seduce her," Emma declared.

"In what world are your little monsters good for that?" inquired an exasperated Elliott with a nod to the car. He took a deep breath, relaxed and smiled, saying smugly, "Besides, you'd be in a world of shit if you pulled the rug out from underneath them at the last minute. And whatever you had planned for today, you can forget that."

Emma sneered but knew Elliott was right. Lanie's beeping of the car horn twice only served to underscore his point. Deciding to cut his sister a break, he relented.

"Besides, four's better for Cedar Point. One adult and one set a' eyes for each kid. It's much safer that way," reasoned Elliott with a goofy grin. Emma shook her head at her brother's cheek as he added, "And you know Toni's good people."

"Just be careful, Elliott," she warned, her own ire evaporating.

"She's taken, I know it and I accept it," said Elliott with the utmost seriousness.

"All right," Emma replied as she raised the white flag. The siblings hugged and she implored him, "Take care of my babies."

"I always do," said Elliott. He hopped off the porch and strode to the LTD. Climbing inside, he winced as the girls cheered, "Cedar Point!"

"Everything good?" Toni asked.

"She didn't hit me, so I'd say yes, everything's good," replied Elliott thoughtfully. The pair shared a knowing grin and Elliott started the car. Pulling away from the curb, he announced like a tour guide, "Next stop, Cedar Point."

Elliott's nieces cheered again and Toni joined them in their excitement. Emma watched the car until it disappeared down the street. She sighed and folded her arms.

"Oh, big brother, why is love always so complicated for you?" Emma asked aloud.

"I wanna go on the *big* swings, Uncle Elliott!" Tessa yelled as she yanked on Elliott's arm and pointed at the Wave Swinger.

"All right, just hang on," replied Elliott as he studied the park map. The first several hours at Cedar Point proved to be whirlwind as the lines were surprisingly short and Elliott's nieces possessed boundless energy. They flitted from ride to ride and worked their way into Frontier Town as lunchtime arrived.

"Wave Swinger's boring," griped Lanie. She stubbornly set her feet and declared, "I'm hungry. I wanna eat now."

"You little monsters are drivin' me crazy," Elliott complained.

"No! Wave swinger!" Tessa yelled. She broke into a sprint.

"Tessa, wait up!" Elliott shouted. Toni sprung into action.

"Race ya' to the line," Toni challenged Lanie with a glance. The ten-year-old's eyes grew wide and, possessing her mother's competitiveness, she lurched forward into a run. Toni, who easily could have overtaken Lanie with her long strides, loped behind her as they pursued Tessa.

"Isn't walking exercise enough?" queried Elliott as he jogged behind them and then plopped down on a bench near the Wave Swinger. He marveled at Toni as she patiently worked her magic.

"I still don't wanna ride this," said Lanie in a snarky tone.

"I don't think you girls are old enough to ride it by yourselves, anyway," ventured Toni.

"*Yes, we are!*" insisted the sisters in unison. An insulted Lanie added, "We're not babies."

Elliott rolled his eyes and exhaled as he heard Emma in Lanie's voice. Toni pretended to be skeptical but soon relented.

"I think we can let 'em, huh, Uncle Elliott?" queried Toni as she outmaneuvered the grade-schoolers.

"I don't know," Elliott answered as he played along. He said with feigned uncertainty, "All right, I guess. Just don't tell your mother."

"And then can we eat when you're done. Maybe get a pizza?" inquired Toni. She placed a hand on her stomach and said, "I'm starving, too."

"Yes! Pizza!" Tessa shouted enthusiastically.

"I'm starting to like you," stated Lanie with a serious mien. Elliott smirked and shook his head while Toni stifled a laugh. Grabbing Tessa's hand, Lanie instructed her younger sister, "Let's go, Tess'. *I* get the outside swing."

Toni walked backward for several steps before turning around and approaching Elliott. She stopped in front of him with her hands on her hips.

"I wish I had a sister," said Toni. She detected the veiled amusement on Elliott's face and asked, "Why're you looking at me like that?"

"You don't wanna know," Elliott said, his smile subtly melting away.

"Tell me," insisted Toni as she examined herself carefully. Elliott observed her and chuckled. Satisfied that there was nothing wrong with her clothing, she inquired emphatically, "What is it, Elliott?"

"I was watching you with the girls," Elliott began with a nod towards his nieces, "and I had one 'a those romantic comedy or sitcom moments. Ya' know, the one where the girl realizes the guy is great with kids and has a bigger heart than she thought."

Toni's cheeks reddened. Elliott spun his index fingers around each other.

"Just in reverse," Elliott said.

"So you didn't think I had a big heart?" asked Toni with an expression of mock offense. She hoped the tone of her question would deter Elliott.

"Anybody who lays eyes on you knows you have a big heart in about half a second," Elliott answered without hesitation. He spread his arms outward and rested them on the back of the bench, adding adoringly, "But that was the first time I saw the mom in you."

Toni struggled with her feelings. She wanted to be honest and expressive with Elliott – he naturally drew those qualities from her – but she belonged to someone else and needed to keep him in his place.

"We shouldn't be talking about this," advised Toni. She turned her head, watched Lanie and Tessa take their seats on the Wave Swinger and stated firmly, "Not when you have that look."

"You wanna have kids, right?" Elliott inquired. Toni hesitated to answer but Elliott raised his eyebrows in a sign of waiting. She begrudgingly took the bait.

"Well, yeah, of course I do," replied Toni. She joined him on the bench, albeit at the far end, and asked, "But what does that hafta do with this?"

"You've got nothin' to worry about, lady, because I'm too old to start a family," Elliott answered with conviction, "so I couldn't be your guy no matter how I look at you. So there's no harm in talkin' about it."

"Guys much older than you become fathers," scoffed Toni, her look of disbelief taking Elliott aback. He swiftly disentangled himself from her logic.

"If I met someone *today*," began Elliott with a pointed look at Toni, "and I rang the baby bell *tonight* . . . ."

Toni grimaced.

" . . . . that kid'd be born when I'm *thirty-eight* and would graduate high school when I'm *fifty-six*," Elliott continued.

"That's not too old to have an eighteen-year-old," Toni admonished Elliott.

"Hey, Em and I've gone 'round and 'round on this lately," replied Elliott. He folded his arms and said, "I've thought it through and being a daddy ain't in the cards."

"You're being ridiculous," Toni asserted with a muted grin on her face and a light in her eyes. She added, "*Grandpa*."

Tessa yelled for Toni so she stood up, took several steps towards the Wave Swinger and returned the eight-year-old's wave on the next pass. When she again faced Elliott, he was standing within her personal space, his unforeseen presence causing her to jump.

"*Elliott*!" Toni exclaimed.

"When I stand this close to you, do you feel anything, anything different than when Bobby is in the exact same spot, looking at you just like I am right now?" Elliott asked her in earnest. Toni's heart fluttered and she felt anxious but, recovering quickly and conjuring an image of Bobby in her mind, she counterattacked.

"Definitely," Toni said with a seductive look. She held it for ten seconds before banishing it and expounding, "I feel like I'm next to a man who'll be a great friend to me, and a great friend to the man I love, and act like a gentleman whenever he's with me, just like he has so far."

Speechless, Elliott simply gawked at Toni. Her words cut him deeply but, impressed by her wit and staunch dedication to her man, he absorbed the pain and threw up his hands.

"My thoughts exactly," announced Elliott with a smirk.

• • • •

NIGHT SETTLED OVER Cedar Point and the foursome traveled towards the exit tucked inside a Sky Ride gondola. Tessa, whose attachment to Toni burgeoned throughout the day, laid her head in Toni's lap and slept.

"She's out," said Elliott. He watched Toni with adoration – a practice he knew was becoming a dangerous habit – as she cuddled Tessa and brushed strands of hair from her face.

Lanie, meanwhile, peered over the side of the gondola and chattered about everything she saw. Elliott gave her a dubious look as her energy showed no sign of waning.

"You are definitely your mother's daughter," Elliott told his niece. She glanced back at him with a befuddled expression.

"Who else's daughter would I be?" Lanie asked precociously before turning her attention back to the park below. Toni squelched a chortle, the movement causing Tessa to stir.

"Damn, she's beautiful," Elliott thought, the word seeming woefully inadequate. He observed her against the backdrop of the night sky and a multitude of colored lights – some flashing at varying speeds, some shining without pause – and, in a moment he would never forget, his deep infatuation morphed into love. She noticed his attention but, instead of becoming uncomfortable with it, she offered him a muted, innocuous smile.

"Another place, another time, Elliott," thought Toni.

Debarking from the Sky Ride, they soon passed through the front gates with a sea of other patrons. Elliott carried a sleeping Tessa to the car while Lanie, much to his surprise, walked hand-in-hand with Toni and prattled on about the events of the day.

"You should come swimming at our house," Lanie said while she waited for Elliott to gently put Tessa in the back seat and fasten her safety belt. She bragged, "We have an *inground* pool *and* a hot tub."

"Look out Kennedys," said Elliott as he emerged from the car. He threw a thumb over his shoulder and said, "You're next, kid."

"You just can't come over when Donna is there," Lanie advised nonchalantly while ignoring Elliott's direction. He grimaced. Pulling Toni down to her level, she whispered in her ear, "Mommy says she still likes Uncle Elliott."

Toni squatted down. Looking Lanie in the eyes, she grasped both of her hands and squeezed them.

"Your Uncle Elliott and I are just friends," Toni assured her, "but I promise I won't come over when Donna's there."

Elliott watched his niece and could see her working out his relationship with Toni in her head. Her epiphany arose so suddenly that he could not intervene.

"Don't say it, kid," thought Elliott with look of warning. Lanie again ignored him and leaned into Toni.

"I think Uncle Elliott likes *you*," Lanie whispered into Toni's ear. She then scurried into the car and, desperate to avoid the moment, Elliott ensured she was properly buckled amid her complaints. Lanie griped, "Stop it. I can do it myself."

Equally eager to escape, Toni hurried around the car and climbed inside. She slid into her seat, buckled her seat belt and looked forward. Pretending to people watch, she gazed through the windshield with her hands in her lap when Elliott settled into his seat.

"Ready?" asked Elliott.

"Ready," Toni replied.

Lanie's talking became infrequent until it altogether ceased. Elliott pretended to focus on the mass of cars swarming around him while keeping Toni in his peripheral vision. She drifted mentally and quietly reflected on the day. He stole a quick glimpse of her.

"It's gonna be over too soon," Elliott said to himself.

• • • •

THE TRAFFIC THINNED as Elliott drove west and the homeward journey proved to be quiet and uneventful. The silence wore on both Elliott and Toni but she spoke first.

"You're pretty good with them," Toni commented. Elliott glanced at her doubtfully and she added with a grin, "In your own quirky way."

Elliott checked the backseat via the rearview mirror. Lanie joined Tessa in a deep slumber.

"My own quirky way, huh?" replied Elliott. Toni studied him as he returned his eyes to the road and said, "Yeah, I guess I love the little buggers or somethin'."

"I wanna ask you a question," Toni said with a gravity that caused Elliott's heart to plummet into his stomach. Realizing her overdramatization of the moment, she shook her head and insisted, "But don't feel like you have to answer."

Elliott glanced at Toni and she at him. Her sheepish expression caused him to chuckle.

"Uh-oh," replied Elliott in jest.

"It's not like that," Toni scolded him playfully.

"Okay, then let's hear it," Elliott said.

"If you're so convinced you're too old to have kids," began Toni with a thoughtful expression, "then what would you've done if you and Nora ended up together? I mean, she's really young and probably wants a family, or will want one."

Elliott deflated. The specter of Nora was an unwelcome one especially when it emerged from Toni's lips.

"We never made it that far. Not even close," Elliott responded after letting Toni's query hang in the air for ten seconds. She felt a twinge of jealousy and, despite warning herself against it, she asked the question perched on her tongue.

"How far did you get?" inquired Toni with bubbling curiosity.

"Wow, are you really asking me that?" queried a vexed Elliott.

"I'm not talking about . . . ," Toni said before trailing off. She peeked into the back seat and, satisfied that Lanie and Tessa were asleep, continued quietly, "About *sex*."

"Oh," said Elliott, his annoyance defused. He thought about Nora and, despite his discomfort with the subject, explained, "We were never together – Em made damn sure of that – but we did . . . ."

It was Elliott's turn to hesitate. Toni held her breath in anticipation of his revelation.

"We did have this one, really incredible kiss," admitted Elliott. Inadvertently smiling, he drifted back to the moment of the kiss, shifted in his seat and said, "One night at the club, in the parking lot."

"In the parking lot?" asked Toni, her implication being that Elliott and Nora were in his car. He took her meaning and shook his head in the negative.

"No, not like that," Elliott corrected her. He took the steering wheel with both hands and extended his arms to stretch them, saying, "She was taking out the garbage . . . well, she took it out to get away from me because I was comin' on pretty strong that night, and this stray cat jumped outta the dumpster."

Elliott's wistfulness prickled Toni greatly. She nonetheless kept her eyes glued to his face.

"I was at the front door, getting some air, when I heard her scream," Elliott said. He heard the scream in his mind, chuckled and continued, "That damn cat scared the hell outta her, and she jumped into my arms and, after I calmed her down, we kinda looked at each other . . . and it just happened."

"That's sweet," Toni remarked in admiration. She said with a small measure of envy, "You rescuing her like that. That really seems to be your instinct, to protect her. It's romantic."

"It was just a cat," Elliot said dismissively.

"Not to her, not in that moment," Toni said. She pondered a pairing of Elliott and Nora for thirty seconds and then queried, "So why didn't it happen for you two?"

"Em badgered the hell outta her. That's what happened," said Elliott bitterly. Stewing over his sister's constant interference in his love life, he added, "And fixed her up with a guy her own age, some kid from Dave's shop."

Elliott's anger ebbed. He shrugged.

"He seems like an okay guy, I guess, and she swears he's good to her," Elliott explained. He added in defeat, "So I guess it was for the better."

"Do you still have feelings for her?" Toni queried, her voice subtly creaking. Elliott did not answer for over a minute, his failure to speak causing Toni distress.

"I was thinking about this at work the other day," said Elliott slowly after the bizarre pause. He grew fey and expounded, "I think it's possible for you to have feelings – strong feelings even – for a few different people at the same time, but the right moments for each person come and go, and the times frames overlap, but they never directly line up."

Toni felt oddly calmed, almost hypnotized, by Elliott's explanation. She observed him with a blank expression.

"They're like strands blown in the wind, and they flutter all around you, all the possible endings," continued Elliott with his glazed eyes staring forward. He shifted in his seat again and continued, "Some people grab one and hold on for dear life, other people move from strand to strand. Some decide which strands to grab and others, well, they just flail around and grab whatever ones they can."

"I had no idea you were so deep," Toni said, her compliment sounding more like a slight.

"Eh, it's all bullshit. Just stuff that creeps into my head during my boring days at work," muttered Elliott. He sidestepped out of his strange mood, looked to Toni and asked, "So, whatcha gonna do tomorrow?"

"Sleep in, for sure, and then church," Toni replied after her own pause. Cognizant that the window into Elliott's heart had closed, she meandered with him into comfortable small talk for the remainder of their trip home.

. . . .

EMMA AND DONNA SAT on the front porch of the Hastings' house, the friends conversing softly and drinking wine in the dull, yellow glow of the porchlight. The temperature dipped into the high sixties and thick clouds, ushered by a muggy breeze, inched across the sky. Only occasionally did they grant a view of the twinkling stars.

"Are you sure we should do this?" asked Donna guiltily when she noticed Elliott's LTD slowly approaching. She nursed a glass of wine.

"She needs to know he's off limits," Emma sneered.

"But you said she's not interested in him, Em," reasoned Donna. She sipped her wine and said, "She's got an almost fiancée, right?"

"I need to push her away early before anything happens," Emma insisted, "so *please* just play along."

"I'm not going back to Elliott," argued Donna convincingly, "and I'm happy with Ben."

"I'm just keeping your options open," Emma replied. Donna tilted her head dubiously at her best friend's scheming. Failing to relent, Emma turned her attention to Elliott's car and added in annoyance, "*You're welcome.*"

"Damn it, Em," muttered Elliott upon seeing Donna. He pulled the car into the driveway, its redness dulled by the yellowish glow of the nearest streetlight.

"That's Donna, isn't it?" Toni inquired while studying Elliott's ex-girlfriend.

"Yep," replied Elliott as he glanced at her, "that's Donna."

Elliott's headlamps washed over the porch's two occupants before he shut them off and shifted into "Park". He left the engine running.

"I think I'll stay in the car," Toni said uneasily as a smug Emma smiled at her and waved. She forced a weak grin of her own and returned it. Surprising them both, Elliott reengaged the headlights and temporarily blinded Emma and Donna.

"Elliott!" Emma admonished him as Donna shielded her eyes. Cognizant of the volume of her voice, she lowered it and demanded, "Turn those off!"

"What're you doing?" Toni queried.

"Are we gonna be friends or what?" asked Elliott pointedly while staring into the dashboard. Echoes of a similar moment with Nora reverberated in his head. Toni gaped at him in disbelief.

"I'm not sure this is the best time to talk about it," Toni replied anxiously. Elliott turned to her and rested his arm on the steering wheel.

"Look, we either commit to this now . . . ," urged Elliott before pausing in response to Toni's optical rebuke. He quickly continued, ". . . to this *friendship*, I mean, and give it right back to Em or we throw up the white flag and say our goodbyes tonight."

"Do we have to decide that *now*?" Toni asked.

"Yes, because Em's gonna do everything she can to run you off," Elliott said. Resisting the urge to affectionately grasp her thigh, he implored her, "And the only way we're gonna beat her is together."

Toni's mind raced. Quivering with the sudden gravity of the moment, she unfastened her seatbelt and turned her body towards Elliott.

"Platonic friends?" Toni asked gravely. She shook her head and warned, "No secret plan, no trying to woo me away from Bobby."

Toni's words skewered Elliott's heart but the adrenaline rush he experienced in anticipation of her answer dulled the pain. He placed his hand over the wound as if to hide it.

"Swear it," Elliott confirmed.

"I really could use a friend like you," Toni said as her demeanor softened. She offered him a warm yet muted grin and said, "Let's do it."

"Are we home yet?" asked a groggy Lanie after a dramatic yawn and stretch. Elliott killed the headlights and turned off the engine.

"Yes, ma'am," answered Elliott. He looked to Toni, simultaneously disappointed and contented with her place in his life, and said, "Help me get these two little buggers moving."

Buttressed by their newfound friendship, Toni confidently disembarked and rounded the front of the car. Emma prepared to fillet Elliott but Toni disarmed her.

"Em, your girls are *so* much fun," Toni gushed. She looked to Donna as she spun around and walked backwards towards Elliott, saying, "Hi. I'm Toni."

"Hi. Donna," replied Donna meekly with a raised hand. Elliott assisted Lanie from the backseat and maneuvered the dazed and unsteady ten-year-old towards Toni.

"Go with Toni," urged Elliott as he handed Lanie her backpack. She took it and insinuated herself underneath Toni's outstretched arm. Leaning into her for support, she made her way to the house with Elliott's words on her heels: "There ya' go."

"C'mon, sweetheart," Toni said while steadying Lanie. Returning to the backseat, Elliott unbuckled Tessa's seatbelt.

"Up ya' go, ya' little monster," said Elliott as he lifted her and removed her from the vehicle. He lowered himself enough to procure her backpack from the floor and added, "Got it."

Escorted by Toni's caring guidance, Lanie zombie-walked onto the porch while Elliott carried an unconscious Tessa. Emma initially bristled at Toni's involvement with her daughter but the sight of Elliott and Toni caring for her little ones like loving parents stifled the feeling.

"Hey, sweetie," Emma greeted Lanie. She drifted into an embrace with her mother and received a kiss on the top of the head. Soaking in the affection of her child, Emma asked, "Did you have fun today?"

"Yeah," answered Lanie in monotone. Oblivious to Donna's presence, Lanie released her mother and stumbled towards the front door, saying, "Toni's gonna come swimming in our pool."

"Great," Emma replied as she opened the door for Lanie. Refusing to look at Toni, she motioned to Elliott and instructed him, "Let's take Tess' right to bed, Uncle Elliott."

"*Jawohl*," replied Elliott. Tessa stirred and awoke.

"I want Toni to tuck me in," whined Tessa. Emma managed to contain her displeasure and held the door open.

"Oh, maybe next time, honey," Toni assured her. She caressed the top of her head and added, "Sleep tight."

"Hey, Dee," said Elliott as he passed by her and entered the house with his precious cargo. Tessa was asleep again before he crossed the threshold.

"Hey," replied Donna. The door closed and Toni and Donna stood alone on the porch. All was quiet in the neighborhood. Donna ventured, "So you're the singer."

"Yeah, that's me," Toni replied as she found herself eagerly awaiting Elliott's return, "*I'm the singer.*"

. . . .

"WE DID IT!" EXCLAIMED a beaming Toni as Elliott's LTD accelerated away from Emma's house. She and Elliott high-fived one another.

"Ya' did good," Elliott lauded her with an adoring grin. He turned left onto Goddard Road and proceeded west as he continued, "And it really chapped Em's ass the way the girls took to you."

"Oh, no," said Toni concernedly. Her enthusiasm dimmed and she asked, "Did she say something?"

"Nah, but she was pretty cold to Uncle Elliott," Elliott answered. He chortled and said, "She knows once Lanie gets something in her head, she's as obstinate as Mommy. Expect a swimming invitation soon."

"Not sure I'm ready for that," replied Toni with a laugh. They made the traffic light at Pardee but, when they arrived at Telegraph Road, the signal was red. Toni glanced at Elliott and opened her mouth to speak but then hesitated.

"Donna's not over you," remarked Toni as the vehicle rolled to a halt. Elliott considered her response for several seconds.

"Geez, she'll be asking me about my seventh-grade girlfriend, next," Elliott thought. He finally inquired, "Did *she* say something?"

"No," replied Toni. The light changed and Elliott traveled through the intersection. Toni watched the slowing southbound traffic approach Goddard and commented, "But she was *really* uncomfortable when we were alone on the porch. Honestly, I was, too."

"So you're not over me, either?" Elliott asked with a smirk. He immediately regretted the question and swiftly apologized, saying, "Sorry, that was stupid."

"Yeah, it was," scolded Toni. She sternly reminded him, "You promised."

"I know, I know," Elliott replied while raising his right hand in a sign of acknowledgement. He nodded and said, "I'll be good."

"I'm sure Donna knows how we feel, I mean, how *you* feel, ya' know, about me," said Toni as she struggled to explain the situation. She averted her gaze to the houses as they whizzed past and uttered, "Given your history, I'm sure it's weird to see you with another woman, girlfriend or not."

"How *do* you feel about me?" Elliott inquired. He gestured and said with increasing frustration over his inability to express his thoughts, "I know you don't love me, or like me, or whatever. But, I guess I mean . . . never mind, I don't know what I mean."

"I have to admit, Elliott, I was really anxious this morning," confessed Toni. She expounded with the turn signal clicking in the background, "The girls really helped, especially at first. They're so funny. Tessa's a little angel and Lanie, she's such a trip."

"She's Emma, Junior, that's for sure," Elliott quipped. He turned right onto Beech Daly Road.

"But, as the day went on, I got to know more about you. What type of person you are," said Toni with her elbow on the windowsill and her head on her hand. She declared with a glowing mien, "And I think we could great friends. Maybe even best friends."

Elliott caught his breath. Toni realized the import of her words and quickly recanted them.

"Well, Bobby will always be my *best* friend," Toni corrected herself. Elliott winced but, as she absorbed his reaction, she sat up and comforted him, "But I think our friendship can be something special . . . as long as you behave yourself."

"I think I can handle that," Elliott responded despite his disheartenment. They shared weak, uncertain smiles. A thought struck Toni.

"I need to give you my number," said Toni. Reaching into her purse, she pulled out a pen and a silvery gum wrapper. Smoothing it out on the dashboard, she wrote her number on the paper side, tore it in half and then handed it to Elliott, "There ya' go. Now, what's yours?"

The next two minutes hurtled by him as Elliott provided his number to Toni and they shared addresses. He soon turned into her driveway – too soon for his liking – and shifted the car into "Park".

"I am definitely sleeping in tomorrow," sighed Toni after a yawn. Elliott decided to gamble.

"I suppose a goodnight hug would be too much?" queried Elliott. Being alone with Toni, at night and in his car, aroused him. Every fiber of his being felt the centripetal force of her presence and, to make matters worse, every single one of them pulled against Elliott's willpower like a rabid dog against its leash.

"That's probably not a good idea, but how about a rain check?" suggested Toni. She unbuckled her seatbelt and continued, "Let's make sure you can handle being friends. And then, if you can do that . . . *yeah*."

"Fair enough," Elliott responded. Feeling foolish, he added, "I can live with that."

Toni exhaled. She was tired yet did not wish for the evening to end.

"Thank you for everything, Elliott," said Toni gratefully. She exhaled and then gushed, "You've been wonderful, the girls were wonderful, and . . . I had a fantastic time today. And I really needed it."

"Any time," Elliott replied, his tone sounding as if he merely gave her a ride to work. His look of concern touched her as he asked, "You gonna be all right?"

"Yeah," said Toni. She reached out, squeezed his arm and then, expecting him to make a move, swiftly opened the door and exited the car. Toni leaned back inside but kept her distance, adding, "Good night."

"Night," Elliott said. Toni closed the door and strode to the side entrance of her house. Elliott watched her longingly until she was safely inside and one-by-one interior lights appeared. He rubbed his tired eyes, glanced at the house once more and backed out of the driveway. Toni's house soon faded into the night.

"And just like that, it's over," Elliott sighed.

Walking On A Thin Line

Nursing a Grumpy Old Man at Johnny Dubs, Elliott daydreamed about Toni. The newfound friends saw each other infrequently since their Cedar Point excursion but spent inordinate amounts of time on the telephone. Elliott burned many hours with the telephone cord stretched from the kitchen wall to the couch and spent the remainder of his time craving their next conversation.

"Of course, all we do is talk about *him*," Elliott mused in reference to Bobby. The calls always centered on Toni's relationship with him and how, despite his marriage *faux pas*, she drifted back into it. Elliott sighed, indulged in a brief fantasy of he and Toni and, returning to the present, said to himself, "Forget it. You'll never pry her loose. It's one of those incredible things about her. Total faithfulness."

Toni, as if summoned by Elliott's thoughts, strode through the open doors of Johnny Dubs. She paused to let her eyes adjust to the dark and acquired Elliott in her vision. A tingling in Elliott's spine announced Toni's arrival and he rotated his barstool towards her. She smiled at him, an innocent smile that one good friend gives another, and its platonic nature plunged into his chest.

"Still, if I ever lose that face . . . ," Elliott thought with a feigned grin of his own. He stuffed the hurt into the farthest corner of his heart: relegation to the status of friend, although a prison he willingly entered, was a prison nonetheless.

"Are we clear?" queried Toni as she searched the bar for signs of Emma. Elliott rose to his feet.

"Yep, we're clear," Elliott answered. He placed his hands in his pockets when she approached him and explained, "The girls have an open house at school tonight so the queen has left the castle. You wanna get a table?"

Elliott pointed at a nearby table. Toni moved close to him and, to his great surprise, gave him a hug.

"Bar's fine," said Toni. It took every ounce of Elliott's willpower not to return her embrace but he managed to keep his hands in his pockets. Toni quickly released him and teased, "I wouldn't wanna make you leave your precious spot."

"You really get me," Elliott replied, the words tasting unpleasantly metallic on his tongue. Toni made no mention of their embrace; he took it as a sign he was behaving himself to her satisfaction. Elliott politely waited for her to sit before sliding back onto his barstool and asking, "You guys all set for the party?"

"Totally," replied Toni with wide eyes. Her excitement burgeoned as she continued, "We've never played *outside* before, believe it or not. The guys are really stoked. If it works out, we might try to play some outdoor festivals next year."

"And I'll be able to say I knew you before you were famous," Elliott said while he absorbed Toni's vivacious energy. There was a dissonant wave in that energy, however, and he felt as if there was more behind her visit.

"How's the planning going?" inquired Toni. Luke sidled down the bar with an open Bud Light and set it in front of her.

"On the house, beautiful," Luke said. Toni blushed.

"Thank you, Luke," she said with mock disapprobation. Elliott's eyes burned with jealousy though the rest of his face remained inert. Failing to notice it, Toni took a drink and then stated, "Okay, back to the party."

"Well, I'm no party planner, so Donna and Dave are handling that end of it," Elliott said. He drained the last of the liquid in his glass and, while setting his elbows on the bar, continued, "*And* playing secret agents, although Donna's taking the lead on that. She's pretty damn good at keeping Em off the trail. God knows she's had a helluva lotta practice."

A sly smile came to Toni's face. Elliott pushed his glass away and gave her a quizzical, sidelong glance.

"What's that for?" he inquired.

"Nothing. I just bet she's enjoying working with you," suggested Toni impishly. Elliott scowled.

"I told you, she's into that Ben guy," Elliott scoffed. Luke swooped up his empty glass but did not offer him another drink as he added, "He's a whack job . . . but, I gotta admit, he seems like a great guy."

"Are you *really* sure you two are done?" asked a skeptical Toni. Her rare incursion into his love interests aroused his suspicion.

"Are you gonna keep pawning me off on other women?" countered Elliott. He knew the question would get him in trouble and Toni did not disappoint; she scalded him with harsh look. Surprisingly, it quickly faded.

"I guess I had that coming," admitted Toni begrudgingly. Her mood became serious and she said, "But you can talk to me, too, ya' know. You're my friend, not my counselor."

"You sure about that?" Elliott asked in jest. Toni feigned a sour mien but then laughed.

"Hey, Toni," Nora said as she breezed past them with a tray of food and drinks. She hazarded a brief glimpse of Elliott's face and then pretended to focus on her tray as it wobbled.

"Hey, Nora," Toni said. She waited for Nora to pass out of earshot and then added, "I think that flyby was intentional."

"She assigned me to her friendship roster, too, so don't even go there," Elliott replied in annoyance.

"Did I strike a nerve?" asked Toni playfully.

"Yeah, so knock off the girlfriend bullshit," Elliott complained, his stinging rebuke draining the emotion from Toni's face. Instantly remorseful, Elliott turned to her and placed a hand on her shoulder, saying, "Look, *I'm sorry*. But I told you. A relationship's just not in the cards right now."

Elliott grabbed his glass and shook it. The degraded ice cubes clinked against its sides.

"At least not this year," Elliott added in defeat. He held up his spiritless glass and offered a toast: "Here's to 1986."

"I'd like to invite Bobby to Emma's party," blurted Toni. Her declaration was a punch to Elliott's solar plexus. Slowly lowering his arm, he gaped at her as she continued, "I mean, if it's okay with you."

"You sure that's a good idea?" Elliott asked. He had yet to consider Bobby in his calculations.

"I've already told him about you, how we're friends," advised Toni. Elliott gave her a doubtful look to which she replied, "You two are gonna have to coexist for this to work – that's what I want – and . . . he said he understands."

Elliott intentionally dropped his glass on the bar, the resultant noise drawing the attention of several patrons. Ice cubes popped out of it and scattered.

"Oops," Elliott said to veil his protest. Gathering the ice cubes, he inquired, "So, was he telling the truth?"

"Absolutely," replied Toni. She watched the gears of Elliott's mind smoking and implored him, "You're both adults, and you both care about me. *You guys can do this.* He knows you've been a gentleman and completely respectful of my relationship with him."

"Does he know all of it?" Elliott queried shrewdly. He dropped the ice cubes back into the glass.

"He knows you were interested," answered Toni vaguely. Elliott considered questioning her further but, deciding he did not want to know anything else, he punted.

"All right," Elliott said. Loathing the thought of Bobby's attendance of the party, he conceded, "If that's what you want, let's do it."

"He's a little jealous still, understandably, but if I can get him to do a few songs with us, and interact with you some, I really think it'll help," said Toni hopefully. She seemed, at least to Elliott, to be at peace with the situation.

"Hey, what could go wrong?" asked Elliott with a shit-eating grin.

• • • •

DAVID RENTED AN AREA of Elizabeth Park in Trenton for Emma's surprise birthday party, the 162-acre park providing the perfect setting for an outdoor event. The wooded spot they chose overlooked the Trenton Channel, the waterway breaking away from the Detroit River, flowing past the island of Grosse Ilse and then reuniting with its parent on their journey northward to Detroit. David utilized Emma's police connections to pull a few strings so the party could run later and include alcohol.

"Here we are," Elliott announced to his nieces as he parallel parked his LTD on the road that traveled in a large circle through the park. The Autumn weather cooperated with sunny skies and daytime temperatures in the sixties; however, the wind tossed tree branches and occasionally absconded with light, unattended objects. Elliott noticed a rolling foam cup and complained, "This wind's gonna be a pain in the ass."

"Swear jar!" bellowed the girls in unison.

"Your mother's jurisdiction doesn't extend to this car," replied Elliott with a roll of his eyes. He noted the girls' befuddled expressions but was soon distracted by the sight of Toni and her bandmates. They set up their equipment underneath the green-roofed pavilion.

"Toni's here!" Tessa shouted excitedly. He, like his nieces, felt the magic of her presence and it greatly improved their moods. Tessa and Lanie unbuckled their seatbelts, threw the front passenger seat forward and hurled open the door.

"Yeah, I know, kid," uttered Elliott. His demeanor soured as he remembered Bobby's impending arrival. Driven by childhood impetuousness, Lanie and Tessa spilled onto the grass.

"What's she doing?" asked Lanie. She did not wait for an answer as the two grade-schoolers charged towards the band.

"Hold on, maniacs!" yelled Elliott, his words barely overtaking the girls as they sprinted towards the pavilion. He popped his trunk, pulled out two grocery bags full of party supplies and then, with the trunk left open, walked down the paved path.

"Toni!" Tessa yelled as she slammed into Toni with an emphatic embrace and nearly toppled her.

"Hi, girls!" a beaming Toni greeted them. Dressed like the quintessential country girl, she wore a man's collared shirt of powder blue with the sleeves haphazardly rolled up and the long, pointed hems tied together. Toni's dark blue jeans had rips and tears in all the right places and she donned her usual cowboy boots.

"What're you doing?" demanded Lanie, the ten-year-old fascinated by the band's assembly of its instruments and equipment. Channeling her mother, she inquired suspiciously, "And who're these guys?"

Eddie, Oscar and Ryan stopped their preparations and gave Lanie feigned looks of intimidation. Remaining undaunted, she defiantly returned them.

"These are my friends, Lanie, and we have a band together, called Morning Cloak," Toni answered. She pointed to each of her bandmates in turn, beginning, "This is Eddie."

"Hey, there," said Eddie with a nod, his expression easing as he greeted them.

"And Oscar," Toni continued, after which Oscar tipped his cowboy hat.

"Little ladies," Oscar said.

"Hi," said Tessa as she wandered amid the band's equipment and studied it with great interest.

"And this is Ryan," Toni said. She chuckled and shook her head as Lanie and Tessa examined the scene, saying, "These two are Emma's little darlings, Lanie and Tessa, if you haven't figured that out already."

"So which one's your boyfriend?" asked Lanie in a snarky tone.

"God, Lanie, knock it off," scolded Elliott as he strode up to them. He glanced covetously at Toni before throwing her bandmates an upward nod and saying, "Hey, guys."

"Can we go to the swings?" asked Tessa as she pointed across the road.

"No, there's too much traffic and it's too far away," reasoned Elliott. He lifted the bags and asked, "So, instead, why don't you guys make yourselves useful and go get more of the bags outta my trunk?"

"Nooo!" Lanie and Tessa pouted.

"Go!" insisted Elliott as Tessa maneuvered back through the band's equipment. She broke into a run once clear of it. Lanie exhaled in frustration and stomped off in a huff. Elliott called after them, "And come right back!"

"Geez, Uncle Elliott's grumpy today," Toni remarked with a smirk.

"How's it goin', bumpkin?" asked Elliott with a mischievous grin. His eyes darted away to track the girls and then moved to Toni's boots. Raising his gaze slowly, Elliott indulged in her long, alluring form.

"Bumpkin?" Toni queried in mock offense.

"Adorable bumpkin," added Elliott in a low tone, the wind carrying off his words before they reached Toni's bandmates' ears. Her cheeks warmed and her spine tingled.

"Stop it," Toni admonished him good-naturedly while escorting him away from the band and towards a nearby picnic table.

"He still coming?" inquired Elliott. He set the bags on the table. Toni pretended to sneak a peek at the snacks inside them.

"Yeah," Toni confirmed. She gave him a penetrating stare and queried gravely, "You still able to handle it?"

"Of course," replied Elliott with an irked smile. Lanie and Tessa, tussling over a bag of plates and utensils, dropped it. Its contents scattered, the commotion causing Elliott to say, "And now, if you'll excuse me, I have two little monsters to kill."

Toni laughed despite feeling ill at ease. When she returned to the band, its members watched her with dubious expressions.

"Walking on a thin line, there, aren't ya?" asked Eddie, the disapproval evident in his tone. She composed herself with great difficulty.

"Yep," acknowledged Toni to her friends' surprise. Meeting each of their gazes and then bowing with dramatic flair, she added with a flash of pretend haughtiness, "And pulling it off flawlessly."

• • • •

DONNA AND DAVID ARRIVED shortly after Elliott and the triumvirate labored quickly to prepare Emma's birthday bash. David, after firing up several charcoal grills, began dumping ice into metal washtubs and filling them with beer while Elliott assisted Donna in setting up the tables. When his preparations were complete, Elliott watched Lanie and Tess interacting with Toni as David and Donna began grilling.

"You really sing?" Tessa asked in wonder.

"I do," answered Toni. She insinuated herself into her guitar strap, lifted the instrument and added, "And I can play this, too."

"Can you teach me to play?" Lanie inquired while reaching out to touch the guitar. Thoroughly enjoying the children's rapt attention, Toni grinned.

"Of course I can, sweetie," answered Toni. She played several chords to the amazement of Elliott's nieces.

"She's really good with kids," commented Donna as she appeared next to Elliott. The former lovers leaned against the short end of a picnic table and, as if rehearsed, maintained the same position with arms folded.

"Eh, I don't know," Elliott replied. He loathed Donna's intrusion into his observation of Toni so, seeking to dodge an uncomfortable conversation, he said, "I think Lanie's just good with adults. She's ten goin' on forty."

"She's precocious, to say the least," said Donna with chortle.

"And Tess' is such a little sweetheart she can make friends with anyone, kid or adult," Elliott continued.

"They're such great girls," said Donna adoringly. She stole a glimpse of Elliott's face as he watched Toni and, after several moments of thought, she inquired with a tinge of sadness, "How long have you been in love with her?"

"Don't go there, Dee," Elliott warned. He massaged his eyes with his left hand and added bitterly, "Just, don't."

"She won't admit it, but Em's terrified of the whole thing," said Donna. Elliott returned his attention to Toni who played an upbeat guitar solo for Lanie and Tessa. The girls danced wildly.

"Which is ridiculous," Elliott said.

"Why's that?" asked an unrelenting Donna. She stepped in front of Elliott to garner his full attention.

"Because, just like you, and just like Nora, she's taken," Elliott answered with a stern mien, "and completely faithful to her man."

"She sneaks little peeks at you, kinda like you do when you don't have an excuse to look at her," offered Donna. Her jealousy prickled her, and she felt guilty, but her feelings for Elliott had not died.

"Then that's bad news for me," Elliott replied.

"You really think so?" asked a confused Donna.

"She'll shut it down, Dee," Elliott said. Filtering into a fey mood, he patted Donna on the cheek, smiled sadly at her and said, "And I'll be out."

Elliott's forlornness rendered Donna speechless. He turned and walked away from her.

"I'm gonna go help Dave with the burgers," Elliott said over his shoulder.

• • • •

A MULTITUDE OF GUESTS poured into Emma's birthday bash twenty minutes prior to her arrival though it was one in particular who vexed Elliott. Bobby's appearance, and Toni's vigorous celebration of it, caused him to teeter on his emotional edge. Both Donna and Nora noticed Elliott's distress but were unable to intervene due to the presence of their own significant others. Elliott also kept his distance from them and his butterflying through the crowd kept anyone from engaging him for too long.

The familiar roar of "SURPRISE!" went up from the crowd upon Emma's arrival. The now thirty-six-year-old, led blindfolded towards the pavilion by Rose and Tom, was overwhelmed and touched by the reception. Her daughters tackled her and she indulged in every ounce of their love.

Morning Cloak immediately launched into a countrified performance of The Beatles' "Birthday" with Toni and Bobby singing lead vocals. Elliott, meanwhile, took over the grilling operation for David while he greeted his wife. He remained hidden in the background behind the sea of people and a pall fell over him as Toni and Bobby masqueraded as the perfect couple.

"Wonder how much trouble I'd get into with an Irish exit," Elliott thought. He nixed the idea of escape and said aloud, "Eh, the burgers'd burn."

Despite Elliott's attempts to restrain his eyes, they always returned to Toni and Bobby and the obvious onstage chemistry they shared. He did not see Nora and Bart watching him and failed to detect their approach.

"Hey, Elliott," said Nora, the twenty-two-year-old wearing one of her denim outfits and a red bow in her hair.

"Hey, Nora," Elliott greeted her. Seeing Bart, he tensed and hesitated.

"What's up, Elliott?" asked Bart who, while wary, did not seem hostile. The young man, in contrast to Elliott's unpolished t-shirt-and-jeans look, appeared clean-cut and wore a collared polo shirt.

"Not much, Bart," Elliott answered as he returned to the task at hand, "how's it goin'?"

"Can I talk to you for sec?" asked Nora. Elliott froze in a comical pose with the metal spatula in one hand and a plate in the other. Nora offered him a muted smile and said, "Bart'll take over for you."

"Okay, then, sure," Elliott agreed uneasily. He relinquished his grilling gear to Bart and said, "Thanks, man."

"No problem," responded Bart. Following Nora to a group of trees outside of the radius of the partygoers, Elliott wondered what she wished to discuss. A series of glances over his shoulder revealed that Bart tracked him closely but, to his surprise, did not appear upset.

"You sure lover boy's okay with this?" Elliott queried after another glance at Bart. Nora's bearded paramour held up the spatula in a sign that all was under control.

"Bart's fine, trust me, especially after the last fifteen minutes," Nora assured Elliott. She mouthed "thank you" to Bart.

"The last fifteen minutes?" Elliott asked suspiciously as he placed his hands on his hips and turned to face Nora. She folded her arms, stepped closer to him and paused.

"Because he's been watching you hawk Toni and seen how hopeless you've looked since Bobby showed up," answered Nora bluntly. Her accusations briefly paralyzed Elliott but, after a surge of jealous anger, he threw up his hands.

"What *is it* with everyone today?" asked Elliott in irritation.

"Hey, *relax*," Nora replied concernedly while motioning for Elliott to lower his voice. Bart noticed the dust-up but Nora waved to him to signal that she was okay. Returning her attention to Elliott, she said, "I'm just worried about you, that's all . . . and about what's gonna happen if Bobby figures out you're in love with his girlfriend."

Nora spoke the final few words with a carefully-veiled sadness. Her performance was so stellar that Elliott doubted his perception of it. A powerful chorus by Toni, however, washed away any consideration of Nora and the lingering desire she might have for him.

"I should just get the hell outta here," Elliott said weakly as he watched Toni sing and bled for her. It irked him that his feelings for her were easily discerned and only his love for his sister kept him at the party.

"Don't do that," Nora gently advised him. Elliott could not tear his gaze away from Toni so Nora, after checking that the coast was clear, grabbed him by the chin and redirected his eyes to her face.

"I forgot how cute she is," Elliott said to himself. The thought quickly passed and Nora released him.

"You've gotta keep it together, Elliott, or your eyes are gonna give you away," warned Nora.

"Why do you care?" Elliott inquired.

"Cuz' I don't wanna see you get hurt," declared Nora emphatically. She struggled with her thoughts on the matter but managed to organize them and said, "You and Toni being friends, especially as close as you seem to be getting . . . I don't think it's a good idea. But, I don't know, I also think maybe you're already too far into it and dropping it now would, like, devastate you."

"C'mon, that's overstating it a bit," Elliott replied.

"Is it?" queried a conflicted Nora. She leaned against a tree and said, "Maybe it could work, this whole 'friends with Toni' thing. But you're gonna have to know, like, where the line is, and stay on the right side of it . . . and not let Bobby find out how you feel. Can you do that?"

"You're way too young to be this on-target," Elliott griped. He scowled and punched the air, snarling, "How did I *get* here?"

Nora paused, waited for Bart to look away as he slid hamburgers onto awaiting plates, and then grasped Elliott's hand. Their old emotions, lying dormant for many weeks, suddenly leapt up like raging flames.

"Elliott, no matter what happens, to you, or to me," explained Nora with a squeeze of his hand, "I will *always* be here for you."

Befuddled by Nora's assertion, Elliott stood motionless as she released him and hurried back to Bart. He did not watch her retreat but instead meandered to the river's edge. Finding a picnic table placed precariously close to the shore, Elliott seated himself on top of it with his feet on the bench. He stared into the passing water.

"Is it too much to ask for someone my own age, attractive, without any love interests or hang ups, sweet and selectively naïve like Nora . . . easy to please like teenage Donna . . . *incredible* and loyal like Toni . . . caring as all three of 'em . . . *and* who Emma approves of?" Elliott asked God aloud. He repeated the words in his head, glanced at the sky and said in defeat, "Yeah, I guess it is."

. . . .

"WHERE'VE YOU BEEN, Big Bro?" Emma asked Elliott as he slithered through the crowd. She hugged him and kissed his cheek and he threw an arm over her shoulder.

"Manning the grill so Dave could enjoy himself a bit," Elliott lied. After his discussion with Nora, he left the grilling duties to Bart and spent thirty minutes watching the water of the Trenton Channel flow past the park.

"Thank you for the party," Emma said affectionately.

"Eh, Donna and Dave were the driving force," deflected Elliott. He lifted his gaze to Toni and wistfully watched her perform from a distance, saying, "I just helped with some odds and ends."

"Like Toni," Emma replied with a hint of displeasure. Elliott sneered.

"Like Toni," sighed Elliott.

"I forgive you," Emma said, her remark only half in jest. Joining Elliott in his admiration of Toni's talents, she added, "She and the boys are really making this party something."

"Em! Come here for a minute!" bellowed David from across the crowd.

"My adoring public calls," Emma joked. She and Elliott shared a half-hug before she strode towards her husband. Because he watched Toni so intently, Elliott missed Bobby's approach.

"So you're Elliott," Bobby said with poorly-concealed detestation. Elliott steeled his will, swallowed his pride and turned to Bobby with an extended hand.

"Hey, Bobby," said Elliott. Though Bobby scorned his handshake attempt, he continued convincingly, "Glad you could make it."

"Yeah, right," Bobby rejoined. Elliott studied his surroundings and, confident that no one paid them any attention, nodded for Bobby to follow him. Bobby stood his ground.

"Look, man, that girl loves you, and she'd boot me as a friend in a second if I was even thinking about making a move," Elliott explained with all the earnestness he could muster. He raised his palms in surrender and swiftly added, "Which I'm not. Not at all. I swear it."

Bobby scanned the vicinity. Satisfied that no one could hear them over the music, he leaned towards Elliott.

"*I'm* booting you now," Bobby said, Toni's paramour knowing Elliott would not cause a scene at Emma's birthday party. Glowering at him, Bobby demanded, "I don't care what you have to tell her, but get lost, and get lost soon."

Bobby's sudden and unexpected maneuver against Elliott briefly stunned him. Seconds later, his ego erupted.

"Whaddaya gonna do if I don't?" Elliott queried sharply and defiantly. Bobby's face went red and, perceiving his advantage, Elliott took a shot he immediately regretted, "Refuse to marry her again?"

Bobby's rage bettered him and, with a swift, powerful swing, his fist crashed into Elliott's face. Elliott saw stars and crumpled to the ground. The sudden violence paralyzed everyone in the crowd save David who charged towards them from a distance. The band played for another few seconds and then ceased.

"Bobby!" screamed Toni as he descended upon Elliott and punched his face a second time. David rumbled up to them and tossed Bobby to the ground.

"What the hell?" Elliott groaned. He saw the blood pouring from his nose and staining his shirt in his blurry vision. Emma flew into her own rage and barreled towards Bobby as he returned to his feet.

"Hold on!" shouted David while grabbing his wife around the waist. He picked her up and held on tightly.

"Let go!" Emma demanded as she vainly battled against his grasp. She screamed, "Let go!"

Elliott, meanwhile, recovered from Bobby's attack. The throbbing pain and his realization that he was just humiliated in Toni's presence ignited the same inner inferno as when Gregg slapped Nora. Shaking free of his spaciness and with his nose bleeding profusely, Elliott leapt to his feet to assault Bobby.

"Elliott, don't!" barked David.

Elliott realized Bobby readied his next punch and prepared to block it while balling his fist for his own strike. The slightest glimpse at Toni, who stood with her guitar hanging from her shoulders, and the horror in her eyes stayed his hand. He dodged Bobby's next swing and backpedaled. The delay permitted Bart to intercede, the young man pinning Bobby's arms to his sides and holding him in place. None of them saw Lanie hurtle into the fray.

"Leave Uncle Elliott alone!" Lanie bellowed. She rushed Bobby and, with a short hop for upward momentum, delivered a snap-kick to his testicles. The crowd emitted a collective gasp.

"Didn't see that coming," commented Elliott before using his t-shirt to wipe blood from his face.

"Lanie Michelle!" exclaimed Rose, the grandmother mortified by her granddaughter's resort to physicality. An astonished Bart released Bobby who dropped to his knees and cradled his aching testicles. Thinking quickly, Nora grabbed a towel, scooped ice from one of the beer tubs and ran to Elliott. She applied the makeshift ice pack to his nose.

"Hold your head back," Nora directed him. Emma began fighting David's grasp again. Toni crawled out of her paralysis, unslung her guitar and set it on the ground.

"Em, enough!" David bellowed. His commanding voice cowed the crowd as he said, "It's over."

David released Emma once she was calm and she rushed to her brother as did Toni. Emma rose up and emphatically pointed to the line of parked cars on the park's main road.

"Get him outta here!" Emma snarled.

"Don't lean your head back, Elliott," instructed Toni as she helped Nora steady him. She adjusted the ice pack and continued, "Pinch your nostrils closed, not the bridge."

"You just get him outta here," Emma commanded. A tearful Toni hesitated but, offering Elliott a look of heartbroken apology, she turned and moved towards her boyfriend.

"Don't talk to her like that," growled a recovering Bobby. Emma's effulgent eyes scintillated with anger.

"You'd better get outta here or I'll have my eight-year-old finish the job," Emma countered vitriolically.

"Oh my God, Bobby! Go!" Toni yelled at Bobby with a hard shove forward. He stumbled into a fast walk and she forcefully escorted him to his car. Emma exhaled in frustration as the party devolved into small groups and hushed conversations. She watched Rose and Tom taking the girls to the Channel's edge.

"Well, at least he didn't retaliate," said David as he straightened his shirt. Emma watched Bobby's car disappear into the park.

"That's what worries me," Emma finally replied.

· · · ·

ELLIOTT STAGGERED TOWARDS his porch with his bandaged face aching. He refused pain pills at the emergency room so, much to Emma's chagrin, he could drive himself home. Obscured by the shadows, Toni sat in a chair on his patio.

"Toni?" asked a surprised Elliott. Toni slowly stood up and, seeing his bandaged nose, permitted tears to fall from her red, puffy eyes. Elliott, who held a white paper bag in his fist, queried, "What're you doing here?"

"*Elliott*," whimpered Toni as he stepped out of the shadows and the extent of his facial injuries became apparent. She sobbed and gushed, "I am *so* sorry."

"It wasn't you who socked me in the face," Elliott said nonchalantly. He squiggled his nose, the movement causing him profound pain, and added, "Actually, it probably would've been better if it *had* been you."

"How bad is it?" inquired Toni gingerly despite knowing the answer. Her coworkers kept her abreast of Elliott's condition throughout his hospital visit but his bruised, battered face was also telling.

"Well, he broke it in not just one place, but two," Elliott answered with feigned enthusiasm. His cheek caused him to wince.

"Damn it, Bobby," griped Toni. Elliott saw her mind shift gears and she inquired gingerly, "Don't take this the wrong way . . . are you gonna press charges?"

Elliott chuckled the slightest of chuckles. He paid for his mirth with a sharp pain shooting up his nose.

"So *that's* why you're here," Elliott said with smirk.

"You have every right to pursue it, Elliott, and I won't blame you if you do," said Toni gravely. She returned to her seat and lamented, "But it could really mess up his life. He's never done anything like that before, at least since I've known him. He made a mistake, a huge mistake, but that's not who he is. I swear it."

"Don't worry, your *boyfriend's* safe," Elliott replied thickly. He walked unsteadily to a chair, slumped into it and said, "He kicked my ass and made me look like a schmuck in front of everyone I care about. I sure as hell don't wanna relive that."

"I'm so sorry, Elliott," repeated Toni with more tears. Elliott hated to see her cry.

"Hey, while I won't call it fair and square," Elliott said with his face throbbing, "I lost and he won. And that's it. It's over. I'll be fine."

"He didn't win anything," countered Toni in irritation.

"Yeah?" Elliott asked skeptically. Setting the bag on the table, he leaned back, stretched out his legs and queried, "How's that?"

"What Bobby did was childish and stupid," replied Toni.

"I thought you liked that stuff," Elliott said.

"I never said that," argued Toni. Her anger with Bobby flared as she bluntly expounded, "He didn't punch you after you slapped me on the butt. He was just acting like a jealous jerk and sucker punched you for no reason. He was being possessive, not protective."

"I guess," Elliott sighed. His eyelids, which he realized were heavy, tried to close several times. The sounds of nighttime insects and cars traveling on Beech Daly Road nudged aside the silence. Elliott dozed. Toni watched him with pity until he returned to consciousness.

"Bobby and I, well, we're . . . we're taking a break," advised Toni.

"So do I get a shot now?" Elliott asked mischievously. The physical and emotional exhaustion of a long day wore on him and degraded his judgement.

"Elliott, please," scolded Toni though in a forgiving manner.

"It was a joke," Elliott replied loudly, the force of his response tweaking his injured nose. He muttered, "Damn it. I gotta stop doing that."

"We promised not to see anyone else," added Toni cautiously.

"*You* promised not to see *me*," Elliott corrected her in annoyance.

"Yeah," confessed Toni guiltily. She returned to her feet and paced, expounding steadfastly, "But also I told him if he sees anyone, we're done. This is not a 'see other people' break, Elliott. It's for both of us to think, and reflect, and really decide what we want from this. And for him to decide what type of man he wants to be."

"He seems like an asshole to me," Elliott remarked. Toni's offended response prompted him to add, "I said *seems*. I guess I don't know him that well. But he did punch me in the face. *Twice*."

"There is so much more to him than that, and he's a good man, and he always treats me so well," explained Toni, "but he does have a conceited streak and occasionally it gets a little ugly and-."

"A little?" Elliott interrupted, the subject of Bobby a bitter one with which he did not want to deal. He rose with great difficulty and continued,

"Toni, my face hurts, my heart hurts, and I'm exhausted. I just wanna get hopped up on pain meds and be unconscious until work on Monday."

A moment of silence crept over them and they retreated into their own thoughts. Toni abruptly came to life, kneeled in front of Elliott and grabbed his hands.

"Let me take care of you," pleaded Toni earnestly. She thought better of her impetuousness and asked, "*Can* you let me take care of you? Ya' know, and still act like a gentleman."

Elliott studied Toni, his scrutiny making her uncomfortable. He pulled free of her grasp and removed a pill bottle from the bag.

"I'll be fine," Elliott assured her. He unsuccessfully attempted to open the bottle's child-proof cap.

"I'd really like to stay tonight," begged Toni. She stood up and took the bottle from Elliott.

"You don't have to do that," Elliott said. Opening the bottle, Toni obtained a pill and handed it to him.

"I'd feel better checking on you every couple hours or so, keep an eye on that concussion," explained Toni. Elliott realized he never told her about the concussion but let the matter lie. She returned the cap to the bottle and the bottle to the bag, declaring, "I'll sleep on the couch."

"You can have the bed," Elliott replied. He grabbed the bag, shook it and said, "A few extra of these puppies and I could sleep on the roof."

"You'll sleep in your own bed," Toni corrected him. She took the bottle from him and, making no pretense that she had monitored his condition, added, "And you'll take exactly what Dr. Jennings prescribed you."

"Yes, dear," said Elliott. Toni narrowed her eyes to rebuke him but the expression melted into a grin.

"Let's go, funny guy," Toni instructed with a nod to the front door. She escorted a woozy Elliott up the front step, onto the porch and through the door. Desiring a subject change, she chuckled and asked, "What'd you think of Lanie?"

"I think there're two Emmas now," responded Elliott as his face smarted, "and the world better watch the hell out."

Toni exited a staff entrance after her fourth consecutive twelve-hour shift and, though tired, it was her growling stomach that was foremost on her mind. The wind tussled her with warmer-than-normal October air, the temperature hovering in the mid-sixties as gray clouds traveled across the sky. The first shades of night gradually settled over Southeast Michigan and the rain from earlier in the day said its goodbyes with fading mists and sprinkles.

"*Elliott*," Toni sighed in mild frustration when she noticed his red LTD idling next to the sidewalk.

"You even make scrubs look good," called Elliott as Toni approached his car. She stopped several feet from it.

"Remember you promised not to visit me at work unannounced?" Toni asked with feigned disapprobation.

"Remember that your car's in the shop?" inquired Elliott as if speaking to a six-year-old. Changing schticks, he asserted in a serious tone, "Maybe you should go back in and get a CAT scan."

"I told you Joan's giving me a ride," Toni countered with a begrudging grin.

"And she told me that she's working over a few hours, and you need a ride," explained Elliott. The wind blew drizzle into Toni and she indulged in its cool, refreshing feel against her skin.

"Gee, that's funny," Toni replied with good-natured suspicion, "because she didn't tell *me* that."

Elliott lifted a finger towards the entrance. Joan, grinning proudly, waved at Toni who scowled and narrowed her eyes. Her friend laughed and quickly disappeared.

"I sense a conspiracy," Toni said as she turned back to Elliott. He glanced forward at two hospital personnel crossing his field of vision.

"*She* called *me*," insisted Elliott. Returning his attention to Toni, he reasoned, "Look I live close and so do you, so it's not a big deal and I ain't got a damn thing to do, especially on a Saturday night."

Toni hesitated while studying Elliott. He waited for a mere ten seconds.

"So you comin'?" urged Elliott. Toni pondered her situation, heard her stomach protest yet again and exhaled.

"Yes, I'm coming," Toni relented. She opened the passenger door, pulled the front seat forward and placed her jacket and purse in the backseat, querying, "Can we *please* stop and get food?"

"Yeah, sure," replied Elliott. Toni returned the front seat to its upright position and fell into it, declaring, "I haven't eaten in hours and I'm starving."

"Whaddaya want?" inquired Elliott.

"McDonald's and beer," Toni gushed. She pulled the passenger door closed and said, "Oh, yeah. McDonald's fries sound *soooo* good right now."

"How do you have such a great bod-," Elliott said before halting mid-sentence. Toni rolled her eyes and stifled a chuckle as Elliott offered her a rough, apologetic look.

"Oh, just say it," Toni replied. Hugging her stomach dramatically, she added, "I'm too hungry to care."

"I was just gonna ask how you stay in such great shape eating what you eat and drinking beer," said Elliott. He composed himself, depressed the brake pedal and shifted the car into "Drive".

"You don't see all the salads and water," Toni explained with a dissatisfied mien, "and being on my feet twelve hours a day doesn't hurt, either. But tonight, I'm eating as much fat, salt and carbs as I can."

"Far be it from me to keep a hungry lady waiting," Elliott said as he set his gaze forward. He lifted his foot off the brake and pressed the accelerator, announcing, "Next stop, McDonald's."

• • • •

"OH, MAN," SAID ELLIOTT as he pulled his car into the McDonald's parking lot. The lengthy drive-through line stretched nearly to the road and loads of kids debarked from two school buses and filed inside.

"Noooooo," Toni whined. She slumped in her seat.

"I could run inside for you," suggested Elliott doubtfully as he watched children swarming the interior of the building. He considered their options and said, "Or we could hit the one on Allen Road, or run up Telegraph to the fifties McDonald's."

"No, I'll live," Toni replied disappointedly. The line rolled forward and she commented, "It looks like it's moving some."

"Ya' sure?" asked Elliott. Seeing the willingness to care for her in his eyes, even regarding such a small matter, brought a warm smile to Toni's face.

"I'm sure," Toni said. Her exhaustion, her hunger and the comfortable moment conspired against her and she said, "Thank you, Elliott."

"They're both like only ten minutes away," deflected Elliott. He knew Toni referred to something greater but stuck to his guns, continuing, "No big deal."

"I meant for being such a wonderful friend, and not pressuring me, even when you want so much more," Toni expounded with admiration. She slid out of her shoes and pulled her legs onto the seat, saying, "I know it's not easy."

"You'll always have me, no matter how hard you try to get rid of 'ole Elliott," he said flippantly with a shit-eating grin. His attempt to dodge the moment failed. Realizing the import of his words, the friends' feelings for each other welled within them. They leaned towards one another and nearly kissed. Toni came to her senses first but, while retreating physically, she nonetheless moved forward emotionally.

"Are you free on Monday night after work?" asked Toni gingerly. Elliott sensed both the conflict and the nervous excitement bubbling within her.

"That depends," Elliott answered despite having no intention of declining her invitation. He queried coyly, "What did you have in mind?"

"I shouldn't have said anything," said Toni remorsefully. She scooted away from Elliott and focused on the moving line of cars, uttering, "Forget it."

"What is it?" Elliott pressed her.

"Well," began Toni sheepishly, "the Country Music Awards are on Monday, and I happen to have that night off, so . . . I want you watch them with me."

"I don't know. It's a school night," Elliott quipped while rolling down his window. He set his elbow on the windowsill and rested his temple on his closed fist, saying, "And you know how much I love country music."

"Come on," Toni urged him, her mood improving, "there must be some country songs you like."

"I love any song that comes from those purdy little lips 'a yours," Elliott said in a mock country accent. Toni laughed.

"Aren't there *any* county songs you liked before you met me?" asked Toni. The light shining from her eyes and the sudden energy seeping from her body enraptured him.

"No," Elliott replied but, as soon as the words left his lips, he realized there was one song. His smile faded and, after an uneasy pause, he said, "Well, I guess there's one."

"Really?" asked a pleasantly surprised Toni.

"Hard to believe, huh?" Elliott said, his mood dimming. Toni's buoyant demeanor fizzled in response.

"I just brought up something you'd rather not talk about, didn't I?" inquired an embarrassed Toni. She frowned and said softly, "Sorry."

"You're fine," replied Elliott. He let his foot off the brake and rolled forward one car length, stating, "It's, just . . . *complicated*."

"Old girlfriend?" asked Toni sympathetically. Her thoughts turned to Donna.

"Dead Dad," Elliott answered bluntly. Toni's stomach hit the floor.

"Oh my goodness, Elliott, I'm so sorry," pleaded Toni. She admonished herself, "That was dumb."

"You're right, I usually don't like to talk about it," Elliott said. Toni prepared to profusely apologize but he added earnestly, "But I think I'd like to tell you."

Elliott glanced at Toni anxiously and then averted his gaze. She maintained her focus on him, however, and scooted closer.

"I think I'd like you to tell me," said Toni tenderly. Her heart fluttering, she took his hand and squeezed it.

"Do I hafta take you home right away?" Elliott queried, his confidence buttressed by her kindhearted gesture.

"Well, you're gonna eat with me, right?" answered Toni. He squeezed her hand and then released it before it progressed any further.

"Yeah, I know the perfect place," Elliott replied. Pulling up to the speaker, he and Toni exchanged unsettled grins before he asked, "So, whatcha want?"

. . . .

ELLIOTT WIPED THE REMNANTS of the rain showers from the hood of his car so he and Toni could enjoy their feast of McDonald's and Bud Light while watching the evening's air traffic. They sat close, but not too close, and faced Metro Airport with their legs folded beneath them.

"It's beautiful here, Elliott," Toni commented while watching an airplane roar towards the airport and touchdown on the runway. She stuffed a bunch of French fries into her mouth, her unladylike manner of eating prompting a laugh from Elliott. Raising her hand to her mouth, she shielded it from view and exclaimed, "What? I'm really hungry!"

"I noticed," chuckled Elliott. He washed down a bite of his Quarter Pounder with a gulp of beer. Toni did the same.

"So, tell me, what's the song?" Toni inquired with burgeoning curiosity. She switched from her fries to her sandwich.

"Kenny Rogers sings it," Elliott said as his eyes glazed and the lights of the airport became blurry. He swallowed and said, "*The Gambler*."

"Really? That's a great song," said Toni. She immediately resolved to learn the song and play it for Elliott. Contemplating its lyrics, she asked carefully, "It reminds you of your Dad?"

"Yeah," Elliott replied. He drifted away for ten seconds and then returned, explaining, "Dad died in March of '75. That was a bad year and it hit us outta the blue. I was fighting with Dad a lot over the bar, but Emma was pregnant with Lanie, and we were all focused on the baby and all the craziness that comes with that. And then Dad suddenly had the heart attack and he was gone. Just like that. We were still reeling when Mom died in May. Killed in a car accident on the way to the damn grocery store, for God's sake. Nineteen seventy-five sucked."

Elliott went pale and numb. He finally turned to Toni and, seeing her crestfallen visage, he suppressed his own grief for her sake.

"Sorry, it's way too early to bleed all over you like that," said Elliott. He took the last bite of his sandwich.

"It's not. Not at all," Toni assured him, the urge to tell Elliott about her own father's death festering in her heart. She set down her beer bottle on the hood and caressed his arm, commending him, "It's nice you can be so open with me about something so painful."

"Well, anyway, I can jump ahead," Elliott said, Toni's gesture making him uncomfortable. He shook his head to clear it and continued, "A few years ago, I ran into my Uncle Larry, my Mom's brother-in-law, in a bar. And, ya' know, we talked about Mom and Dad, and the old days. After we'd had a few, he said 'What'd that Kenny Roger's song, *The Gambler*, say? *It's best ta' die while sleepin'?*' He got the words wrong, but what he said stuck with me, and I'll never forget that moment. Because Dad died in his sleep, peacefully. It gave me at least a little comfort, knowing he didn't suffer."

"Come here," Toni said with a wave of compassion that swept over Elliott and eased his pain. Leaning forward, she embraced him tightly.

"Mom and Emma found him that morning," stated Elliott as a grimness descended upon him. He returned Toni's hug and the force with which he squeezed her increased as he explained, "When I got to the house they were still waiting for him to be picked up. So I went into his bedroom, alone, and closed the door, and saw John Warden for the last time. I'll never forget it."

Toni released Elliott and sat down in front of him, their knees touching and his hands protectively encased in hers.

"I just looked at him for like, I don't know, a minute or so," said Elliott. His eyes watered slightly but he shed no tears as he added, "And it seemed like I could just reach out and touch him and he'd wake up. I gave him a kiss on the temple, and hugged him, and that's when I knew. He was cold. Skin had this weird gray tint to it. The life was gone. He was gone."

Toni, with the patience of an experienced therapist, permitted the silence as Elliott stared into their clasped hands. He finally stirred and then looked to her contentedly.

"But that song," said Elliott with a surge of joy. His muted grin engendered Toni's own as he elucidated, "Since then, whenever I hear that song, it reminds me of him. In a good way. A really good way."

"That's so . . . *wonderful*, Elliott," replied Toni with an enviousness in her tone. She shook his hands gently and said, "Having something that brings back fond memories of your Dad."

The cooling wind brought with it a light shower, the breeze striking Toni and causing her to shiver. Elliott realized he had spent too long in his past and the abrupt return of the rain provided the perfect excuse to escape it.

"I should get you home," said Elliott though he wanted no such thing.

"We could just get into the car," Toni suggested. Her desire to tell Elliott her own story roiled beneath her emotional surface and she could no longer contain it.

"Are you sure?" asked Elliott. Toni released his hands and slid off the hood. Collecting the McDonald's wrappers and containers, she offered him a stolid mien.

"Yes, we can *watch the planes*, and *drink beer*, and *talk* inside the car," Toni declared firmly yet kindly. She moved towards the passenger door.

"Let's *do it* then," Elliott countered, the sexual innuendo clear yet also in jest. He grabbed the six pack of beer.

"Let's not," Toni admonished him as she opened the car door, "and say we didn't."

Toni slid into the car. Elliott let the rain moisten his clothing and exhaled.

"Right," said Elliott.

· · · ·

THE WIPERS WHIRRED to life and removed the veneer of raindrops from the windshield. Toni popped the last of the refuse from their meal into the McDonald's bag, crumpled it closed and then obtained two bottles of beer. She opened one with the bottle opener and handed it to Elliott.

"When did your dad die?" Elliott asked as he took the beer. Toni was stunned.

"How did you know he died?" inquired Toni with wide eyes.

"When I talk to someone about my parents dying, and their parents are gone, you can see empathy in their eyes, not sympathy," Elliott explained before taking a drink. Toni opened her beer as he said simply, "You had the look."

Toni hesitated and kept her gaze downward. She gathered herself with several gulps of Bud Light and returned her attention to Elliott.

"You know, to look at you, Elliott, and maybe talk to you once in a while, you seem like a regular guy, with a regular job, living a regular life," Toni expounded with a keen expression, "but . . . you're so much deeper than that. So much more intuitive. So much more than I ever suspected."

"Tell me about your dad," Elliott requested gently as he sidestepped Toni's assertions. Shedding a few tears, Toni struggled with the right beginning for her story.

"I wish I could say I loved my dad, 'cuz I wanted to, and I think I did when I was little. Until I was four or five, maybe," said Toni sadly. She took another pull from her bottle and added, "But I didn't after that, and I don't now. I still want to, though."

Elliott's heart shattered for Toni. He placed a hand on her shoulder and, as if he touched a button, she immediately lurched into him and clung to his body. Elliott felt Toni trembling and wrapped his arms around her.

"Marvin Cullen," stated Toni bitterly. She cuddled into Elliott and continued, "He was quiet, and stern, and not affectionate at all. He had a mean streak that was usually reserved for Mom and I, though Mom took the brunt of it. She did her best, and shielded me whenever she could, but sometimes that nastiness was too much to hold back."

Toni sat up, sipped her beer and, looking at it strangely, returned it to the six-pack container on the floor. She kicked off her shoes and, using Elliott's thigh as a pillow, she laid on the seat with her knees bent.

"I love the bench seats in these old cars," commented Toni during a temporary break in her angst. Uncertain of where to place his right hand, Elliott laid his arm on the back of the seat as she resumed her story, saying, "Butte was a big mining town, and he was a maintenance worker for one of the mining companies. Until he punched out his supervisor and got fired. And arrested, too. Luckily, my mom was really active in our church. She managed to convince the priest to hire him as a maintenance man at the Catholic school where she taught. But he was never the same, and things got worse. He would at least try to be a dad once in a while before it happened. But after? He just became more isolated and pretty much ignored me."

Toni used her thumb to crack the other four fingers of each hand, a habit signaling she was deep in thought. Elliott remained silent and attentive.

"Unless he was mad," added Toni bitterly. She folded her arms and cried angry tears, saying, "He abused us verbally, emotionally. He never hit me, but he hit Mom a few times. I saw it once and heard it a couple others. And that's when I was done. I kicked him outta my heart that day and I haven't let him back in since. I'm not sure I ever will."

"Man, Toni, I'm sorry," Elliott said though he felt his words were feeble and inadequate. He placed a caring hand on her folded arms and continued, "Whining about my life when you had to go through all that."

Toni's eyes flipped up to Elliott. She extended a hand to his face, caressed it and smiled weakly.

"We all go through what we go through, and how serious someone else might consider it to be doesn't make it any less painful to who's going through it," replied Toni with a wisdom beyond her years. Her grin burgeoned and her mood improved as she expounded, "And my story isn't quite so sad, because Mom and I had a guardian angel. Great Aunt Agnes. When she found out about my dad, she convinced my Mom to get a divorce and moved us to Michigan with her, and my life got a whole lot better. She was a nurse, too, and that's what inspired me to be one."

"That's a helluva plot twist," Elliot responded. Toni took his right hand between her own and held it against her stomach. Fighting his arousal, he waited patiently for her to finish the story as her father's death had yet to be revealed.

"Life was good, and I didn't hear anything about Daddy until years later," said Toni. She patted his hand, saying, "Mom didn't say anything and I never asked. I grew up here, and Michigan became home, and he faded into the past."

Toni closed her eyes and conjured old images in her mind. Elliott felt as if he would jump out of his own skin.

"But then he came back," sighed Toni. Cognizant that the physical contact toyed with Elliott's emotions and libido, she sat up and moved to the far end of the front seat. She leaned her back into the passenger door and hugged her knees into her chest. Toni's retreat tweaked Elliott's ego but he doused the feeling with beer and let her continue, "My college graduation gift was a call from the Butte police because I was his next of kin. Dad put a shotgun in his mouth and pulled the trigger."

"Damn, Toni," Elliott replied, "that's rough."

"Mom was relieved. I think, for her, it represented freedom," said Toni. She hugged her legs tighter and stated, "He couldn't make a sudden reappearance in our lives any longer. See, that never worried me, though. It wasn't his style."

"So you did okay with it?" Elliott queried.

"I was ambivalent at the time," answered Toni. The distance Toni imposed between them taunted Elliott but he squelched the urge to approach her as she said, "Now, it changes. Sometimes I'm sad, other times angry. Most of the time, though, I just don't care. The only connection I share with him is my last name."

"Bobby know all this?" Elliott inquired, his mention of her estranged boyfriend spurred by envy.

"He knows my dad's gone," responded Toni.

"But not all of it?" Elliott asked. Toni sensed the line blurring and noticed they had steamed the windows of the car. She lowered her gaze.

"We can't do this again," said Toni forlornly, "because it's not fair to Bobby, and it's not fair to you."

"Hey, I thought I was good," Elliott replied with raised palms.

"You were," Toni cooed. She again lunged at him and embraced him. Trying to extricate himself from Toni's grasp, he struggled but failed. She continued to cling to him and rest her head on his shoulder.

"Please just give me tonight, though," Toni pleaded, "and I promise, I won't put you through it again."

"Whatever you need," said Elliott, their physicality becoming painful. Despite the pain, he knew he could never refuse Toni and wondered if she was aware of that fact.

"So, about the CMAs," said Toni as she redirected the conversation to a lighter topic.

"You'd better have popcorn," Elliott sighed.

• • • •

"SO, YOU'RE ELLIOTT," Katherine Cullen said when she opened the door and gave Elliott a once-over. She closely resembled her daughter in build and countenance despite her longer, graying hair but was careworn beyond her years.

"As far as I know," replied Elliott with a weak grin. Toni thought better of spending time alone with him so she shifted the location to her mother's house. Elliott accepted the installation of a chaperone without complaint.

"Mother, invite him in," Toni scolded Katherine. She squeezed past her mother, gave Elliott a welcoming smile and a big hug, saying, "Hey, I'm glad you're here."

"Me, too," said Elliott while wallowing in the embrace. He caught Katherine examining him and appraising Toni's emotional buoyancy. Returning his focus to Toni, Elliott noticed the hoodless, blue-and-gray sweatshirt she wore.

"I didn't know you were a Tigers fan," stated Elliott with interest. Toni's cheeks flushed and she bit her lip, the display prompting him to say, "Oh. Bobby's a Tigers fan."

"Ouch, that was painful to watch," remarked Katherine blithely. Reclaiming her place in front of Toni, who was mortified by her mother's unfiltered commentary, she took Elliott by the arm and escorted him into the house. She lightened the mood with the declaration, "That earned you a beer, young man."

Everything about the next ninety minutes, save for Toni's usual radiant presence, proved either mediocre or grating. Katherine placed Elliott on one section of the L-shaped sectional while she and Toni occupied the other. Dominating the conversation and insisting for quiet during the musical performances, she drank several glasses of wine and frequently interrupted Elliott. Toni remained quiet but fumed over her mother's rudeness.

"She's got a bad habit of dating men like her father," Katherine said bluntly when Toni left to make more popcorn at her mother's request. She penetrated Elliott's very spirit with her gaze and stated sternly, "Guys who don't deserve her."

"Well, I sure as hell don't deserve her," replied Elliott without hesitation. Displaying a quirky grin, he said, "But I'm just her friend, so thankfully that bar's a lot lower."

Katherine chuckled.

"You know they're getting back together, right?" Katherine inquired.

"Oh, yeah," answered Elliott. He outwardly demonstrated composure but inwardly ached. Katherine held her glass close to her body after sipping her wine.

"He'll get over the cold feet, and the fear of commitment," Katherine explained, "and come crawling back with a ring."

"I told her the same damn thing," responded Elliott, his ire with Katherine leaking into his words.

"Really?" Katherine said with piqued interest. Her body language changed and she stated, "Frankly, I'm surprised she's stuck to her guns and forced him to decide, if you can really call it a decision. Spend your life with that tenderhearted angel or not? You men are so dumb sometimes."

"Not a tough call, is it?" sighed Elliott. Tortured by the threat of a wedding, he looked away. Katherine displayed the first traces of a smile and gazed on him with approbation.

"What's not a tough call?" Toni queried as she returned to the living room with two fresh bowls of popcorn. Katherine launched into a convincing performance.

"Giving Hank Williams, Jr. the Video of the Year award," Katherine said while pointing to the television. The bearded artist gave his acceptance speech.

"Damn, she's quick," thought Elliott. Toni smirked.

"I didn't realize you were a connoisseur of country music videos," Toni said skeptically. She handed the larger bowl to her mother and surveyed Elliott with suspicion.

"Oh, yeah," Elliott replied, the two words all he could muster. Katherine came to his rescue.

"You promised the man popcorn, dear," Katherine jokingly rebuked her daughter. She nudged Toni with her foot.

"Okay, Mom, geez," snapped Toni with uncharacteristic impatience. Rolling her eyes and then widening them to convey her annoyance, she handed the smaller bowl to Elliott and said, "As promised."

"Thank you," replied Elliott who, on a whim, caressed Toni's hand upon accepting the bowl. The moment caused a brief crackling of romantic energy between them and their spines tingled. Toni retreated from it and returned to her seat.

"Kenny Rogers," said Kris Kristofferson as he introduced the live performance of the former.

"Okay, quiet kids," Katherine demanded.

"Mom loves Kenny Rogers," advised Toni.

"Shhh," Katherine hushed her. Kenny Rogers launched into the premiere of his music video for "Morning Desire" and, while Toni and Katherine attentively watched the video, Elliott saw nothing. His eyes divided their time between the beer in his hands and Toni as the song's words described the joy of waking up next to the love of one's life. He suddenly heard Katherine's words in his head.

"You know they're getting back together, right?" Katherine warned. The image of Toni peacefully sleeping next to him shattered and he drifted into dark thoughts.

• • • •

"WILL YOU CLEAN UP, dear?" Katherine asked Toni as she passed the kitchen entranceway. Calling from the hall, she stated with the slightest slurring of her words, "I'll escort the handsome gentleman to his car."

"*Mother*," griped Toni. She threw the dish rag on the counter.

"You look so much like her," began an amused Elliott while approaching Toni, "but that's sure as hell where the similarities end."

"Why am I always apologizing to you?" queried Toni, her embarrassment evident on her face. She kissed him on the cheek and sighed, "*Sorry*. The whole thing kinda backfired on me, and she was terrible. *On purpose*."

"Eh, I'm fine," replied Elliott despite feeling the effects of the gauntlet that was their evening. Seeking to encourage Toni, he assured her, "You gotta remember, I'm a regular resident in Em's doghouse, and that's as rough as it gets."

Katherine reappeared in the entranceway wearing a light jacket. She leaned against the wall and impatiently folded her arms.

"She's not usually this bad," Toni whispered. She offered him an apologetic expression and added, "Thanks for putting up with it."

Elliott decided to gamble. He took Toni's chin between his thumb and forefinger, moved his lips close to hers and, at the last millisecond, stopped. Katherine and Toni both tensed.

"Any time," said Elliott with a loving yet piercing gaze. His play made, he exited the kitchen while throwing Katherine a haughty look. Toni melted where she stood.

"Oh, Bobby, you're running out of time," a conflicted Toni thought. Katherine recognized her angst but, leaving her daughter to her ponderings, she quietly slipped out of the kitchen. Catching up with Elliott, she took his arm and escorted him outside.

"Look at you, showing a little confidence," Katherine lauded Elliott. They descended the porch steps and she added, "I knew you could do it."

"Well, Katherine, thanks for the hospitality," said Elliott when they reached his car. He wanted to leave posthaste but she led him onward.

"*Hospitality*," Katherine scoffed. They turned left at the sidewalk as she confessed, "I was a complete bitch to you most of the night."

"Nah, not at all," said Elliott. He admitted in response to her dubious mien, "Yeah, little bit."

"Well, I have good news," Katherine announced. She released his arm and said, "You passed the first test."

"So *that's* what tonight was," said Elliott. A dog barked at them through a chain link fence. Katherine ignored it.

"Blame me, not her," Katherine stated while maintaining a steady pace. She chuckled and added, "She didn't know it was coming until it was too late."

"It's hard to blame your daughter for anything," replied Elliott with a longing in his voice.

"She probably thinks I'm drunk," Katherine said.

"You did drink almost two bottles of wine," offered Elliott.

"Over four hours," Katherine replied with a dismissive wave of her hand.

"Are you an alcoholic?' asked Elliott nonchalantly.

"Nah, not at all," deadpanned Katherine. She then admitted with a smirk, "Yeah, little bit."

"Why are we taking this walk, Katherine?" inquired Elliott, his patience waning with their meandering conversation.

"Bobby'll hurt her," Katherine stated gravely, "and you're gonna need to be there for her when it happens."

"I will," replied Elliott with conviction.

"I don't mean as her friend," Katherine countered. They stopped and turned towards each other as if by silent agreement.

"She doesn't want that, and part of the deal is I don't push it," argued Elliott edgily. Throwing a thumb back towards the house, he insisted, "She wants him, not me."

"Let me tell you something about my daughter," Katherine stated firmly. She expounded with watery eyes and a sudden vulnerability, "It's nothing short of a miracle that she became the incredible, strong, big-hearted person she is, Elliott, given who her father was, and what she went through as a child."

Katherine traveled into the past. A pleasant journey it was not; she sneered.

"I was like that once, and I let that black hole of a man chew me up and spit me out," Katherine grumbled. Her mood improved and she resumed their walk, saying, "But Toni's stronger than I am, though that big heart gets in her way a lot. It's on you to accept her when she's strong and stand up for her when she's not."

"Oh, so no pressure," said Elliott with a shrug.

"Grow a pair, Elliott," Katherine snapped.

"Katherine, you just met me," protested Elliott. He stopped and gestured incredulously, saying, "How the hell could you know I'm right for Toni?"

Katherine took two more steps and rotated towards Elliott. Her seriousness garnered his complete attention.

"Had I treated Bobby like I treated you tonight," Katherine replied chillingly, "he'd have taken it out on her."

Katherine's contention rendered Elliott speechless. She nodded to the house.

"Let's head back," Katherine said, "so I can sleep this off."

"Yeah," muttered Elliott, "let's do that."

"Oh, I'm sorry," Toni pouted when she saw Elliott's pale, tired countenance. He slumped into the Senate Coney Island booth and immediately keyed on the coffee steaming in front of him.

"For what?" asked Elliott after taking it in both hands and greedily sipping it. He moaned, "Oh, sweet caffeine."

"For waking you up so early on a Sunday," Toni answered while watching him with pity. A twinge of jealousy arose in her heart and she queried, "Were you at the club last night?"

"No, I was monster wrangling," replied Elliott as he rubbed his face with both hands. Indulging in another gulp of coffee and wincing at the burn, he elucidated, "Lanie and Tess' were *all* geared up last night – more than usual if you can believe that – and Em and Dave were later than they thought, so I crashed at like two a.m."

"Well, I was gonna ask you to go to church with me this morning," Toni said, her statement garnering a skeptical mien from Elliott, "but I'll spare you this time."

An older, heavyset waitress appeared with two plates, one in her right hand and one balanced on her arm. She held a pot of coffee in the other hand.

"Good morning, hon," she greeted him with a naturally gruff voice. She began pouring his coffee but still asked, "More coffee?"

"Hell yes," replied Elliott while watching the coffee level rise in his mug. The waitress slid the first plate in front of Toni. Elliott gushed, "*Thank you.*"

"Two eggs, sunny side up with wheat toast," the waitress said. She set the other plate in front of Elliott and said, "Corned beef hash and biscuits."

"Thank you," Toni said with an endearing wink at Elliott.

"Anything else for you two?" the waitress asked.

"I'm good," said Elliott.

"Me, too," Toni said, "thanks."

"All right," the waitress said as she spun away with surprising agility, "enjoy."

"I took the liberty of ordering your usual," Toni said as she happily watched Elliott dig into his food, "and it's *my* treat today."

"So what's up this morning, Ms. Cullen?" Elliott inquired in between bites.

"We didn't talk much this week," Toni answered while cutting an egg, "and I guess I wanted to hang out for a bit and catch up. Thanksgiving week's always busy for me and I may be out of touch."

Elliott was simultaneously struck by anxiety and a yawn. Toni frowned.

"I won't keep you long," Toni assured him, "I promise."

"You've got me as long as you want me," responded Elliott with words that intentionally carried greater import. Toni blushed and averted her eyes so he pivoted and queried, "Why ya' gonna be out of touch? You and your Mom goin' outta town or somethin'?"

"No, our Thanskgivings are pretty boring," Toni answered. She pushed some egg around her plate and reminisced before saying forlornly, "Since Aunt Agnes died, it's just Mom and me and we don't do anything, really."

"Why don't you two join the Hastings' Thanksgiving?" suggested Elliott as he lifted his mug to his lips. He drank and then said, "The monsters would love the opportunity to pester the hell out of you for an afternoon."

"Thanks, but we couldn't impose like that," Toni replied while holding up her egg-laden fork. Elliott opened his mouth to argue but she quickly added, "Besides, we have a Thanksgiving tradition. I pick up extra shifts and work the entire weekend but I stay at Mom's and she feeds me."

"Wow, that sucks," said Elliott, his bluntness driven by his exhaustion. They each shoveled a forkful for food into their mouths.

"Yes and no," Toni sighed. Her demeanor lightened and her eyes shimmered as she expounded, "It's a little grueling, but the paycheck's nice. I get to spend time with Mom and she takes care of me. It's kinda like being in school again. It's not so bad."

"That woman's really grown on me since I met her," said Elliott. It pleased him that Katherine was such a rock for her child, both a sword and a shield advocating staunchly for her daughter.

"I'm still mad at her about that night," advised Toni with a sour expression.

"Eh, she was protecting her little girl," said Elliott in defense of Katherine. He thought of his late mother, Lillian, let his focus drift and said, "Love it while ya' got it."

"So what's a Hasting's Thanksgiving like?" Toni queried in an attempt to maneuver Elliott away from a painful subject. He recognized and appreciated the diversion.

"Well, since the night before is the biggest bar night of the year, Em needs the sleep more than the control, so Rose gets a holiday of her own," Elliott replied. He heaped corned beef hash onto his last biscuit half and explained, "Em sleeps in Thanksgiving morning while Dave takes the girls to the parade in Detroit. Then we all convene at Tom and Rose's, maybe watch the Lions game, eat ridiculous amounts of great food and then lay around complaining about how full we are. Typical Thanksgiving I guess."

"Sounds wonderful," Toni said with longing in her voice. Elliott nodded in agreement as he chewed his food.

"Which is why, next Thanksgiving, you guys need to come with me," urged Elliott after a dramatic swallow. He sent more caffeine into his veins and added, "You could still work Friday to Sunday."

Toni hesitated and became uncomfortable. Elliott frowned and set down his mug.

"Oh, yeah," said Elliott. He sat up straight and conceded, "You'll probably be with Bobby next year."

"Actually, that's not what I was thinking," Toni corrected him. She gathered her thoughts and feelings on the matter and said forthrightly, "Elliott, I may not be with him next year."

"Yeah, you will," replied Elliott. His hands trembled in anticipation so he dropped them into his lap.

"I mean it, Elliott," Toni countered. She gave him a pointed look and said, "I don't know who I'll be with next year."

"What're you saying?" inquired Elliott as realization percolated within him. Toni lost her tight grip on her emotions and struggled for the right words. Terrified by his surging hopes and fluttering elation, Elliott pointed at Toni and warned, "Don't make promises you can't keep."

"I'm not promising anything," Toni replied sharply while grabbing Elliott's hand and lowering it to the table. A strange tension arose between them before Toni deflated and said anxiously, "I shouldn't have said anything."

Neither Toni nor Elliott said a word or looked at the other for over a minute. They ate in silence with an occasional sip of coffee. Elliott finished his breakfast, nudged his plate aside and looked to Toni.

"No promises, no discussion, nothing," Elliott offered thoughtfully, "until 1986."

"What?" asked a confused Toni.

"Whatever we were just gonna talk about," answered Elliott with burgeoning confidence, "we just don't . . . until 1986."

Toni sifted Elliott's proposal in her mind and he watched her warily. She finally raised her eyes to him.

"No expectations, either?" Toni bargained. Elliott pondered the amendment and, though the uncertainty prickled him, he nodded in agreement.

"No expectations," stated Elliott firmly. Toni paused.

"Okay," Toni responded slowly as she continued to contemplate their arrangement. She nodded, too, and her apprehension eased. She raised her coffee mug and, sensing her heart turning towards Elliott, she continued, "*To 1986.*"

Elliott lifted his mug and clinked it against Toni's coffee. They shared nervous grins.

"To 1986," Elliott repeated.

• • • •

ELLIOTT AND EMMA TOILED in the kitchen to clear the aftermath of Thanksgiving dinner while David and Tom snoozed in the den with the Dallas Cowboys game flickering on the television. Rose, her Thanksgiving efforts at an end, sipped a Martini and watched Lanie and Tessa play Atari games in the living room. A sudden surge in their excited chattering caused Emma and Elliott to chortle.

"Dining room table's clean and clear," Elliott announced dutifully as he ferried the last serving dish to the counter. Emma finished slicing the turkey but, seeing his sister working as if at Johnny Dubs, Elliott urged her, "I got this, Em. You shouldn't have to be in a kitchen on your day off."

"It'll give us a chance to talk," replied Emma without looking at her brother. She added with the slightest hint of rebuke, "Haven't seen you much in the last few weeks."

"No one has," Elliott sighed. He raised his eyebrows, set the dish with the rest of them on the counter and explained, "Overtime and a nasty sinus infection. *But you already knew that.*"

The siblings danced their usual post-Turkey-day dance as they efficiently wrapped leftovers and stored them in the refrigerator. Elliott assisted Emma in disposing of the turkey carcass.

"All right, food's taken care of. Let's get these dishes done," said Emma as she washed her hands. Taking up their normal positions, Emma soaped a large serving dish and inquired, "Talk to Donna at all?"

"There it is," Elliott said. Emma rinsed the dish which he took and dried as he admonished her, "You know I haven't."

"You should," countered Emma swiftly.

"You just don't wanna admit she found a great guy without your help," Elliott jibed his sister.

"No, I really don't," replied Emma as she and Elliott exchanged affectionate smirks. Her mirth faded and she inquired, "Are you seeing anyone?"

"Not exactly," Elliott answered cryptically. The siblings continued their efficient wash-and-dry cycle.

"Oh, god," replied Emma with a mock pout, "please tell me you didn't pull another bar whore outta the club."

"All your bar whores are safe, Sis," Elliott said sardonically. Emma stopped in mid-dish and glowered at him.

"Tell me you're not seeing an actual whore," Emma snapped.

"I'm not," Elliott grumbled in response, "but it's nice you think so highly of me."

Lanie's boisterous cheers erupted from the living room. Tessa's groan revealed the winner of their current game.

"Inside voice, Lanie!" Rose scolded her. Emma paused and listened. Satisfied that her daughters obeyed their grandmother, she returned to the task at hand.

"Okay, I'm sorry," relented Emma, "but will you just tell me what's going on with you?"

Elliott hesitated and carefully chose his words. Emma beat him to the punch.

"You've been seeing Nora, haven't you?" asked Emma accusatorily. She studied him and asserted, "That's why you've been in a better mood lately."

"*No.* I haven't even actually *seen* Nora in weeks," answered an irritated Elliott. He dried a pot and inquired, "Why would you think that?"

"Oh, you didn't hear?" replied Emma with mild surprise. She began washing the good plates and thrust one at Elliott, saying, "Careful with those. She and Bart split up."

"Really?" Elliott queried. He stopped drying and turned to Emma, saying, "Why?"

"Apparently he was getting too serious too fast," advised Emma. She set another two plates in front of him and posited, "In my opinion, that's *not* the whole story. Couldn't tell you what it is, though. She's been pretty tight-lipped about it."

Emma watched Elliott to gauge his response. Aware of her intentions, he did not take the bait on Nora. Emma's tiredness frayed her nerves and she lost control of her emotions.

"Elliott, I love you, so much, and you know you've got a big piece of my heart," a teary-eyed Emma explained, "but there're three in line ahead of you when it comes to my time and energy, and you need someone to take care of you. But more important than that, you need someone to take care *of,* and give you some purpose in your life. You're too old for this depressed, floating-through-life bullshit."

"Geez, Em, tell me how you really feel," Elliott replied. Emma exhaled in frustration as she washed a pot, her angst prompting him to admit, "I've been hanging out with Toni a lot. Just as friends right now, but I think something's starting to change."

Elliott's admission was a cathartic one and his countenance softened. Emma, her hands submerged in soapy dish water, stopped to again glare at him.

"Honestly, Elliott, right now I feel like beaning you in the head with this pot. Maybe it'd knock some sense into you," growled Emma. Misty-eyed yet red-faced, she preached, "Can't you find someone in their thirties? Or, hell, early forties, even. Toni is too young, too energetic, *too positive*, and, real soon, she'll be too engaged."

"She's not with him right now," Elliott informed Emma with particular relish. Emma lowered her eyes and pretended to focus on washing silverware as he added, "That punch knocked them off the rails. Bobby won the battle but he may've lost the war."

Emma groaned. The girls heard it and became quiet to eavesdrop.

"Elliott, if she's not with him, then why isn't she with you?" questioned Emma in a low tone but with her brilliant eyes shimmering. She dried her hands on some paper towels and asked skeptically, "What's she waiting for?"

"Let's just say Bobby's runnin' outta time," Elliott said though he did not feel as much confidence in the statement as he expected.

"Oh, so you're good with being her *second* choice?" inquired an exasperated Emma sharply. Elliott slapped his dish towel onto the counter.

"I'd be fine with being her tenth choice," Elliott replied angrily. His answer was too much for his sister and she briefly faltered; angry tears rolled down her face. Elliott dried his hands and, turning her away from the sink, hugged her. She accepted the affection and laid her head on his shoulder.

"You're so damn stubborn," uttered Emma. She let her waterworks flow freely and griped, "You wouldn't let Daddy give you the bar and you won't let me give you the girl. And because of it you've got nothing in your life."

Elliott moved Emma away from him but maintained his grip on her upper arms. She averted her gaze.

"Look at me, Em," Elliott demanded. She initially refused but he shook her and ordered, "Look at me."

Emma obeyed with narrowed eyes. Her tears ceased.

"I've never felt like this before," Elliott stated emphatically. He relinquished his grip on her arms and turned around. Gently hitting a fist on the counter, he continued, "Not about Donna, not about anyone. I'm in love with her, Emma – hopelessly and stupidly in love with her – and, like it or not, you're gonna hafta accept that."

Elliott rotated to face Emma and was met with a silent scowl. Realizing he achieved only a temporary stalemate, Elliott watched his sister contemplating the lesser of two evils. The siblings finished the dishes without saying another word.

· · · ·

TONI, FRESH OFF HER Thanksgiving Day shift, sat with her mother at the kitchen table. Katherine watched her daughter eat with her chin setting in one hand and a glass of white wine in the other.

"I can't believe you wanted Macaroni and Cheese for Thanksgiving dinner," remarked Katherine as Toni eagerly devoured a heaping, steaming bowl of it.

"Your homemade Mac and Cheese is the best," Toni replied through her food. Wearing her usual blue scrubs, she scooped up another forkful and said, "It's one of my best childhood memories. You making it for me, and us sitting in that little kitchen and talking."

"Take a breath, dear," urged Katherine, Toni's mother stubbornly refusing to meander into the past. She added the admonishment, "You shouldn't goad your food."

"I don't think that's the proper usage of the word *goad*, Mother," Toni replied in between bites. Katherine rolled her eyes.

"What's Elliott doing for Thanksgiving?" inquired Katherine. She had been not-so-subtly pushing Toni towards Elliott since she met him.

"Dinner at the in-laws," Toni answered. Katherine noticed the hint of sadness in her voice as she said, "He actually invited us but I was already scheduled to work."

"Well, then, we have our plans for *next year*," declared Katherine. Toni flashed her an expression of rebuke though it lost some of its forcefulness with the dollop of cheese in the corner of her mouth.

"I think we'll wait until *next year* to make that call," Toni replied. A knock at the front door interrupted their conversation.

"I wonder who that could be," said Katherine, her tone sounding devious to Toni.

"Did you invite him over?" Toni inquired with a dubious mien.

"No, but I should have," responded Katherine. The unexpected visitor again knocked.

"I'll get it," Toni said. Dabbing her mouth with a napkin, she missed the dollop of cheese. She slid her chair from the table, rose to her feet and walked out of the kitchen.

"Perfect timing," Katherine said aloud before sipping her wine. Toni arrived at the front door and peeked through the peep hole.

"Bobby?" asked Toni aloud. She gradually opened the door and, to her surprise, her boyfriend stood on the porch. Katherine scowled and drained her wine glass.

"Hi, Toni," Bobby greeted her with an adoring yet nervous smile. The sight of a dozen red roses in his right arm sent a shockwave through Toni. It conjured a cavalcade of thoughts, the most prominent being an engagement ring and Elliott's haggard face.

"What's this?" Toni asked with a glance at the flowers. She stepped onto the porch, pulled the door closed behind her and folded her arms in the chilly air.

"Toni Amanda Cullen, I've been a complete fool," began Bobby. Toni caught her breath but the words she expected were not immediately spoken as he remained standing and continued, "You're the most incredible, loving and special woman I've ever known, but I've treated you like you were lucky to be with me, and that's just not true."

A tear ran down Toni's cheek but she found herself unable to move or utter a single word. Katherine, her demeanor darkening, entered the hallway and listened intently to Bobby's monologue.

"I was wrong," declared Bobby. He took Toni by the hand and explained, "*I* am lucky to be with *you*, and so incredibly stupid for not seeing that. And, you know, I realize these are just words, and don't mean anything."

"Too slow, Elliott," muttered Katherine bitterly, "too damn slow."

"So, starting tonight, you're gonna see a change . . . you're gonna see *a lot* of changes. I've already started making them," said Bobby with a squeeze of her hand. Toni struggled to maintain her composure as he promised, "No more selfishness. No more taking things out on you."

Toni felt lightheaded. Bobby, in mere minutes, was surrendering every position he had fiercely defended during the course of their relationship. He released her hand and placed his own over his heart.

"I will sing with you whenever you want," swore Bobby. His grin evaporated and he paused to force out the bitter words he did not wish to say.

"I'll even apologize to Elliott," said Bobby resolutely. Toni unsteadily backed into the door and leaned against it; she felt as if she might faint as he stated, "I'll pay for his medical bills if you want me to. And if you wanna be his friend, that's cool with me, and I'll try to be his friend, too. I can't promise anything but I'll try."

Carefully setting the roses on the patio chair, Bobby buttressed Toni. His presence and arguments overwhelmed her.

"I started seeing a counselor, too," advised Bobby with a measure of embarrassment, "ya' know, to deal with how angry I get, and how self-centered I can be."

"You're kidding," Toni gushed.

"Been goin' for a month now," said Bobby. Unable to withstand him any longer, she embraced him wholeheartedly as he vowed, "Whatever it takes for me to make it up to you, and be the man you deserve, I'll do it."

"I don't know what to say," a tearful Toni whimpered.

"How about yes?" suggested Bobby. Relinquishing his grasp on her, he retrieved a ring box from his jacket pocket and sunk to one knee, querying in a strong voice, "Toni Amanda Cullen, will you be my wife?"

Toni and Katherine both went numb. Bobby raised the ring box closer to Toni who trembled. The problem of Elliott abruptly interrupted her thoughts the second he flipped it open.

"No," Toni said with a dramatic exhale. Katherine perked up.

"What?" asked a flabbergasted Bobby. Toni, who did not look at the ring, closed the box.

"Ask me again, soon," Toni directed Bobby. Katherine threw a befuddled look at the closed door.

"Have you lost your mind?" queried Bobby. He rose to his feet and, nearly dropping the box, asked incredulously, "I thought this is what you wanted."

"You said you'd do whatever it takes," Toni replied calmly, her clement response melting Bobby's frustration. She touched his cheek and expounded, "You made this wonderful effort, Bobby, and I am so touched by it. You won't need to do it again. Give me a little time, keep doing all the things you're doing, and ask me again. I'll say yes. I don't care where it is, or how you do it. *I'll say yes.*"

Toni's heart lurched. A thought struck her.

"Just do it before 1986," Toni insisted.

"Before 1986?" queried Bobby.

"Before 1986?" said Katherine quietly.

"Yeah," Toni said, the fallout from Bobby's proposal attempt already needling her.

"Whatever you want is what I'll do," replied Bobby steadfastly. He lowered his gaze and pondered the last few minutes. Returning his attention to Toni, he handed her the roses and said, "These are for you."

"Thank you," Toni replied, both a sense of relief and a sense of dread washing over her. Bobby took her head in his hands and looked into her eyes.

"I will always love you," stated Bobby. Toni froze. She knew the words on her tongue, whether said or unsaid, would end a relationship.

"I love you, too," Toni replied. She surrendered to Bobby's assault on her heart and kissed him before sighing with happy tears, "Oh, Bobby."

Katherine slowly exhaled upon hearing the love in Toni's voice. Bowing her head, she returned to the kitchen and poured another glass of wine.

• • • •

"I FIGURED YOU'D SHOW up eventually," Emma sneered while throwing her feet up on her desk and leaning back in her chair. She folded her hands on her stomach and added snidely, "Even after your asshole boyfriend sucker punched my brother and broke his nose."

Toni hovered near the door to Emma's office. The latter's hostility made the former doubt the efficacy of her visit.

"What Bobby did was horrible, Em, and trust me, he paid for it," replied Toni deferentially. Feeling honor bound to defend her man, however, she said in defense of Bobby, "But he's truly sorry for what he did. He's even offered to apologize to Elliott."

"He's lucky my brother's so stupid crazy about you," advised Emma, the words tasting foul in her mouth. She glowered at Toni and said, "He should've pressed charges and had Bobby thrown in jail."

Emma smiled an evil smile. Toni shivered and stepped backward.

"I got a few friends on the Trenton PD who would've made his stay one to remember," Emma said in wicked amusement.

"I'm not here to fight, Em, and I wish you'd forgive Bobby for what he did," pleaded Toni. Changing her tone, she steeled her will and said, "But that's not why I'm here, either."

"Oh, I know," Emma replied on the heels of Toni's words. She declared with considerable hauteur, "You're here because you're going back to Bobby and you want me to help Elliott stuff his heart back in after you rip it out."

Emotionally staggered by Emma's foreknowledge of her intentions, Toni took another physical step back with her mouth agape. Emma simply smirked at her.

"'Tough problems require strong drinks,'" Emma proudly quoted John Warden. She spun her chair around, unlocked the cabinet behind her desk and retrieved the bottle of moonshine and two shot glasses.

"I don't want anything to drink," said Toni nervously.

"Yeah, ya' do," Emma snapped. Rotating her chair around again, she set the moonshine and the glasses on her desk, uncorked the bottle and added with gradually easing ire, "You obviously care enough about Elliott to risk coming here. I mean, for all you knew, I was gonna pull a Bobby on you. Of course, I wouldn't need a sucker punch to break your nose."

Emma filled one shot glass and then the other, her harsh demeanor devolving into resignation as she did. When Toni maintained her distance, Emma nodded to the guest chairs in front of her desk.

"Oh, relax, I'm not gonna hurt you. Elliott'd never forgive me if I did," Emma coaxed Toni. She cautiously approached Emma who urged her, "Have a seat, country girl."

Toni obeyed and carefully settled into the left guest chair. Emma slammed back a shot.

"All right, let's start at the beginning," Emma sighed. She refilled the glass and inquired, "Did Bobby propose?"

"How do you know that?" uttered a shocked Toni.

"Given my brother's luck with women, I always assume the worst . . . for him, I mean," Emma answered discontentedly. Toni's shock melted into sadness.

"Yeah, he proposed, but I said no," said Toni. Her reply surprised Emma and, in response, she admitted, "Well, I guess it was more of a 'ask again in a few weeks.'"

"And, when he does, you're gonna say yes," Emma stated matter-of-factly.

"Yeah, unless you tell me something that changes my mind," responded Toni meekly. Emma laughed.

"I'm gonna make the decision easy for you, that's what I'm gonna do," Emma said. Launching into an impassioned monologue, she proclaimed, "Toni, I know Elliott better than anyone. And I know a little bit about you. My brother likes his routines, and his schedules, and mulling around the little Downriver borders he's set up for himself and, eventually, if you two got together, they'd become a cage you'd wanna break out of."

"That's not true," countered Toni though without much confidence.

"Oh, it is, chickee. And I'll tell you something else. He's not a go-getter," Emma said with a serious mien. Discomfited by memories of her father, she explained bitterly, "He should have taken this place over, not me. Daddy was old-fashioned and he wanted to pass on the bar to his oldest son. But Elliott wasn't interested."

"Elliott told me they fought about it a lot," stated Toni. She laid her hands in her lap and fiddled with her fingers.

"They fought a war," Emma replied. Leaning back in her chair, her eyes became hazy and she complained, "They were both so stubborn."

Toni stifled an abrupt chuckle. Emma smirked again.

"Yeah, I know, I suffer from that disease, too," Emma confessed, "and I guess I was more like Daddy than Elliott, which is why I'm sitting here now, and not him."

Emma drifted into the past while staring into her desk. Sitting up, she returned to the present and lifted her gaze to Toni.

"But getting back to you and Elliott . . . when you got to that point where you felt trapped and bored, he'd get stubborn and refuse to change," Emma said. She felt foul and, to combat it, she threw back her second shot before stating, "Things would deteriorate, and you'd eventually escape, and take off to be with some fun guy your own age, and it would devastate him."

"I would *never* do that," argued Toni.

"But you'd want to, and that's the point," Emma parried. Toni despaired and having, pity on her, Emma stated, "So, do it now, and he may actually get over it."

Toni began crying and cleared her eyes with her sleeve. Emma pushed the shot glass towards her.

"Is there anything we can do?" asked Toni. She shed a few more tears before composing herself.

"Look, when you cut him loose, he's gonna crawl even deeper into that dark shell of his, he always does," Emma warned Toni.

"Dark shell?" queried a frazzled Toni. She grasped the shot glass, paused and then drained it with a grimace and then a shudder.

"The place he's been since Daddy died, and the place he cemented himself into when Mom died a few months later," Emma explained. She became misty-eyed and continued, "1975 tore our hearts and our insides out. I had a husband to help me stuff it all back in, but Elliott had no one. I mean, Dave and I did what we could, but I was grieving, and dealing with a newborn, and he was helping me get through it all of it. So Elliott closed down. Crawled into the *dark shell*. And this, well, it'll drive him deeper in."

"So what do we do?" demanded Toni with considerable distress.

"Why does everyone always ask me that?" Emma asked. She wallowed in the booze drifting to her head and coursing through her veins before expounding, "*We* do nothing. *I* need to find someone to crawl in there with him, stuff his heart back in and then lead him out."

"Donna?" asked Toni.

"There's no doubt in my mind," Emma lied.

"How do I know you're not just saying all this because she's your best friend?" asked Toni. Her question frustrated Emma and her eyes sparkled with energy.

"Look at me," Emma ordered. Toni delayed but then complied as she stated firmly, "If I thought Donna was wrong for him, I'd personally put her on the next plane outta Metro."

Toni bit her lip. She surrendered to her sorrow and again wept.

"And Donna'll be there to crawl into his cage and sit happily by his side?" queried Toni sorrowfully.

Emma hesitated. Given Donna's new approach to her brother's hermitage, and her strong feelings for Benjamin, she was not certain Donna would, so she did not answer verbally but instead shook her head to confirm Toni's statement. More of Toni's tears fell.

"Is Bobby a good guy, ultimately?" Emma inquired as she pressed her advantage. Toni shook her head in the affirmative.

"Yeah, he is," answered Toni.

"Then say yes," Emma urged her. She recorked the moonshine bottle and said, "Bobby seems like the right guy for you and trust me, you're way over Elliott's head."

"Are you saying I'm too good for your brother?" asked Toni in disbelief.

"*No*," Emma replied emphatically. Her mood deflated and she confessed, "And yes."

"Em, that's crazy," protested Toni. She rose to her feet and, with dramatic gestures, said, "There's more to him than you give him credit for. He just needs some guidance, some motivation."

"Maybe, but he's not your problem, and you need to be with Bobby," Emma responded calmly while Toni wiped away her tears. She focused intently on Toni and asked, "So whaddaya say?"

"*I say this is bullshit*," erupted Toni. She stormed out of Emma's office and slammed the door behind her.

"Stubborn with anger issues," Emma said with an exhale. Returning the bottle and glasses to the cabinet, she muttered, "Maybe they do belong together."

Separate Lives

T oni dallied after the first knock on her front door. She knew who stood on the other side and was not prepared for the encounter. The second knock spurred her into action and she reluctantly granted her visitor access.

"Where the hell've you been?" an irked Elliott asked. Gentle snowflakes fell around him and he looked like a scruffy, fallen angel in the porchlight. Stepping closer to Toni, Elliott admonished her, "My next stop was your Mom's house. I was gettin' pretty damn worried."

Elliott's vision adjusted to the dark. He realized Toni had long been crying.

"What's wrong?" Elliott inquired with a touch of panic in his tone. Toni offered him a pained mien and then burst into tears. Elliott gaped at her in utter disbelief as she barreled to the couch, collapsed upon it and bawled. Regaining his senses, he stepped into the house and closed the door. He asked again, "Toni, what's wrong?"

"*Elliott*," whimpered Toni. Elliott hurried to the couch and kneeled beside her.

"Toni, tell me what's goin' on," Elliott implored her while laying a supportive hand on her shoulder, "*now*."

"This wasn't supposed to happen," muttered Toni amid her sobs and sniffles. Reaching out to a tissue box on the far end table, she snagged two tissues. She laid her head on a throw pillow and scrunched her body into the fetal position.

"*What* wasn't supposed to happen?" Elliott queried, his worry for Toni causing his heart to pound in his chest. He permitted her to weep for over a minute before urging her, "Toni, you gotta tell me what's goin' on."

Toni, with Elliott's tender assistance, dragged herself into a sitting position. She composed herself, wiped her eyes and nose with the clump of tissues and then grasped Elliott's hands. Despite the warmth of Toni's grip, the aura emanating from the rest of her body chilled him to the bone.

"I," began Toni with a hard swallow and a shake of her head, "I can't."

Realization struck Elliott harder than Bobby's fist. He extricated his hands from hers and lowered himself to a sitting position on the floor with his arms resting on his knees.

"Ya' don't need to," Elliott said, his face becoming pensive. Toni remained centered but tears streamed down her cheeks. Neither of them would look at the other.

"I don't know what to do, Elliott," mewled Toni. Elliott experienced a feeling he had never felt before. His love for Toni tore his spirit in two, half of it being pulled by his desire to be with her while the other half was wrested in the other direction by his wish for her happiness.

"I do," Elliott declared.

"You do?" asked a confused Toni. He cocked an eye at her with a half-smile on his face.

"I love you, Toni Amanda Cullen," Elliott stated.

"*Elliott!*" Toni scolded him. She began trembling at the prospect of a competing proposal.

"And if I expect you to believe that," Elliott said grimly, "then I gotta do this."

"Do what?" queried Toni. She took two quick swipes at her watery eyes as Elliott rumbled to his feet.

"Say goodbye," a defeated Elliott replied. He displayed no emotion, and in fact felt none, his imminent loss of Toni rendering him hopelessly numb.

"*No,*" gushed Toni as she fell to her knees and embraced Elliott. Her tears stained his shirt and she pressed her cheek into it.

"We don't have a choice, here, Toni," Elliott corrected her. She clung to him even tighter.

"There's always a choice," insisted Toni. Elliott guided Toni to her feet and then carefully yet firmly moved her away.

"I won't ask you if you love me," Elliott said. He ran a hand over his face, balled it into a fist and then continued, "I just won't do that to you. Or to me. But I will ask you this: do you love him?"

Toni hesitated. Goaded into an answer by Elliott's piercing eyes, she faltered and nodded in the affirmative.

"I don't wanna lose either of you," Toni bleated. She attempted to again hug him but he held her at bay.

"Look, Toni, us meeting was some type of huge cosmic mistake," Elliott said. His words injured Toni as he stated, "All it did was mess up our hearts and our heads and got you all mixed up in my bullshit."

"*It wasn't a mistake*," argued Toni. Elliott contemplated her words and his countenance became thoughtful.

"Eh, maybe you're right," Elliott conceded. He soaked in as much of her intoxicating presence and simple beauty as he could, saying, "Maybe I was just the jolt Bobby needed to get his act together, which I'm guessing he did."

Toni lowered her eyes and nodded again. Elliott placed a brief kiss on her lips and sat her down on the couch. She futilely and feebly resisted his efforts.

"Elliott, stay," begged Toni despite having no viable way for him to do it. He lifted her chin with a finger.

"Be happy," Elliott implored her, "or none of what I'm about to go through will mean a damn thing."

Elliott turned and walked to the front door. Toni grabbed the throw pillow and hugged it but was unable to watch his departure.

"Well that was fun," Elliott muttered after he pulled the door closed. He winced when the locking mechanism clicked. Standing dejectedly on Toni's porch, he sensed his emotions balling inside. The pulsing and festering center of negative, depressive energy slowly grew and he said aloud, "It's gonna be a long road back."

· · · ·

"I FIGURED YOU'D BE here," said Emma as she walked up to Elliott with her shoes crackling on the frost-bitten lawn. Her brother stood on the grounds of Our Lady of Hope Catholic Cemetery in Brownstown and stared at his parents' graves. Emma wore a heavy purple coat with pinkish-purple earmuffs and gloves to combat the cold morning air.

"To be honest, it's been a little while," Elliott revealed with a measure of shame. He wore a black winter hat and his peacoat with the collar turned up and his hands stuffed in the pockets.

"Brought ya' a coffee," said Emma as she handed it to him.

"Thanks," Elliott replied. He accepted the Styrofoam cup and indulged in the warmth it radiated through his bare hands.

"You don't look good," advised Emma as she appraised his paler-than-normal skin, the dark circles around his eyes and the several days of stubble on his face.

"Never have," Elliott uttered.

"Stop it," replied Emma. The silence prickled her so she said, "Look, I know you really like Toni-."

"*Love*, Em," Elliott snarled. He repeated with less vitriol, "*Love*."

"Okay, whatever, Elliott," replied an irked Emma. When Elliott threw her optical daggers, she relented and said, "Fine. *Love*."

Elliott peeled back the opening of the cup's lid and took a cautious drink. The coffee was comfortably hot so he took several gulps.

"When're you bringing out their Christmas wreathes?" Elliott queried in an attempt to avoid a fight. He brushed some snow from John Warden's gravestone.

"It doesn't matter whether it's like or love, Elliott," reasoned Emma ardently. Unable to surrender her point, she continued, "She was never gonna be with you, and you've gotta know that."

"Drop it," replied Elliott acerbically. Emma decided to switch from defense to offense.

"Sure, I'll drop it," said Emma, "*if* you do something for me."

"You're worse than Dad was," Elliott remarked. He set his coffee on the frozen ground and returned his hands to his pockets. Emma rolled her eyes.

"I'm John Warden's daughter, not his clone," said Emma in a snarky tone. She picked up the cup, took a sip and asked, "Anyway, do you remember Tessa's friend Brittany?"

"Uh, yeah, I think so," replied Elliott. He inquired in puzzlement, "She's the little quiet one, right?"

"Yeah, you remember," Emma said while setting the coffee cup on the gravestone behind her. Pulling off her glove, she searched for something in her coat pocket and stated, "Well, I was hesitant about this, but, her Mom, Colleen, is divorced and-."

"*You're insane*," Elliott chastised his sister.

"What?" replied Emma while feigning innocence. She produced a Polaroid and displayed it to Elliott proudly, saying, "She's a little younger than me, and really pretty – here's proof – and really nice. She's kinda, like, a homebody, too, which might be more your speed."

"Do you ever stop?" Elliott inquired in disbelief. He folded his arms and remarked carelessly, "Besides, I'm not sure I'm Dad material."

"You'd better be Dad material," snapped Emma. She stuffed the picture in her pocket and returned her hand to its glove.

"Yeah? Why's that?" Elliott replied with a dubious glance.

"Because you had one helluva role model who gave you the playbook, idiot," growled an offended Emma. Her anger cooled but her countenance grew more intense and, with greenish-blue flames burning in her eyes, she stated, "And if Dave and I bite the big one, you're getting our kids."

"Wait, what?" a confused Elliott asked.

"That's right, Uncle Elliott," said Emma as she went nose-to-nose with her sibling. Elliott, feeling threatened, stepped back a pace as she excoriated him, "And you'd better snap outta this and be the best damn uncle in the world."

Elliott spun around so quickly and addressed Emma with such emotion that it was her turn to step backward. He threw an index finger at her.

"I can do that without a wife!" Elliott snarled.

"Of course you can, Elliott," Emma answered. She reversed her retreat and pleaded, "But I want my kids to grow up in an intact family, like we did."

"Well, sorry, but I'm all they're gonna get," snapped Elliott angrily. Flinging the rest of his angst into their argument, he barked, "And if that's not good enough for you, Queen Emma, maybe Donna and Ben can take 'em."

Emma's furious glare flashed to Elliott for but a fraction of a second before she charged him. Slapping him hard across the face, she then repeatedly smacked his chest.

"Emma, stop it!" demanded Elliott as he blocked several of her attempts.

"You *will* raise my girls," Emma stated with cutting authority. Elliott managed to corral her swinging arms.

"You and Dave aren't gonna die!" countered Elliott as the siblings struggled. Emma finally relented while a tear escaped her left eye and tumbled down her cheek.

"We thought the same thing about Daddy and Mom, yet there they are," Emma said with a wavering voice and nod towards her parents' graves. Channeling all her emotion away from her parents and to her brother, she implored him, "For once, Elliott, go out with someone who's your age, and acts like it. No interference or pressure from me . . . well, *after this* . . . and no history to deal with. A complete clean slate. And a chance at something real."

"Give it up, Em, damn it!" Elliott yelled.

"It's one date, Elliott!" shouted Emma in return.

"Just back off!" Elliott bellowed. Enraged and hurting, he marched past his sister and knocked the coffee from the gravestone.

"Elliott, stop," Emma called but her summons was in vain. Elliott climbed into his car, slammed the door and squealed his tires as his LTD sped away. Emma helplessly watched him depart with angry tears in her eyes and then turned to her mother's grave.

"What do I do with him, Mom?" Emma sighed. She stubbornly composed herself and wiped away her tears, saying, "I just can't strongarm him like I used to, like Daddy used to. You're the only one who could really talk to him, get into his head. Who's gonna do it now?"

. . . .

"WELL, HO-LY SHIT," said Brandy as Elliott walked solemnly into North End Bar, a hole-in-the wall establishment on Ecorse Road in the northern portion of Taylor. She dried a beer mug with a cigarette in her mouth and asked, "That crazy sister of yours know you're in here?"

"Didn't expect to see you in this place," Elliott answered weakly while approaching the bar. He did not see the blonde smoking and drinking vodka in a shadowy corner. Brandy's eyes darted to her and then back to Elliott.

"Great to see you, too," said Brandy with a sneer. Her countenance softened and she added, "Actually it's not because you look like refried shit."

"It's been a rough day, week . . . year," Elliott said. He settled onto a stool and rested his elbows on the bar, asking, "So, how the hell'd you end up in this 'crappy little bar'?"

"Missed rippin' on drunks like you," replied Brandy snidely before easing her tone, "and Neil needed someone to run the bar a couple days a week.

Loser knocked up some girl and they're gettin' married. Can ya' believe that? And she's a nice girl, too. *Neil*. Got a nice girl."

"No shit," Elliott replied as his spirit sunk lower. Brandy, regretting her careless words, began fixing him a Grumpy Old Man.

"So what're we drinking to tonight?" asked Brandy as she added a small amount of cheap ginger ale to the glass. Picking it up, she moved to Elliott and swiped the area in front of him with a white towel. She then set the drink down and asked pointedly, "Woman trouble?"

"*Women* trouble," Elliott answered as he sampled his cocktail, "*women* trouble."

"Well, I'll have mercy on you and only ask this: two strikes or three?" queried Brandy. Elliott dropped his gaze to the bar.

"Three," Elliott confirmed bleakly. Returning his attention to Brandy, he uttered, "And Em and I are at war, so that makes life even better."

"You sure are a trainwreck, Warden," said Brandy with a slow shake of her head. She said in a voice of mock enthusiasm, "But don't worry, things are about to get worse."

Elliott suddenly smelled a familiar fragrance as Brandy scowled and melted away. He bowed his head.

"Well, if it isn't my old boyfriend, Elliott Warden," said Macayla, Elliott's ex-girlfriend arriving next to him with a cigarette hanging in one hand and a vodka and tonic in the other.

"Hello, Macayla," Elliott replied. Instead of irrevocably crushing his spirit, her impromptu appearance amused him.

"Emma finally kicked you out of her precious club so you had to slither into this dump, huh?" gloated Macayla.

"You seem to like this dump just fine," interjected Brandy from the other end of the bar. Macayla threw her a quick glower. Elliott drained his glass.

"I gotta hit the john," Elliott grumbled. He slithered off his barstool and headed for the men's room.

"Macayla, leave him alone," scolded Brandy after Elliott disappeared.

"Why?" Macayla snapped. She seated herself in Elliott's place and said, "He's just like any other loser who crawls in here."

"That's bullshit and you know it," answered Brandy as she approached Macayla. She whisked up Elliott's glass, bored into Macayla with her eyes and stated firmly, "He's a good guy in a really bad spot and you, like any drunken tramp, will just make things worse."

"I know all about Elliott," said Macayla indignantly. Brandy offered her a dubious look. Undaunted, Macayla smiled deviously and raised her eyebrows, saying, "And he owes me."

"Whatever," Brandy said while shaking her head in disapproval. She said no more and began making Elliott another drink.

· · · ·

ELLIOTT RETURNED FROM the restroom, grabbed his new drink and moved further down the bar. Macayla chuckled, shook her head and then sidled up to him. Claiming the next barstool, she stared at Elliott while he stared blankly into the mirror behind the bar.

"What's it been? Eight, ten months?" asked Macayla. She lit a cigarette and began puffing on it.

"Go away, Cay," Elliott grumbled.

"I guess Em couldn't find you Ms. Right," taunted Macayla. She turned her head and blew smoke away from Elliott.

"You're such a bitch," Elliott replied acerbically. Macayla laughed. Brandy entered a meandering conversation with the only other patron in the bar but hawked them from a distance.

"Never knew you to be a mean drunk," said Macayla with a snide half-smile. Allowing her countenance to become serious, she leaned into Elliott and explained, "Ya' know, us bar sluts don't have feelings so you can't hurt us by being an asshole. We kinda like the abuse. It turns us on."

The smell of the vodka on Macayla's breath wafted over Elliott. He inhaled to chastise her but, before he could utter a syllable, she gave him such a poignant look that he could not respond. It was as if she lifted his darkness, crawled under it like a blanket and pulled it over them both.

"We're both lyin' in the gutter tonight, so that gives us somethin' in common," reasoned Macayla. She grinned lustily and added, "And the sex was always good, so there's that."

"Are you really going there?" Elliott queried.

"You catch on fast," jibed Macayla. She stood up and added, "Think it over while I pee."

"Always a lady," Elliott muttered as he watched her stumble to the women's restroom.

"You really wanna make that mistake twice, Elliott?" warned Brandy when the restroom door closed behind Macayla.

"I'm runnin' outta people to make mistakes with," Elliott said with his eyes glued to the restroom door.

"I'm not one to interfere with a guy gettin' a little tail," explained Brandy with a tilt of her head, "but you know that slut's not worth it."

"That I do," Elliott asserted before draining another drink.

"You sure about that?" asked Brandy. She leaned over the bar and expounded, "She's on disability for a bad back but takes a different guy outta here almost every week, and that back's never worse for wear. Then there's her pain pill addiction, which goes really great with the alcoholism."

"None of that's new, Brandy," Elliott replied dismissively. Brandy stood up straight.

"Oh, she does coke now, too," rejoined Brandy.

"That *is* new," Elliott said. He slid his empty glass towards Brandy and admitted, "Well, at least I could never confirm the rumor."

"What *is* new is that she's tryin' to get her hooks into someone permanently," Brandy replied in her final salvo.

"Yeah, and if I'd a' just let her do it the first time, I coulda' skipped the last eight months," Elliott stated, his assertion sounding strangely profound in his head. Unable to change his mind, Brandy faded into the background as Mackayla emerged from the restroom. Elliott, firmly in the grasp of the alcohol, sized up Macayla and thought, "Ms. Wrong is still a Miss."

· · · ·

DESPITE THEIR INTOXICATION and rushed second courtship, Macayla and Elliott spent the most engaging and passionate night they had ever experienced together. They anticipated each other's desires and satiated all of them with interludes of surprising tenderness and affection. When their lovemaking finally ended in the wee hours of the morning, they fell asleep in each other's arms.

Elliott awoke first as morning passed into afternoon. Plagued by a hangover, he cautiously eased himself out of Macayla's bed to avoid waking her. The room smelled of sex, alcohol and cigarettes, the foul taint in the air sullying his memories of the past twelve hours.

Macayla gradually pushed aside the cobwebs of sleep and watched Elliott dress with one eye open. When he finished, she sat up with the covers pressed to her chest.

"You're leaving without saying goodbye because you're late for work, right?" Macayla asked despite knowing the answer.

"Yeah, and I didn't wanna wake you up," Elliott lied. Holding back the confession on his lips that he had already taken the day off work, he added, "That's all."

"Why don't you call off and we'll get some breakfast?" suggested Macayla as she scooted backward against the headboard. The paramours studied each other carefully in the seconds that followed, each one noticing how rough the other appeared. Macayla glanced at the alarm clock on her bedside table and said, "Or lunch, I guess."

"Yeah," Elliott responded, "yeah. We can do that."

An awkward silence followed. Elliott sat on the end of the bed while Macayla lit her first cigarette of the afternoon.

"Last night, as wonderful as it was," said Macayla as she read Elliott's worn countenance and discerned his lies, "wasn't for me, was it?"

"What're you talking about?" Elliott replied despite taking Macayla's meaning.

"Nothing. Forget it," Macayla said. She and Elliott watched each other longingly, both of them realizing they shared a loneliness that gnawed at their insides. They peered into a possible future together but, at the same instant, their faces became sullen and they forsook it. Macayla yawned and said, "We're both burnt. I'll take a rain check on lunch."

"Ya' sure?" Elliott queried while masking his relief. He regretted his drunken dalliance with Macayla and thought of Toni. The prospect of her sharing a similar night with Bobby arose in his mind and his nausea worsened.

"Yeah, don't worry about it," said Macayla before exhaling a plume of smoke. She held the cigarette away from her, slid her hand under the sheets and grasped her thigh. Wishing to depart, Elliott pulled on his coat and then turned to her. Telling her own lie, Macayla tapped her cigarette on an ashtray and said, "I'll see ya' soon."

"Yeah," Elliott replied, "see ya' soon."

He stood up, left her bedroom and closed the door. The click tweaked both of their hearts.

"Bye, Elliott," said Macayla softly. Sliding her hand gradually up her leg, she paid particular attention to the feel of her own skin. Her hand passed her pelvis, lingered on her stomach and then moved between her breasts. She made a fist, rested it on her chest and uttered, "Hope ya' get her."

Macayla extinguished her cigarette in the ashtray. Laying down again, she closed her eyes and fell into a deep sleep.

• • • •

ELLIOTT MADE A BRIEF, impromptu appearance at the Hastings' house on Christmas Eve to give his nieces their gifts. His inability to experience joy in the blazing light of their excitement proved telling and he faked an illness to gain Emma's begrudging dispensation from his Christmas Day obligations.

"Feel better, Elliott," Emma said through the telephone. She added with a flash of disapprobation, "And Merry Christmas."

"Yeah, Sis, you, too," replied Elliott. He hung up the telephone and said aloud, "I'm gonna pay for this one until next Christmas."

The holiday dawned bleak and frigid with intermittent snow flurries. Elliott spent it alone in his apartment, dulling his pain with half a bottle of cheap rum and flat Coke and subsisting on two-day old pizza. He occasionally heard voices outside or the passing of a car but for most of the day only the sounds of the television broke the silence.

December twenty-sixth brought the threat of snow later in the day so Elliott, nursing a hangover, surrendered his solitary existence for a couple hours and visited the Senate for a greasy breakfast. His favorite restaurant served few patrons and the closest of them sat two booths away from Elliott.

He ate his meal in contemplative silence until a familiar figure sauntered up to him.

"Katherine," said a surprised Elliott. He set his fork on his plate with a clink and remarked, "Didn't know you ate here."

"I don't, but you mentioned this place once," Katherine said as she unslung her purse and tossed it into the booth. Taking the cushioned bench opposite Elliott, she stated, "So I figured the cat may have dragged you in here. And, from the looks of it, it dragged you a long, long way."

Elliott chuckled and raised his mug. Katherine waited for his response.

"If only you were twenty years younger," joked Elliott before sipping his lukewarm coffee.

"Well, aren't you the charmer?" Katherine replied with a dubious mien. Flipping a mug into an upright position, she said, "Of course, if you were twenty years older, and lived in Montana, you could've saved me from that asshole ex-husband of mine and the years of misery he brought me."

Katherine's eyes lost focus for a second. They strengthened suddenly and she offered Elliott a smile.

"But then we wouldn't have our precious Toni," Katherine mused. Elliott winced; he did not "have" Toni at all. A mousy, bespectacled waitress arrived at the booth as Katherine added, "She's the only good that man ever did."

"You eatin', hon?" asked the waitress bluntly. She pulled out her notepad and pen.

"Pumpkin pie, extra whipped cream, and a coffee, black," Katherine stated. She glanced at Elliott and queried, "Should we make it two?"

"Why not?" said Elliott. He finished the last of his breakfast and handed the empty plate to the waitress.

"You got it," replied the waitress without writing anything down. She stowed her pen and pad in her apron with one hand and meandered away with the plate in the other.

"Have a good Christmas?" asked Elliott when he found no other words to say. Afraid to mention Toni's name, he drained his mug of its contents.

"I'm not one for holidays," Katherine answered with mild disdain, "but I suppose it was okay. Any day with my daughter is a good one."

"Yeah," agreed Elliott softly. The pair drifted into a brief silence until the waitress returned with two slices of pumpkin pie and a fresh pot of coffee.

"If you want to know, I'll tell you, Elliott," Katherine said when the waitress left, "but it has to be your decision."

"It's why you're here though, isn't it?" replied Elliott with an angst-ridden frown and a downward gaze. A foulness settled over him and he suspected that Toni was now beyond his reach.

"Yes," Katherine confessed with pity, "it is."

"So why ruin the tragic ending?" asked Elliott rhetorically. Smirking in contravention to the way he felt, he opined, "Eighty-five's already been a shit year, so I'll take the hit now and maybe save eighty-six . . . *maybe*."

Elliott raised his eyes and gazed upon Katherine. Her face twitched with sadness before she squelched the uncomfortable emotion.

"Bobby proposed Christmas morning, in my living room," Katherine said as if guilty that the proposal occurred in her house. Her expression became pained and she added, "And Toni said yes."

Elliott went pale but remained outwardly emotionless. He shrugged.

"It's what she wanted," Elliott said while raising his mug in her honor, "and I'm happy for her."

"No, you're not," Katherine scolded him. Elliott lowered his mug when she did not raise hers.

"I am, I really am, Katherine," replied Elliott in earnest. His spirit dying, he uttered hopelessly, "I'm just not happy for me."

Bellied up to the bar, Emma sat alone and enjoyed a quiet moment, a Diet Coke and a club sandwich of her own making. She reviewed the plans for Johnny Dubs' third annual New Year's Eve dinner party in her head, scratched some thoughts onto a cocktail napkin and made last minute adjustments. A knock on the door broke her concentration.

"We're closed," Emma said in a raised voice. Toni's bandmate, Eddie, cracked open the door and poked his shaggy-haired head into the club.

"Even for your second favorite guitar player?" asked Eddie with a goofy expression.

"Oh, hey, Eddie," Emma greeted him with a confused expression. She shook the event preparations out of her head and waved him forward, saying, "C'mon in."

Eddie slipped inside the club and strode up to Emma on his long shanks. She took a drink of her Diet Coke.

"Got a minute?" asked Eddie. His eyes settled on the uneaten half of Emma's club sandwich.

"Yeah, sure," Emma replied despite secretly resenting the intrusion on her private time. She rotated her barstool towards him and queried, "What's up?"

Normally unflappable, Eddie became nervous and lowered his gaze. He scratched his cheek and then thrust his hands into the back pockets of his jeans.

"Well . . . Toni wanted me to run something by you," began Eddie.

"I'm kinda busy today," Emma replied as some irritation slipped from her tongue. She folded her arms, tilted her head and added, "She coulda' just called me."

"Well, given all the shit that's gone down between her an' Elliott, she was a little nervous about doin' it herself," explained Eddie. Emma's mien became one of puzzlement.

"Nervous?" Emma asked. She stretched out her long legs before her, her shoes almost touching Eddie and asked, "Why the hell would she be nervous?"

"Well, ya' see, Toni wanted me to check if the band could take January off," advised Eddie cautiously with a backward step. Emma returned her feet to the floor.

"What, is she worried about seeing Elliott?" Emma inquired. Feeling her blood boil over the effect of Elliott's indiscretions on Johnny Dubs, she said, "Cuz' she shouldn't be. I don't think she'll run into him here, at least not for a while."

"Well, that's part of it," admitted Eddie. The import of Emma's words finally struck him and he asked, "What's goin' on with Elliott?"

"I haven't seen hide nor hair of my big brother in a week," Emma answered bitterly. She wrinkled her nose in disapprobation.

"Well, that's probably for the same reason we're out in January," said Eddie with a knowing expression. He grew quiet despite Emma's expectant look.

"And that reason is?" Emma asked impatiently.

"Cuz' Bobby popped the question Christmas morning," said Eddie, "and our girl's goin' on a little Car-ri-be-an cruise to celebrate."

Realization hit Emma like a punch to the solar plexus. She winced, exhaled and then massaged the radix of her nose as if battling a headache.

"*Damn*," Emma griped emphatically. Panic fluttered in her heart but she repressed any outward expression of it and asked, "Can you chill for a minute? I gotta make a phone call."

"Yeah, no prob," said Eddie, the hungry musician oblivious to Emma's angst. His eyes reacquired her sandwich and he queried, "You gonna finish that sandwich?"

"Go ahead," Emma said with a wave of surrender. The wave turned into a pointed finger aimed at the beer coolers and she added, "You can pull a beer outta the cooler if you want, too."

Emma slid off the barstool and hurried towards her office. Eddie eagerly took her place but Emma suddenly stopped in her tracks without turning around.

"*One* beer, Eddie," Emma said.

"Damn it," muttered Eddie through a mouthful of club sandwich.

• • • •

"OH, THANK GOD YOU'RE finally here," Emma gushed when she met Donna at the entrance to Johnny Dubs. The club hummed with preparations for its New Year's Eve party and workers scurried around like ants. Noticing the stunning red dress that Donna wore, she momentarily lost focus and complimented her, "You look fantastic."

"Thanks," replied Donna with a tinge of embarrassment. She carefully laid her new coat over a chair and said, "But I'd really like to know *why* I'm here."

Emma scanned the vicinity and then pulled Donna into the small area in front of the coat check room. Nora, who had been cleaning in one of its unseen corners, stopped moving and listened intently.

"I need you to check on Elliott," Emma pleaded quietly.

"Why? What's wrong?" inquired Donna in a hushed tone.

"Please, just go over to his apartment," Emma said before pausing to fend off tears. Biting her lip to repress her worry, she continued, "And maybe stay with him for a while tonight. I mean, this is one of our biggest nights of the year, and this whole dinner buffet thing is new and crazy, and Dave's got the girls and four of their friends tonight because Rose and Tom are in Chicago. He's probably just drunk and pouting, but . . . if I'm wrong . . . ."

Emma trailed off, looked around the club erratically and, in a rare lapse of sanity, started to panic. Grasping her by the arms, Donna pulled down on them and stared into her eyes.

"Emma, *slow down*, and breathe," instructed Donna. She squeezed Emma's arms reassuringly, demonstrated a few deep breaths and said, "The first thing you're gonna do is tell me what's going on with Elliott. Is he okay?"

"Em, caterer's here," beckoned Sean from across the club.

"Damn it," Emma whimpered. A few tears escaped but Donna stepped in front of her.

"Sean, can you get them started?" asked Donna deferentially. She gestured towards her best friend and pleaded, "I really need Em for a few minutes."

"Oh, yeah, no problem," Sean said, Emma's young second-in command dutifully taking charge.

"Thank you," replied Donna with a smile. Pulling Emma closer to the coat room, she inquired, "Okay, now you have a few minutes, so *what's wrong with Elliott?*"

"He not dealing well with this whole Toni thing," Emma said with distaste. Donna's strength in the moment calmed her and she recovered, explaining, "At first, I thought he'd just do the usual moping, maybe for a little bit longer, but he's getting worse."

"When's the last time you saw him?" asked Donna as her worry deepened. Nora drifted to the coat room wall and stood next to the window.

"He made an unannounced visit on Christmas Eve, gave the girls their Christmas presents and then left, and he barely spoke to me," Emma answered. She waited for two of her employees to pass before she added, "He faked the flu on Christmas day – I should've pressed him on it but I was so busy I didn't – but anyway, it's been a whole week. I called him a few days ago but he didn't pick up the phone."

"Okay, why are you worried about him right now?" inquired Donna firmly.

"One of the guys from Toni's band stopped in here a little while ago," Emma said. Recounting the story made her feel panicky once again as she continued, "Bobby popped the question on Christmas morning, and she said yes. She's engaged, Donna."

"How did Elliott find out?" queried Donna skeptically.

"I have no idea," Emma said. She began more emphatic gesticulations and continued, "But I think something's wrong and that's why I need you to go see him, because he just won't talk to me."

"Em, it's *New Years Eve*. Ben's waiting for me in the car and we have plans tonight," said Donna. Emma grimaced but Donna held up her hand and stated, "But you know him. I'm sure he'd be willing to stop by Elliott's and check on him with me. We'll go right now."

"He won't answer the door if Ben's with you," Emma countered.

"I can't go there alone," resisted Donna. She squirmed under Emma's resolute gaze and protested, "That's not fair to Ben. I just can't."

"Fine, I'm calling one of my guys on the Taylor PD then," threatened Emma. She turned to walk away but Donna grabbed her arm.

"That'll really set him off, especially if he's drunk," Donna warned. Struck by impulsivity, Nora exited the coat room and approached Emma and Donna.

"I'll go," Nora volunteered in her young, sweet voice.

"Were you spying on us?" Emma demanded.

"Look, Em, we all care about Elliott," Nora explained, "but I should go. I'm the only one who *can* go."

"In case you haven't noticed," Emma objected with a sweeping gesture, "it's New Year's Eve, which is one of our biggest nights of the year. All hands on deck. All cylinders firing. All that stupid jazz."

"Yeah, and it's a terrible time to be alone and hurting," said Nora with burgeoning concern for Elliott. She motioned to the west, in the general direction of his apartment, and reasoned, "Somebody's gotta be there for him tonight and it's gotta be me."

Donna moved to speak but the words stuck in her throat. She forced them out.

"She's right, Em," urged Donna with a wince.

"God, I can't wait for 1985 to be over," Emma griped. Appraising Nora's youthful appearance, accentuated by the silver, glittery bow in her hair, she stated, "You're closer in age to my eight-year-old than to Elliott."

Nora and Donna both gazed at Emma with grave miens. She remained undaunted.

"You're not going," Emma declared.

"I broke up with Bart because I couldn't stop thinking about Elliott, and it was just wrong to lead him on like that," Nora confessed with reddening cheeks. Angst etched itself into her face as she expounded, "I thought I was too late because of the way, like, things were going with he and Toni. But maybe it's not. Maybe I'm, like, supposed to get him through tonight. Through all of this."

Nora's admission and deep concern for Elliott softened Emma's heart. Her ire melted.

"She may not want him, Em," continued Nora desperately, "*but I do.*"

Jealousy welled within Donna as she saw the love in Nora's eyes. Emma, meanwhile, studied Nora before taking her chin in her hand as if she instructed one of her daughters.

"You do this, and you're one of us – *I mean it* – and that's not always a good thing," Emma said with the utmost gravity, her words branding Nora's heart. She squeezed Nora's jaw and warned, "I'm dead serious, little girl. You ready for that? You ready for him?"

Nora pondered Emma's warning as a disquieted Donna covetously watched and squirmed. A warm smile came to Nora's face and, elated over her second chance with Elliott, she removed Emma's hand from her jaw.

"Yeah," Nora replied without the slightest hint of doubt, "I am."

"Then go take care of my big bro," Emma relented, her concern for Elliott washing over her. She pointed at Nora and ordered, "You call me the second you know he's okay."

"I will," promised Nora earnestly. She untied her server's apron as she scurried along the outer edge of the bar, rounded its far end and ducked behind it. Grabbing her purse and her coat and discarding her apron, she dodged caterers and vanished down the hallway leading to the east doors.

"You okay?" inquired Donna. Her stomach rumbled as the tantalizing scents of the catered food wafted throughout the club.

"I don't know," Emma answered as she turned and leaned her back against the coat room's outer wall. She set her sights on Donna and remarked, "Mark my words. This'll lead to an engagement or a train wreck."

"So which one would you bet on?" asked Donna.

"Knowing my idiot brother," Emma said snottily, "*both*."

• • • •

WHEN ELLIOTT ANSWERED his apartment door, his condition horrified Nora. He had lost weight, his skin was pallid and his eyes were dark-ringed wells of hopelessness. He shivered as the cold swirled around him; his shorts and t-shirt provided little protection from the winter weather.

"God, Elliott!" Nora gasped. His deterioration broke her heart.

"Shouldn't you be working?" asked Elliott in a cutting tone.

"Emma's worried sick about you," Nora advised him. She attempted to enter his apartment and said, "A lot of people are worried sick about you."

"Toni's not," Elliott said as he blocked her advance. Nora smelled the alcohol on his breath as he continued, "Emma must be pretty damn desperate to send you to do her dirty work. Well, you can tell her I ain't interested in anything she has to say and to leave me the hell alone."

"*I'm* worried sick about you," Nora replied firmly. Elliott paused to consider her words but, overwhelmed by his depression, he dismissed them as meaningless.

"It's cold, so I'm closing the door now," Elliott informed her. He waved at her weakly and said, "Go away."

"*Elliott*," Nora pleaded. He ignored her and closed the door. The young woman, in a rare burst of assertiveness, forced the door open again and entered his apartment. Her unexpected initiative surprised Elliott and caused him to stumble backwards.

"What the hell are you doing?" protested Elliott. Nora closed and locked the door behind her.

"Bringing you back from the dead," Nora answered. She smelled his stench, which hung in the stale air of the apartment, and asked in disgust, "When's the last time you showered?"

A weary Elliott surrendered and fell onto the couch in a semi-sitting position. He closed his eyes.

"I dunno," muttered Elliott. Nora noticed a lone, grease-stained pizza container on his kitchen table as he muttered pathetically, "A few days, a week. Doesn't matter."

Nora kicked off her shoes. She then removed her jean jacket and tossed it over the recliner near the door.

"You're not staying," warned an irritated Elliott while struggling to his feet. Nora said nothing but pulled off her glittery, black-and-white sweater and let it fall to the floor. Her bra soon followed. Tearing his eyes away from her, Elliott subsequently snuck lustful peeks while Nora revealed her nubile figure.

"I'm going upstairs to call your sister and tell her you're alive," Nora announced as she slid off her spandex pants. She maintained eye contact with Elliott but he shrugged and fell back onto the couch.

"Fine," he grumbled. She hesitated before removing her panties. Elliott averted his eyes again and muttered, "Whatever."

"And then I'm gonna take a shower," Nora said as she pulled the silvery bow out of her golden locks and shook out her curls. Elliott remained on the couch. Firing optical daggers at him, Nora demanded with a conviction that would have made Emma proud, "Get up, idiot."

"Why?" asked Elliott as he reluctantly obeyed. Nervous yet determined, Nora locked her focus on Elliott's startled face and held out her hand.

"Because you're coming with me," Nora said.

The End (of 1985)

NOVELS BY JOSHUA R. FIELDS

THE MILLSTONE CRUSADE. *". . . but whoever causes one of these little ones who believe in Me to stumble, it would be better for him to have a heavy millstone hung around his neck, and to be drowned in the depth of the sea." The Gospel of Matthew 18:6.*

Shocking abductions of ones they hold dear unite Catholic teenagers Judas Trent and Ursula Baumé and thrust them into the evil world of human trafficking. Mentored by a whiskey-drinking, cigar-smoking priest, the headstrong psychokinetic and the disfigured healer lead their friends against a local sex-slave operation in Southeast Michigan and Northwest Ohio.

Together, Judas and Ursula take the fight to those who would harm and enslave children and score early victories against their enemies. Yet as the dangers of their Millstone Crusade against human trafficking increase and their feelings for one another are continually frustrated, they are forced to consider one simple question.

Can they stay together?

• • • •

A DOG AMONG THORNS. Descending on the post-apocalyptic city of Kaiser in a flurry of vulgarity and vitriol, the towheaded demon Miriam hunts the weak in spirit and the unlucky in love. Men mired in turbulent romantic relationships lose more than their faith in God as she manipulates them into taking their own lives. None of Miriam's victims survive her wily ways. Her latest mark, the brooding and sinful Jacob Gottschalk, seems easy prey until she discovers the Holy Spirit wards him from her very touch. Miriam's devious webs fail to ensnare him and she, instead of causing his downfall, becomes his reluctant-yet-loving protector. That impassioned defense, however, raises the ire of the most powerful person in Kaiser: Elizabeth Nicks, Jacob's wife and the city's Constable.

The resulting war between the two women threatens to destroy them all as Miriam's penchant for carnage flourishes and Elizabeth confronts the dangers of the demonic world. Hurtling towards their intertwined destinies, the three troubled lovers enter a tempest of gory violence, romantic intrigue, shifting political alliances and the evil schemes of conniving spiritual beings.

• • • •

GIRLS WITHOUT GODS. Emerging from the fog of her war with Elizabeth for Jacob's heart, a victorious Miriam departs Kaiser with her prize. The demon and her unlikely paramour travel to the fantastical skyscraper of Chinese Peak, an opulent casino that flourishes in the post-apocalyptic world. Miriam's evil nature and savage jealousy, however, clash with Jacob's spiritual growth and reluctance to abandon his marriage. The resultant emotional conflict threatens to tear their fledgling relationship apart at the seams.

Elizabeth, meanwhile, remains in Kaiser, the Constable refusing to pursue her husband and his "demon whore." Yet the spiritual world forces her hand when Miriam's former handler, the demon Marcion, possesses her teenage daughter and absconds with her. Desperate to rescue her oldest child, Elizabeth travels to Chinese Peak seeking the aid of Jacob and Miriam in hunting down her child's abductor. Thrust together once again in sea of unbridled decadence, Jacob, Elizabeth and Miriam encounter a constantly evolving kaleidoscope of nefarious schemes, political intrigues, old lovers, new threats and alluring temptations. The deadly demonic gauntlet through which they tread promises but one simple truth: loss is inevitable.

• • • •

A DOG RETURNS TO ITS OWN. Months after banishing his demonic lover, Miriam, to the Abyss, Jacob Gottschalk travels into the frigid Canadian wilderness to rescue the corpses of his possessed stepdaughters and properly lay them to rest. The violent and insatiable Sophie lures him from the narrow way, however, and, blinded by his waning faith, he fails to detect the terrible secret she hides. His fortunes seemingly improve upon his arrival at New Oneida, an esoteric Christian settlement located in a pristine river valley. Its leader, Dr. Irinushka Zhukova, tempts Jacob with many beautiful vessels of spiritual purity and seeks to create in him a wellspring of the Holy Spirit. Unbeknownst to them all, a greater spiritual storm stains the skies of their future and threatens all those who dwell upon the face of the earth. Facing a terrible new evil and the destruction of everyone he loves, a stoic Jacob holds on desperately to the words of Christ: "But the one who endures to the end, he shall be saved."

www.ingramcontent.com/pod-product-compliance
Lightning Source LLC
Chambersburg PA
CBHW070318260626
47160CB00003B/879